# MARY
### OF
# CARISBROOKE

## Praise for Margaret Campbell Barnes

"Mrs. Barnes has found a rewarding field in English history, retelling royal lives with sympathy and skill."

—*New York Herald Tribune*

"We find in *Mary of Carisbrooke* the same warmth of feeling and adherence to historical fact which mark the previous historical works of Margaret Campbell Barnes and which have made her in *The Tudor Rose*, *Brief Gaudy Hour*, *My Lady of Cleves*, and other novels one of the most widely read and best loved of contemporary writers."

—*Toronto Globe & Mail*

"In a day when so many cheap historical novels are being written, one should be all the more grateful for those books which combine a thorough knowledge of backgrounds with a just assessment of life and character. Mrs. Barnes' are among the best."

—*Chicago Tribune* on *Brief Gaudy Hour*

"A cunning fusion of historical fact and humanizing fiction. So skillful indeed is the welding that only a scholar can detect where the documental leaves off and the fanciful begins. Smoothness of narration, however, is but one of Miss Barnes' literary virtues. She has a notable gift for blowing the dust off antique and colorful settings. Her characterizations are vital. Her dialogue, though at time anachronistic, is always assured and frequently witty."

—*Philadelphia Record* on *My Lady of Cleves*

"Rich in detail and flows beautifully, letting readers escape into Anne's court and country life. It is a must read for those who love exploring the dynamic relationships of Henry VIII and his wives."

—*Historical Novels Review* on *My Lady of Cleves*

"Mrs. Barnes captures the flavor, pageantry, and colors of the Middle Ages. One can hear the blare of trumpets, the shouts of

crowds, and the clash of arms in tournaments; one can see the knights, the armor, the castles, the towers, the banners; one can sense the intrigue and misrule of princes and politicians."
—*Philadelphia Inquirer* on *Within the Hollow Crown*

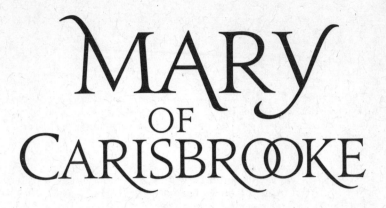

# MARY
## OF
## CARISBROOKE

*The Girl Who Would Not
Betray Her King*

## MARGARET CAMPBELL
## BARNES

Cover and internal design © 2011 by Sourcebooks, Inc.
Cover design by Pete Garceau
Cover images © James Walker/Trevillion

Published by Sourcebooks Landmark, an imprint of Sourcebooks, Inc.
P.O. Box 4410, Naperville, Illinois 60567-4410
(630) 961-3900
Fax: (630) 961-2168
www.sourcebooks.com

Originally published in Great Britain in 1956 by Macdonald & Co. Ltd.

Library of Congress Cataloging-in-Publication Data

Barnes, Margaret Campbell.
  Mary of Carisbrooke / Margaret Campbell Barnes.
    p. cm.
  1. Charles I, King of England, 1600-1649—Fiction. 2. Carisbrooke Castle (England)—Fiction. 3. Women household employees—Fiction. 4. Isle of Wight (England)—Fiction. I. Title.
  PR6003.A72M37 2011
  823'.912—dc22

                        2010052890

         Printed and bound in the United States of America.
              VP 10 9 8 7 6 5 4 3 2 1

To the beauty and
unspoiled courtesy of the Wight

# PROLOGUE

———— ⟁⟁⟁ ————

I N THE EARLY HOURS of a November morning four horsemen
drew rein outside the village of Bishop's Sutton on the road
to Southampton. Their horses were sweating and their dark
cloaks sodden with rain, but they knew that fresh mounts awaited
them and that only twenty miles separated them from the Solent.
As the sun rose redly through the mist the thoughts of each of
them strained forward hopefully across the water to the low,
wooded coastline of the Isle of Wight.

"It is the safest place from which to bargain with Cromwell,"
urged John Ashburnham, who had done his share of fighting in the
beaten Royalist army. "Although the new Governor was appointed
by Parliament, surely he cannot forget that his father was one of
your Majesty's chaplains?"

"All the s-same I would have you and Berkeley go ac-c-cross
and sound him first," said the small man with the slight stammer.
He had need of caution because, being the King of England, he
had everything to gain or lose. "Meanwhile Colonel Legge and
I will make for Titchfield House," he decided, "and beg a night's
hospitality from the Countess of Southampton."

They had escaped from the lenient bondage of Hampton Court
and been in the saddle all night. All four of them were half dead
with weariness, but behind them Cromwell's Ironsides might be in
hot pursuit. So Berkeley whistled cautiously outside the inn for their
waiting accomplice, and they changed horses without waste of words.

"What are the islanders like?" asked the man called Legge, as the four of them were about to part company.

"Loyal, I should say. My father once sent me over there to review their militia," recalled King Charles the First, with a touch of nostalgia for those carefree days. "Sir John Oglander, the Deputy Governor, was certainly a genial host. It was a summer's day and from the keep of Carisbrooke Castle the whole island seemed to be spread out like a lovely sunlit map. I was little more than a lad, and after dinner they let me fire off some of their ordnance. There was a young gunner who loaded for me, I remember—a pleasant-spoken, curly haired fellow not much older than myself…"

Whatever further recollections Charles Stuart may have had were cut short by the urgency of his plight, or lost in the beat of hooves as he and Legge turned aside towards Titchfield while their two companions spurred onwards towards the coast.

# CHAPTER ONE

---

I N THE SERVANTS' QUARTERS at Carisbrooke Castle on the Isle of Wight, the housekeeper's niece, Mary Floyd, was tucking a frightened little chambermaid into a truckle bed. "I'll send the slut packing!" Mistress Wheeler, the housekeeper, had declared as soon as it became evident that the hired wench was pregnant. But Sergeant Floyd, Mary's father, had gone on imperturbably checking the morning's supplies from Newport. "What can you expect, with Roundheads being brought into the garrison?" he had asked of no one in particular.

Mary herself, whose tender heart yearned over every sick dog on the island, had made no comment. She had picked up the pieces of a water pitcher the girl had dropped and quietly helped her up the backstairs and put a hot brick to her feet.

"Where shall I go if Mistress Wheeler turns me out?" sobbed the erring, orphaned Libby.

"Why not to your lover's folk?" suggested Mary. "Where does he live?"

"Somewheres over on the mainland," moaned Libby, retching over the bowl which her employer's niece had produced. "He be one o' the escort who came over from London with the new Governor and Captain Rolph."

"An *overner,*" snorted Mary, very conscious that there had been Floyds and Wheelers on the Isle of Wight for generations. "When I give myself to a man I'll make right sure he's an islander!"

At seventeen it is so easy to be sure.

But Libby had lived two years longer, and with no solidly respected relatives to care for her. "Tom's a right persuasive sort of man. And this love-making isn't anything a girl decides about. It just happens," she stated, out of her dearly bought experience.

Mary stood wondering about it. She recalled the slick-tongued Londoner whom the other soldiers called Tom Rudy, and involuntarily her mind made pictures. What secret trysts had these two kept, slipping out into the darkness from warm kitchen and rowdy guardroom? What ecstasies had bright-eyed Libby found out there in the shadows of some bastion or hayloft? And had the magic of those encounters been worth all this apprehension and shamed morning sickness? To a girl who had been strictly brought up by Sergeant Floyd's widowed sister, such passionate moments were as yet but figments of occasional curiosity.

As if to dispel such unaccustomed thoughts Mary crossed to the small attic window, and, pushing open the lattice, let the sweet air of an autumnal morning sweep through the stuffiness of the room. "Aunt Druscilla's roses are still out," she remarked, looking down into the herb garden. But in the mild climate of an island nestling beneath the southern shires of England there was nothing remarkable about roses blooming in November, and Libby's interest was focused upon immediate necessity.

"There's the Governor's bedroom to be done," she muttered, struggling to get up; for although Colonel Hammond, the new Governor, might be quiet in manner, soldiers and servants alike were beginning to mind his quietness more than the hearty blustering of any of his predecessors.

"Lie still awhile. I will do it," promised Mary, taking pity on her plight.

"And you'll try to persuade your aunt to let me stay?"

"I will ask my father to," promised Mary.

Libby slid gratefully back against the straw-filled pillow. Silas Floyd might be Sergeant of the Garrison, but she was far less afraid of him than of his sharp-tongued sister, Mistress Wheeler. "Tell them Tom Rudy says he'll marry me if ever he has the money," she urged, with small conviction.

On the floor below Mary knocked on the small service door between backstair passage and best bedroom. Having lived in the castle all her life she knew the room well, but now she would have preferred to find it empty. Light streamed through the five arched lights of the big west window. Facing it was a tapestry-covered wall and above it, set back over the backstair passage, a disused music gallery. In the far corner a larger door led into the long living room. To Mary the big state bed looked very grand, and long familiarity blinded her to the fact that its hangings were faded. It was a lovely room, she thought, needing only the cheerfulness of a fire crackling in the fine fireplace. But Colonel Hammond was a man of austere taste. He sat at his writing desk dealing with official documents, a tall, plainly dressed man whose soldierly bearing was belied by a sensitive face. No book or picture betrayed some private facet of his mind, no trailing garment lent the place a homeliness. Only a pair of immaculately polished riding boots stood ready by the empty hearth.

As unobtrusively as possible Mary made the almost unrumpled bed, and swept the broad oak floorboards. While drawing the hangings again so that they should not show the place which she had darned so laboriously last winter, she recalled how the last Governor but one, Lord Portland, had been wont to pinch her cheek and call her "Floyd's little wench." She had been little more than a child then, of course. But this new Governor, sent by that all-powerful body of men called Parliament, had no merry quips for children—nor for women either, the maidservants said. Although he had married an important Parliamentarian's daughter, he must have left her behind in London or be a widower like her own father, Mary supposed, for only his sweet-faced mother graced the foot of his table in hall.

She was glad enough to climb the stairs again to tidy the house-keeper's room, which was immediately above. And glad to find her aunt deep in conversation with Mistress Trattle from the "Rose and Crown," since a friend's gossip might distract her from noticing that it was her niece, and not Libby, who did the work.

"And what is the new Governor really like?" Mistress Trattle was asking, as everybody did who came in from the nearby town of Newport.

The high-backed settle before the fire hid all but the two women's laps from Mary's view, but she could imagine the judicious pursing of Aunt Druscilla's lips. "A quiet-living man," was the verdict. "Keeps a good table, but none of the roystering supper parties milord Portland used to have. This one is all for discipline and seeing that the bolts and portcullises work smoothly, my brother says."

"His father was one of the royal chaplains," recalled the hostess of the "Rose and Crown."

"So he may have been. But Parliament appointed him, and father and son often take different sides now."

"But surely the Colonel's sympathy must be with the poor King, dictated to by a lot of traitors and separated from all his children. He's kept almost a prisoner at Hampton Court now, my relatives on the mainland say, and the Queen fled back home to France to have her last baby—"

"I heard she had it in Exeter before she sailed."

It was evidently going to be one of those long discussions about the civil war over on the mainland, and someone called Oliver Cromwell who had usurped the power of King Charles. The bitter arguments which had caused so much bloodshed were beyond Mary's ken. Edgehill, Marston Moor, Nazeby, and Hampton were no more than names to her. All she knew was that the King stood firm for the Church of England and that Parliament refused to grant him enough money. The Puritan's side of the matter she had scarcely heard. She stood by the window looking out upon her simpler and more immediate world. Down in the courtyard her father's spaniel, Patters, lay scratching herself in the sunshine, and the horse upon which Mistress Trattle had ridden pillion behind her servant was tethered to the gate of the herb garden. Soldiers came and went unhurriedly between guardroom and stables, or sat in the shadow of the arched gateway whistling as they cleaned their accoutrements. The great iron-studded doors stood wide, and from the top storey of the Governor's lodgings which butted out into the courtyard she could catch an enchanting glimpse of green fields beyond the drawbridge. Within the wide girdle of the battlements the familiar scene was leisurely and sun-washed. Even the gilded weathervane above the chapel scarcely stirred.

Coming out of her reverie she realized that the voices of the two women on the settle were murmuring on. "Safer to keep one's real sympathies to oneself these days," Mistress Trattle was saying.

"Or suffer for it like poor Sir John Oglander," agreed Aunt Druscilla. "The best Deputy Governor we ever had. And imprisoned twice and almost ruined by those Roundhead traitors in London!"

"Well, at least he came back to Nunwell House alive."

"But the strain of it killed his poor wife, Bess Oglander says."

Because Agnes Trattle was the daughter of a knight impoverished in the wars and Druscilla Wheeler was the widow of one, they liked it to be known that they were on visiting terms with Sir John's cousin, who kept house for him. There was a creak of the settle as buxom Mistress Trattle leaned forward to admire her friend's collar. "A treat to see such lovely lace after the hideous plain collars of these sour-faced Puritans!" she said. "And how beautifully laundered!"

"I never allow anyone but Mary to launder my caps and collars."

"I had no idea she was so clever."

"Oh, she is clever enough with her *hands*."

Mary heard the faint disparagement in her aunt's voice. She knew without envy that she was not quick and gay like pretty Frances, the Trattles' daughter, who met so many interesting people in her father's inn.

"But your Mary is so kind," defended Frances's mother, with her usual generosity.

"Too kind—to any mangy cur or lazy good-for-nothing with a likely story! Why, only this morning when that brazen strumpet Libby began swooning and vomiting—" The clatter of a falling warming-pan reminded her that someone was tidying the room, so that she looked round the corner of the settle and added in vexation, "Why, Mary, surely you are not foolish enough to be doing the drone's work for her! At least I hope you have not been making the Colonel's bed?"

"Libby was sick, and I have nothing special else to do," said Mary. She spoke with deference, but her aunt recognized the same steady voice and level gaze which had won the day when the foolish girl had insisted upon setting free a lamed doe the men had been baiting. For one so gentle, she could be amazingly persistent, and her aunt thought it deplorable the way her father allowed her to roam about the place talking to the soldiers and servants. Mistress Wheeler rose angrily. "Do you suppose I like a niece of mine performing such menial tasks for a mere Parliamentarian? I, whose husband was killed fighting for the King at Nazeby?" she scolded.

Warming-pan in hand, Mary stood silently rebuked, and was grateful when Mistress Trattle intervened good-naturedly. "If Colonel Hammond is as diligent as you say, I wager he did not notice *which* wench it was," she laughed, gathering up her cloak. "And since Mary says she has no special duties this morning why not let her ride back with me and spend the day with Frances? I think she has some outing in mind. You have not been down into Newport all this week, Mary, and Frances counts you her best friend."

Mary Floyd flushed with pleasure. Although she and Frances had played and gossiped together since childhood, she had always been filled with shy admiration for the innkeeper's daughter whose graceful vivacity made her feel uncouth and whose dark, carefully tended hair seemed a reproach every time she remembered to brush out her own mop of tawny curls. And her aunt, she knew, approved the friendship, inventing small errands so that the girls should meet at least once a week. For was not Edward Trattle a member of the Corporation of Newport, with its busy wharves along the Medina river whence laden ships sailed out to sea at Cowes?

Down in the stables one of the men-at-arms stopped grooming his horse to saddle her white pony. Any one of them would have done the same for her. To them, as to the previous Governor, she was "Floyd's little wench" who always asked after their wives and cared for their sick children. Although now she had grown into the slender girl who smiled at them all impartially as she gentled her mount through the gloom of the guardroom gatehouse.

So large a part of Mary's life was confined to the twenty acres within the castle walls that setting forth into the outside world never failed to seem something of an adventure. Down the steep lane close under the fortifications she went, following Mistress Trattle and the manservant, until their mounts splashed through the, clear, brown brook at the bottom. Through Carisbrooke village and along a mile of country road, and then into the bustle and excitement of the island's principal town. Cattle were being driven in to market, and boys, newly released from their books, came running and shouting from the doors of Newport Grammar School. About the doors of the "Bull Inn" and the "George" clustered farmers and drovers, and in the Square beside the church stood the "Rose and Crown," a comfortable-looking hostelry with dormers projecting from the sloping roof, and the greenery of a climbing rose softening the grey stone of its walls.

Outside in the sunshine Edward Trattle was superintending a delivery of casks from his brewhouse in Lugley Street, Frances was already mounted, and a tall, mettlesome-looking black horse was being walked up and down by Jem, the red-headed ostler. Trattle helped his wife down from the saddle, and called a cheery greeting to Mary.

"I am so glad you have come," said Frances. "Captain Burley is going up to Brighstone Down to inspect the look-out post and help plan out this month's manoeuvres for the militia, and he says he will take us with him."

"He seems to think all our defences will fall to pieces now he has retired," laughed the innkeeper indulgently.

"Time hangs heavy for him after being in charge of Yarmouth castle, I expect," said Agnes Trattle. "What with a Governor sent by Parliament and the ranting kind of Mayor we've got, it's good to see so loyal a servant of the King! Ah, here he comes, all booted and spurred at seventy."

With a pleasant mixture of affection and anxiety she turned to berate a stocky, naval-looking man who was emerging from the inn door and whose weather-beaten face looked all the ruddier because of his crisply curling white hair. "You know very well that Dr. Bagnell says you should rest and not excite yourself with such things, Captain Burley. Where's the good of my letting you my quietest room and giving you the most comfortable bed in the house if you can't leave someone younger to look over the militia?"

Being an obstinate old man, he only patted his hostess's plump white hands as she fastened his cloak. "You spoil me, all the lot of you," he chuckled. "But if those Parliamentary fools who retired me think I'm too old to do things myself, at least I know how they ought to be done. Which is more than you can say of some of those landlubbers they've put in charge of our lookouts."

"Well, if you must go sweltering up on to the hills—"

"And this pretty poppet of yours has been plaguing me to let her and Mary come along too, though no doubt 'tis only to make eyes at the young militia officers."

Because of increasing puritanical prejudices. Agnes Trattle thought often of the youthful fun she had enjoyed in her father's palmier days. "I think you had better both go along if only to see that the Captain remembers to eat some of those pasties you have packed," she agreed indulgently.

So the two girls set off on their ponies, one on either side of the Captain on his big black horse, climbing up and up along the chalky hill paths, exclaiming with admiration at the gold and russet of the wooded slopes and listening to Burley's hair-raising stories about sea battles with the Spaniards. When they reached the summit of Brighstone Down they let their tired beasts crop the short, sweet turf, while Mary unpacked the saddle bags and saw to it that the vigorous old man really ate something before inspecting the look-out station. From where they sat he could point out to them several others strategically placed on the highest points of the island from which approaching enemy ships could be sighted, and from which messages could be sent to raise a militia two thousand men strong. He took delight in explaining the whole system of defence which had served the island so well in the past, and outlined the mock battle which was to take place when all the companies, each under the command of its local squire, were to meet upon Brighstone Down for their next exercise.

"But what is the use of it all when we are not at war?" asked Frances, biting into a succulent pasty.

To Mary, a soldier's daughter, the whole scheme was familiar. "All successful attacks come suddenly," she said, quoting words she had often heard her father growl at some slack sentry. "When the French landed unexpectedly and pillaged Newport the whole island might have been taken if the castle's garrison hadn't been prepared. They ambushed scores of them in Noddies Lane."

"And before that the Frenchies had slipped into the creeks along the north shore and occupied Shalfleet for months," corroborated Captain Burley. "They sacked Yarmouth harbour in the west and burned down the church. Out in the Channel you can hear our Yarmouth bells ringing out from some church steeple in Cherbourg."

"But that was a hundred years ago and more," yawned Frances, for whom life was mostly glittering daydreams of the future. "Nothing exciting ever happens here now." The old Captain had stumped off to greet a little group of militia captains, and she was disappointed because Sir Henry Worsley's good-looking son was not among them.

"There are fairs and summer days down on the beaches, and the big ships coming in at Cowes, and sometimes the militia march through Newport with their band," enumerated Mary, feeding Blanche, her pony, with an apple. "And days when all the gentry come up to dine at the castle," she added, hearing her friend sniff at such rustic pleasures.

"My father says they don't go as often as they used. Doesn't the new Governor invite them?"

"Yes, I think so," answered Mary, gathering up the remains of their meal. "But so many of them seem to make excuses."

"One could scarcely blame the Oglanders!" said Frances, whose mother was an out-spoken Royalist. Since all the militia captains had moved away, and were interested only in field-pieces and demi-culverins anyway, she pulled off her new plumed hat and lay sulkily watching a little brig tack out of the mouth of the

Medina river towards Southampton. "I wish I were going over to the Main."

"Not to *live*!" protested Mary, scarcely less surprised than if her friend had proposed crossing the Atlantic to Virginia.

"Why not? My mother lived there before she was married and a right good time she had. There was music and dancing at my grandfather's manor, and sometimes fashionably dressed young men came who could pay a pretty compliment and who had been to Court. I should like to meet some men who had really been to Court."

"But, Frances, there is Mr. Newland. I thought it was all arranged that you and he—"

"Just because he is one of the wealthiest merchants in Newport! But he is old—forty at least—and thinks only about his trade on the Medina and his money."

Mary often saw John Newland up at the castle, of course, when he came to discuss supplies of corn and coal for the garrison and the Governor's household. Both there and at the inn he always spoke to her pleasantly. But certainly he was neither young nor fashionably dressed—not the exciting sort of lover she would have wished for her friend. Mary could scarcely imagine a sober-looking merchant like Master Newland being passionate. From him her thoughts shifted involuntarily to Tom Rudy, the plausible young Londoner with the persuasive smile. "Our Libby is going to have a baby," she said, with apparent irrelevance.

Frances sat up at once, displaying mild interest. "Will they send her away?" she asked.

"The poor thing's father was drowned at sea and her mother was a drab."

"And so I suppose your silly tender heart will drive you to champion her?"

"I promised her I would do what I could. You see, she has absolutely nowhere to go."

"She should have thought of that before," said Frances, with a toss of her sleek, dark head.

Mary tugged thoughtfully at a tuft of grass. "Do people stop to think? Would we, do you suppose?" she asked with shyly averted eyes, remembering what Libby had said. "Supposing, I mean, the man was young—and very persuasive—"

Frances, who met so many personable young men coming and going at the inn, leant forward impulsively to kiss the serious fair-skinned face so near her own. "Oh, Mary Floyd, what a dear innocent you are!" she laughed, between affection and exasperation.

To hide her embarrassment, Mary got up and stood watching the group of men gathered about the little stone look-out station. The afternoon sun was warm upon her bare head and a fresh sea breeze was tugging at her skirts. From the top of Brighstone Down the whole lozenge-shaped outline of the Wight was visible. Eastward stood the imposing mound of the castle, below steep cliffs to the south stretched the Channel in a blue expanse of white-capped waves towards France, while westward the long spine of hills tapered to the thin peninsula of the treacherous Needles' rocks. Down in the valley the Medina flowed like a silver streak from Newport out to Cowes and beyond the smooth waters of the Solent lay the southern coast of England, so clear and close some days that Mary could see the houses at Portsmouth and shipping coming out from Southampton Water. One hand shading her eyes, she stood and gazed, all smaller issues forgotten. Strange to think that over there civil war had been raging, with the King detained in one of his palaces, and people hating and killing each other because of their politics or their religion. Whereas here, as Frances said, nothing ever happened. Here the farms were folded peacefully into the sheltered hollows of the downland, only the cloud shadows chased each other across the green slopes of the hills and the white gulls screamed overhead or swooped hungrily upon the rich, red earth of newly furrowed fields. Here was beauty, security and home. The only known land, the place that held a beloved father and good friends. Unlike Frances, she had no desire to be anywhere else.

To-day, she thought, rousing herself at the sound of the returning Captain's blustering voice, has been another ordinary, happy day.

# CHAPTER TWO

———— ⬥⬥⬥ ————

N EXT MORNING, LIBBY BEING fit to work again, Mary went to
the well-house as usual taking tid-bits for the donkeys who
took turns at treading the great draught wheel to raise
the water, a task in peacetime no longer performed by prisoners.
It had needed infinite kindness and patience, but the men knew
that she had a way with animals. "Get in, Jacob! " she said quietly,
and at sound of her clear young voice the waiting donkey pricked
his ears. His small hoofs clattered across the stone floor and then
thudded softly into the wooden wheel. "March!" she ordered; and
obediently Jacob began to march, moving forward not at all, but
effortlessly turning the mighty wheel until old Brett, leaning over
the well top, called to him to stop.

Mary was always well content to be in the company of Brett,
whose back was bent by humble, cheerfully accomplished tasks.
She loved to stand in the cool shadows of the well-house and watch
his gnarled hands guide the pulley rope until each bucket came to
rest upon the stone coping, and then detach it from the iron hook
and fix an empty bucket in its place. And since childhood she had
listened with delight for the delayed, far-off splash as some of the
water slopped back down the thirty-fathom shaft. One of the young
soldiers, with bare brown arms and leathern jerkin, would come
striding in to heave two freshly filled buckets on to the yoke across
his shoulders and then tramp off with them towards the kitchens.
Then another empty bucket would be swung down and either she

or Brett would call to Jacob to tread the wheel again, until the morning's task was done and the wheel finally creaked to rest.

"He do obey 'ee better 'n me," allowed Brett handsomely.

"Only because I bribe him better," laughed Mary, giving the donkey his reward. "Do you know where my father is, Brett?"

"I zeed 'un ridin' out to Nippert afore you come in, Mistress Mary. Don't 'ee allus go in after the stores and such come Zaturday?"

"Yes, Brett, but not as early as this. And I specially wanted to speak to him."

The old man went on coiling up the slack of the rope, sensing her disappointment. "Was it zummat you wanted special like?" he asked, as he always had since she was a baby, in the hope that it might be something he could get for her.

"Oh, no, not for myself. It was just that I promised someone—"

"Not that minx Libby?"

Mary turned in surprise. "Why, how could you guess?"

"She come to me cryin' soon as she knowed. An' last night when I was bankin' up the kitchen fires she told me how kind you bin, doin' her work an' all."

"It was nothing. I'm stronger than she is. And I don't want my aunt to turn her out as if she were really a wanton. I thought perhaps if my father would speak for her."

"I reckon her never had a chance—not with the glib type o' Roundhead us be getting' in garrison now. Fair dazzled, like a coney with a stoat, a girl'd be." He nodded his grizzled head in the direction of the kitchens whither Tom Rudy, who happened to be on well-house duty, was carrying the buckets. "I bin thinkin', little Mistress," he added, "if you was to talk Mistress Wheeler into keepin' the wench, maybe I could talk my sister down in village into takin' her in when her time comes—"

Mary turned to him with shining eyes and laid a hand upon his bare, wet arm. He might be only the castle odd-job man but she valued his shrewd kindliness and counted him her friend. "There be someone in a terbul hurry clatterin' over the drawbridge now," he said, uncomfortably staving off her gratitude. "But it could scarce be Sergeant yet."

Sergeant Floyd's daughter stepped out into the sunshine to make sure. The well-house doorway faced the main gates of the castle and she could see two horsemen talking to the sentry and some of the guard gathering round to listen. A sudden unusual stir seemed to have broken the morning's peaceful routine. With one arm still resting upon the donkey's neck she waited to hear what it was all about. Old Brett stood watching in the doorway behind her; and Tom Rudy, coming round the corner from the kitchens, pulled up short beside them, the chains hanging empty from his yoke.

The two horsemen and the sentry were coming across the courtyard, the taller of the two strangers still gesticulating.

"Who can they be?" asked Mary, who knew the island gentry by sight.

"Overners," snorted Brett. "An' in a fair firk 'bout zummat! Look how blown their poor beasts be."

"I'll wager they're from Court with those fancy clothes," put in Rudy. Although no one had asked for his opinion, he spoke with assured experience and with a Cromwellian's contempt for Royalist laces.

"A pity Frances is not here!" thought Mary, remembering her friend's desire; but even if these visitors had really come from Court they were no younger than Master Newland and seemed far too hurried for any romantic dalliance.

"Anyone seen Captain Rolph?" the sentry was bawling through cupped hands.

"I'll go seek him," offered Brett, ambling off towards the officers' quarters.

"Our business is with the Governor, not your Captain," fumed the taller, more excitable of the two gentlemen.

"But I tell 'ee, sir, Colonel Hammond be gone into Newport," repeated the worried sentry. "If you will but go in and rest, sirs, I am sure that Mistress Wheeler will—"

"When will he be back?"

"This afternoon, like as not."

The older cavalier made a gesture of exasperated fury and the younger one said more reasonably. "Had we not better ride back into Newport, Jack, and try to find him?"

"But the dolts say they don't know where he is."

They sat their sweating horses irresolutely, staring up with frustration at the front of the Governor's lodgings. There was no sign of old Brett having found the Captain, who might at least have preserved the castle's hospitality by receiving them with some show of authority. And seeing the annoyance on their faces change to deep concern, Mary overcame her shyness sufficiently to step forward. "Colonel Hammond rode out about half an hour ago on private business," she told them, bobbing a countrified curtsy and uncomfortably aware that Jacob was clopping at her heels. "But my father went with him to order stores for the garrison, and he may well have seen which way the Governor went. And you would almost surely find my father with the corn merchant, Master John Newland, down by the quay, or else at Master Trattle's malthouse in Lugley Street."

The two men's tired faces lit up with relief. They raised their be-plumed hats at the pretty sight of her. "And what is your father's name?" one of them asked.

"Silas Floyd, Sergeant of the garrison here," said Mary. "But will you not, as our sentry suggests, let us give you some refreshment before you go?"

They thanked her but excused themselves, saying that their business brooked not a moment's delay, and wheeled their weary horses immediately. But in passing her the tall man bent from his saddle and kissed her hand as if she were some fine lady. "It would be difficult to tell you how grateful we are," he said, his voice unsteady with emotion. And, looking up, she saw that there were actually tears in his eyes.

As she stood watching them depart she was surprised to see Tom Rudy approach them. He was leading a horse and buttoning his hastily donned tunic. "If I might show you gentlemen the way about Newport, sirs, it would save time," he suggested, with his ingratiating smile.

They accepted his offer readily enough. It was common sense, of course; but only the quick-witted Londoner, for some reason of his own, had thought of it.

"Heaven help you when Captain Rolph hears of it—leaving the castle without orders!" jeered the passing trooper whose horse he had borrowed.

But as Rudy vaulted into the saddle, he grinned down at him. "I wager you Captain'll not be too grieved!" he said, and galloped after the departing visitors with so much assurance that both the inner and outer sentries supposed he had been sent.

"Well, of all the impudence!" exclaimed Mary, goaded beyond prudence. "A stranger scarcely come into the island taking it upon himself to play guide when there's twenty of you here, mostly Newport born!"

The trooper, who had been standing open-mouthed, laughed ruefully at her vehemence. "Your father'd have zummat to zay, Mistress. But 'twould be like a slimy Puritan's luck to get back before 'un. And with a silver pound in his pocket for his pains as like as not."

He offered to lead Jacob back to his stall for her, and Mary stood wondering what business could have been so urgent as to bring tears of gratitude to a fashionably dressed middle-aged man's eyes. For a moment she had seemed to stand on the brink of some exciting happenings, and felt oddly frustrated now the courtyard was quiet and deserted again; but was soon brought back to the everyday level of life by a casement being pushed open sharply behind her. "Who were those people making such a to-do down there?" Mistress Wheeler called to her.

"Two gentlemen wanting to see the Governor, but they could not wait," explained Mary.

"You should have called Captain Rolph, child."

"Brett did go for him."

"Pah! Brett is as slow as a wet week."

"He is getting old," defended Mary.

"Well, he and his donkeys seem to have wasted enough of your morning. Better come up here and help with some of this mending."

Mary found the housekeeper's room strewn with sheets. Her

aunt had been going through the linen presses. "No more than half a dozen pairs fit to use in the best bedroom," she was lamenting. "And two of those need some of your darning. Your very finest, mind. Sit you down by the window where the light is good, while I cut out patches for the rest."

It was warm and pleasant in the top-floor room and they worked in companionable silence. Thanks to her aunt's training Mary was an excellent needlewoman and as she drew the thread back and forth her thoughts roamed easily. The crackling of the fire and the homely sound of scissors grating against the table were but a lulling accompaniment. But when less than an hour had passed and in imagination she was living over again yesterday's happy hours on Brighstone Down she became aware of hurried footsteps on the stairs. The door opened quickly and to the astonishment of both of them her father stood there.

"Why, Silas, what brings you back from Newport so soon?" exclaimed Mistress Wheeler, turning from the table with the big scissors in her hand.

Silas Floyd shot the bolt behind him and leaned against the door. He was a man renowned for calmness in any emergency, but his breath came quickly and he looked almost bemused.

"Have you had some bad news?" asked Mary quickly.

"God knows whether it be good or bad. To me it is just—unbelievable." By an effort his abstracted gaze returned to them as if seeing them again as familiar individuals. "Colonel Hammond sent me back to tell you that the King is coming," he said.

His sister dropped the scissors with a clatter and the sheet spread across his daughter's lap slid to the floor. "Coming *here*—to the island?" they cried in unison.

"Here, to Carisbrooke." Although he had ridden back from Newport with the news, he seemed scarcely to have had time to credit it himself. "King Charles is just across the Solent, at Lady Southampton's house," he added, setting his steel helmet on the table and crossing to a cupboard to find himself a drink. His sister poured it for him with an unsteady hand. "You mean they have let him leave Hampton?" she said.

"He escaped. It seems there was some plot against his life and his friends thought he would be safer here." Floyd emptied his tankard at a draught. "Two gentlemen came to me when I was settling our weekly account with Trattle. They said you sent them, Mary."

"I understand now why they were in such a state. Who were they?"

"A Master Ashburnham and Sir John Berkeley, both formerly officers in the King's disbanded army. Seems they were sent over in advance to sound the Governor as to whether he would keep him safe."

"And you found the Governor?"

"I'd seen him go into the Mayor's house. Couldn't have been a worse place. This Master Ashburnham seemed confident that if he could get the King to Carisbrooke before nightfall their troubles would be over. But the less a Puritan fanatic like his Worship Moses Read knows about the King's movements, the better, say I!"

Mary came and refilled his tankard. "How did King Charles escape from Hampton Court?" she asked.

"My dear child, how should I know? There never has been such hustle and commotion on the island since the French came. I could hear them conferring in Master Read's best parlour while I kicked my heels outside along with that Roundhead fellow Captain Rolph brought from London. All I know is what the Colonel told me when he came outside to give me my orders. And by the way he drew me aside I reckon he didn't want the two Court gentlemen to hear. I'd a feeling he was as fair stunned as I was, and none too pleased to be drawn into the matter. 'Hurry back to the castle, Sergeant,' he said, 'and tell them to prepare for the King's coming. And tell Captain Rolph I am going over to Southampton with these gentlemen. I want him to ride straight to Cowes Castle and meet me there so that I can take him and the Cowes Captain along with me. To ensure the safe conduct of the King, of course.' "

"Captain Rolph is mounting his horse already," said Mary, looking down from the window. For her the jumped-up Parliamentarian Captain's departure always brought a vague sense of relief, for of all the men in the place only he, with his bold apprising glance, made her feel vaguely afraid.

"But what are we to do? Where are we to house the King? And how feed him?" demanded Druscilla Wheeler, momentarily distraught.

"I've the Governor's orders for you too," said Floyd. "You are to prepare the best bedroom for King Charles, and the Colonel will move into the officers' quarters in the old wing. His Majesty will take his meals in the long parlour over the great hall. And rooms will have to be prepared for Sir John Berkeley and Master Ashburnham, of course, and for a Colonel Legge, I think he said, who rode from Hampton with the King and is waiting with him now. And a meal must be ready upon his Majesty's arrival."

"But how should we know what royalty eats?" asked Mary.

"And how make up four beds with only six good pairs of sheets?" demanded Mistress Wheeler, looking round desperately at the half-sorted contents of her poorly stocked linen cupboard. "And the bedroom needs fresh tapestries and hangings."

Sergeant Floyd picked up his helmet and set it in the crook of his arm. Domestic arrangements, thank God, were no concern of his. He had all the military detail to attend to, and twenty men to drill into the performance of some kind of reception parade fit for royalty, of which performance he was none too sure himself.

"If it's a matter of moving things or nailing hangings, I can spare you a couple of men to help," he offered. "I shall be in charge until they return with his Majesty."

"And when, in the name of a merciful God, will that be?" asked Mistress Wheeler, facing him squarely.

"Sometime to-morrow, I imagine, if the tide serves."

"*To-morrow!*"

"If you were the King wouldn't you be anxious to put three miles of Solent and the good will of us islanders between yourself and such pestilential enemies?" asked Floyd, from the doorway. But when he had drawn back the bolt he turned to enquire more sympathetically, "You will be able to have the place ready, Druscilla?"

His sister took a grip on herself and regarded him from across the room with a mixture of pride and affection. Even her social and housekeeping experiences as chatelaine of a small manor on the mainland were not going to help her much now, so she guessed that her brother, who had never been off the island, must be as scared as she was at the thought of preparing a reception for a king. "Have we Floyds ever failed to do our duty when the time comes, Silas?" she asked, drawing herself up to her full height. "I pray you, have someone go to the chandlers for six gross more candles. The best tallow kind. And send Brett and Libby and the rest of the maids to me as you go past the kitchens."

"We could get extra help perhaps from the village?" suggested Mary, gathering up a pile of folded sheets in her strong young arms as soon as he was gone.

"I make no doubt we could. Wouldn't every lily-fingered, gossip-lapping woman among them give her eyes to come up here now?" sniffed the competent housekeeper of Carisbrooke. "But we will manage very well with such wenches as we have. At least I've trained them myself."

The excellence of her training was to be severely tested during the next twenty-four hours. For the rest of the day the castle household ate cold viands picked from the buttery at odd moments. The cook and his underlings prepared dishes which they had not made since Lord Portland's day, the scullions scoured every pot and the best silver dinner set was brought out. Maids scurried about making up beds, and a couple of stalwart troopers got in their way moving furniture. Mary stood with her aunt in the middle of the best bedroom considering what to do. Somehow the four poster did not look so grand now, only rather shabby and faded. "There are those red velvet hangings milady Portland was wont to use in the winter," Mary remembered suddenly.

"Red velvet?" In the ferment of the afternoon's work aunt and niece had each come to respect the other's ability, so that much of the authoritative manner and the meekness were gone.

"Yes, Aunt Druscilla, do you not remember? They had little silver stags embroidered on them, which I adored. They may be in one of the attics. I know they were all packed up ready to take to France but milady had to leave so much behind when the Parliamentarians turned her out of the castle."

The material had been as brave and beautiful as the Governor's wife who had owned it. So the attics were searched and the four-poster rehung with crimson velvet, which looked quite suitable for a king. By nightfall the Colonel's business-like writing desk had been removed and a prie-dieu put in its place because everyone knew the King was pious. Real wax candles, borrowed from the chapel, stood upon his table because it was said he liked to read. The best chair in the castle had been placed beside the wide hearth and the fire which old Brett had laid burned cheerily, throwing kindly, dancing shadows upon the faded tapestry on the wall facing the window. "The servants will have to walk quietly along the backstairs passage behind that partition wall, with no courting and no tittering," decreed Mistress Wheeler, surveying the main scene of their labours with a critical but not unsatisfied eye. "And you and I will have to make the bed."

Terror seized shy Mary. "You mean—come in here—with the King of England sitting maybe in that chair?" she asked with bated breath.

With a rare demonstration of affection Aunt Druscilla pushed her down upon the carved chest set for the accommodation of the King's clothes at the bottom of the bed. "You are tired, child," she said. "To-morrow it will not seem so alarming. And who else is there to do it? We could not have Libby in here, and in any case she will have the other beds to do."

So Libby would not be sent away. There would be no need to plead for her after all. Having been on her feet since before noon, Mary sank down on the chest, digesting that unexpected fact with thankfulness. The ways of the Almighty were indeed exceeding strange. For instance, who would have dreamed this time yesterday that she would be making a bed for a king? And once his Majesty came here what would life be like? Would he be allowed to live in peace or would all the harrying and disturbances from the mainland follow him?

She was still sitting there before the fire almost too tired for thought when she heard her father's deep, cheerful voice. By the sound of it she knew that his part of the preparations must have gone well. And now he was inspecting his sister's handiwork and commending her with the same warmth which encouraged his men.

"And how goes the State bedroom?" he was asking laughingly. "And my tired little daughter?"

"Do you suppose the King will think it all very strange and simple after Hampton Court?" she asked sleepily.

Floyd smiled down at her. "He has been here before, you know."

"Why, of course. When I was quite small, you used to tell me at bedtime about the day Prince Charles came. But I have almost forgotten."

Floyd had had a worrying day himself and was glad to sit down on the carved chest beside her and gather her drooping form to his side. "He came across to review the militia and watched them having a practice battle, the same as they're practising for now up on Brighstone Down. Except that he was King James's son he wasn't very important then because his elder brother, Prince Henry, was still alive. And after the review Prince Charles came up to the castle to dine."

Mary leaned in weary comfort against her father's side. She could scarcely keep her eyes open. "And what was he like?" she asked.

"A rather frail-looking lad with a limp. Though he sat a horse well. He'd a shy way with him but he took everything in. And when he went round the battlements after dinner he asked Sir John Oglander, who was Deputy Governor here then, if he might touch off one of our biggest guns. He was but an eager lad and 'twas I who primed it for him. 'Twas my first year with the garrison and I mind how proud I was."

For the first time the King for whom all this preparation had been going on began to take on a human personality, and to awaken pity. He had been young and shy and eager. "And now he comes back to us an escaped prisoner," murmured Mary compassionately. And because she had worked far too hard and was dearer to him than anyone else in the world, the Sergeant of the garrison picked her up in his strong arms and carried her, already sleeping, to her bed.

# CHAPTER THREE

⌘

LTHOUGH IT WAS SUNDAY and the chapel bell was ringing, few people up at the castle had time to attend morning service. In the long room above the great hall the table was being laid with the best napery and silver, and down in the kitchen everyone from cook to turnspit was in a state of nervous tension. No one knew when the King would arrive. "The wind should serve," said Mistress Wheeler, glancing out across the court-yard at the chapel weathervane. "So even though they were not able to cross to Cowes last night, they may still be here in time for dinner." So close a contingency shook even her determined semblance of composure. Being uncertain how people ought to sit at table with royalty and fearing that her arrangements might not be sufficiently formal, at the last minute she sent her niece down to the "Rose and Crown" to beg the loan of an imposing salt cellar which had been part of Agnes Trattle's dowry.

"How strange it seems that we had the news this time yesterday and have not yet had time to tell even our best friends!" said Mary, hastily pulling on her cloak.

But there was no need to tell the Trattles or anyone else. She soon found that the amazing news had already seeped through the little village at the foot of the castle and spread to the town of Newport. People coming out of St. Thomas's church were all discussing what the parson had told them, and others stood about the streets in animated groups or ran in and out of each other's houses asking if it could possibly be true that King Charles was coming to Carisbrooke. At the "Rose and Crown" Agnes and Frances had donned their best gowns, and Captain Burley was pacing up and down their parlour as though it were a quarter-deck. "I'd train my guns on all those houses with shuttered windows and the scum who listen to that fanatic preacher and deny our King a welcome!" he kept muttering. Only Edward Trattle, unwillingly observing the new Puritanical ruling that customers should not be served upon the Sabbath, kept outwardly calm.

As soon as Mary arrived everyone crowded round her because she had come from the castle. With proud heart and willing hands Agnes wrapped up the cherished salt cellar. "What a pother you must all have had to get the rooms and table prepared!" she sympathized, half enviously. "And now your poor harassed Aunt will have to work like this every day. When she came back to the island mourning her lot as a war-impoverished widow little did she think she would soon be housekeeping for a king!"

"She says that you and Frances must come up soon and get a sight of him," said Mary.

"I should like to come back with you now and help," offered Frances, her eyes alight with excitement. "I would work my fingers to the bone for him!"

"It is an idea, Frances. I am sure that Mistress Wheeler can do with more help," agreed her mother, feeling that once some fine gentleman from Court set eyes upon her pretty daughter, a fine match could be arranged for her. Something more suitable for a girl of Langdale blood than her husband's idea of marriage with a local merchant.

"Oh, do ask her, Mary!" urged Frances.

Although Mary felt dubious of the value of her friend's domestic services, she would readily have promised to do so had not the innkeeper himself intervened. "You'll bide here, my girl," he told his daughter with unusual firmness.

"Oh, father, would you not have us all serve the King?" pouted Frances, whose whims were so seldom denied her. And even Mary felt surprised and not a little shocked.

"Probably for the moment we can all serve him best by going about our own work as usual and keeping a quiet tongue in our heads," said Trattle, with an anxious eye on the excitable old Captain who was stamping restlessly out into the street.

"But it would be such a chance for Frances," persisted her mother. "Other Royalists are bound to gather here and it would be like living at Court."

"For a time, perhaps. But don't forget that even over here there are some who wish him ill," answered Trattle, watching the furtive movements of a sour-looking, tall-hatted Puritan on the opposite side of the street.

Further argument was stopped by the sudden appearance of Captain Burley's grizzled head at the open window. "Frances, child! All of you! Come out quickly!" he called. "There is a party of horsemen coming along the road from Cowes. And I can hear cheering. I believe it is the King himself."

They all crowded through the door and out into the street to find everyone gazing in the direction of Cowes. Certainly there was cheering and it was coming nearer; but it sounded spasmodic and half-hearted. People still refused to believe the fantastic rumour that the King was coming. Some of the older folk assumed importance because, like Silas Floyd, they remembered his coming as a young prince; but as most of them had never seen so much as a painting of him they would not know him even if he did come. The more soberly dressed men and women of Cromwellian persuasion stared in silence and even the majority of loyal islanders seemed uncertain what to do.

Mary, lined up among the Trattle family and servants, stared wonderingly too. She had taken it for granted that when the King arrived she would be up at the castle, under the direction of her father or her aunt. Here, in the capital of the island, there was a feeling of being caught unawares. After a stormy night, thin sunshine was making a wet radiance of the rain-washed cobbles. Shading her eyes against it she could see a little cavalcade of six trotting smartly towards her. Two of them, she supposed, must be the gentlemen whom she had directed the day before. Colonel

Hammond, of course, was easily distinguishable on his tall roan, and bluff Captain Baskett from Cowes she knew by sight. And riding between the two of them but a pace or two ahead was a man of much slighter build with a pale, thoughtful face and small, pointed brown beard. His clothes were neither militarily severe like Hammond's nor flamboyant in the cavalier style, but in such quiet good taste that all eyes were drawn to him. And each time he rose in the saddle the glittering insignia of some order showed beneath the plain dark cloak he wore. "Is *he* the King? That little man in front?" Mary asked involuntarily.

"He is a better horseman than any of them. The best in England." Captain Burley flung the words at her over his shoulder, having noted the faint disappointment in her voice. Stepping forward, he almost elbowed her aside. "Let us welcome his Majesty to Newport!" he called, raising both hands commandingly so that nearly all the people about him broke into a really rousing cheer. The King slowed his mount to a walking pace. Cheers could not have been too plentiful of late, for a look of pleasure warmed the still composure of his face. Mistress Trattle, making a charming picture against the homely walls of the inn, picked up the skirts of her best plum-coloured satin and swept a splendid curtsy which Mary, standing a little behind her, tried self-consciously to imitate. The irrepressible Captain drew smartly to attention and saluted. Some prentice lads standing near threw up their Sunday caps into the air. The maid servants of the "Rose and Crown" flung wide an upper casement to wave, while their master stood respectfully, cap in hand, his keen knowledgeable eyes searching his Sovereign's face.

Colonel Hammond's horse reared a little and swerved at all the noise and commotion; or more probably, thought Mary with her close understanding of animals, because of some nervous tension passing from man to beast. Although etiquette demanded that he must ride a little behind the King, it seemed almost as though the Governor were hurrying him forward. And just at that moment, the sour-faced man Trattle had been watching stooped down behind a knot of people, his white-cuffed arm shot upwards and a handful of mud splashed against the King's borrowed cloak, some of it even spattering the sparkling George beneath.

Charles Stuart disdained to notice it, but Mary saw his face tighten with angry hurt at the indignity.

"Oh shame!" cried the women in the crowd, while their men, furious at the slur upon the hospitality of their town, closed in to catch the mud-slinger. But he was too quick for them, or lived too close. The front door of his house banged in their faces. And it was not for them, without the Governor's orders, to break it open. Ashburnham pricked his horse forward and would have wiped the mud away with his handkerchief, but the King stayed him with an authoritative gesture. The people of Newport stopped cheering, feeling that part of the shame was theirs.

In the sudden silence before the royal party had time to ride on, Frances Trattle's wit and facile emotion told her what to do to efface the insult. With a sure sense of the dramatic she turned to pull one of her mother's damask roses from the inn wall and ran forward with it into the middle of the street. Without any formality she held it up to the King. All the freshness of youth and the impulsiveness of loyalty were in the gesture. She looked lovely as a rose herself in her close-fitting cap and pink-tabbed gown. The King's set face broke into a smile. With quick courtesy he drew off a glove to take the stiff-stemmed bloom, lifting it delicately to his nostrils to inhale the sweetness of its perfume.

"He has a daughter of about her age from whom he has so recently been forced to part," murmured Agnes Trattle, her eyes abrim with tears.

Hammond looked annoyed and was clearly as anxious to terminate this kind of demonstration as the other, but short of running Frances down he was forced to rein in his horse.

A murmur of admiring approval ran through the crowd. Only a few Newport girls, less fortunate than she, muttered something about Frances Trattle always knowing how to put herself into the picture. For a moment or two cavalcade and onlookers kept still, so that King Charles and Frances seemed to be momentarily alone and the centre of all attention.

"God bless you, my child, for this good omen!"

Their King's pleasant, cultured voice came to them clearly in the stillness before he rode on towards Carisbrooke with the red rose in his hand.

Agnes Trattle was beaming with maternal pride. Captain Burley almost pranced with jubilation. Mary was torn between admiration and envy. "Oh, Frances, how splendid of you!" she cried, running to embrace her friend. Frances herself began to laugh self-consciously, her cheeks aflame. As soon as the riders had passed on and the staring crowds closed after them everyone crowded around her. A few hours ago none of them had expected ever to behold a king, and now the Sovereign of Great Britain had actually spoken to young Frances Trattle, and given her his blessing.

"It is something that will always be remembered about her," prophesied the doting old Captain.

"If only I could think of things like that and do them without becoming tongue-tied and clumsy!" thought Mary, suddenly conscious that she, unlike the rest of them, had not even had time to change from her workaday clothes.

Presently they were all indoors again drinking to the King's health, and to the safety of young Prince Charles over the water, and then—upon Burley's fond insistence—lifting their glasses laughingly to Frances. "Now you *must* let her go back with Mary to help Druscilla—now that the King himself has noticed her!" exulted Agnes Trattle, slipping persuasive arms about her husband's shoulders. When she smiled like that it was easy to see from whom Frances inherited her coaxing ways, and difficult to deny her. But Edward Trattle was a long-thinking man, not readily moved from his convictions by the emotions of the moment. Gently he detached Agnes's clinging hands. "'Twas prettily done and I was as proud as you, wife," he admitted. "But maybe 'twas unwise."

His wife stared at him in amazement. "Edward Trattle, you'd never be chicken-hearted enough to fawn to the opinions of these ranting Puritans?" she gasped.

"Or be thinking of your own skin?" joined in Burley indignantly.

"'Tis Charles Stuart's skin I am thinking of," answered the

innkeeper, thoughtfully twirling the contents of his half-empty glass. "Many's the time I've seen it happen in a brawl that you can help a man better if you are not suspected of being his friend." He looked up to make sure the door was shut and the servants gone before attempting to explain a half-formulated idea. "Men come and go in my house. Men of all kinds and parties. Their tongues are loosened with my good liquor, so that whether I will or not I hear a mort of things. The 'Bull' has a definitely Cromwellian trade. Jackson of the 'George' hears many a royalist toast raised over his tankards. A time may come when it will be wiser for the 'Rose and Crown' to cater for no particular party."

"Meaning that you want the trade of both?" accused Burley, because his blood was overheated by excitement and a good deal more of his host's good Burgundy than his doctor would have allowed.

Mercifully Trattle, who knew all the old man's weaknesses, was both morally and financially above any need to defend himself. "I mean because no one is sure which side the Governor himself is really on," he said quietly. "On Saturday before he left for the Main he told some of us councillors that he had insisted upon going with those two gentlemen to escort the King across so as to ensure his Majesty's safety. Yet as you saw just now he did not have that mud-slinging crop-head clapped into the stocks. So who knows but what—should the King stay here long—it may not prove useful for his friends to be able to come into my house without being labelled royalists?"

The serious moment passed, and was soon relieved by Mary's anxious insistence that she must get back to the castle. Attention focused upon her now because she would presently be in the place where all their thoughts were. "You will see the King every day!" they said.

"And I suppose she may even help make his Majesty's bed!" pouted Frances enviously.

"And perhaps be allowed to launder that priceless lace collar he was wearing!" sighed Agnes Trattle, wishing that she had brought up her own daughter to be less decorative and more domesticated.

But Mary only laughed as she kissed her friend's flushed cheek.

"Even if I do is it likely that his Majesty would ever be aware of my existence? Much less speak to me as he did to you," she said comfortingly. "And truly, Frances, I should feel like sinking through the floor if he did!"

Edward Trattle rode part way home with her lest there should be any roughness among the crowd, and once back in the castle, her estimate of her own unimportance seemed to be only too correct. She had missed the garrison's diligently drilled reception, which she would have been so proud to watch, and was scolded for loitering because the imposing Trattle salt cellar was only just in time for the King's table. And far from gazing at their important guests, she spent the rest of the day obeying her aunt's instructions and running up and down the backstairs trying to help the flustered servants. From time to time, as the dishes were being carried in, she caught the sound of men's animated voices. And once when she paused to rearrange a dish of fruit which one of the men servants was carrying, she heard Colonel Hammond saying very politely that he trusted his Majesty would not find island hospitality too inadequate after the luxury of Hampton Court, and then, before the door shut again, that quiet voice which she now knew to be the King's assuring him that it was a comfort indeed after the inn at Cowes where they had been obliged to spend the previous night.

The momentous November day darkened early and after attending evensong his Majesty was pleased to retire to the room which had been so carefully prepared for him. All three of his gentlemen went in, too, to undress him. To Mary, so completely ignorant of the complicated etiquette of courts, it seemed strange that one man—even a king—could need the services of three people to prepare him for bed. But perhaps, she thought, they wanted to talk among themselves without their host. She could not know how near the truth she was. All she knew was that most of the servants would have given anything to go to bed, too. But there was the royal supper table to clear as well as the ordinary tables for the household in the hall below, the fires to be damped down and the best silver to be put away. Relieved at last of his formal duties the Governor himself was standing looking uncertainly at the closed door of the King's room when he found himself waylaid by Mistress Wheeler and the head cook wanting their orders for the morrow.

"Must we prepare for any more guests?" asked the housekeeper.

"I suppose that all the island gentry will expect to come up and pay their respects," said the Governor, passing a hand over his high forehead. "Certainly Sir John Oglander. His Majesty had been asking for him. He seems to have expected to find him here."

"Whether he comes or not we shall need more poultry," announced Cheke, the cook, firmly.

"To-morrow I will see what I can do," promised the harassed Colonel, heading for his hastily arranged quarters in the officers' wing.

"If he would just give one word of praise for all our work!" sighed Druscilla Wheeler. At any other time she would not have demeaned herself by discussing even a Parliamentarian governor with any save her own intimate friends; but she was nearing sixty and had been on her feet since dawn.

"When Lord Portland gave a dinner party he drove us much harder," recalled Cheke, looking disapprovingly after the tall departing figure of his present master. "But he always let us know afterwards what he thought of the sweets and the sauces, and often came down and drank a glass of wine with us afterwards."

"The trouble with this one is that no one knows what he thinks about anything!" agreed Mistress Wheeler.

Aunt and niece began to mount the backstairs to their well-earned rest. This day, so utterly different from all others in their lives, would soon be done. But as they tiptoed past the best bedroom the door opened quietly. To their surprise, Mr. Ashburnham stood tall and solemn in the lamplit passage with something white held across his extended arms. "There will be his Majesty's shirt to wash, madam," he said, holding it towards the castle housekeeper as reverently as though it were the Holy Grail.

"To-night?" stammered that weary lady, taken aback.

Ashburnham's features relaxed into a sad, propitiating smile. "Having left Hampton so hurriedly, he has no other," he explained simply.

It was a plight they had not thought of. "Perhaps Colonel Hammond could lend—" she began; but one glance at the exquisitely stitched garment and the recollection of the Governor's severely starched linen dried up the words. "But how could we get it laundered and aired before his Majesty rises?" she asked instead.

"And his Majesty's collar," insisted Ashburnham imperturbably. "We rode hard from Hampton and he has already been obliged to wear it two days."

"The servants are at last gone to their beds," objected Mistress Wheeler, feeling that this day she could do no more.

"It does not concern the servants. No one at Court, Madam, touches his Majesty's linen save the royal laundress."

For once Druscilla Wheeler was at a loss. In all her careful planning, this was a contingency which she had overlooked. There was no royal laundress at Carisbrooke. Only the giggling, clumsy laundry maids. "My niece is clever with her hands," she said, falling back in her weariness upon a familiar phrase.

"Old Brett has not yet damped down the fire in your room. I could dry them by that," suggested Mary, in a small tired voice.

"It will mean sitting up half the night to get them just right for pressing," her aunt reminded her, turning away as though the matter had passed beyond her control.

All Mary longed for was the small, hard bed in her little attic room next to the maidservant's dormitory; but she found herself obediently stretching out her arms in unconscious imitation of the King's confidential friend, while very carefully he laid the King's shirt across them and placed the elaborate lace collar on top of it. "What shall I do with them when they are ready, sir?" she asked, with her usual common sense.

"Bring them to this door before the King breaks his fast, and one of us will take them." His master's need provided for, John Ashburnham smiled down at her like the great gentleman he was. "This is the second time I find myself indebted to you," he added gently.

Aunt Druscilla was already halfway up the stairs. Standing there with the lamplight shining on her ruffled curls and the

King of England's garments in her arms, Mary looked very childlike and uncertain. "I pray God I will do them aright!" she murmured anxiously.

The weight of a far greater responsibility had already deepened the lines on John Ashburnham's face. "Since it was I who persuaded the King to cross the Solent, I too have good reason this night to pray God that I have done aright," he said, sharing her burden and drawing her unwittingly into the companionship of a cause.

# CHAPTER FOUR

⚬⚬⚬

W HEN MARY WOKE NEXT morning it was full daylight and
Libby was standing beside her with a plate of bread and
honey and a mug of milk. "The King's shirt—" Mary stammered, struggling up in bed although still heavy with belated sleep.

"Mistress Wheeler found it where you'd set it to air and took it
to them," Libby reassured her. "She said not to waken you. That
you'd done right well."

"Did she really, Libby?" A warm feeling of happiness filled
Mary at such unaccustomed praise. Eating her bread and honey
she savoured the luxurious novelty of not rising at dawn and
considered the prospects of an unpredictable Monday morning.
"To-day will be even busier," she prophesied. "The Governor said
that Sir John Oglander and all the other gentry might be coming."

"He's already sent two of the men to fetch them to meet him in
Newport. To ask 'em up here to dinner, I reckon. And your aunt's
invited the folk from the 'Rose and Crown' to see 'em arrive."

"Then I must be getting up."

"I reckon 'er won't be sendin' me away now?" Libby asked.

"I am sure she cannot spare you," said Mary. "That is one good
thing the King's coming has done."

The chambermaid's dark eyes softened behind half-lowered
lashes as she waited to take the plate. "All the same, you was
mortal kind, Mistress Mary. And I b'aint one to forget—not if
there should ever be any ways I could do ought for *you*."

Embarrassed by the girl's gratitude, Mary got out of bed and began washing her face at an earthenware basin. But Libby still lingered, the empty mug and platter in her work-roughened hands. "Tom Rudy b'aint come back," she said.

"Maybe Captain Rolph left him at Cowes," suggested Mary, sensing the anxiety behind the flatly uttered words. "I did hear my father say something yesterday about Colonel Hammond wanting the ports watched."

"That'll be it, I expect, because Captain Rolph b'aint back neither."

"Now you say so I don't remember seeing him at supper last night. But we were all so busy."

"I should ha' thought you would ha' noticed."

The girl's quizzing glance brought the colour to Mary's wet cheeks so that she hid them quickly with a towel. "Why should I?" she asked defensively.

Libby, so much more sex wise than she, turned on her heel and lifted the door latch. "Because of the way he looks at you."

"What way?" asked Mary, standing in the middle of the room in her shift.

"The same as Tom used to look at me," said Libby, opening the door with the point of her heavy shoe and letting it bang behind her.

Her words lay menacingly at the back of Mary's mind throughout a busy morning. For some weeks she had known them to be true; and the uncomfortable knowledge had been the beginning of womanhood.

While she helped her aunt to make the King's bed they both looked from time to time from the window to see their royal visitor walking in the herb garden or climbing the steps on to the battlements with his gentlemen. They supposed he must have slept well because he looked brisk and cheerful and seemed to be admiring the view.

"Where do you suppose his crown is?" asked Mary, glancing round the unchanged neatness of the room.

"How should I know, child?" laughed her aunt. "Surely you did not expect him to ride the best part of a hundred miles in it, or to bring it in his saddle bag?"

"He does not seem to have brought anything except his Bible."

Even in the haste of his escape from Hampton Court he had found time and space to bring *that*. The exquisitely bound book lay upon his table. Together they stood and admired it. "He is very considerate and gentle and thanks people for quite ordinary services," said Mistress Wheeler, her sharp-featured face softening. "This morning he sent for me and said he hoped his sudden coming had not caused us too much trouble. And he even had a word for old Brett when he came in to make up the fire."

Mary touched the worn leather cover of the Bible with reverent fingers. "Perhaps he is one who really lives by it instead of just quoting it at other people," she said, remembering how fiercely the new Puritan preacher had hurled texts at her and Frances for dancing with some of the young men at the Michaelmas Fair.

Now that the King was really with them and making none of the difficult demands which they had expected, the Castle household became less flustered. And after all the Governor did not invite any of the island gentry to dine. He had told them quite frankly that the coming of the royal party had caught him unawares and that the Castle larder was already sadly depleted, and most of them had promised to send poultry and game from their own estates. And after dining with them in Newport he brought them back with him to be presented to the King, which gave nobody any trouble at all. From the window of the housekeeper's room Frances and Mary, with Mistress Trattle, watched them arrive, led by kind, portly Sir John Oglander. Most of them were only squires of small country manors, but to the two island girls they seemed to make a brave show.

"Here comes young Mr. Worsley riding through the gateway now!" whispered Frances, squeezing Mary's arm. "How handsome he is! Do you suppose he will look up?"

"I like the look of Barnabas Leigh," whispered back Mary. "And look, there is your Captain Burley. I am so glad for him that he was able to come."

"They all look so solemn and nervous one would think they were going to an execution!" giggled Frances, all unaware how swiftly jesting can sharpen into reality.

They all disappeared into the Governor's lodgings to kiss the King's hand and afterwards Floyd, who was on duty, told the women how gracious his Majesty had been and how quickly he had set them all at ease. And when they left, the King himself came out and walked across the courtyard with Sir John Oglander and stood talking apart with him by the gateway.

"His Majesty has arranged to go and visit the Oglanders at Nunwell next Thursday," Silas Floyd told the little company in his sister's room, as soon as he was free to join them.

"I warrant he wishes Sir John were still Deputy Governor," said Mistress Wheeler.

"If you ask me I think none of them from Hampton Court realized how thoroughly Parliament had clipped his wings," said Floyd.

"You mean that had they known they would not have come?" asked Agnes Trattle.

Sergeant Floyd went and stood by the window, running a playful hand through his daughter's curls. "I would not say that," he answered thoughtfully. "This Ashburnham seems to have high hopes of Colonel Hammond's help, and no one can say but what he has acted very properly. He told the militia captains to hold their companies ready in case of any trouble, and gave orders that any large groups of people are to be dispersed. And he has set guards at Cowes and Yarmouth and Ryde to keep all suspicious strangers out."

"Then he means to keep the King safe from another wicked attempt upon his life," concluded Agnes Trattle with relief.

"He certainly means to keep him *safe*," agreed Floyd, more grimly. "But it may have occurred to his Majesty by now that the same guards could keep him in."

"Perhaps that is why he is so anxious to visit Sir John privately," suggested Druscilla Wheeler.

The Governor showed his unwanted guest every possible civility. He accompanied him about the island, visiting at Gatcombe and Billingham, and going hunting with him in Parkhurst forest. In fact, it looked at times as if he did not want to let him out of his sight. But when the day came for the Nunwell visit Hammond was obviously a very worried man. Sir John had not invited him and there was nothing he could do about it. And the King's pleasure, as he mounted his horse and rode away, could not be hidden.

Hammond saw him off, standing respectfully hat in hand. Sergeant Floyd rapped out an order and the men of the garrison sprang to attention. The household watched discreetly from open windows. But the moment King Charles and his handful of friends had ridden out beneath the barbican the Governor strode back to his apartments and bolted the door, Floyd dismissed his men, casements were clapped shut and after the strain and excitement of the last five days everyone in the castle sagged almost visibly with relief.

"How long will he say at Nunwell?"

"Will he come back?"

"Will he try to join the Queen in France?"

In hall and guardroom and kitchen there was time now to ask such questions. But no one asked them half so earnestly as the Governor himself. "I could not forbid him to go. He is still the King," he defended himself, pacing up and down the room where his mother sat.

"And your father was his favourite chaplain," the old lady reminded him from her high-backed chair beside the fire.

"It would be easier for me were that not so. If I had not been brought up with this feeling that the person of a king is sacred."

Her pretty, faded blue eyes searched his face. "You would not betray him, Robert?"

"I am the servant of Parliament." The words, which had been held so steadfastly in his mind during the past week, fell heavily into the quietness of the room. "It is they who gave me this appointment."

"Not from any favouritism because you married John Hampden's daughter, and are related to Oliver Cromwell. You earned it as a soldier. Cromwell and General Fairfax both think highly of you."

Robert Hammond picked up one of the frail hands lying in her lap and kissed it absently, a smile for her swift maternal pride momentarily relieving the anxiety on his face. "It is a good appointment. Or was—until the King came. I am a plain soldier and was only too glad to get away from all the bickering on the mainland." He took a turn or two about the room, then added. "I have sometimes wondered why they got rid of the last Governor so suddenly and gave it to me. Now I think I know."

Mistress Hammond patted the settle invitingly and her son sat down beside her. Because of his position there was no one else on the island whom he could speak to unguardedly. Leaning forward, his fine strong hands clasped between his knees, he stared into the fire. "Suppose Cromwell *meant* him to escape from Hampton Court? Meant him to come here?" he suggested.

"Why should you think that?"

"Because they got away so easily. It is true that his Majesty is a good horseman and they had a good start, but no one seems to have pursued them. I know what well-trained Parliamentarian troops could do in a few hours if Cromwell *really* wanted to catch anyone so important. I believe that they made me the Governor of the Wight hoping that the King might come here."

"But why should they want him to, Robert?"

"Of that I cannot be sure. If there really was some plot on his life Cromwell may have wanted to save him; or the rumour may even have been spread in order to drive him here. It seems to me that having gotten himself all the power he needs, cousin Oliver would be spared much embarrassment if he could get the King out of the country. And how much better for him if his Majesty went voluntarily!"

"You mean that from here he might get right away to France?"

"The nights are dark. Even now while he is at Nunwell he may persuade this Oglander to get him a ship."

"It would make the poor Queen very happy," murmured Mistress Hammond, who had known her at Whitehall.

Hammond kicked at a fallen log. "Who wants to make the Queen happy? Has not the accursed Frenchwoman made enough trouble for us all? It is now only a question which party loathes her most—Parliament, the Army or the Royalists themselves."

"Yet she has been a loyal and courageous wife."

"A Papist meddler!" He got up restlessly, his mind back on his own immediate problem. "If only I knew Cromwell's mind in this! Whether he would have me play host or gaoler. I would rather let the King escape, but if not I must be given the necessary authority to hold him fast. God knows I did not want the responsibility!"

"Most men would be thinking of it as an unlooked for chance of preferment."

"It can also be my undoing if I let him slip through my fingers when such is not their wish!"

With a deep sigh Mistress Hammond rose and faced him across the table. "It is strange to think that while we have been so occupied in receiving his Majesty here, all England must be wondering where he is," she said. She was watching him and his very stillness betrayed him. "Or do they already know?"

She saw her son turn to her impulsively as though it would be a relief to confide in her, much as he had been wont to do as a youth when uncertain of the uprightness of his actions. But divergence of political opinions had come between them, driving him in upon himself. "I sent Rolph and one of his men to London," he told her after a surly pause.

Tears rose to her gentle eyes. "Oh, Robert, did you have to tell them—so soon?"

"I am the servant of Parliament," he repeated.

"But your father—"

"He will understand that a man cannot cheat the hand that feeds him." There was an obstinate look in his eyes and he was going towards the door. His mother put out a hand to detain him. "Do Mr. Ashburnham and the others know?" she asked, thinking that if they did they would surely try to get away to France.

Hammond shook his head. "I made up my mind on the boat and sent Rolph the moment we landed on the mainland. So now, until his return, I must go on playing the pleasant host—like Judas," he said bitterly, and strode from the room to make his daily inspection of the battlements. But for once his mind seemed to be less upon flintlocks and culverins than upon the weathervane and the view. He stood for a long time on the northern wall of the castle facing Southampton, searching the water for a ship coming into Cowes.

That evening when the lamps were lit and Mary was coming from supper, Libby ran towards her from the kitchen. Her eyes and cheeks were bright. "Oh, Mistress Mary, Tom Rudy has come back!" she announced.

"And Captain Rolph with him?" asked Mary involuntarily.

Libby nodded but was too full of her own news to tease anyone. "Tom says he will marry me" she announced breathlessly.

Mary turned immediately and kissed her, thinking that the self-confident overner could not be so bad after all. "Oh, Libby, I am so glad for you! Come into a quiet corner of the hall and tell me about it."

The servants had finished clearing the long tables and the two girls stood just inside the serving screens. "He alus said he would if he had the money, and now he has five silver pounds in his pocket!" boasted the chambermaid.

"Oh, Libby, you don't think that he—"

The girl whose mother had been a common troll was quick to understand Mary's fear that he had stolen them. "They was given to him by somebody important in London," she said defensively.

Mary stared in surprise. "Then he and Captain Rolph haven't been on duty in Cowes all this time?" she exclaimed. "What were they doing in London?"

Libby began to speak of something else so quickly that Mary felt sure she had been told not to mention London. "Brett's sister says I can have that room in her cottage," she babbled on. "But I don't want to go till my time comes. It be more exciting helping here since the King came. Will you ask Reverend Troughton to marry us this very week?"

"Of course. And I am sure he will. But Rudy will have to ask Captain Rolph's permission."

Libby laughed boldly. "Won't be any difficulty there," she said. "Tom's in Captain's favour. But will you see parson *now*, Mistress Mary?"

"It is late," demurred Mary. "And surely your Rudy has a ready enough tongue to do his own asking."

Libby put a coaxing hand on her wrist. Some of her confidence was already beginning to ooze away. "I'm not sayin' but what Tom had been celebrating a bit," she admitted. "Dead sober, he might change his mind."

# CHAPTER FIVE

———⊗⊗⊗———

THE GOVERNOR SAT AT his writing table, his inscrutable face and fairish hair illuminated by the light of two tall candles. However little he liked Edmund Rolph personally, he was glad to have his second-in-command back. "You delivered my letter to the Speaker?" he asked, immediately the Captain came into his room.

"I went straight to the House of Commons, sir." Rolph handed him Parliament's reply, still warm from contact with his own body, and stood watching him break the imposing-looking seals. His sharp, inquisitive mind noted with what nervous urgency Hammond's hands unfolded the contents, and how deeply the last few days had etched tell-tale lines of sleeplessness about his eyes. Why should a man worry, he wondered, when the chance of a lifetime had just fallen into his hands? And a fine reward as well, no doubt, judging by the jubilation he had seen at Westminster. "Had I the luck to be in his shoes I would know very well what to do. And enjoy doing it," he thought. "I would use my authority to humiliate that so-called king until he learned that he is no better than other men—not turn out of my own room for him and let him go hunting while others work. Nor let him slip out of my hands to pay visits." Being too mannerless to wait until the Governor had finished reading, he said aloud and with truculence. "I hear you have let the Stuart go?"

"I am not his gaoler," replied Hammond evasively, without

looking up. The man's tone, taken in conjunction with the two Houses' stern intent, seemed to condemn him.

"It looks as if you soon will be. *If he comes back.* Did you have Nunwell watched?"

It was what Rolph himself would have done; but then he was not hampered by any of those instincts which make a man shrink from spying upon his guest. Before the civil war had opened up undreamed of possibilities for workmen with initiative, he had been a bootmaker. Knowing this, Hammond ignored his over-familiarity. "You are already acquainted with the contents of this letter, then?" he inquired coldly.

"In part, sir, by things they said to me at the time." Rolph despised himself for still being subservient to the rebukes of his social superiors. He both resented and envied the advantage which their controlled way of speaking often gave them.

Aware of his unfair advantage, Hammond made an effort at geniality. "You must have had a hard ride, Captain. Sit down," he invited, "and help yourself to some wine." With his eyes still upon the all-important letter before him, he pushed a flagon of Bordeaux towards him and—although a temperate man himself—was startled by the violence of the man's refusal. "'Tis a lure of Satan's. Intoxicating liquors were the ruin of Rupert's army!" the Roundhead Captain exclaimed in the jargon of his kind, pushing the good red wine away so vigorously that he almost upset an inkwell.

Hammond remembered that the man did not drink, and that Sergeant Floyd had recently reported complaints from the garrison because their ale ration had been cut down by the new Captain's orders; but all the commotion of the last week had put such trivial matters out of his mind.

"Are we to keep the King prisoner?" asked Rolph, breaking an awkward silence.

"He is to stay here, yes. Parliament considers it will be the safest place, and I am not to allow him to depart without their orders."

"Then are we to set a guard about him?"

"Not obviously."

"A polite kind of guard takes twice as many men. We shall need reinforcements, sir. Good trusty Ironsides."

Although he could not like the man, Hammond found it a relief to talk with someone of his own party. Someone who shared his knowledge of the political pattern of a wider, outside world. "Do you suppose we shall have any trouble from the islanders? When they realize it is—something more than a visit?"

"We shall if the King is allowed to ride abroad and talk to them. Even if it wasn't that they are mostly for him at the moment," answered Rolph.

"Their loyalties seem to have remained unchanged since the beginning of the Long Parliament!" laughed Hammond. The word "uncontaminated" had occurred to him because he had so often heard it on his father's lips, but he was careful not to use it.

"It is queer how he turns people's heads," Rolph was saying. "I have seen it happen in London. For months they'd be grumbling about his Ship Money being levied on inland towns and his forced loans and the way they always got his troops billeted on them if they didn't pay up, and then he'd come riding through the streets and speak civilly to some old woman, or perform some of that idolatrous wickedness when he makes himself out to be God and touches them for the Evil, and suddenly they'd all seem to be under a spell and forget about their cruel wrongs. Stagecraft, it is, like they bemuse people with in those iniquitous theatres. I was there at Twickenham when he was allowed out of Hampton to meet his two youngest children. A lot of hysterical women wept their eyes out over young Princess Elizabeth because they thought she looked frail and needed a mother's care. And even the men helped to strew the streets with flowers. You should have seen it, sir."

Robert Hammond, who could just remember seeing the Stuarts gay, happy, and secure at Whitehall, was glad that he had not. "All his family have a kind of charm, you know," he explained. But when Edmund Rolph made the rude kind of noise he had learned in the backstreets of his boyhood, Hammond clutched firmly at the safeguard of common sense. "A good thing for Cromwell that you and I, Rolph, are not susceptible to it," he commented, with his thin smile. He leaned back in his chair and stretched his long legs more comfortably under the table. "Life here is going to be very different," he went on. "Carisbrooke will become a miniature Hampton Court. I see that Parliament has very generously voted five thousand a year for the upkeep of his Majesty's household."

"Five thousand! Why, a hundred poor families could live on that!"

"Too true. But it is to be expected that his Majesty will keep up something of his accustomed state."

Edmund Rolph muttered something about his Majesty being cheaper dead.

"Thirty of his attendants from Hampton are being sent here," added Hammond, consulting the Speaker's letter.

"And the attendants' servants, no doubt," sneered Rolph. "How do they expect you to house them all?"

"God knows!" sighed the harassed Governor. "You had better send Mistress Wheeler to me when you go."

For a moment or two they sat in silence, each considering his particular part of a mutual problem. "Everything has gone well in the guardroom while I have been gone?" asked the garrison Captain, rousing himself.

"Floyd has done excellently."

"A fine sergeant. Has the confidence of his men," allowed Rolph. "A pity he isn't twenty years younger with some knowledge of New Model Army methods!"

Hammond looked round the old stone walls of his room, and with his mind's eye saw the much older keep and fortifications outside. "Imagine this great place being held for years by a mere score of men!" he said.

"Most of them nearly as old as their muskets!" grinned Rolph.

"All the same, in a tough place I would not mind being with them. There is something about these people of the Wight," mused their new Governor. "They are trustworthy and ingenious. I suppose they need to be, since every man among them is half-sailor, half-farmer. And they have a natural courtesy." His glance flickered with momentary distaste over the thick-set figure facing him. "They quarrel among themselves, no doubt. But to you or me no islander would ever give another away. At a word from this Sir John Oglander, because he is one of them, they would slaughter their best cattle or launch a boat when the sea around their treacherous coast is like a cauldron. But I sometimes wonder if a lifetime of just ruling would be enough for an overner like me to be accepted by them."

"You have been here but a bare two months, sir," Rolph reminded him. "And, anyhow, why should you care?"

"Except that at times it makes one feel like an exile," smiled Hammond, marvelling at his own loneliness. Perhaps if he were to unbend to people more or give them more encouragement. "I appreciate the speed and secrecy with which you carried out this important mission. I trust that Parliament—er—appreciated it too," he began, embarrassed at seeming to pry into the private affairs of a subordinate.

"To the tune of five hundred pounds!" Rolph told him, without any embarrassment at all. And as his boastful frankness elicited no response he gave rein to his curiosity, unconscious of offence, "I hope they have treated you as generously, sir."

"With the future of the country pushed into my hands I shall have much added responsibility," Hammond said stiffly. He had been even more overcome by the generosity of Parliament than his messenger, but he preferred to think of the thousand pounds and the annuity they had promised him as an increase in salary rather as a reward for betrayal. Receiving it had started the old argument in his conscientious mind. "The King put himself voluntarily into my hands," he thought, "or rather he sent Ashburnham and Berkeley to sound me and I said I would do what I could, and I forced his hand by insisting upon going back with them and taking Baskett with me. Before ever I met him at Southampton I had betrayed him by giving Rolph secret orders. But it was not betrayal. It was my duty to Parliament. As a paid soldier on a battlefield, sure of my convictions, I have been fighting against him for years. Why must it seem different here? Why must their thousand pounds feel like thirty pieces of silver?" Hammond pulled his mind back to his companion and rose. "You must have had a hard journey. Have you eaten?" he enquired, in order to terminate the interview.

"At Cowes, while Rudy was getting us horses. A useful fellow, Rudy." Rolph lingered for a moment, smiling reminiscently. "Too promising to throw himself away on a rustic chambermaid."

"One of our servants?"

"He spoke of marriage. But I should imagine he has had all he wants of her."

"Then see that he *does* marry her," ordered the Governor sharply. "We do not want our Puritan army to get a Godless reputation for pilfering and raping."

"No, sir."

Captain Rolph went down the stairs and out into the courtyard, intending to send one of his men to tell Mistress Wheeler that the Governor wanted her. Seeing no one about, he strolled towards the barracks. Some of the lights in the castle had already been put out. The Solent had been smooth and the sky was starlit. He paused by the well-house, struck by the stillness of the evening. After the bustle of mainland towns the quality of the silence on the island seemed tangible, and was almost disconcerting to a town-bred man. He was glad when it was broken by the occasional rhythmic tramp of a guard on the battlements, or by a sudden burst of rough laughter from the barracks. And then by quick footsteps, much lighter than the sentry's. Peering through the darkness he was able to discern the figure of a girl hurrying towards him from the direction of the chapel. The hood of her cloak was thrown back, and he knew by the starlight on her short mop of curls that it must be Mary Floyd. With quickened interest he calculated that whether she were bound for her aunt's room or merely going to bed she must pass him. He stepped back into the shadow of the well-house and waited, so that she ran almost into his arms before being aware that anyone was there. When she shrank back with a startled cry, he caught hold of her, pretending to steady her; for even in his wenching Edmund Rolph tried to cover his sensuality with the moral hypocrisy of his kind. "What tryst have you been keeping so late, my pretty one?" he asked almost sternly.

"I have been to see the parson."

"That for a likely tale, with a score of lustier men about the place!" he laughed coarsely, still holding her.

"About Libby and Tom Rudy," she explained, sounding almost stupid in her confusion.

"That fellow Rudy has all the good fortune. At least I warrant she gave him a warm welcome. I, too, have been gone a week. Have you not missed me?"

It was the first time Mary had been held close against a man. Fear set her heart racing, and she hoped he could not hear it. "I—I scarcely noticed—" she stammered.

He threw back his cropped black head and laughed. "Scarcely noticed!" he mocked, sure of his masculine power. "Then what reddens your cheeks every time I look at you across the supper table?"

"Let me go," she begged. "*Please*, Captain Rolph!"

"'Twas you who put yourself into bondage," he teased. "What if I make the ransom a kiss?"

She had the sense not to struggle. Either a belated recollection of the Governor's parting words or the preacher's reiterated talk about hellfire restrained his lustfulness, and to Mary's surprise he released her. "You are only a foolish child," he said, hiding behind the age-old pretence that his feelings were paternal. "But I did not forget *you*. See, I bought you something when I was on the mainland." He reached down into one of the capacious pockets of his buff army coat and pulled forth a string of beautifully carved amber beads. Drawing her towards the light of a lantern hanging above a doorway, he held them out to her; and Mary gave a little gasp of admiration, for they were even finer than the ones which Master Newland, the merchant, had given to Frances. "Such things breed vanity, but I overheard you admiring your friend's," Rolph said.

She had done more than admire them. She had sighed with envy because they were just the colour which suited her best. And because she had never possessed any jewellery. It had been clever of him to choose them, but Mary called to mind her aunt's warnings and tried to avert her gaze. "I cannot possibly accept anything so expensive," she excused herself.

"I can well afford it," he bragged. "And other trinkets. And maybe perhaps a visit to the mainland—if you will be kind to me." She knew that he was talking to her as Rudy must have talked to Libby. "My father would not let me wear them," she protested.

"Your father takes his orders from me."

Although her aunt had married into a titled family, it was true. Since the civil war the social life of the country had become muddled up like that. She must do nothing to prejudice her beloved father. Reluctantly, almost as though he had placed a snake in her hands, Mary let the cool beads slide through her fingers.

"You can wear the thing when you go into Newport—or when you are alone with me. Let me put them on for you," he urged. He was a long time fumbling with the clasp and she could feel his hands exploring the smooth whiteness of her neck.

"I do not want to go to the mainland," she said, jerking herself away. "And why should you, the Captain of the Guard, need kindness?"

The ingenuousness of the words drew something of the truth from him. "It is not only my men who miss their home life. You do not suppose, do you, that I *wanted* to leave London and be stuck on this God-forsaken island?"

"Do you suppose *we* wanted any of *you?*" she flashed back at him, stung to local loyalty.

She was a lovely young thing when the colour came into her cheeks, and the sparkle into her golden-brown eyes. Rolph decided to take the Governor's message himself, and walked close behind her as she began to mount the stairs. "At least we liven things up," he chuckled, clutching at her in the darkness.

But Mary was too fleet for him. "Why are you following me?" she demanded breathlessly, having reached the security of her aunt's doorway.

He straightened his belt and resumed his normal air of authority. "Because I, too, have occasion to see Mistress Wheeler."

Inside the housekeeper's room they found Silas Floyd, tunic unbuttoned, taking his ease before the fire, while his sister stood by the table fashioning some garment. Both occupants of the room looked surprised to see the overner, and Floyd, off duty, rose to his feet just deliberately enough to convey the impression that his presence was an intrusion. "Do you want something of me, Captain?" asked Mistress Wheeler.

"It is Colonel Hammond who wants you, Mistress," said Rolph, with cheerful civility. "It seems that all the trouble royalty has caused you is as nothing compared with what is yet to come."

"You are pleased to speak in riddles, Captain."

"To be more explicit, a batch of courtiers are coming from Hampton."

The sorely tried housekeeper laid down her measuring tape and stared at him across the table. "How do you know this?" she asked.

"The Governor himself told me just now, and I thought it only kind to prepare you before you see him. Moreover, I myself have just come from London."

"From London?" exclaimed Floyd. "Then they know that the King—"

"Sooner or later they had to know. In my opinion, the man who advised him to come here was a fool."

"But surely having his own people sent here means that his Majesty will be properly treated, sir?"

"If you ask me, Sergeant, it means that the trap is closed," grinned Rolph, lifting Mary's cloak from her shoulders with an exaggerated air of gallantry. "An island twenty-four miles long by fourteen wide can be very effectively patrolled."

Druscilla Wheeler sank into a chair and Mary went as far from her admirer as she could and sat upon the window seat. Edmund Rolph would have liked to sit down among them, but no one invited him to do so. Thick-skinned as he was, he was uncomfortably aware that although these islanders always spoke to him politely, they never did anything to make him feel welcome.

"How many are coming?" asked Mistress Wheeler, averse from showing him their anxiety for the King.

"About thirty, I understand. But do not fear that you and Mary will be over-worked. Most of them will bring their own servants."

"We are not afraid of work, but where shall we sleep them all?"

"I imagine that is what the Governor wants to talk with you about."

"I will go down now. We shall have to turn some of the servants' quarters into guest rooms, I suppose."

"The barracks are half empty. I could let you have the top floor for the men servants."

Silas Floyd was looking thoughtfully at his daughter. He could wager she had not heard a word they had been saying, and he noticed her heightened colour. When the Captain had taken her cloak her hand had gone quickly to her throat, and now the fire-light was sparkling on a string of expensive-looking beads. "There is also Mary's room," he said. "She had better come in here, Druscilla, and sleep with you." The words sounded like an order. They were addressed to his sister, but as he said them he turned and looked straight at the Captain of the Guard.

Rolph reddened angrily and moved towards the door. "You might remind the Governor," he said to Mistress Wheeler, "that accommodation in the barracks will be available only *until General Fairfax sends our reinforcements*."

"Reinforcements?" Mary spoke for the first time as soon as he was gone.

"A sensible precaution—for the King's safety," said her father quietly. It would mean more overners. Other Sergeants, poking about contemptuously among his outdated cannon. Cromwell's Model Army types, out to teach old dogs new tricks. And he himself was not so young. All the same he took up the Captain's half-spoken challenge. He crossed the room and laid a hand on his daughter's shoulder. "How did you come by the fine necklace, Mary?"

Her clear eyes looked up straightly into his. "Captain Rolph gave it to me just now. He bought it for me in London. I think he and Tom Rudy must have had some sort of reward, because Rudy is going to marry Libby, Aunt Druscilla. I—I did try not to take it, father," she added. "But the Captain reminded me that you were under his command."

"The swine!" He swung away with an oath and began pacing the floor, but soon came back to her. "And so you thought you had to obey him—for my sake." Very gently he cupped her troubled face in his hands. "My little tenderheart! But you must give them to me."

Reluctantly Mary unclasped her first piece of jewellery. "They are very beautiful," murmured her aunt, with womanly understanding.

"But very dangerous," said Floyd, still holding out his hand.

"What will you do with them?" asked Mary, laying them upon his open palm.

"Give them back to him, of course. And tell him that if my daughter wants for trinkets before she gets herself a good husband, I will give them to her. To me you seem still a child...I blame myself for not thinking of it before."

Mary was on her feet immediately, her arms about him. "It is not the beads I am thinking of, but you. I saw him kick Patters once because she snarled at him for treading on one of her pups. Such men can be vengeful."

"Do not worry, my dear," said her aunt. "At least the Governor is a just man and your father knows his trade."

"And how to look after my own!" laughed the Sergeant, pulling his daughter against him in a rough embrace. "But I must get back to the barracks. Now go and bring your gear down here and get you to bed."

They watched her go and then, before parting, turned back to their own urgent thoughts. "God help his Majesty, they lost no time in betraying him!" cried Druscilla Wheeler.

Sergeant Floyd crunched the beads almost absently in his muscular hand. He had been in a Stuart's army since he was a lad, but he had never been so consciously a Royalist before. "If Rudy came back with money enough to make an honest woman of that Libby of yours, and this lechering bootmaker can buy amber in the hopes of raping my daughter, how much did the Governor get?" he demanded savagely.

# CHAPTER SIX

———∞∞∞———

T HE KING'S LAUNDRESS!" REPEATED Agnes Trattle, her amused voice lending warmth to the comfortable inn parlour. "Little did I think, when we were learning our lessons together, that prim little Druscilla Floyd would ever be called anything so imposing!"

For the first time since the King's return from Nunwell Mary had found time to visit her friend's family, and she was enjoying an unaccustomed sense of importance because they were all agog to hear news from the castle.

"And what do they call *you*?" teased Frances, fluttering round her with offers of refreshment.

"The King's Laundress's Assistant, I suppose," laughed Mary. "At least I do all his Majesty's washing and mending."

"And do all the important people from Hampton have fancy titles like that?" asked Mistress Trattle.

Mary nodded as her strong white teeth bit into a tempting apple. "There is a list of them hanging in the great hall." She began checking them off on her fingers. "Master Mildmay, Carver—Master Murray, Groom of the Bedchamber—Master Cressett, Treasurer—oh, I cannot remember the half of them!"

"Then his Majesty is treated properly in spite of all his attendants having been chosen by Parliament?" concluded Captain Burley, from his place beside the fire.

"Indeed, yes, Captain," Mary assured him. "The Parliament

people have even sent over some of his furniture. You never saw such changes, Mistress Trattle! The best bedroom is now the State room and has fine rugs on the floor and a new red-and-blue tapestry against the serving passage wall, and when I take in his Majesty's clean nightshirt of an evening Master Ashburnham himself takes it from me and warms it before the fire. His Majesty's meals are served in the great hall and we have to call it the Presence Chamber. And one of the gentlemen who is called a Sewer tastes each dish before the King touches it!"

"As if honest islanders would poison him!" muttered Burley.

"Poor Cheke could not if he would," laughed Mary. "He is like to burst himself with fury, poor man, because a Roundhead cook from Hampton has been put over him. Though in fact, with so many to feed, there must be work enough for both."

"I hear from the 'Bull' that all their rooms are full up with Parliamentary Commissioners from London," said Trattle, who had come into the parlour with Master Newland to hear the Carisbrooke news.

"Aye, and some from Scotland as well. You'll be having some of them along here to-night, Mistress Trattle," added John Newland. "They came over in my brig *Vectis*. It seems that as soon as his Majesty found Colonel Hammond had given away his whereabouts, he wrote openly to Parliament, urging some further negotiations by which he hoped to come to terms with them. And now, so my skipper tells me, both these Scots and our own Commissioners have brought Bills for the King to sign."

"Does he owe them a great deal of money?" asked Frances, and flushed with annoyance when her father laughed and said, "Not that kind of bill, my pretty."

"Terms of agreement, Frances, in exchange for which they will give him their support," explained Newland, who was no mean driver of bargains himself.

"And if his Majesty signs them perhaps we shall have peace at last, and they will let him go back to Whitehall," sighed Agnes Trattle.

"Anything that comes from Cromwell now is more likely to be in the nature of a victor's ultimatum," said her husband less hopefully.

"What right have such scum to dictate terms to an anointed king?" burst forth the irascible Burley.

"We should not forget that he *did* levy taxes without consulting them," pointed out Newland.

His words started off a heated discussion, and Mary remembered that her aunt would be needing her and kissed Mistress Trattle good-bye. "I wish I could stay over Christmas," she said, looking round the hospitable room already decked with holly. "The castle is so full of strangers. We used to roam about wherever we liked, but now it does not seem at all like home."

"But it must be much more exciting. More exciting than anything we ever dreamed of," said Frances, going with her to the street door. With a glance over her shoulder to make sure that John Newland was still talking too heatedly to overhear her, she asked eagerly, "What are they like, these courtiers?"

"I scarcely know them apart as yet," confessed Mary. "They all bow a lot and wear huge plumes in their hats and talk differently from us. But truly, Frances, I do not think that you are missing much; for all of them are appointed by Parliament and most of them are middle-aged."

But that evening Mary encountered one who was young. In his early twenties, at most. He was tall and slender and almost red-headed. And he was laughing as he called back some bantering remarks to someone in the King's ante-room. Everyone had been so worried that there had been little laughter in the castle for weeks, and Mary's unusual depression lifted suddenly at the sound of it.

The cheerful young man came into the deserted hall where she had supped carrying a pile of papers with an inkhorn poised precariously on top. And suddenly all was confusion. A servant, carrying out the last of the dishes, let the opposite door slam and a draught blew the papers all over the floor and sent the inkhorn flying. "Devil take all clerking!" yelled the young man, diving after them. In trying to save the inkhorn from upsetting over a chair he trod on Floyd's bitch Patters, who lay suckling her latest litter before the hearth. The bitch yelped and flew at his ankles. And Mary noticed with approval that instead of kicking at her as

Captain Rolph had done he gathered her up and felt each of her paws with dog-wise hands, seeming more concerned lest he had injured her than because a black splash of ink was spreading over the seat of the chair. "I doubt if she is really hurt. She always flies out like that," said Mary, crossing to the hearth. A week or two ago she would have been too shy to address anyone in so modish a coat, but her world had enlarged since then.

Together they examined the foolish little animal, who was already struggling to lick the young man's face. He put Patters down and they considered the chair. "We Parliament people will be less popular than ever," he said ruefully.

"Perhaps I can embroider over the stain," suggested Mary. "It is the chair my aunt sits in at meals."

He took the empty inkhorn from her and threw it into the fire and, in spite of her protests, began wiping her ink-stained fingers with a flamboyant silk handkerchief. "Your aunt is Mistress Wheeler, isn't she?" he asked. "And you are Mary?"

"How did you know?"

"Colonel Ashburnham told me. He said how beautifully you laundered the King's shirts."

"He is very kind. I did not know he was a Colonel."

"He commanded a regiment in the King's army. But that is all over now." Having wiped each of her fingers very carefully, he tucked the handkerchief back into his cuff. They were standing very close together and, being young, took stock of each other. "My name is Firebrace," he said. "Harry Firebrace."

Mary smothered a little spurt of laughter. "It is rather an odd name," she said apologetically.

"A very good name," he countered. "Obviously of Norman vintage. *Bras de Feu*, you know. Or Strong Arm."

"Your arm could not have been particularly strong when you dropped all those papers," smiled Mary. "Where were you taking them?"

"To the Court room." Together they began gathering them up and between grovelling under benches and agile dives beneath the empty supper tables he tried to explain. "The Parliamentary

Commissioners are to wait upon his Majesty to-morrow, and they will need a room where they can hold their private discussions and write their reports. Colonel Hammond asked me to see that it is in readiness for them. I was to have got one of the servants to help me, but they all seem to have gone to their suppers." As Mary handed him a bunch of quill pens she had retrieved he scratched his smoothly shaven cheek doubtfully with the feathered ends of them. "Come to think about it, I do not even know where the Court room is."

"I will show you," offered Mary.

She led him down a flight of stairs to a large room on the ground floor. "The Governor holds sessions here and people come from all over the island," she told him. "As it is not often used between times, I had better have someone light a fire."

Harry Firebrace regarded the room with interest. It was barely furnished with old chairs and a long table but coats of arms carved round the fireplace gave it an air of official importance. "This would be exactly under the King's bedroom, would it not?" he asked. "And where does that outer door lead?"

"To the back of the castle, by the old keep. The people come in that way. It saves their muddy feet traipsing all through the house. This stone floor can easily be scrubbed."

His mind seemed to be upon less domestic considerations. He crossed the room, unbolted the outer door, and looked out into the darkness. He appeared to be a very inquisitive young man. "Do you find our island God-forsaken?" she asked, still sore from the slighting way in which the Captain of the Guard had spoken of it.

"God-forsaken? Lord save us, no! " He had bolted the door again and come back to her all in what seemed to be one swift movement, and she supposed that anyone with such unbounded vitality would scarcely find a desert dull. "But then," he added reasonably, "I have only just arrived. My friend Osborne and I came over with the Scottish Commissioners."

"Aboard the *Vectis*?"

"How did you know?"

"She belongs to Master Newland, and he said that she was in."

He seemed to be readily interested in the affairs of others. "Is he a particular friend of yours?" he asked.

"Oh no. But he is betrothed to my best friend, Frances Trattle. It was she," added Mary proudly, "who stepped out of the crowd the day the King arrived and gave him a rose."

He gave her a swift searching look, then began doling out some of his papers along the table. "The *Vectis* was a trim little craft. Built for speed," he remarked casually. "I suppose this Newland would have others?"

"Oh yes. There are usually several being laden or unladen in Medina river. He is one of the busiest merchants in Newport."

"Then I suppose your friend lives in Newport too?"

"Her father keeps the 'Rose and Crown'."

"And you often go to see her there?"

"About once a week. But no one has had time for visiting lately."

He jerked forward a stool for her and perched himself on the edge of the table. It was as if he threw off some preoccupation of his own in order to offer her a more personal and sympathetic interest. "One forgets that this is your home and we have invaded it," he said more gently. "Have you hated our coming very much?"

Mary found herself answering him as though he were a friend of long standing. "Everything is so formal and different," she said. "To-morrow will be Christmas Eve. Other years we have had the men bringing in a yule log and the maids and I have been decorating the hall with holly. The last Governor used to let us get up a masque. Everybody would have been joking and laughing. That was why when I heard you laughing just now—"

He leaned forward and took one of her hands. "You poor disappointed child!" he said.

"I am seventeen," she told him with dignity.

Immediately he let go her hand with a friendly pat. "And now everybody seems to have forgotten it is Christmas time and instead of masques we shall have only a posse of solemn lawyers and Elders of the Kirk making a lot of long speeches. Though I daresay they will manage to be quite as amusing."

For a custodian sent by Parliament he was remarkably

irreverent. "I daresay you Puritans would not have permitted the masque anyway," she sighed.

"Everybody who works for Oliver Cromwell is not a kill-joy," he said, and because he sounded really hurt and had been concerned for Patters she made him the most friendly overture she could think of. "Would you care to come and watch the well-house donkeys one morning?"

"The donkeys?"

"They work the great wheel. Old Brett and I trained them."

"Is he the bent old man who brought in the logs for the Presence Chamber this evening?"

Mary nodded, thinking how observant he was.

"I will come to-morrow," he said. "Or rather, the next day. To-morrow, being Christmas Eve, we will go gathering holly and you must take me to the 'Rose and Crown' to meet your friend."

"But you will not have time," objected Mary, although her eyes were bright with anticipation.

"Even a royal attendant has *some* hours off duty. Or perhaps Richard Osborne will take my place and help us decorate the hall."

A sudden thought sobered the happiness of her face. "No, I think not," she said quietly. "It would be too sad for the poor King."

"The contrast with other Christmases, you mean?"

"He will be thinking of his children."

He looked at her with very real liking. "Mary, how sweet you are!" he said. "We will just go and drink a Christmas wassail at the 'Rose and Crown'."

Perhaps he was missing his home life, she thought. "I suppose everything here must seem very strange to you, too," she said. "I know the soldiers who came over with the new Governor feel as if they were in exile."

Harry Firebrace stood up and took a final look at the table where matters of such vast importance to the King would be argued out. "It is not so strange to me as you would think," he said. "You see, I have been his Majesty's page of the backstairs before—at Holmby and at Hampton."

His voice sounded quite different, as if all the laughter had gone out of it—almost as if he were worshipping in church. She looked up and saw his face serious and dedicated in the candlelight, and an odd little pulse of excitement stirred in her. "And now?" she whispered, scarcely knowing what she meant.

"Now I have been promoted to be groom of the bedchamber," he said. Suddenly he smiled at her gaily. "So since my royal master is here, I do not feel at all as if I were in exile, little tender-heart," he assured her, unconsciously using the name by which her father so often called her.

He insisted upon seeing her to the household entrance and as they crossed the courtyard they passed Captain Rolph going his nightly rounds. She expected him to be surly because she was with another man, but her companion called out something flippant and both men laughed. Firebrace seemed already to be on good terms with him.

Mary found the housekeeper's room deserted, and when she had blown out the candle and climbed into her side of her aunt's big bed she parted the curtains so that she could see the stars. There was one just above the chapel roof which seemed to be winking at her very merrily. "Perhaps Frances was right after all," she thought, "and life here before the King came *had* been a little dull."

# CHAPTER SEVEN

————∽∽∽————

WHAT A CHRISTMAS! DO none of those Commissioners have homes of their own in which to spend it?" sighed Sir John Berkeley, closing the state room door against the very memory of them.

"God knows they did not bring much peace and good will *here*—arguing and haranguing for their own ends for days on end!" exclaimed John Ashburnham, sick with disappointment.

"Well, at least they are gone at last!" said Colonel Legge, setting the King's chair closer to the cheer of a good fire.

But Charles remained standing, still torn by the wordy conflict which would have worsted any man of less unwavering principles. "They would have had me sign away the last vestige of my power to Parliament for the next twenty years. The country would have been ruled by laws made without authority. The Church of England would have been left defenceless. Nothing in the world—not even force—would have persuaded me to it." Hands resting on the carved stone chimneypiece, he stood for a moment or two gazing down into the red heart of the crackling logs; then, squaring his slight shoulders, turned to face his three loyal friends. "And now it is done," he said. "And they must be already halfway across the Solent bearing my refusal."

"Yes, now it is done," repeated Ashburnham, seeing only too clearly what must come of it.

"Would that I, too, could be riding back to Westminster! With

Whitehall as it was five years ago, and my family about me. But, gentlemen, you too have homes—abandoned for my sake." With that charming smile which made men willingly do such things he seated himself and began to speak more crisply. "You feel that this new usher Osborne is to be trusted? When he handed me my gloves the other day I found a note inside assuring me of his loyalty, but with Cromwell's creatures all around us who knows whether it be a ruse?"

"He is related to Sir Peter Osborne who governed Guernsey and is a friend of Harry Firebrace, who long ago came over to your Majesty's side," Berkeley reminded him.

"Then that should be enough. Let us have them both in," decided Charles; and while the two young men who had come in from the ante-room were bowing he looked searchingly at the darker, more strongly built of the two. "You gave the Commissioners my sealed reply as near to the last moment of their departure as possible, Osborne?"

"As you bade me, sir," said Richard Osborne. "But they insisted upon unsealing it."

"*Insisted?* Is there no courtesy left in England?" The red of anger dyed the King's cheeks, but remembering the helplessness of his circumstances and reading fresh anxiety in the faces around him, he added more mildly, "Then Hammond already knows that I refused to sign?"

"Yes, sir."

"It would have given us a few days' valuable time had he been kept in ignorance as your Majesty planned," said Berkeley.

"He has ridden with them as far as Newport," volunteered Osborne.

"No doubt discussing the matter as they go," growled Legge.

There was a tenseness about them all.

Ashburnham came and stood before his master. "Since there is no longer any chance of agreement, your Majesty's safety lies only in escape. And *now* is all the time we have. An hour or two at most—" he said, in a voice that shook.

"When Hammond comes back, knowing that all this week's negotiations have been wasted—and how those curs at

Westminster are likely to reply—he may take more precautions," warned Berkeley.

Ashburnham went down upon his knees. "Your Majesty, it must be now—while you are still free to ride abroad. I beseech you—"

"My dear Jack—"

Feeling a hand upon his greying hair, the King's confidential adviser nearly broke down. "It was I who urged your Majesty to come hither, but I fear we are fallen into a cunning trap," he admitted humbly. "Since that day when Hammond came to Titchfield House and you exclaimed, 'Why, Jack, you have undone me!' you have never once reproached me. I counted on Oglander still having influence here and thought that Robert Hammond, because he was your favourite chaplain's son, must be at heart upon our side. But he is a true servant of Parliament. Again and again I have tried to win him over, but now that I know it to be useless the burden of my ill-advising is more than I can bear."

"We all bear the burden of mistakes," said Charles very gently. "I, too, thought that this might be a good place to bargain from—without leaving the country. But, as you know, I have here that which may help me to do so." Pulling his friend gently to his feet, Charles produced a much-folded paper so that the others might see it too. "The letter which that man fishing in the mill stream slipped into my boot as we rode to Yafford yesterday."

"Although he was huddled in a patched coat with a hat over his eyes, I could have sworn he was Captain Bosvile who was sometimes at Hampton," said Berkeley.

"And you would have been right," smiled Charles. "Humphrey Bosvile has a rare aptitude for disguise, and has smuggled me many a private letter under the very noses of our enemies. This particular one is from my wife."

"From the Queen!" exclaimed the two younger men, drawing closer.

"Straitened as her Majesty is and living on the charity of her relatives at the Louvre, she has managed to send a French ship, with a skipper bribed to do our bidding. Since he dare not weigh anchor here he is making a show of unloading a cargo of French wines at Southampton." Involuntarily, six heads turned to consult the chapel weathervane. "And the wind is set fair for France," breathed Charles, as though he were offering up a *Te Deum*.

"And the name of the ship, sir?" asked Firebrace eagerly.

"'Tis in code, but we can work it out. You found means to get me across the Solent, Jack?"

"Firebrace has found a man—"

"'Twas Christmas Day and the wassail bowl had gone round before I met him," admitted Firebrace. "But I judge him to be the type of person who will risk much for money and who, once sworn, will stick to his bond."

"There is the purse of gold Sir John Oglander gave me for just such an emergency," said Charles.

"I persuaded this man Newland to leave one of his smaller craft in a little creek below those meadows they call Fair Lea."

"Is he to be trusted, Harry?" asked Ashburnham anxiously.

"He is betrothed to the girl who greeted his Majesty with a red rose."

"Heaven send her happiness with him!" murmured the King.

"Sir, I made it my business to visit her father's inn," went on Firebrace. "Captain Burley, who waited upon your Majesty, lodges there, and the whole family appears to be hotly Royalist. They are friends of Mistress Wheeler and her niece. So I told some of my best war stories to the menfolk, and from there it was only a step to talking about ships."

"In spite of all my political misfortunes, few monarchs were ever so fortunate in their friends," said Charles, smiling at the capable young red-head. He tucked the Queen's letter back within his coat, and sat thinking. He had not intended to leave England. It meant drawing up the last stake he had in his kingdom. And now that it came to the point he felt an emptiness at the prospect of parting with this handful of men whose lives had been disrupted in his cause, and who had for months past provided all the sense of home and security he had. But beyond their pleasant company, freedom beckoned. His mind conjured up a picture of the dark, vivacious wife whom he had not seen for four years. He was beset by a desire to look upon the baby daughter, born to her during her flight, whom he had never seen at all. And torn by memories of his tall, affectionate eldest son. What a life for a lad—dragged from battlefield to battlefield, then sent hurriedly to Jersey away from all home influence, and now, in his earliest manhood, an exile in France! The elder Charles roused himself to the urgent present. "Bring me my riding boots, Harry," he ordered.

"What if Captain Rolph should have been told that nothing was signed?" demurred Ashburnham, grown cautious as the great moment approached.

"He will suspect nothing. It is his Majesty's usual hour for riding," Berkeley reassured him.

"Would it not be as well, sir, to borrow the Governor's pack of hounds quite openly and set out for Parkhurst forest before doubling back to the river?" suggested Firebrace, kneeling to pull on his master's boots. "At first, when your Majesty does not return, Rolph will only suppose that the hounds were a long time finding."

"It is well thought of," agreed the King, with rising spirits. "And your cozening tongue is just the one to ask the favour. We will wait here until we hear from you that all is well."

"I will go and make love to the Governor's adorable mother," said Firebrace, rising nimbly to the occasion.

"He could probably wheedle the keys of heaven out of Saint Peter!" grinned Berkeley as the door closed behind him; and his feeble jest was greeted with the gusty, over-easy laughter which cloaks men's nervous tension.

"We must seem to saunter—" decided Charles, beginning to pace up and down. But in the midst of drawing on his gloves he stopped abruptly before the window and gripped painfully at Ashburnham's arm. "The vane!" he exclaimed aghast. "Look! It has swung right round."

"The wind must have changed with the tide," said Ashburnham in a choked sort of voice, staring over his shoulder.

They all crowded to the window and stared. It was as though they could not credit their misfortune. Although nearly a quarter of an hour must have passed they were still standing there, motionless and silent, when Harry Firebrace came back. "The old lady says your Majesty is more than welcome to take the hounds. The horses are being brought round—" he began exultantly.

"The wind has veered to south-south-west," cut in Berkeley flatly, without turning. "Until it changes again it will be impossible to make France."

Even Firebrace stood silent and deflated. "Then shall I tell them at the kennels—" he began, when the first bitterness of the moment was past.

It was at such times that Charles Stuart showed himself supremely royal. Keyed up at last to go, he accepted disappointment. Although the others would have waited, hoping for yet another change, he counted upon no miracle. Turning from the window, he walked towards the door with complete composure, pausing only for Richard Osborne to place his riding cloak across his shoulders. "While the sun still shines we will go hunting as arranged," he said, "for God alone knows how long it may be before I hunt again."

And however little his friends' hearts may have been in it, there was nothing for it but to follow him and try to borrow something of his unruffled dignity.

It was almost dusk and raining hard before the Governor returned from Newport, followed by Tom Rudy. His black horse was flecked with sweat, and his own temper vile. "Sergeant!" he shouted, before he was well out of the saddle. Having heard how hard he was putting the animal at the steep rise to the drawbridge, his groom sprang to take his horse and Floyd appeared from the gatehouse almost on the instant.

"Rub him down well and give him a hot mash," Hammond barked at the groom.

"Has the King ridden out to-day?" he demanded of the Sergeant.

"He went hunting an hour or so after you left, sir."

"And he is back?" The Governor's glance had gone immediately to the lighted window of the state room.

"Well before sundown, sir. And all his gentlemen with him."

"Ah!" The ejaculation held all the relief of one who has been enduring a torment of anxiety, and orders followed in premeditated spate. "Bolt the gates for the night, and keep them bolted. No one is to go out even during daylight without a pass from Captain Rolph or myself. No one, save members of my own household. Double the guard and make half-hourly inspection of the battlements. Ask Captain Rolph to report to my room immediately. And have a couple of men stand by at the windlass of the outer portcullis."

"Now, by Heaven, what foul fiend has bitten him?" demanded a hirsute giant of a trooper, poking a cautious head out of the guard-room as soon as the Governor was out of earshot.

"It seems the royal bird meant to fly the cage," Rudy told him, sliding from his saddle. "There's been a French ship hanging around Southampton, very suspicious like. Colonel got wind of it somehow just after the Commissioners had left, so me and him went cantering down to the quay to see if there was any sign of a strange ship on this side waiting to take the Stuart over. Else we'd ha' been back before now."

"And did you find any strange craft?"

"Not a smell of one. Only the usual barges being unloaded for local merchants. Two of 'em offered to help us. Said they knew every craft that had a right to tie up in Medina river. And a long-winded pair they was, wasting the Colonel's time and he fair sweatin' with impatience."

"Which merchants were they?" asked Floyd, from the foot of the winding stone stairs which led up to the portcullis chamber.

Rudy took off his helmet and scratched the damp hair on his forehead. "Newland and Trattle, or some such outlandish names, so far as I can remember. Why did you want to know, Sergeant?"

But Sergeant Floyd did not satisfy his curiosity. "Bring me half a dozen more muskets from the armoury and see that all the guardroom lanterns are replenished before you go off duty," he ordered curtly.

He had been about to go off duty himself. He would have liked a word with his sister and had been looking forward to spending a quiet hour with his daughter; but with this new development and the Governor behaving as though some foul fiend had indeed bitten him, he would be lucky if he got to bed this night.

Mary, hoping that he would come, had been sitting alone in the housekeeper's room, stitching by candlelight. She was making a belated wedding-dress for Libby, who was to be married as soon as the Commissioners were gone and the Governor's young chaplain, Troughton, was freed from the additional duty of helping to entertain them. As her needle moved in and out of the soft homespun material a small, secret smile curved her mouth—but it was not of Libby's happiness that she was thinking. She was going over again the happy hours of Christmas afternoon when Harry Firebrace had walked down with her into Newport. It had been his suggestion that they should walk, and she recalled with pleasure how delicately the bare branches of the beech trees had been etched against a pale sky and how the frosty fields had sparkled as the great red ball of a wintry sun went down. And with a special secret delight she remembered how, when she had slipped a little on a frozen patch going down the steep lane, he had pulled her arm through his to steady her.

True, her happiness had faded a little as they approached the "Rose and Crown." Although political opinions had not seemed to matter before the coming of the King, feeling now ran as high as upon the mainland, and she had been afraid that Mistress Trattle would not welcome one of "Cromwell's minions" as she termed them. And she had been afraid, too, of Frances Trattle's charms. For had not Firebrace suggested the visit in the first place because he wanted to meet the girl who had had the lovely thought to give the King a rose? And was he not the kind of young man for whom Frances would use her lures to the utmost? But her fears had been groundless. Their visit had proved a vast success. She had been so proud to bring him, and Firebrace himself had known just how to please his hostess, kissing her hand and paying her intelligent compliments. Because John Newland was present he had shown Frances only the respectful admiration due to any pretty girl, and although he had a way of making all women feel precious, he had spent most of the afternoon deep in congenial conversation with the lucky merchant and his host.

Coming home through the early darkness had been even best of all, decided Mary, living it all over again. Just at first

Firebrace had seemed preoccupied, and she had walked beside him in contented silence, thinking of the care with which he had wrapped her cloak about her, and of how he had smiled into her eyes as he pulled the hood up over her curls. And as they climbed the hill to the castle the church bells had begun to ring, and he had taken her arm to help her over the frozen patches again, and they had laughed together at the everyday absurdities of their strangely altered lives. And although she had been alone with him in the darkness and tingling with a new excitement, she had felt safe; so that the ugly memory of Edmund Rolph's exploring hands and the fear of his hungry staring were quite wiped out.

In spite of there being neither masque nor decorations, it had been the happiest Christmas Mary had ever known. The exquisite thrill of it remained so vividly that, though stitching the hem of some other girl's wedding-gown, her cheeks glowed softly pink as though it were her own. But it was then that her happy dreams were rudely shattered by the sudden clamour of the Governor's return down in the courtyard. She heard shouting, a sharp clatter of hooves, and her father's voice giving a string of sharply rapped-out orders. Then the sound of a horse being led past to the stables.

"The Governor has come back," she thought. Though why with such an unusual commotion she could not imagine.

She laid aside her work and hurried to the window. But the weather had changed. Rain dashed across the panes, running in rivulets down the glass so that, peer as she would, she could make out nothing save the bobbing lights of lanterns going to and fro. She heard the Governor's quick footsteps cross the courtyard towards the officers' quarters. And although it was barely four by her aunt's cherished clock, the great doors beneath the barbican banged shut, the iron bolts slammed home. And then she was aware of a strange rumble from the gatehouse, and the groan of heavy chains.

"Listen, Aunt Druscilla!" she called out, as Mistress Wheeler came into the room. "Surely that is the portcullis going down?"

Her aunt came swiftly to stand beside her, listening. "What

times we live in!" she exclaimed. "Never once since milady Portland defied Mayor Moses and his mob has that portcullis been lowered."

"It is like being in prison," whispered Mary, apprehensively.

And in the room immediately below the King of England heard it too. Sitting at his writing table, alone, he heard it with far more apprehension than did his little laundry maid. He pulled a sheet of paper towards him and, laboriously consulting his code, began to pen an answer to his wife.

"Dear Heart" he wrote, "By the mischance which always dogs me the wind changed even as I drew on my boots to come to you. Though it should veer again the ship your devotion provided may well have to sail without me. To delay over long at Southampton may provoke suspicion. I know not at the moment by what means this poor letter can reach you, but by reason that my circumstances here have veered also I fear that it must reach you in my stead."

# CHAPTER EIGHT

**A** GUARD MUST BE set at each door of the State Room and Presence Chamber," decided the Governor, sitting down to a hasty meal which had been brought to his room.

It was a precaution which the Captain of the Guard had been wanting to take for days, but he realized well enough the reason for the Colonel's worried agitation. "With only twenty-two men and one sergeant?" he said derisively.

"The master gunner can relieve Floyd. And, as you know, I have asked for reinforcements. Several of the Commissioners have promised to support my request."

"How aptly was the end of the Long Parliament dubbed the Rump!" grumbled Rolph, warming himself before the fire. "If General Fairfax were free to act without consulting them, we should have had a well-trained company of foot by now."

Hurriedly picking at a chicken leg, Hammond spoke of the thing which had been worrying him most. "This morning we have seen what may happen so long as the King is allowed to ride abroad, yet can I risk keeping him in close custody until these reinforcements come? If the islanders never see him outside the castle they may imagine that we are keeping him in the dungeon or trying to murder him, in which case they will probably raise some kind of revolt; and—as you say—what have we but twenty-two men and a sergeant?"

"There is the militia," said Rolph, who had made it his business to watch one of their exercises. "Adequately manned and remarkably well organized."

"But captained for the most part by gentlemen of old island families who have always been for the King." Pushing aside his plate, Hammond brought himself to appeal for advice to the stockily built *parvena* standing over-familiarly before his hearth. "You go about among them more than I do, Rolph. How would you say the majority of the ordinary people here feel about this matter?"

Rolph thrust out a full lower lip and shrugged contemptuously. "I would say they have always been too remote from what goes on on the mainland to care much either way. Of course, things may be different now, with most of them all worked up by so much unheard-of excitement. But in any case they lack a leader."

"At the moment, yes." It was a comforting thought, particularly to a man who was beginning to have a very high idea of their intelligence and resourcefulness. Warmed by a good draught of wine, their Governor rose from the table and reached for his sword belt. "But if there *should* be any trouble all demonstration must be suppressed before it spreads, and the ringleader dealt with ruthlessly."

"Meaning that the velvet glove may now be exchanged for the mailed fist?" grinned the Captain, slapping the buckle of his own belt.

"Hardly that, I hope. But Ashburnham, Berkeley, and Legge must go immediately."

"And those two bishop-ridden chaplains?"

The Governor stood absently fingering some papers, then turned away from the table with a sigh. "Parliament would probably wish it, but I should have liked to leave him that much consolation. Probably," he added, with his wry, thin smile, "because my own father happens to be a bishop-ridden chaplain, as you call it."

"Do you suppose that these household gentry sent from Hampton are to be trusted, sir?" asked Rolph hurriedly, to cover his tactlessness.

"Most of them are strangers to me. Master Herbert and Master Mildmay are, of course, beyond doubt. And the two young men who have just joined us—Firebrace and Osborne—seem sound enough."

"They certainly brighten up our exiled lives!" laughed Rolph. "But there are too many ushers and servers and such. What does a throneless monarch need with so much state? Besides—"

"Besides what, Captain?"

Edmund Rolph gave a short, embarrassed laugh. "I was only remembering what you once said about the Stuart charm, and thinking that men exposed to it for any length of time *have* been known to change their coats. And that one unrecognized enemy can be more dangerous than a dozen in the open."

"You are very right. But at least their opinions are not my responsibility, since they have been selected by Parliament."

"All the same, if I might suggest it, sir, I would try to cut down the size of this make-believe court. And in so doing you could get rid of any of them whom you felt might be suspected of Royalist sympathy."

Although Hammond knew that party spite prompted the words, they clothed sound advice. "Sympathy is not incompatible with duty," he said, almost as though he were speaking to himself. "Thomas Herbert and Anthony Mildmay know how to combine the two. They must often be torn as I am."

Rolph looked at him with momentary alarm. "But you *will* tell the King his friends are to go?"

"Set your mind at rest, my good democrat. I will tell him to-morrow. Immediately after I have arranged for their dismissal. Though I admit there are few duties I would not sooner perform."

"It is the Lord's judgment on him, and I am quite willing to deputise for you," offered Rolph.

"I make no doubt you are," said Hammond, regarding him with ill-conceived distaste. By the nature of their appointments it was inevitable that there should be a certain amount of confidence between them. He himself had been so much harassed of late that, contrary to his normal habit, he had felt the need to consult someone; and at least Rolph was an efficient officer, incorruptible in the cause. For that one should be more thankful, Hammond supposed. "I hope for your sake that the reinforcements arrive soon. I myself will relieve you with the night watch," he promised stiffly.

"And to-morrow morning you had better send Sergeant Floyd to ask the five gentlemen in question to come here as soon as they have broken their fast." Floyd, he knew, could be counted upon to deliver the message with courtesy.

Dismissed, Rolph went willingly to his duties, but stopped before reaching the door. His fingers had touched the cold smoothness of beads in his pocket. He was not accustomed to being thwarted. His manner became aggressive as he clumsily seized the occasion to make a bid for the impossible. "From something that was touched on when I was in London," he said. "I am hoping that Fairfax may send us my own company of foot. I take it that my sergeants, with their modern training and equipment, will rank senior to Floyd?"

But, as Mistress Wheeler had once told Mary, the new Governor was at least just. He met the irrelevant query with a look of cold surprise. "Floyd has been Sergeant of the Guard here for ten years or more," he said, "and has, to the best of my knowledge, always carried out his duties satisfactorily."

The following morning was one of wild excitement and conjecture throughout the castle. The servants were surprised to find the gates shut and to see baggage being piled into a cart before the royal lodgings. The Governor absented himself from dinner, scarcely anyone spoke throughout the meal, and most of the dishes were carried down to the kitchen untouched. In view of the impending parting, constraint between men of opposite parties was inevitable. And immediately afterwards it was the King who sent for the Governor. He was whitely furious. "Why do you use me thus, sending away my friends? Where are your orders for it?" he demanded. And having as yet received none, Hammond had no answer.

"When I came here it was of my own free will," went on the King, facing him across the uncleared table and dispensing with all formality. "And did you not promise me that you would not take advantage of my predicament?"

"I promised only that I would do what I could," said Hammond. Angry colour flooded into the King's pale cheeks. It was so unusual for him to raise his voice that his gentlemen in the ante-room kept complete silence, straining to hear. "You equivocate, Hammond," he accused. "You pretended to a very different spirit then. And immediately betrayed me."

Before that slight figure so assured of divine right, the Governor of the Wight felt—and looked—like a prisoner at the bar. "My spirit towards your Majesty is no different now," he defended himself. "But I am the servant of Parliament."

"You are my subject," snapped Charles. "Your father received every kindness from me, yet you presume to shut your gates upon me and dismiss your betters!"

Irritation rose hotly in Robert Hammond, dissipating his unwilling awe. "Your Majesty knows very well why I am now forced to do so—since yesterday," he said firmly.

It was Charles Stuart's turn to have nothing to say. Since Ashburnham and the others had been summoned to the Governor's room, he had been allowed no opportunity to speak with them in private. He could only guess at how much Hammond knew of their plans, but he could not doubt the reason for their dismissal. Nor could he really expect that any Governor in his senses would allow them to stay. "Will you not at least allow my chaplains to remain?" he brought himself to ask, reluctantly admitting his custodian's power if not his authority.

Because in common humanity he wished to do so—because he realized the comfort a chaplain could be to a cornered man—Hammond stood in silence, merely making a small, helpless gesture with his hands.

His attitude seemed to infuriate the king more than anything which had gone before. "You—who broke away from the traditions of your family because you pretend to stand for liberty of conscience!" he cried, his voice rising so that the very servants crowded outside the door waiting to draw the cloths could catch some of his words. "Am I to have none?"

"It is not for religious reasons," said Hammond, ignoring the personal jibe. "But I cannot—I sincerely regret that I cannot—allow them to remain."

Charles banged down the tasselled walking stick he was holding upon the table and turned away to the window. "Then you use me neither as a Christian nor a gentleman," he complained.

Although Hammond felt him to be unreasonable, the accusation hurt. "May we not talk of this when—"

"When they are gone, and it is useless?" interrupted Charles.

"I was about to say when your Majesty is in a better temper," concluded the Governor evenly.

Realizing the disadvantage under which his rare loss of temper placed him, Charles made a great effort to control all outward signs of it. "My conscience being clear, I slept well last night," he said almost banteringly, sitting down on the window seat. "I would remind you that it was not I who fumed round the battlements half the night for fear the King's friends would get him out or his loyal island subjects rise up in indignation and come into fetch him."

The recaptured dignity and cool smile did more to humble Hammond than any previous anger. "Have I not always used you civilly?" he demanded earnestly.

"Then why do you not do so now?" enquired Charles, unable to deny it. As the Governor would not argue with him, he picked up a book that was lying on the window seat and drew it on to his knees, as though the matter were of small account. But the littleness of his world seemed to be closing in upon him. And there was one thing which still mattered supremely. "Under this new regime," he asked, making a show of turning over the pages, "shall I have liberty to ride out and take the air?"

Both men realized that to do so was the only possible gateway to a larger liberty. There was a weighty silence while it seemed that Robert Hammond still struggled with his conscience. "No, sir. I regret I cannot grant it," he said at last.

"Then am I a prisoner indeed!" sighed Charles.

"Your Majesty will always be free to walk upon the walls or in the extensive place-of-arms," Hammond reminded him tentatively.

But the King was not listening. With the book open before him he sat staring across the courtyard at the sad dripping trees against the herb garden and at the fast-closed gates. "The prisoner of

Carisbrooke," he murmured, trying the words over as if wondering how they would sound to the outside world, or perhaps to posterity.

Seeing him so downcast and withdrawn, Hammond went quickly from the Presence Chamber. It had not been easy to exert his authority over such exalted personages. His morning had been made up of painful interviews and he had had enough. He did not wish to witness the farewell for which he would feel responsible. In the ante-room he found Captain Rolph with the five gentlemen who had received their dismissal, and drew him aside. From now on the ordering of the affair would be his, and no doubt he would enjoy it. "Let them go in and bid his Majesty good-bye, but stay with them until they are outside the castle," he said. "Show them every courtesy, but see to it that no one speaks to him in private lest they hatch some further plot.

When everyone streamed back into the Presence Chamber, Rolph took up his stand near the King. Not only did he keep well within earshot of the sad little group by the window, but he tormented them by bringing various servants into the room upon unnecessary errands concerned with their departure. Seeing Mary hesitating by the serving screens with a pile of freshly laundered napkins for the King's table he called to her to come in and set them down. Besides wishing to show his authority, he seemed intent upon allowing the King and his friends as little privacy as possible.

Royal formality was ironically forced upon the King when all he wanted was to say good-bye to the dismissed courtiers as well-tried friends. Each of them knelt and kissed his hand, but Charles himself was too full of emotion to say more than a few words. Master Mildmay and Master Herbert, loyal servants of Parliament as they were, moved to the far end of the room, unwilling to pry upon their mutual grief. Mary, embarrassed at being there at all, stood as near the door as she could, the pile of laundry still outspread upon her arms. After one curious and pitying glance she looked away from the King, and noting with what a vigilant and scoffing eye Captain Rolph stared at him she loathed the man more than ever. She could not imagine how she had ever wished to keep his necklace.

She knew that kind Master Ashburnham and some of the others were being sent away, and that perhaps it was merciful that the time allowed them for farewells was short. Someone said something about the tide, and a servant came hurrying in to whisper to the Captain that the horses had been brought round. The King stood with quiet dignity watching his friends and chaplains depart. They came down the long room towards Mary and in the silence there was only their reluctant tread and the smothered sound of Master John Ashburnham's shamed weeping.

And suddenly into the saddened hush came the shocking sound of approaching laughter. The cheerful, chaffing laughter of high-spirited young men. She recognized the voices of Harry Firebrace and Richard Osborne. They were coming round the serving screens. They must both be off duty, and usually at this hour the King would be out taking the air. How appalling that they should know what was happening! "They will be utterly disgraced. The King will never forgive them. I must slip out and warn them," thought Mary.

But it was not easy for a laundry maid to turn and walk out before a procession of such important people; and before she dared to do so worse befell.

The two young men burst into the hushed room and Richard Osborne, coming up from behind, caught her teasingly round the waist and kissed her. Mary had heard that he had a reputation for levity. Still clutching the pile of clean linen, she stood crimson-faced and helpless. Rolph, coming down the room close behind the dismissed courtiers, glared at him; and Firebrace pulled up within a yard of them. Apparently becoming aware, to his horror, that they were in the King's presence, he made a frantic effort to suppress his friend's exuberance, pulling at his arm in order to distract his attention from Mary. He was not usually clumsy, but in doing so he bumped into Sir John Berkeley, knocking the plumed hat from his hand. He apologised profusely and bent down to retrieve the hat. As Ashburnham and the others went out through the door, Berkeley and Firebrace were very close together, while Osborne— seemingly stricken with embarrassment—stood blocking the

Captain's way with his broad shoulders. Firebrace prolonged the confused moment still more by dusting the ill-used headgear with his sleeve, and insisting upon smoothing out the sweeping plume. Mary stood watching the odd scene, fascinated. She was marvelling that she, quiet Mary Floyd, should have been drawn into the circle of such colourful people and dramatic events. She saw Sir Charles Berkeley, with his back to Rolph, say something quickly to Firebrace, and it had nothing to do with the hat. He spoke in a whisper, but he was so close to her that she overheard. "Tell his Majesty that Edward Worsley of Gatcombe will act in our stead," he said; and added something about "despairing of an opportunity to speak" and "horses on the other side."

When Sir John Berkeley and the impatient Captain had gone out to their waiting horses she was still thinking what an extraordinary thing it was for an ardent Royalist to say to an attendant appointed by Parliament.

Forgetting Osborne's boldness and her own embarrassment, she stood staring at Harry Firebrace; but she was seeing him in an entirely new light. She began trying to fit into the puzzle the memory of various things which he had done and said. Realizing that she must have overheard, he turned and met her searching gaze. And as though divining her thoughts, he shrugged his shoulders almost imperceptibly and smiled. He seemed confident that she would not betray him. And Mary felt suddenly elated, as though some strange, secret bond had been tied between them.

When Richard Osborne set the pile of linen down for her and asked her pardon she forgave him absently because she supposed it had all been part of the purposeful play-acting.

"I ask no pardon for kissing you, only for choosing so public a moment," he was careful to explain.

He smiled down at her, and she thought his voice singularly attractive. With the mild, preoccupied appreciation of a girl already in love, she noticed that his mouth was reckless and his brown eyes kind.

But when the King retired to the State Room and beckoned to his auburn-haired Groom of the Bedchamber to attend him, showing no sign of annoyance at the disturbance he had created, Mary's exultation was mixed with fear. "Now he will give him Sir John Berkeley's message," she thought. "There is something real which is going on, and from now on there will be real danger."

But it was of Harry Firebrace's danger she thought, not the King's.

# CHAPTER NINE

———∞∞∞———

"T HEY ARRESTED HIM AND took him away. Our kind old Captain Burley—handcuffed as though he were a felon!" sobbed Frances Trattle, burying her frightened white face in her arms as she huddled over the parlour table at the "Rose and Crown."

"And there were not enough of us to save him from the Governor's soldiers," confirmed her mother, wiping her eyes by the inn window.

"It was a hopeless venture anyway," said Edward Trattle sombrely, from the hearth.

Although most of the excitement of an abortive rising had died down, people were still standing about in the streets outside, or gaping from their doorways, and at that moment a couple of patrolling troopers trotted briskly past.

"What really happened?" asked Mary, who had been sent by her aunt to get a first-hand account of things. They had both seen Captain Burley being brought into the castle. At first it had been supposed that all Newport was marching furiously to Carisbrooke to set the King free, but from the escort which had arrested him on the road to Carisbrooke they had been able to elicit only garbled stories.

Seeing that his wife and daughter were still too agitated for coherency, Trattle drew Mary to the settle and sat down beside her. "It all began with Master Ashburnham and his two friends coming here while they waited for a boat," he explained. "Rumour'd already got around that they were being sent away, and people kept crowding about the door, sympathizing and shouting out what they'd like to do to the Governor. I served the three gentlemen with drinks myself, and I'll say no one ever looked more in need of them. But presently two of them went off—to say good-bye to a friend, they said."

"And I asked poor Master Ashburnham to rest awhile in here," said Agnes, coming to warm her hands at the fire. "But it seems it was the worst thing I could have done."

Mary, who loved her, hated to see her so distressed. "Why, surely 'twas only human, Mistress Trattle!" she said.

"Yes. But you see, child, Captain Burley was in here too. He'd been taking his afternoon nap by the fire. And seeing they'd met up at the castle, the two of them fell to talking. Master Ashburnham began telling him all that's been going on up there, and you know how excitable the poor dear Captain is—"

"Seems he got it into his head that as soon as his Majesty's friends had been got rid of, these Parliament folk meant to do the King some mischief. 'I've served him all these years,' he said, 'and retired or not, I'm not going to stand by now when his Majesty's life is in danger!' And out he rushes into the street and starts haranguing the crowd."

Agnes Trattle sat down and put a shaky hand on Mary's knee. "He sent a lad for the town drum and had him beat it in the Square and up and down the town; while he himself called on everyone to rise up and rescue the King—"

"'For God and King Charles!' he kept shouting in that great quarter-deck voice of his," sniffed Frances, beginning to dry her eyes and rearrange her disordered hair.

"As if he could have taken the castle, poor old gamecock!" smiled Trattle, the realist, sadly regarding his lodger's empty chair.

"There's no more than a dozen or so in the garrison, Mary always says," argued Frances defiantly, coming to join them. "If only people would have rallied round as they said they would, and old Mayor Moses had not interfered—seizing his drum back and sending to warn the Governor!"

"'Twas but a poor following anyway," said Trattle. "Many of 'em women and children like yourself, and only the Captain's sword and one musket between the lot of you."

Now that Frances was standing up, Mary could see that her skirts were mudstained and torn. "Did *you* go, Frances?" she exclaimed admiringly. For it seemed almost as spectacular a thing to do as presenting the King of England with a rose. So much more splendid than anything which she herself would ever dare to do.

"He was always so fond of her," murmured Agnes. "I was for following myself—"

"Until I put a stop to it," said Trattle. "And only just in time, too. Rolph's men arrested him before he was well out of the town."

"It seems you will never raise a finger for the King!" accused his wife angrily.

"Not unless I see some reasonable hopes of success. A forlorn hope like this may well do him more harm than good, as Master Ashburnham was telling the people just now."

"Where are Master Ashburnham and the others?" asked Mary.

"Captain Rolph chartered a ship for them. He would have liked to pin this disturbance on to them if he could. But although that Roundhead cur who lives opposite—he who threw the mud at the King, you remember—piped up and said Master Ashburnham had been leaning out of this window inciting the people to rise for the King, everyone gave him the lie. They swore that he had only been counselling them to keep quiet, and they were in such a dangerous mood by then that Captain Rolph was only too glad to hurry him and his friends aboard for the mainland."

"Let us hope he will be safe from Cromwell," said Mary, who had never cared about what happened on the mainland before.

"He told me he hoped to find refuge at Netley Abbey," said Agnes. "But what of Captain Burley? Was he brought into the castle before you left? Did they take off those awful handcuffs?"

Mary hesitated. She could not bring herself to add to their distress. "He was taken straight to the Governor's room," she said.

Agnes Trattle gave a sigh of relief. "Then undoubtedly the Governor will see that he is just an excitable old gentleman and will let him go. After all, nothing *came* of his enterprise. We shall probably have him home before the day is out."

She began cheerfully setting the disordered room to rights, but her husband was watching Mary. He felt sure that she was holding something back. "It is getting dark and, with all this commotion in the town, I am sure your father would like me to see you home," he said.

Frances, smoothing out her muddied gown, was almost her bright self again. "Didn't that handsome Master Firebrace offer to bring you again this time?" she teased.

"Only those of us who live there are allowed out without a special pass," said Mary, colouring becomingly.

"It is iniquitous!" declared Agnes, kissing her good-bye. "But at least *you* will still be able to come and see us."

Trattle led Mary out to the inn yard, and called to his ostler to saddle a horse. It was already dusk and as he took a lantern from its hook outside the kitchen door the light fell on her face, so fair and serious in the soft darkness of her hood. It occurred to him that she had grown up surprisingly during the last few weeks, outstripping his own daughter in maturity. For the first time he found himself thinking of her as a woman, and one who knew when to speak and when to hold her tongue. "What did they really do to Burley?" he asked.

"He was put down in the dungeon."

"Merciful God! And he close on seventy. You did right not to tell them."

"Aunt Druscilla thinks it was to frighten others from following his example. The Governor has been like a cat on hot bricks since the King came."

"It sounds more like Rolph's work, persecuting an old man."

"Try not to worry, Master Trattle. My father will see that he is properly fed, and there is scarcely one of the men who does not sympathize with him. Perhaps he will be set free before the reinforcements come."

"Reinforcements?"

"They are expected any day. The garrison can talk of nothing else."

"These New Model Ironsides?"

"I suppose so. Our men hate the thought of it."

To Mary that score of middle-aged gunners and musketeers were personal friends.

"Everything will be tightened up. But at least you are still able to come and go," said Edward Trattle, unconsciously echoing his wife's words. "The Governor must be a bigger fool than we supposed." For a moment or two he stood thoughtfully swaying the lantern, then shrugged as a man will who comes to an unwilling decision.

He kicked open a door to the crowded public room of the inn and beckoned to someone inside. A sudden buzz of conversation and laughter, a stale warmth and the smell of spilled ale assailed their senses; and through the shaft of yellow light briefly streaming across the cobbles a shabbily dressed man lurched out into the yard. "Here is someone who is going back to the castle," Trattle told him quietly, as the door swung shut again.

The man might have been a valet or a barber who had seen better days. In a thin whine he began a tale about wanting to get a message to his master who had gotten himself a fine appointment up there and owed him a month's wages. But his host cut him short. "No need for that, Major," he said. "Mistress Mary is one of us, and if she is to do it I will not have her hoodwinked." At the sound of horseshoes clopping from the stable Trattle glanced over his shoulder, but his ostler had stopped to tighten a girth. "This is Major Bosvile, Mary. And the letter is for the King," he told her tersely. "Bosvile is already suspected and there is grave risk. I would not have you take it unwillingly or unwarned."

Cold fear struck at Mary's heart. A sense of unreality gripped her. "How could *I* give a letter to the *King*?" she whispered, conscious of how eagerly they were both watching her.

"I do not ask you to," said the man who had lurched out. His voice no longer whined and he was quite sober. "Do you know a young Groom of the Bedchamber called Firebrace?"

Mary nodded. Cold fear gave way to warm excitement. She remembered the sense of being specially trusted which she had experienced when Harry Firebrace had last smiled at her. She would do anything to enter yet more fully into that joyful confederacy.

"He is an ingenious young man," the disguised Major was saying. "If you give him this letter he will somehow find means to deliver it."

In the half light she saw him delve into the pockets of his patched coat and draw out a purse. She could hear the ostler whistling through his teeth as he brought the horse. The whiteness of a letter showed momentarily in the shifting lantern light; then she felt its crispness being thrust into her hand. It seemed incredible. Only a short while ago she had thought Frances a heroine for greeting the King as an acknowledged Royalist before an uncertain crowd; and for following, mud-splashed and romantic, in an old man's loyal rising. That had been splendid and spectacular, of course. But mere play-acting, compared with this. This was real. And dangerous, as Trattle had so gravely warned. And within that charmed circle of danger stood a young man with a devastating smile.

Mary tucked the letter down inside her bodice, against her fast-beating heart. "I do not want your money," she whispered brusquely, waving the diffidently proffered purse away.

Trattle took the reins and mounted and Jem the redheaded ostler thrust out a palm for her to scramble to the saddle behind him. She took the lantern in one hand and held on to Trattle's belt with the other. As they passed out under the archway into the road she looked back; but save for old Jem, with the inevitable straw in his mouth, the inn yard was empty. There was only the sharp pricking of the letter between her breasts to convince her of the reality of the task she had undertaken.

She and Trattle rode through the town and out towards Carisbrooke in silence. At the foot of the lane by the water splash he drew in his horse under the shadow of the great beech trees which grew beneath the escarpment. "Better that I am not seen with you," he muttered; and then, as he stretched an arm backwards to set her down, he added remorsefully, "I would not have drawn you into this, Mary, could I have seen any other way. That letter is about another ship to take the place of the French one at Southampton. But I beg you do not speak of it to my wife and Frances."

"Why do you let them suppose that you do nothing for the King?"

"Because I can be of more use that way." He was surprised by the radiance of Mary's upturned face, and smiled down at her more easily. "My Frances has not your gift of reticence, and the dangers of the mainland are now spread to the island. Go now, my dear, so that friend Floyd may know I have brought you safely back."

Hurrying eagerly up the path to the drawbridge, calling back friendly "good-nights" to the sentries, walking in under the great gateway with all the lights from the castle window giving her welcome—all was pleasantly familiar. And yet different because of the letter.

"Why, you are all out of breath, my poppet!" called her father, who was talking with the master-gunner just inside the gateway.

"The way up is so steep," said Mary.

"No steeper than it has been these last seventeen years," grinned Floyd, glad to have anything at all to grin about on such a misfortunate day.

"Let's hope it will blow some of the breath out of this new batch of know-all Ironsides!" muttered Howe, the old master-gunner, fervently.

"Tell your aunt they have landed and should be here before nightfall," the Sergeant of the Guard called after her.

Mary understood her father's more than ordinary zeal that nothing should be found amiss. Anxious as she was to tell him about the letter, there was no opportunity—nor could she have found it in her heart to add to his burdens at such a time.

While brushing out her hair before supper, she looked searchingly into her aunt's mirror. She had fastened about her neck a string of beads which her father had given her. They were not real amber like those which Captain Rolph had brought her from London, but she touched them with a loving smile. And the smile curved her wide mouth to tenderness and lent a soft lustre to her eyes. "Of course, I am not *really* lovely like Frances—" she thought, turning shyly from a reflection which almost pleased her.

There was a new look about her—something more soignée, more secret and mature. And Captain Rolph was quick to notice it. At supper he managed to sit next to her. "Although you would have none from me, those yellow beads suit you," he said, in his mannerless way. "Did Richard Osborne give them to you?"

The way she seemed to draw herself out of some private dream piqued his desire still further. "Richard Osborne?" she repeated vaguely. "Why?"

"I saw him kiss you after dinner, and you did not seem to mind."

The kiss had meant nothing. It had merely achieved its purpose of distracting his attention. Mary laughed, but remembered in time that she must not say so. From now on there would be other things one must remember not to say. She must learn to guard her tongue, to think more quickly.

Rolph frowned, taking her laughter for flirtatious acquiescence. "Osborne's kisses are as lavish as his love tokens. If your father hopes to get you a good husband I wonder he does not draw the line at a man of his reputation." His thigh pressed hers as he reached ostentatiously for the jug of water which was always set before him.

"Is it true that reinforcements have landed?" asked Mary coldly.

"Two sergeants from my own company rode in. Where were you that you did not hear the excitement?"

"With my friend in Newport."

"You should have let me take you."

"You were on duty."

"Too true. Rounding up a lot of hysterical Royalists."

"And humiliating one brave old man with handcuffs."

"As a lesson to the other crazy rustics," admitted Rolph sheepishly. "But how did you know?"

"The people of Newport are mostly our friends and neighbours."

"How you islanders do hang together!"

Mary would have liked to escape his attentions by going to her aunt's quiet room; but as soon as supper was over she knelt down by the hearth and began playing with the spaniel Patters and her fast-growing pups. And presently, as she had hoped, Harry

Firebrace came through the room. She knelt upright, with a small spaniel cuddled in each arm and the firelight on her hair, deliberately attracting his attention. She might have been a wanton playing one man off against another. "See how they have grown! Are they not adorable, Master Firebrace?" she called, in the middle of whatever Edmund Rolph was saying.

The young Groom of the Bedchamber came over to her at once and set the other two fat, lumbering pups racing for walnuts which he had filched from a passing servant. He minded not at all that the Captain of the Guard scowled at him, resenting the interruption and thinking such amusements childish.

"I have something for you," Mary managed to tell him softly, as they both made a lunge after a rolling walnut.

"A letter?" asked Firebrace, apparently absorbed in preventing the pick of Patters' litter from choking himself.

Mary looked up with flushed cheeks. "I cannot give it to you now," she whispered. Rolph was standing with his back to the fire, watching her.

The Captain's lascivious glance was for the white budding of her breasts at the top of her gown, but all her apprehension was for the King's letter. She felt that even beneath her best green worsted it must be apparent to his gaze. But it was useless to run away. She had undertaken to deliver it and she must act, as Firebrace and Osborne had acted earlier in the day. For the first time in her life she dissembled. Sinking down upon one of the hearthside benches, as though out of breath, she laughed up at Firebrace. "Oh, I am too exhausted to play with the Patters family any more, after being in Newport all the afternoon! And to-morrow morning Brett and I have to begin training another donkey because so much extra water will be needed for the new troops."

Firebrace picked up his cue immediately. "I must come and watch," he said. It would be quiet and dark in the well-house, and only gentle old Brett would be there. But to Mary's momentary horror—because he always played for disarming all possible suspicion—Firebrace turned invitingly to Rolph. "Have you ever watched the clever little beasts turn the wheel? Of course, you must be extra busy just now, Captain. But you really should one day. It takes so much skill and patience to train them."

But, as he had safely reckoned, the dark-jowled Captain of the Guard had no interest in donkeys.

"God knows it takes me all my time to train the human variety!" he laughed, his good humour restored.

# CHAPTER TEN

$\sim\!\!\infty\!\!\sim$

Materially, Edward Trattle's prophecy proved true. After the failure of Captain Burley's ill-considered rising, the King was kept in much closer confinement. A special commission was set up at Derby House in London to deal with his captivity, and from their Speaker Hammond received his orders. Half the officers of the royal household who had come from Hampton were dismissed, and from the remainder he was bidden to choose four of the most trustworthy to act as wardens of the King's person. Pompously, the gentlemen of Derby House called them conservators, insisting that one or other of them must always be on guard outside the two doors of the State Room. Every night their beds were pushed one against the main door and one against the backstairs entrance so that, once his Majesty had retired, he could not come forth without their knowledge and neither could any unauthorized person enter. For the first time Hammond not only had full backing for his orders, but the power to enforce them; for General Fairfax had sent two companies of foot, and the castle barracks were full to overflowing.

But in more subtle ways the arrest and imprisonment of Captain Burley had exactly the opposite effect. The harsh way in which he was treated swung public sympathy towards the Royalist cause which he so courageously represented. During his captaincy of Yarmouth he had been popular with the people, and even those who were normally indifferent to politics were moved to indignant pity. "If the Governor had dispersed the crowd and let the old sea-dog go, no one would have been any the worse off," they said. "But he allowed that wild-eyed Mayor of Newport to persuade him."

And Hammond himself saw, too late, that reporting the affair had been a bad error of judgment; for after doing so the Captain's fate was out of his hands. There was nothing he could do to mitigate it, however much he might regret its cruelty. His own genuine desire to make pleasant contact with the islanders was doomed. Just as he himself had done in the first place, Parliament used the unfortunate Burley as a scapegoat and an example. And by sending him to an unjust trial at Winchester they presented the King he so fearlessly upheld with scores of secret sympathisers. No decent man on the island or in Hampshire would be a party to that travesty of a trial. And when at last by some legal chicanery the excitable Captain was condemned to death, an executioner had to be sent down from London because no one else would carry out the foul sentence.

"Hanged, drawn and quartered—that kindly, upright old man! The Trattles must be heart-broken," lamented Druscilla Wheeler, staring out unseeingly at the bleak February day.

"And on a charge of high treason, of all absurdities! The one true man among a pack of traitors!" added her brother, thankful to be for an hour or two where he could speak his mind away from the king-hating, Psalm-singing type of men now in barracks. "The Governor dare not go out to Yarmouth Haven, where all the ships' pennants are at half-mast. And down in Newport almost every inn and shop is closed. He pretends not to notice, but I wager he wishes the whole miserable business undone."

Mary crouched in the window seat, sick with pity, cradling her favourite spaniel pup in protective arms. Death to her had always seemed too far away to think about, a vague frightening shadow which would one day threaten her in some unapprehended state of illness or old age. How could people face it, in full health, seeing its certain approach? How summon the courage to walk out to meet it, while the sun shone and the birds still sang? How keep their brave defiance unbroken, as ruddy-faced Captain Burley had done, knowing the horrible, unspeakable things that were to be done to him? "I shall always remember the day he took Frances and me on the downs," she said, her hot tears splashing on to the small dog's head. "It was such an ordinary, *happy* day. The last day before the King came and everything on the island changed."

Everywhere in the castle the execution at Winchester was being discussed. Four of the younger courtiers, waiting about in the ante-room to accompany their royal master on his morning walk, were equally concerned. "If your Parliament can twist words to take the life of an unimportant retired officer, what may not the *canailles* attempt against the King himself?" propounded Abraham Dowcett, the French Clerk of the Kitchen, who had long ago conceived a great admiration for Charles Stuart.

Firebrace began gathering up his master's stick and gloves. "Before Christmas I had the honour of meeting this Burley at the inn where he lodged, and the impertinence to think of him as a white-haired old eccentric whose day was done," he said. "But he shames us all. Whether it succeeded or not, at least he *did* something. And when those butchers came to drag his entrails from him he still shouted to the crowd 'Serve God and the King!'"

"A brave motto!" allowed Captain Titus, one of the new conservators.

"I know which party I would sooner serve!" declared Cresset, the Treasurer, emboldened by his words. "They say the heartless bastards will not allow Burley's family a penny from his estate."

"How does his Majesty take the news of his execution?" asked Titus.

"Master Herbert says that he has been at his prayers for hours, and has scarcely eaten or spoken to anyone," answered Firebrace. "Here they come, and—being sick at heart—I warrant the King will walk round those walls more quickly than ever!" The State Room door opened and Charles came out, accompanied by Mildmay and Herbert. He was dressed all in black and took stick and gloves without a word. Briskly, the four young men followed him. Downstairs and across the courtyard they went in heavy silence; but as they mounted the stone steps to the southern side of the battlements Firebrace slipped a hand through Titus's arm. "Did you truly mean what you said just now—about the brave motto?" he asked, in an eager undertone.

Titus, son of a God-fearing Hertfordshire squire, turned and looked him straight in the eyes. "Do you suppose I enjoy earning my living by snooping at a good man's door?" he asked with unexpected bitterness. "I could not well refuse; but the more I see of the Stuart the more I respect him. He never complains about all the things he must miss nor vents his irritation on us. And even towards Hammond—"

Seeing the Governor ascending the steps close on their heels Firebrace nudged Titus to silence. "This evening I may find means to relieve you," he whispered hastily.

At the top of the steps both young men stood aside for the Governor to pass, and then Cresset and Dowcett fell back a pace or two to rejoin them. "The perfect host cannot bear his guest to be out of his sight," chuckled Dowcett, as they watched the tall, lean Governor pursuing the slight, swiftly moving figure of the King.

"And there is nothing his Majesty hates more," grinned Francis Cresset.

But seeing that his Majesty had the courtesy to stop and talk with Hammond, the four of them took the opportunity to stop too. It was beautiful on the south battlements on a sunny morning. A soft, almost springlike breeze blew in from the Channel, and the sparsely inhabited country away to the back of the island was spread below them. Apart from a few scattered farms and villages, they could see only softly rounded hills, small oaks stunted by the wind, and a winding lane leading from the wild Channel coast at Chale towards the north coast on the smoother Solent. Harry Firebrace's gaze rested thoughtfully upon the winding lane. He leant over the fortifications, looking down at the steep escarpment and the narrow moat below. To the Cromwellian sentry tramping past he appeared to be only another soft-living courtier poetically admiring the view. But Firebrace's eyes were keen and calculating and when the sentry had passed he still leaned there, drawing his three companions closer with a beckoning motion of his head. "Given a stout rope and a strong confederate up here, the drop should not be impossible," he said.

"And those trees on the other side of the counterscarp would hide a couple of horses," murmured Cresset.

For as long as they dared they stood there looking down, sharing the same fascinating thought. But King and Governor were moving on, followed decorously by Herbert and Mildmay, and the four younger men had perforce to hasten after them. "In all this rabbit warren of a castle is there no safe place where we can talk?" demanded Dowcett, in whose impatient Latin blood the desire to be doing something was already fermenting.

That evening Harry Firebrace found such a place, safe and convenient beyond their hopes. And he was offered it almost by accident.

He was always so good-natured and accommodating that it seemed quite natural he should offer to relieve one of the conservators for an hour or so. Their hours were long and tedious, and after the King and the Governor had supped and retired to their rooms Firebrace took over Titus's guard, giving him the rare opportunity of enjoying a meal in company with the other members of the household. Happily for his purpose. Firebrace found himself posted at the backstairs door which opened from the King's bedroom into the privacy of a poorly lighted passage. As soon as the second supper was in progress and the whole house quiet he tapped gently on the door, and presently the King opened it. Seeing his devoted Groom of the Bedchamber standing there alone instead of a conservator made an unexpectedly bright ending to a dismal way. Dear as Herbert and Mildmay were to Charles, they were the incorruptible servants of Parliament and there were matters with which he would not burden their consciences. Firebrace, with his adventurous and undivided loyalty, brought hope of contact with the outside world and of eventual escape. Firebrace would tell him who was, and who was not, to be trusted in the enterprise. And—for his immediate comfort—Firebrace would no doubt find means to deliver the letters he had been writing and to bring answers from those whom he loved. Holding the door ajar, King and ingenious Groom of the Bedchamber spoke in hurried whispers, lest the conservator on the outside of the other door should hear. Since the one privilege which Charles had insisted upon was the right to lock both his doors when he had retired for the night, they were safe from interruption from that quarter. But, quiet as the Governor's house was at that hour, anyone mounting the backstairs could see them from the end of the passage. Warily, as he spoke or listened, Firebrace kept an eye upon the stair-head. He knew that he was taking an enormous risk. And even as he turned to take a packet of letters from the King and thrust them hurriedly inside his coat he heard a light step and the swish of a skirt and Mary Floyd was almost upon him. He closed the door quickly and heard the King lock it from within. Mary was as confused as he. "You!" she exclaimed softly. "I had expected to see Captain Titus."

"Do you want him?"

"No. But once before when I was late with the King's laundry and his Majesty had retired early I was allowed to leave it here."

"Was it obvious that the door was open?"

"Yes."

Mary put down the King's shirt and nightcap on a side table and Firebrace, buttoning his coat above the letters, walked back with her to the top of the stairs. Letting out a low whistle of relief, he drew forth one of his gaudy handkerchiefs and began mopping his brow with dramatic fervour. "Thank Heaven, Mary, it was only you!"

"It might have been one of the servants or Captain Rolph."

"God forbid! Though he would scarcely be prowling about the backstairs, would he?"

"He would prowl about anywhere if it suited him. He once followed me upstairs to the housekeeper's room on the next floor. Were you giving his Majesty the letter I passed you in the well-house?"

Firebrace nodded, his mind still upon their hurriedly terminated conversation.

"You could go back while I stay here to warn you."

"And incriminate you? Besides, Titus may be back at any moment. By the way he talks I believe he would not betray me, but a man may pretend to certain sentiments in order to trap one."

Leaning against the wall, Mary faced him provocatively. "Why are you so sure that I will not betray you?"

Serious, yet smiling, he cupped her face between his hands, tilting it upwards, as though searching for the reason. "Because of the candour of your eyes, I suppose, and the lovely kindness of your mouth," he said. "I would trust you with my life, Mary. You are one of us."

To Mary it was as if Michael and all the angels had commended her. She glowed with happiness. "Then there are others—besides Mr. Osborne?" she asked. But she did not greatly care and he did not seem to hear her.

He was looking back along the passage. "Another time I could blow out the nearest lantern and complain afterwards that the servants had let it go out."

"You could not do it twice," pointed out Mary.

Together they sat down on the top stair, considering the problem. In spite of the thrill of his nearness, Mary tried to be practical. "This wall of the State Room is really only a wooden partition, put up to make room for the serving passage," she told him.

"Of course, you are right. We were standing just now underneath the music gallery, which must once have been part of the room."

"When I was mending the old threadbare tapestry beside the bed I noticed how thin the partition wall was. There are small chinks in it here and there. Of course, the splendid red-and-blue tapestry from Hampton hangs over it now."

Modesty overtook her even in her desire to help, but Firebrace urged her to go on. She looked down at her workaday gown and pushed back a straying curl, unaware how well both became her. Had she known that she would be sitting beside him on the stairs she would have stopped grieving for poor Burley and found time somehow to put on her dull red velvet. "I was only thinking," she said, "that with a sharp knife you could easily make one of those chinks bigger. Big enough to speak through or pass a letter. And if one day when I am helping to make the bed I could snip a kind of flap in the pattern of the tapestry—then you would not need to open the door at all."

Harry Firebrace caught her to him in an ecstatic embrace. "Mary Floyd, you are a genius!" he cried. "What should I do on this island without you?"

Mary made no great effort to free herself. "If anyone came along unexpectedly as I did, you would just seem to be standing there—reading a letter, perhaps, by the light of the passage lantern," she concluded with excusable triumph. She had no idea how she would find means to cut the tapestry, she was desperately afraid of all this new exciting secrecy; but to be held close against him with the warmth of his approval flowing over her was ample recompense for the wildest risks she might be called upon to run.

Yet her companion's mind was already back with his master. "Consider what it will mean to him, having letters from his family, even if we cannot yet arrange anything," he said. "The young Duke of York is in Cromwell's hands. And his Majesty often longs for news of little Princess Elizabeth and the boy, Henry of Gloucester, who are always being moved from place to place."

"What do you mean by 'arrange anything'?" asked Mary, a trifle tartly. She would have liked more of his attention herself, and for once other people's misfortunes left her unmoved.

He did not answer her directly. He had twisted his head away from her so as to see the beginning of the next flight of stairs. "Did you say the housekeeper's room was up there? And are there no guards?" he asked.

"Of course not. They are our private quarters. My father comes there when he is off duty."

"Do you suppose your aunt would allow me to come up and visit you sometimes?"

Mary nodded, her eyes shining.

"And to bring some of my friends?"

"You mean—because—of all this?"

"To have some place where we can all meet."

"I think she would," said Mary, more soberly. "She and Mistress Trattle are both Royalists."

"I know. I met the Trattles, you remember. And Master Newland."

A new and chastening idea came to her. "Was that why you wanted to come with me on Christmas Eve?"

He was aware of the hurt hardness in her voice, but liked her too well to lie. "I asked permission to come here in order to serve the King," he said gravely. "But even if there were no question of king or captivity—if life were simple again for both of us—I should always be absurdly happy in your company. You do believe that?"

"Yes."

"Mary, you are adorable! But besides your company I need your help."

"How can anyone so unimportant as I help you?" she asked.

He took one of the hands lying folded in her lap and began gently pushing back her fingers one by one. "Do you not see, my sweet? You have lived here all your life. Everyone—soldiers and servants alike—will do anything for you. You know every cranny in the castle. You can come and go unsuspected. You look so young—so guilelessly young—Hammond probably thinks of you as still a child."

Exasperated, Mary pulled her hand away. "And how do you think of me?" she wanted to ask, as she felt sure Frances would have done. But coquetry was not in her. "I will take whatever letters the King has given you and try to see the messenger at the 'Rose and Crown' again, if that is what you want and if it will keep the King happy," she promised, with a cool perspicacity which belied his stressing of her guileless youth.

Firebrace handed the letters over to her admiringly and watched her tuck them into the bosom of her gown. "Probably he is particularly depressed just now because of poor Burley," he said. "Did they ever meet?"

"A few days before you came. It was Burley's dearest wish to see the King, and when he came up to the castle with all the other gentry his Majesty was particularly gracious to him, my father says. It must be terrible for kings when men die for them."

"They must get used to it, I suppose. So many men die for them in battle." Firebrace stood up, pulling her to her feet with him, so that they stood facing each other at the end of the narrow passage.

"It is more than keeping the King happy in captivity now," he told her abruptly. "There are some who think that what Parliament did to Burley they may try to do to his Majesty."

"Harry!" Mary caught at his arm, incredulous. She pictured that gentle, dignified figure—now so familiar to them all—walking briskly on the battlements, watching the master-gunner's small son playing at soldiers, writing letters by candlelight in his bedroom, as he probably was now. Letters which he, unlike his subjects, was denied means of despatching. Suddenly, poignantly, she saw the possibility of his danger. "Oh, but they could not!" she cried pitifully. "What cruelty has he ever done?"

"Power, in the hands of men who have not had time to learn how to use it, is divorced from reason. They become drunk with it," he told her. "And now Parliament is driven on by the Army, which has already tasted blood."

"You do not really believe that they will ever seek to kill him?"

Firebrace was looking back along the passage towards the State Room. Whether he believed it or not, his face had that pale, withdrawn look which could momentarily quench his gaiety. "It has been done before—every time a sovereign has been imprisoned," he said, as if trying to pile up a backing for his own thoughts. "Edward the Second at Berkeley, Richard the Second at Pontefract, Henry the Sixth in the Tower of London—"

From watching his face, Mary turned, too, to look along the passage towards the King's door. "Then it is more than merely—letters," she whispered. "You mean, he must—"

"Escape."

His firm hands had gripped hers, and they were still standing there when a convivial voice at the foot of the stairs brought them back to the smaller necessity of immediate action. "Titus!" said Firebrace, preparing to take up his stance outside the King's door.

"You sound glad," accused Mary, for whom the intimate moments had sped all too rapidly.

He turned and grinned at her, his ordinary cheerful self again. "I am hungry. I missed my supper," he explained.

"So did I," she confessed. Their healthy young hunger, their exchanged smiles and the warm excitement of shared conspiracy seemed to have exorcized the cold ghost of impending tragedy. With her foot on the first stair of the upper flight and her skirts gathered ready for flight, Mary called back to him in a laughing whisper. "Come up to my aunt's room *now*," she invited, "and I will coax the new bride, Libby Rudy, to bring us some supper by the fire!"

# CHAPTER ELEVEN

⊸∞∞⊸

THE HOUSEKEEPER'S ROOM, WITH its homely atmosphere of domesticity, was the last place likely to be associated in people's minds with intrigue. It was cheerfully bright with dormer windows facing east and west, and sweet with the scent of samples of drying herbs. On a solid work table neatly written laundry lists and notes about needful household stores gave evidence of Mistress Wheeler's prosaic daytime activities, and the discreetly tapestried four-poster suggested only a place for well learned repose.

But as the new year began to slip by the room sometimes took on a different guise. Between dusk and supper, as soon as the curtains were drawn, strangely assorted guests stole quietly up the backstairs. Mary would go round snuffing the candles so that from outside the room appeared to be untenanted, the last arrival would shoot the bolt, and the great bed would be drawn out a little from the wall so as to afford a hiding place in case of any unforeseen interruption. As Druscilla Wheeler poured heartening red wine into her best Venetian glasses and Mary handed it round to the little company the quietly spoken toast would be "The King, God save him!" There would be a warm smile and a nod above each raised glass, and a drawing together of recently acquainted people in a close bond of good comradeship. These were the most exciting gatherings Mary had ever attended, and she no longer envied Frances the gay, inconsequent parties she was invited to in Newport.

While the seven people present finished their wine on an evening early in February, Mary settled herself on a low stool by the hearth and looked round at them, seeing the faces of most of them interestingly illuminated by the firelight. Aunt Druscilla, upright in her high-backed chair, with her white lace collar and severe black gown and a spot of colour on either prominent cheekbone. Captain Titus, the Conservator so implicitly trusted by Parliament, hovering uneasily by one of the windows. Cresset, the Treasurer, and Dowcett, Clerk of the Kitchen, sitting side by side in their fashionable Court clothes on the well-worn settle; with the King's barber and Napier, one of the royal tailors, squatting on the floor near them. And Harry Firebrace, who had answered to his hostess for the reliability of all of them, perched on a corner of her table. At first each of them had been surprised to meet some of the others in that secret coterie; but however different their political professions or their social status, in the housekeeper's room all voiced their opinions freely. Being united in so risky and important an enterprise, each depended upon the absolute loyalty of the rest. "It must be hard for Harry Firebrace," thought Mary, noting Richard Osborne's absence, "if he cannot trust his own friend sufficiently to bring him."

"You say, Madam, that Monday is the best day for us to meet?" the swarthy little tailor was saying.

"Because it is Court day," confirmed Druscilla Wheeler.

"The Governor has to spend most of it trying cases down in the Court Room—millers who have overcharged for grinding people's corn or men caught plundering a wreck," explained Mary, who knew that the little man had only recently come across from London with Cromwell's permission to make the King a generous supply of new clothes.

"Even now, although it is almost dark, they are still coming in," added Titus, holding back a corner of the heavy curtain and peering out. "Judging by the number of lanterns I can see bobbing about, Hammond should be kept down there safely until supper time."

"And what about Busybody Rolph?" asked Dowcett.

"Last time I saw him he was in the officers' quarters talking to

Dick Osborne," said Firebrace, with a hint of amused satisfaction in his voice.

Mary looked at him in puzzled surprise. "They are always together nowadays, thick as thieves," she said. "I had supposed Master Osborne was *your* friend."

"My invaluable friend! " replied Firebrace. "Keeping the gallant Captain of the Guard occupied and no doubt learning things at the same time."

"What sort of things?" asked Mary, feeling that he was making fun of her.

"Oh, how best to wheedle a pass to go outside the gates, and when and where normally humane men of the original garrison are likely to be on guard," replied Firebrace airily.

"And Rolph is like to be learning a variety of things too, if I know Osborne!" chuckled Francis Cresset. "How to pick a wench, for instance—saving your presence, Mistress Wheeler—and how *not* to pick his teeth at table."

"It is odd how these self-righteous, jumped-up Puritans secretly hanker after the very things they affect to despise," agreed Druscilla Wheeler contemptuously. "Master Osborne's good birth and wild reputation with women make even easier bait in that direction than we dared to hope. And the impressive fact that his uncle is Deputy Governor of Guernsey."

Mary was surprised at the reference to Osborne's reputation, but from her lowly stool she looked up at her aunt admiringly. Although older than all of them Druscilla Wheeler had, without fuss or Royalist protestations, entered into their scheme with the same matter-of-fact efficiency that she brought to bear upon her extra household burdens. Several of them smiled at her incongruous duplicity; but their time was precious, and while Titus kept watch from time to time from either window, they came abruptly to the matters for which they were met.

"For the passing of the King's private correspondence Witherings, the newly appointed postmaster, can by no means be trusted," announced Cresset, who had sounded him while arranging for the forwarding of financial accounts to Parliament.

"Did Hammond appoint him purposely in place of some honest island fellow, Madam?"

"We never had a postmaster before," his hostess told him. "The few letters we wrote before you all came were taken across by the coney man who sells our rabbits in the mainland markets."

"How exquisitely casual!" laughed Firebrace. "But mercifully we have other means now. Before coming over here I made sure of two trusty messengers between Southampton and London and so far every letter in or out has arrived safely."

"And Bosvile is often in Newport in some fantastic disguise or other. Friend Trattle always knows where to find him," said Cresset.

"And our Mary here is invaluable, with letters from half the Stuart family neatly folded in the King's clean linen!" declared Dowcett, drawing her back in friendly fashion so that she leaned against his knee.

"In code, I hope!" put in Titus anxiously.

"His Majesty has been using one for months, and since figures are my *metier* I have been helping him to keep it up to date," Cresset assured him. "And besides the code numbers for ordinary words, all those whom he corresponds with—his family, his friends in Scotland, even we here who are prepared to help him escape— are known by letters of the alphabet. Did you know, Mary, that you are called 'B' in the King of England's code?"

"And sometimes referred to as 'asparagus' or 'artichokes'," teased Dowcett, noting how she blushed with pleasure. "You would laugh to hear our conversation at dinner, all of the King's devising, and held quite openly under the Governor's very nose. 'An it please your Majesty I have been able to get some *asparagus* from London,' I say, as a careful Clerk of the Kitchen should. Which means that I have passed a packet of his letters on to you. And if I should add 'Knowing how your Majesty dotes on them, I have also ordered some *artichokes*,' then he understands that you have been able to pass them on to Major Bosvile, and looks inordinately pleased."

"Why, I did not know that he so much as noticed me when I go in to make the bed or bring the linen!" gasped Mary.

"His Majesty is remarkably observant, but for safety's sake must pretend not to be. For the same reason he often looks sourly at me when the Governor or other members of the household are present, and then of his graciousness asks my forgiveness afterwards." Cresset turned more soberly to Firebrace. "Who would you say, of the household, can be counted upon not to betray us even though they take no active part, Harry?"

"Anthony Mildmay and certainly Thomas Herbert," decided Firebrace, after a moment's consideration.

"And, of the garrison, my brother," promised Mistress Wheeler.

"And among the servants old Brett, who can pretend to be deaf as an adder when it suits him. And I think my aunt's maid, Libby," added Mary.

"But you told me she is married to that long Cromwellian fellow, Rudy," objected Firebrace.

"I doubt if Libby notices what a man's politics are so long as his body pleases her," said her Mistress, with an almost tolerant smile.

"It is just that she thinks I was once kind to her," murmured Mary. "And Brett goes in and out of the State Room several times a day to see to the fires. I think I could persuade him—"

Firebrace slid down from the table and came to join her by the hearth. "The castle must be full of people you have been kind to!" he laughed. "What ingenious plan have you been hatching now, Mary Floyd?"

"I thought perhaps if he and the King changed clothes when he goes in last thing in the evening and the King is alone—they are both little men—" In her modesty, Mary glanced round the room, half expecting the simplicity of her idea to meet with ridicule; but seven pairs of eyes were regarding her attentively. And presently they were all discussing the project with animation.

His Majesty would have to pass one of the Conservators," pointed out his tailor.

"It could be Captain Titus," Mistress Wheeler reminded them.

"The plan sounds feasible," agreed Dowcett eagerly. "His Majesty, carrying the empty coal hod, would then walk towards the servants' quarters, I take it? And then make for the little postern gate near the keep."

"How would he get past the sentries there?" two of them asked in unison.

"Brett has a sister in the village whom he is allowed to visit of an evening when his work is done. He wears an old hooded cloak when he goes out and limps a little like the King does when he is tired," Mary told them. "And if the King would deign to smear his face with wood ash—"

"If your plan worked it would give his Majesty a whole night's start," admitted Titus, impressed.

"But what would they do to poor Brett when they found him in the State Room next morning?" At thought of that inevitable sequel the colour faded from Mary's face. She could have bitten her tongue for speaking so glibly on the spur of the moment. Her one thought had been to please Harry Firebrace; but bent old Brett, who had shown her small kindnesses since her childhood, meant more to her than any king. "No, no, we cannot ask the poor old man to do that! " she cried, catching at Firebrace's hand as he stood beside her. "Please, please, forget what I said!"

Firebrace squeezed her hand reassuringly. Besides realizing her distress, he doubted his royal master's ability to act the part or to improvise quickly enough in strange surroundings. Moreover, he had for days been trying to work out a plan of his own. "It seems to me that we who serve his Majesty and wish to save him should bear the risks ourselves," he said, and turned towards the two men seated on the floor. "What was the idea you two were beginning to speak of when we were down in the courtyard and Captain Rolph came prying by?" he asked.

The King's assistant barber, who had so far contributed nothing to the conversation, rose from the hearth and began pressing at the floorboards with his foot as though to test their thickness. "From where we were standing it seemed to us that this room must be the one above his Majesty's bedroom," he said.

"Immediately above," confirmed Mary.

He nodded in the direction of the bolted door. "And outside, on this floor, there would be no guards at all?"

"No. These are our own private quarters," Mistress Wheeler told him. "Why?"

"It occurred to Napier and me that if we could cut a hole in the State Room ceiling—"

"Which no one would notice, of course!" scoffed Titus.

"Neither would they. Not if it was made over the disused music gallery," snapped the little tailor, his eyes shining in the firelight as he sat cross-legged by the hearth. "First thing I saw when I was fitting his Majesty was that gallery, and that no one coming in and out of the room ever thinks of looking up there. A man working right at the back of it would scarcely be seen."

"There is no way up to it since the backstairs passage has been built," Mistress Wheeler told him.

"I could take a length of rope in my bag, and a saw hidden in a bale of cloth. As Groom-of-the-Bedchamber, Master Firebrace is usually the only person in attendance while his Majesty is being fitted."

"And early one morning while I am shaving his Majesty I could choose my opportunity to call up to you and some of you could draw him up," said the barber.

They discussed the fantastic plan and found it over-weighted with difficulties. "If by the ceiling why not by the window?" suggested Cresset.

"And if it be possible by the window, why not straight down into the courtyard and be done with it?" asked Firebrace.

"In full view of the guardhouse?" pointed out Titus.

"We should have to choose a very dark night," conceded Firebrace.

"You have a definite plan?" asked Dowcett.

"Osborne and I have a half-made one."

"Tell us."

"Wait! There is someone outside the door," warned Mary.

Some of them sprang silently to their feet and for a moment or two all stood tense, listening to a faint scratching sound. "It *is* Osborne!" said Firebrace, relaxing. And as the others resumed their places with a sigh of relief, he hurried to admit him.

"I have held your Captain enthralled with all my best bawdy

stories for the best part of an hour. He abhors liquor and I am parched," announced the King's tall Usher. "A glass of wine, I beseech you Mistress Wheeler, before I wilt."

He took the wine from Mary, smiled down at her with a quirk of his strongly marked brows and lounged over to the window seat. All the little company turned eagerly towards him. "We hear you have a plan," they said. But he merely waved his glass in the direction of his friend. "It is Harry who is gifted with powers of invention," he told them, disclaiming all merit in the matter. "I merely clown or play watchdog as I am bid."

For once Harry Firebrace seemed disinclined for speech. His plan was not as yet perfected and even to his optimistic mind certain difficulties presented themselves. The very fact that he felt that it might finally prove to be the master-plan, so far-reaching in effect that it would change the face of history, prompted him to keep it unshared a little longer.

"When we first met here we agreed to lay all our cards on the table," urged Titus, coming to join the intimate little group by the fire.

"And it will soon be suppertime," warned their hostess, glancing at the clock which had once graced her husband's manor on the mainland, and motioning to her niece to hide away the used glasses.

"It is absurdly simple really," began Firebrace, still hesitant.

"All the best ideas are," encouraged Dowcett.

"We plan to lower the King by rope from his bedroom window one dark night," said Firebrace, throwing him a grateful glance, and feeling how trite it all sounded. "I will stand below in the courtyard to guide him to that spot on the south battlement where some of us first spoke of it, and then with another rope I would let him down the escarpment. The moat is dry and narrow, and Osborne and an island gentleman whom he knows will have horses waiting in that little copse opposite and one of them will help his Majesty up the counterscarp. John Newland of Newport can be persuaded, I think, to have a boat waiting on the north shore near Quarr Abbey woods. Once across the Solent—well, the King himself is even now in correspondence about another ship to France or Holland. We may be sure the Queen or the Prince of Wales will contrive to send one."

Something purposeful in Firebrace's unusually quiet manner, coupled with the realization that he must already have discussed the possibilities with the King himself, held the interest of his listeners.

"How will Master Osborne get outside after dark to bring the horses?" asked Druscilla Wheeler after a few moments' silence.

"The same way as I often do, dear lady—with the Captain of the Guard's connivance," grinned Osborne. "To visit my relatives who are staying on the island, or a wench in Newport. Friend Rolph is marvellously sympathetic, providing I sometimes invite him to come along with me."

"Let the cobbler not go above his last," murmured French Dowcett, in his mother tongue.

It was Mary whose practical mind hit upon the real difficulty which had been bothering Firebrace. "Since the Burley rising Colonel Hammond has had bars fitted to the King's window."

"But, as you said just now, his Majesty is a small man," he reminded her, with a confidence he was far from feeling.

"And what about the sentries on the battlements?" asked Cresset.

"We must see that they are fuddled," said Firebrace.

"That should not be difficult with the perpetual thirst they have since Rolph cut down their liquor ration, and the grudge they bear him for it! " said Osborne, reaching out to refill his glass before Mary put away the wine. "And the Clerk of the Kitchen can always produce a bottle or two of something particularly potent, eh, Dowcett?"

"But what about Rolph himself, who drinks water?" asked someone gloomily.

"And goes his rounds at no set time, so as to keep the men up to the mark," added Mistress Wheeler.

That was an unforeseen difficulty. "We could perhaps provide him with some alternative distraction," said Firebrace.

"Our versatile Osborne will not be available, being on the other side of the moat," pointed out Titus.

"Perhaps Mistress Mary—" began Napier, who had been itching all evening to fashion a modish gown to her svelte figure.

"In the middle of the night?" countered Osborne heavily. And at Abraham Dowcett's emphatic Gallic gesture of outraged chivalry the tactless little tailor subsided hastily.

"Why not choose a time, sir, when Sergeant Floyd and some of the original island garrison are on duty?" suggested the assistant barber—rather handsomely, Firebrace thought, seeing that the man was anxious for his own plan to be tried.

But their hostess rose up from her chair, tall and impressive. "No. My brother must not be brought into this," she decreed. "He is loyal to the King. Whatever he may see or overhear by chance, you may be sure he will not speak of; but if my niece and I help you I insist that you do not ask him to take any active part."

Accepting her mandate and their dismissal, her guests began to take their departure. Mistress Wheeler went first to make sure the coast was clear, and they all went silently in ones and twos down the backstairs to appear later from various directions for supper. All but Richard Osborne, who still sat in the window recess, empty glass in hand. "The bell will sound for supper in a minute," said Mary, going to take it from him. To her surprise he grasped her wrist instead. "This is not a game," he warned.

"Why do you say that?" exclaimed Mary, wide-eyed with surprise.

"Because a girl will do anything, however risky, for the man whose love she wants."

A week—a few days ago—Mary would have blushed and stammered in confusion, but the changed circumstances of her life were lending her a new composure. "I had supposed we were all doing things for the King," she said coldly.

"The rest of us may be. But look into your heart, my dear."

She knew that he had hit upon the truth, and hated him for it. "I would do anything for Harry Firebrace, if that is what you mean," she said proudly.

"But what do you know of him?"

"How mean—oh, how mean of you! When he speaks so generously of you and your—morals!"

"God knows I need his blessed generosity! But I was not refer-ring to his morals, which seem to me to be immaculate."

She was too angry to heed him. "That you should preach—you who creep out at night wenching!" she cried childishly, struggling to free herself.

Osborne laughed softly. "I see some kind friend has already been helping us to get acquainted," he said without rancour.

"You bragged of it yourself; just now. About the girl in Newport."

"So I did. Would you like to know what she looks like?"

"Why should I care?" she snapped at him.

"Or why, for that matter, should I care what you think of me?" he questioned, with a sigh. "But for some odd reason I do. It must be those candid eyes of yours, Mary. Or the spitcat hidden beneath your gentleness. Listen, I will tell you what my last night's companion is like."

"I tell you I do not want to hear. Let me go!"

He turned her hand palm upwards and kissed it casually before releasing it. "Dark, six-foot-two, a remarkably good shot and lives at Gatcombe," he enumerated, smiling up at her with narrowed, teasing eyes.

Her furious antagonism simmered down into interest. "You mean—Master Edward Worsley?"

"He will provide the horses," he said negligently, gathering himself up from the window seat. "And if I said things which angered you it was because you are young and inexperienced, and acting without the advice of your father. Do you know how vastly anger becomes you, Mary?"

Suddenly Mary felt forlorn, and would have given almost anything for the comfort of her father's presence. "It is the first time I have ever kept anything of importance from him," she admitted. "Why did my aunt say what she did just now? Why must he not be with us, when you and Harry Firebrace and all of us run risks?"

"As a soldier's daughter you should know." But seeing how little she had thought about the matter, he stood looking down at her gravely, all his bantering recklessness gone. "If Harry or I get caught, probably the worst that will happen to us would be dismissal, imprisonment, or exile. Since we no longer hold commissions in the King's army, we are civilians," he explained. "But if your father were to be caught acting against orders, he would be shot."

"Shot!" Mary's lips formed the word, but no sound came. Her hands flew to her lips as though to stifle it unborn. Her eyes sought his in shocked terror. "You are trying to frighten me," she accused, scarcely knowing what she said. "You are jealous. You do not want me in this!"

They could hear Mistress Wheeler's step and the swish of her skirts coming back from the stair-head. Richard Osborne shrugged and picked up his hat, but before leaving he cupped Mary's chin very gently in his hand. "I do not want you to get hurt," he said.

# CHAPTER TWELVE

T HE LAUNDRY CASEMENTS STOOD open to let out the steam, and at a wooden tub stood Mary, her workaday brown dress bunched up over a gay quilted petticoat, washing the King's body linen. At a table nearby, Libby, already clumsy with her pregnancy, was busy mixing the lye. The two of them were alone, for the laundry maids rose early and had finished the ordinary morning's wash. At the other end of the long, low room shirts and smocks were soaking, packed in folds over sticks, in the huge buck tubs; while the woollens hung stretched out to dry between the hooks of the tall tenter posts.

Libby soaked and strained the wood ash saved from the fires, mixing it in careful proportions with a bowlful of boiled-down fat. To this, for its bleaching properties, she added some droppings scraped from the dovecote. But a small portion of the washing lye she kept apart in a smaller bowl, scenting it with rosemary and lavender, and shaping it into small balls for personal ablutions, as her mistress had taught her. Mistress Wheeler, like most careful housekeepers, usually made the soft soap herself, and liked to keep a good stock of it for giving as seasonable gifts to her friends or to any person from whom she sought favours; but all this week she had been kept in bed with a quinsy. And of late, out of consideration for her condition, Libby had been given some of the lighter tasks.

It was a peaceful hour of the morning which both girls enjoyed. The King's linen was scarcely soiled and needed little rubbing, and the ironing of such fine garments was a delectable art, so Mary sang snatches of songs as she worked. "It seems like it was before they all came," said Libby not very lucidly, admiring a little regiment of her soap balls marshalled in a scooped-out trough on the window ledge.

"The King came in November and to-morrow will be St. Valentine's Day," said Mary, marvelling how ten weeks could have slipped by so quickly and changed her life so completely.

"Day for lovers' tokens, Mistress Mary. Reckon I be carrying *my* token under my apron, but I wager you get a fairing or zummat this year," remarked Libby, with a sly grin.

> "It was a lover and his lass,
>     With a hey, and a ho, and a hey nonino,"

carolled Mary, feigning not to hear her.

"Remember how you said you'd not give yourself to an overner?" persisted Libby.

"I've not given myself to anybody!" declared Mary, rubbing with unnecessary vigour at a royal shirt until her cheeks were as red as the C.R. embroidered upon it.

"The will to give goes half way towards it," chuckled Libby. "What *is* that fancy song?"

"Some play-actor called Shakespeare wrote it," Mary told her casually. "One of the courtiers from London is always singing it."

"Mercy on us, who speak of the devil!" ejaculated Libby, as Harry Firebrace suddenly rounded the corner beneath the laundry window.

"I wasn't speaking of anybody in particular," fibbed Mary, wringing out the long-suffering shirt as though it were one of her father's strong army jerkins.

The good-looking young Groom of the Bedchamber was dressed for riding and held a squirming spaniel pup by the scruff of its fat neck. "So here is where all the real work of the castle is done?" he observed, smiling upon both girls impartially—far too impartially, Mary felt. "This witless little brute of yours was courting sudden death by yapping round the heels of Hammond's ferocious horse, Mary."

"Oh, thank you for rescuing him!" Mary identified the small white creature, with its tail curled meekly up between its legs, as her favourite. "It is Pride of the Litter. He is beginning to get it into his head that he's a grown dog and no longer needs Patters' protection."

"*I* need some more mutton fat for my lye," giggled Libby, picking up a by-no-means-empty bowl and making for the kitchen.

Mary blessed her for going but could have clouted her for the significant giggle. "And while you are there, Libby, tell one of the scullions to bring me some more hot water," she called after her, hoping that the double errand would detain her still longer.

"You were not able to collect the letter yesterday?" asked Firebrace anxiously, the moment the girl was out of earshot.

"I could not go down into Newport, much less meet Major Bosvile. Captain Rolph stopped me at the gate," Mary told him, wishing they sometimes had time to speak about themselves.

"But I thought that you of the Governor's household were free to come and go?"

"I reminded him that I always went once a week to visit my friends. But it was of no use."

"Do you suppose that he—suspected?"

Mary had supposed that Rolph had other reasons but she stirred the suds in her cooling tub absently while considering the matter. "It is odd that it should happen immediately after the tailor and the King's barber have been sent away."

"And poor Cresset, of all people!"

"Why did the Governor dismiss them?"

Firebrace stepped back a pace or two, looking this way and that, to make sure they were still unobserved. "He must have got wind of their crazy plot, even though they had no time to do anything. With Cresset, it could have been something to do with the code, I suppose. We shall miss Cresset. He was a useful man. I am going with Hammond to Cowes now to meet the new Treasurer appointed in his place. Lee, his name is. Dyed in the wool Cromwellian, probably." He tried to speak lightly, but could not hide his anxiety. "I wish I knew what happened. There must have been a leakage somewhere."

The thoughts of both of them turned back to the warm comradery of the housekeeper's firelit room. "Could it be Captain Titus?" Mary brought herself to suggest.

"No, I am sure not. He often urges caution because of his damnable position as Conservator. But I trust him."

"And you trust—Richard Osborne, I suppose? Even when he is being boon companion to Rolph so successfully?"

Firebrace only laughed, so certain was he of his friend's integrity. She ached to tell him that Osborne had seemed to be less generous about himself, but did not dare. And her reticence was rewarded. For the first time Firebrace trusted her with his inmost doubts. "The King himself is sometimes—indiscreet—in his correspondence."

"Oh, but surely he would not endanger men who risk so much for him!" cried Mary.

"No, no, of course not," Firebrace hastened to assure her, though without vast conviction. "It is only that he is inclined to trust too many people—people who were trustworthy enough, perhaps, so long as his fortunes stood high."

It was the first time Mary had ever heard him utter a breath of criticism of his master, and it seemed incredible that the man in whose interests they all worked should not guard his tongue and pen the most; but Firebrace had been Charles's page and should know. "Will it matter very much that I was not able to bring the letters?" she asked.

"Bosvile will probably guess what has happened and contrive to send a messenger. I will leave you this piece of gold for him in case you may need it." He laid it on the window ledge because her hands were wet. "Better stay about so that he may the more easily find you."

"Here is as good a place as any other—where I can see anyone arriving at the gate. Were the letters about something very important this time?"

It made Mary very proud that he did not hesitate to tell her. "It is young James of York his Majesty is so anxious to hear from. He has been urging him to get out of the country."

"In that last letter I took? "

"Yes."

"Is the Duke in danger?"

"I do not think so. It is rather that Parliament and the Army seem to be at loggerheads, and one party or the other plans to strengthen its position by making the lad King and ruling the country from behind a puppet throne."

Mary lifted the King's lace nightcap from the water and stretched it over its round wooden mould to dry. It gave her time to decide whether to prod Firebrace's interest in her by telling him about Edmund Rolph's, and to hope that he would mind. "Captain Rolph may not have suspected anything," she said. "You see, he made some pretext yesterday to draw me into the constable's room—to write me a pass or something—and began to paw me. I think he would have let me go down into Newport—at a price."

Firebrace let the wriggling puppy slip from his arms and swung round, every whit as angry as she had hoped. "The hypocritical swine!" he exclaimed, all his decent manhood up in arms. "It passes my comprehension how Osborne can maintain even the necessary semblance of friendliness towards him." Remorsefully, he came close to the window and covered her wet hands with his own. "Dick Osborne was right. We ought not to have used you—"

"*Used* me?" Mary's lovely amber eyes glared at him as angrily as a cat's, and she jerked her hands away. But as usual his smile caressed her into forgiveness. "Let you risk acting as messenger," he corrected himself penitently.

"We are all in this together. We all take risks," she said, sullenly.

"But there is always one added risk for a girl."

She came back to him, mollified, and leaned towards him through the open casement. After all, it was she who had provoked him to speak heedlessly. "Listen, Harry," she said softly. "These past few weeks have been the most wonderful in my life. Oh, I know it is heartless of me to say it, with all the cruel anxiety they have meant to the King, and to you. But there is a reality—a closer sharing—as though life were lit up. You must not think of listening to Richard Osborne. If anything were to exclude me now I—I don't know what I should do."

Firebrace was deeply touched. He bent his burnished head and brushed his lips against her clinging fingers. "It has been all that you say," he agreed, "though sometimes when I stop to think what I am doing I feel aged with responsibility. But sometime, sweet, it will have to end. God knows I pray it will, and soon—when the King really gets safely away from his enemies."

"But that does not mean that our lives will end," she reminded him with a warm flurry of laughter. "That we must separate—" It was as near an avowal of love as a girl of her sensitivity could make. Her fingers clung to his, her eyes and lips invited him. Slowly, as though drawn against his will, Firebrace kissed her and reluctantly drew away. For Mary the whole promise of love's sweetness and surrender was held in those moments, to be kept sacred through the years.

They smiled at each other in a kind of surprised, wordless liking; only to be drawn back from the brink of ecstasy by approaching footsteps and voices. "Libby and the man with the hot water," announced Firebrace flatly. Why must all their best moments together be interrupted, wondered Mary, and how can he accept it with such ease and common sense?

"I find I shall not need the water now. Set it down for the maids when they come back," she bade the scullion. As the man hurried back to his pots a horse whinnied impatiently in the courtyard and both girls' accustomed ears recognized the distant clatter of sentries springing to attention outside the officers' quarters. "The Governor," warned Libby, going back to her soap-making. And when Firebrace had hurried away to join him and the two of them, followed by a couple of troopers, had ridden out through the archway, Mary stood idly staring out of the laundry window. Pride of the Litter, crazy with new-found liberty and enticed by the whistles of the men clustered about the guardroom, streaked across to them and jumped to their rough play in a frenzy of canine excitement. At any other time his absurd antics would have enchanted her. But her mind registered little of the scene. She was living over again the moments of her lover's embrace. Brief as they were, all her girlhood had been waiting for them, leading up to them. And surely she might think of him as her lover now, since he had so ardently kissed her. She had had her St. Valentine's token indeed. She smiled almost maternally over his devotion to the Stuart. She could afford to now. After the King's escape they two would have all the time in the world to settle their own affairs. Quite understandably, Firebrace must put her and their dawning love second for a time. She wished that she had talked to her father about it, but the two matters were somehow so inextricably mixed and of some things she must not speak. Silas Floyd would be the first, surely, to chide her for wanting to put her womanish desires before the safety of the King. As ever, the thought of the plans in which she had become involved sobered and amazed her. "The whole island talked about Frances Trattle greeting his Majesty with the red November rose," she thought, "and here am I, Mary Floyd the Sergeant's daughter, smuggling in secret letters about affairs of State, and having a number in the King's code which may even be recorded in history!"

"Shall I mix rose water in this next working of soap?" asked Libby. "They do say the King dotes on their perfume."

"If you like," agreed Mary, rousing herself to put away her work. Soon the other maids would be back to push the weighted rollers back and forth across the ordinary household sheets; but she must leave the King's linen until it was just damp enough for expert laundering. Then she would fill the little pan with live red coals and slide it into the iron for his shirts, heat the goffering tongs for the frilled rosettes on his shoes and the round knobbed pressers for his lace cravat and nightcap. Until then she would stay within sight of the gatehouse in case Major Bosvile contrived to send a messenger. It would be tedious, particularly as she had no idea what kind of person to look out for.

But she did not have long to wait.

"Here comes Master Newland's cart with the corn," announced Libby. "Lord, how quickly Saturday mornings come round!"

Even when the great iron-studded oak doors stood wide, the

familiar creaking cart piled high with sacks could only just pass through. It lurched to a standstill just inside while the driver stopped to exchange pleasantries with the soldiers. While the small spaniel barked at it importantly, and the day's news was being exchanged, the driver's mate slid down from the tail of the cart. Instead of staying to help unload the sacks he began to make straight for the residential part of the castle. He was a horsy-looking individual with a tattered hat perched at the back of a tousled, flaming-red head and a long straw hanging from his mouth. Mary recognized him with relief as Edward Trattle's ostler, and stood in the open doorway where he must see her. No opportunity could be better, she thought, with the men all preoccupied and no one near her but Libby, who would only suppose that friends in Newport had taken the opportunity to send her some message.

"Who is he?" asked Libby, peering over her shoulder at the odd, erratically approaching figure.

"Jem from the 'Rose and Crown,'" Mary told her.

"Whoever he be, he's drunk," said Libby.

"Or pretending to be," thought Mary, remembering how Major Bosvile, waiting for her at the inn, sometimes allayed suspicion by making himself look like a sot. He may have told Jem to do the same, but the ostler was over-acting his part; and surely, since the moment was so propitious, it would have been better to approach her as unobtrusively as possible?

But there was nothing unobtrusive about poor Jemmy this morning. Mary realized with dismay that much-hunted Major Bosvile, in his anxiety to get rid of the letter and be gone, must have been over-lavish with his money, and that driver and passenger had probably stopped at the "Castle Inn" on the way. Libby was laughing at his antics. Lurching unsteadily, he appeared to be fumbling for something in the patched pocket of his smock, and having found it he gave a whoop of triumph. It looked like a package of letters, and he immediately dropped it. After falling over several times in his efforts to retrieve it, he finally stuck it, with an air of vast solemnity, in the sweaty band of his hat, and then came rolling on. The corn cart had creaked away towards the barracks store-house and the guards' attention, no longer occupied, was now drawn towards him by his riotous snatches of song. Mary dared not go out into the courtyard and stop him, or be seen with him at all. "Here, Jemmy! I'm here," she called, as loudly as she dared, as soon as he drew level with the laundry.

He heard her and turned. He always had liked her. She never spoke high and haughty to a fellow. She was a real lady and deserved to be treated as one. But he had forgotten his instructions. He bowed elaborately, blew her a kiss with the tips of his dirty fingers in grotesque imitation of the Court gallants he had seen in Newport, and lurched on. On in the direction, not of the servants' quarters or the housekeeper's room, but of the main door to the King's apartments. "Libby! Libby! Stop him!" implored Mary, in panic. "He has a letter…See how the fool has stuck it in his hat for all the world to see." All her invention deserted her. She wished with all her heart that Harry Firebrace were still there beside her to help. He was so quick, so ingenious—and so far away. "*Do* something, Libby," she urged. "Don't let the old zany go any farther. The sentries at the Governor's door will see him."

She was aware of her companion's curious, speculative gaze. Although Libby might understand nothing of the reason, she understood another woman's distress when she saw it. She hurried out after the ostler and waylaid him, pulling at him, cajoling, even walking with him arm in arm. But he disengaged himself and would not listen to her blandishments.

"Important messash!" he told her, waving his disreputable, decorated hat.

"If Libby cannot stop him, no one can," thought Mary, in flat despair.

Libby came dejectedly back, and standing together in the laundry doorway she and Mary saw the sentries challenge him. It seemed that the pair of them were for tolerantly shooing him away. They pointed towards the servants' entrance round at the back but Jem persisted, drawing the packet from his hatband. Laughing at his fuddled state and incurious as to his errand, one of them took the packet carelessly while the other gave him a good-natured prod

with the butt of his pike. "Probably neither of them can read. I may
be able to get it from them afterwards. God is going to be good to
me after all!" thought Mary.

But at that moment Captain Rolph came hurrying down
the steps from the officers' quarters. He held out a gloved hand
for the packet of letters, flayed their drunken bearer with some
well-chosen denunciations from the Scriptures, made a gesture
to the sentries to arrest him and stalked past them into the
Governor's house.

"He could have seen everything from the window of his
room," pointed out Libby gloomily. "Does it matter terribly—
about the letters?"

"It matters—everything." Mary sank back against the ironing
table, covering her eyes with her hands. "They will send me away."

"Away from *him*—from Master Firebrace—you mean?"

Mary nodded without subterfuge. "I don't mind what they do to
me, if only they don't send me away."

Libby remembered saying much the same words. And how
the only person prepared to help her had been Mary. She stood
considering, looking round at Mary's bent head, at the King's grand
nightcap set up like a symbol on its mould, at the glittering piece
of gold which she imagined Firebrace must have left to buy some
love token. She pushed her half-fainting companion down on to a
stool. "You do be all of a fair firk," she said, her warm island voice
full of compassion. "Bide still a while while I go see if I can muddle
their gurt minds."

She picked up the piece of money and slipped it into her pocket,
and went across the courtyard to where Jem waited, already half-
sobered by the Captain of the Guard's biblical epithets.

# CHAPTER THIRTEEN

T HE GOVERNOR OF THE Wight stood by his desk weighing the packet of secretly conveyed letters upon his palm. He would have given a great deal to read the contents. For security's sake the packet had been addressed to Master Mildmay, but when he requested the Conservator to open them before him, they had found that the inner wrapper was addressed to the King. "I am convinced that Anthony Mildmay's amazement was not assumed," Hammond told his mother, who was sitting by the fire. "When I asked him if he would have delivered the packet he told me quite candidly that he supposed he would have done so, but that he had had no part in the deception."

As the Governor laid the packet down, the door opened and Edmund Rolph, hot and mud-splashed from a day-long manhunt, came into the room. "You did not get your man, then?" said Hammond, reading at a glance the dark-visaged Captain's disappointment.

"No, sir. We took a couple of bloodhounds and combed every lane and copse for miles around. From what the messenger said it must have been Major Bosvile who persuaded that sot to bring the letters." Rolph stood in the middle of the room, thumbs in regimental sash, gloomily considering that if he could have caught so useful a Royalist General Fairfax would almost certainly have given him his own majority. "It's my belief he's got clean out of the island."

"It was no fault of yours, Rolph. You did right to go after him straight away without waiting for my return," commended Hammond, wishing that all his subordinates were as vigorous in the prosecution of their duty. "Parliament knows that Bosvile is a master at his game, and I shall make a point of telling them that it was thanks to your vigilance that the letters were intercepted."

"Thank you, sir." Rolph's eyes rested greedily upon the sealed packet. "You have not opened it yet?"

"It is not addressed to me," Hammond told him stiffly.

Mistress Hammond turned to look up at her son approvingly, and Rolph—aware of the slight movement—hastened to remove his helmet, muttering a sheepish apology. "But you will not let the King have them?" he exclaimed anxiously.

"I shall send them to Parliament to deal with as they think fit."

The erstwhile shoemaker had no patience with such punctiliousness. "If I were in charge of this castle," he thought, as he so often had of late, "there would be no polite pandering to the prisoner nor loopholes left for all these silly plottings among his servants." He walked over to the Governor's desk and stared rudely down at his papers, poking at the creased package with a hairy, spatulate finger. "But suppose some of these letters contain more cunning notions for opening the royal bird's cage?" he said aloud.

"Then you may rest assured the Commissioners will waste no time in letting me know," Hammond told him, with exasperated bitterness. For had he not already received warning from Derby House that previous letters had been conveyed to the King by some woman of his household? It galled him that gentlemen sitting comfortably in that smug backwater of the city should profess to know more about his own household than he did himself. He was watchful and conscientious, and it made a mock of his Governorship; therefore it was not a matter which he felt himself called upon to impart to his second-in-command. "I understand that the man bribed to bring the message from Newport was asking for someone called Mary, but that it was the chambermaid Libby who was seen with him?" he asked.

"I saw the girl Libby run out to meet him myself," testified

Rolph. "They were crossing the courtyard familiarly, arm in arm. And my men say that after I had put the drunken ostler under arrest she ran to him and felt in his pockets as if searching for something."

"And the man himself, what does he say?"

"He was too disgustingly fuddled to remember."

"Then it could have been either girl?"

"Not that clear-eyed girl, Mary Floyd!" exclaimed the Governor's mother.

"I cannot think that Sergeant Floyd's daughter could be guilty of such duplicity," said Hammond. "Has the other girl ever had access to the State Room?"

"Since Mistress Wheeler's sickness she has helped to make the King's bed," remembered the old lady.

"This Libby did not deny it, although she is married to one of my men. Besides, a gold piece was found in her pocket, which seems to me conclusive enough," said Rolph. "A girl like that knows only two ways of getting gold, and at the moment—"

"She is pregnant and near her time." Mistress Hammond finished the sentence for him in order to spare herself any more of his coarseness. Having spent much of her life in the cultured atmosphere of Whitehall, she found the manners of some of her son's republican associates hard to bear. "If you should send her away, Robert, I pray you allow me to see her before she leaves the castle, so that I may make sure she has somewhere respectable to go."

Hammond nodded assent. "I must question both of them," he said. "But Bosvile is our main concern. Whoever takes the packet to Westminster can keep a watchful eye along the road to London."

Rolph offered to go himself, a shade too eagerly. Hammond knew that no one else whom he could send would be so efficient, but he did not care for the possibility of the King's letters being steamed open and stuck up again. "I shall need you here," he said shortly. He was beginning to sense the Captain's jealous ambition, and was uncomfortably aware that, given the opportunity, he would make a better gaoler than himself. And that in these desperate times, too fastidious a sense of honour could be a distinct disadvantage.

Dismissing Rolph, he sat down and wrote to the Speaker of the House of Commons, then went down into the courtyard himself to dispatch his messenger. As he stood there giving last-minute instructions to a young lieutenant mounted upon the garrison's fleetest horse, the King happened to come down the steps, followed by Herbert and Mildmay, for his postprandial walk. He gave the Governor a pleasant salutation, making some knowledgeable comment upon the horse's finer points. He even stood for a minute or two watching the high-spirited creature rear and wheel towards the gate, all unaware that the letters he was hungering for were within a few yards of him in the lieutenant's pocket. That after so nearly reaching him in safety, they were being borne away beneath his very eyes to his worst enemies at Westminster.

Involuntarily, a wave of pity assailed Hammond. "Judas that I am!" he thought; and instead of offering to accompany his unwanted guest he turned back into his own quarters, sending for the girl Libby whose manner soon persuaded him of her guilt.

The King went on his way, stopped for a few moments at the stables to give some tid-bits to the donkeys, then passed out through the postern gate to the place-of-arms, his tasseled stick tapping briskly on the stones as he went. The afternoon sunshine was almost springlike, and catkins hung in small golden showers from the hazel bushes along the banks of the moat. With his back to the forbidding walls of the castle it was easy to forget for a while that he was a prisoner. "It is a lovely place!" he exclaimed, pausing as he so often did to admire the immense grass plateau behind the castle, which commanded such fine views all over the island. "It would make a splendid bowling green to alleviate our tedium, but one cannot help picturing the splendid jousts that must have been held here in olden times."

"And the archers practising every evening at the butts before Henry the Fifth sailed for Agincourt or the Spanish Armada was sighted in the Channel," mused bookish Thomas Herbert.

"Always vulnerable, always preparing for the defence of their country, right down to the present day," said Charles, walking on towards a battery where Sergeant Floyd and Howes, the master-gunner, were discussing the mounting of a new piece of ordnance sent from the mainland. Both men sprang to attention as the King sauntered up and bade them a pleasant good-day. "It must have been from about this spot where you showed me how to fire my first cannon, Floyd," he said.

"'Twas that very culverine, over to your Majesty's left," said Floyd, inordinately pleased that he should have remembered.

"How can you tell after all this time?"

"I set a mark upon it the self-same day, and got a fine basting for it," grinned Floyd, coming to show him. "See, here on the under-side of the muzzle, sir."

By bending down Charles could just make out a roughly scratched C on the iron. Because he had to endure so many slights these days, he was so deeply touched that when he straightened himself the view from the ramparts was blurred by tears. "You were very patient. I am afraid I was not a very apt pupil," he said.

Standing with a hand on his beloved gun, Silas Floyd smiled back at him with that attractive mixture of respect and independence peculiar to his island breed. "Your young Highness was not so bad," he recalled without flattery, "except that you killed someone's cow."

It was Charles's own voice that led the gust of laughter. "And you did not tell me!" he said ruefully.

"'Twould have spoiled a happy day."

"And have gone against your native courtesy, no doubt." Charles sighed as he turned away and looked back at the castle. "Ah, well, Floyd," he said, raising his stick in a friendly gesture of farewell, "at least you and Sir John Oglander between you gave me one completely happy recollection of Carisbrooke. It may even have helped persuade me to return."

"God save him! " muttered the master-gunner, when the royal party had passed on.

Across the heavy iron gun-carriage Silas Floyd glanced at him searchingly. "Do you really fear that he—may need saving?" he asked gruffly.

Howes shrugged. "Not from this Governor. But there are those on the mainland who hate him."

"And some over here. One has only to listen to these New Model men talking."

"To say nothing of Captain Rolph! The way he abuses the royal family one feels he would not stick at murder."

Both of them were men who usually kept their thoughts to themselves; but there were many things going on in the castle which gave the Sergeant of the Guard food for anxious thought. He would have liked to speak more openly to a man whom he had known from boyhood, but there always seemed to be some spying Roundhead within earshot; and even now the smith and his mate were coming to work on the new gun emplacement. "You would have laughed to see my little lad drilling his playmates down by the stables yesterday," said Howes, changing the subject as they moved back along the battery to supervise the mounting. "And the way his Majesty delighted him by stopping to inspect them."

"The young Duke of Gloucester must be about your boy's age," remembered Floyd.

"They do say the King eats his heart out for his younger daughter. The delicate fourteen-year-old one, Princess Elizabeth."

"Where is she now?"

"Alone with the boy in St. James's Palace, according to that know-all Rudy."

Floyd stood by giving occasional directions to the smith, but half his thoughts were on the more domestic subject of daughters— his own and the King's. It must be hard to be parted from them. He had always supposed that his Mary would marry an islander and settle down somewhere where he would be able to see her until the end of his days. But now, with all these fine overners about, how could one be sure? They all seemed to like her, teasing her and offering to help her with her tasks. And there was a new radiance about the girl these days, a gayer warmth to her laughter. His shy slender Mary was growing into a woman—and a beauty. He had no notion which of the gallants she preferred. He must speak to Druscilla about it. Women were sharp as needles about such things.

"I'd not be sorry to see Mary wed—not in these unsettled times with lecherous brutes like Edmund Rolph about," he decided. "But Heaven send her a husband who does not want to carry her off across the Solent, for God knows what I should do without her!"

He had meant to talk to her about this unfortunate affair with the drunken messenger for which the girl Libby was being sent away—and to warn Mary not to get herself even remotely mixed up in such things. But now—after his recent meeting with the King—he could not bring himself to scold her. If ever there was anything his tender-hearted Mary could do to lighten the patient King's bondage, would he really have her refuse? She was free to do as she chose, not bound by military duty as he was. But he hoped that she would not take any undue risks. He went to find her; but instead of warning or reproving her, he gave her the key to the room where Libby had been detained. "She asked to see you before she goes," he told her, without comment.

A pack-horse was already being saddled and Tom Rudy was kicking his heels in the courtyard waiting to take his wife down to Brett's sister in the village, so Mary's time with Libby was short. "What made you pretend it was you who were to have received the King's letters? Why did you court dismissal to shield me?" she asked remorsefully.

"You have done a mort o' things for me ever since I came here," muttered Libby, her dark, tousled head averted in embarrassment, "Didn't I zay that if ever there was zummat I could do for *you*—"

"I know. But this is such a big thing."

"I'd have had to go before long anyways to have my baby."

It was true enough, but it went against the grain with Mary to let anyone take blame that should be hers. "I ought to have told the Governor you were lying. But your manner so persuaded him that he never even sent for me."

Libby laughed, swinging her cloak round her shoulders and tying it under her chin. She was well pleased with her cleverness. "What fun can I have anywheres, the way I am?" she said. "'Tis more sense for you to bide, Mistress Mary, seeing you be fair set on a man for the first time in your life."

The colour rushed up under Mary's fair skin. "It is not only that, Libby. Just out of selfishness, I doubt if I'd have let you shield me. It is because I can be of use here—" Hearing Rudy whistling close outside the window, she broke off the half-confidence and added lamely, "In ways I cannot explain—"

"You don't need to explain 'em!" laughed Libby coarsely. "There's more'n one man wants you. Why, only last week my Tom was saying how Captain Rolph—"

"Mistress Wheeler told me to bring you these," interrupted Mary hastily, setting down a basket filled with venison pasties and a piece of well-cured ham in a cloth. "And to say there'll be more for Rudy to bring whenever he comes to see you."

Libby gathered up the toothsome gift with satisfaction. "Her be grown a deal less hard," she commented.

"It must be the King's coming," said Mary, who had more than once speculated about the same phenomenon. "We have all had to work so. We seem more dependent upon each other. Just a handful of us seem more—together."

Libby could hear the pack-horse being brought round and her husband stamping impatiently. She picked up her bundle of possessions but hung back a moment, thoughtfully fingering the rush handle of the housekeeper's basket. "I'd ha' liked to be—together—with you too," she said slowly, betraying that she was not without some inkling of what was going on. "But I be married to a Roundhead. If it han't ha' been for the baby he'd ha' beaten me for havin' any truck with the Stuart's letter."

"But he's good to you?" asked Mary anxiously.

Someone was coming with firm footsteps to order the girl's departure. With her bundle on one arm and the basket on the other, Libby, the trollop's daughter, looked back with the authentic flame of wifely devotion in her eyes. "Though he be as crafty as they come, he do know how to fondle a girl out of her senses, and I'd as lief have him as any other man," she averred.

Mary stood a while in the bare little cell of a room, marvelling with a smile on her lips at the goodness to be found in unexpected places. Hearing Captain Rolph's voice outside, she knew to whom the approaching footsteps had belonged. Drawn instantly from her reverie, she listened tensely to the sound of Libby's departure, hoping to escape as soon as he was gone. But he was in the open doorway before her. "Well, what do I get by way of thanks?" he asked, delighted at his opportunity and her discomfiture.

"Thanks for what?" asked Mary, hoping the coldness of her voice might hide the frightened beating of her heart.

He came to her, lifting her chin familiarly. "You don't suppose I believed a word that bitch of Rudy's said, do you?"

"Then why did you send her away?" countered Mary. He dared not shut the door. Her father would be coming at any moment for the key. But with his eyes he could enjoy every curve of her body at his leisure. "It was either her or you," he said. "My men say the ostler fellow asked for Mary. I don't blame him. Any man would have," he laughed fulsomely. "Do you not suppose that I need some pleasant companionship during my exile in this clannish island?" He pulled her roughly to him. His thick shoulders shut out the daylight. "The Governor relies on me. I could have had you sent away as you deserve. Away from your precious father and that fine lady aunt who has made such a proud prude of you."

Mary saw his hungry lascivious face come closer and shut her eyes, making a stiff unresponsiveness of her body. She felt his hot, moist mouth on hers and had to suffer it. "I protected you," he muttered, half boastful, half self-excusing.

"Is that your idea of duty?" raged Mary, struggling like a wild cat to free herself.

"Duty? You need have no fear that Edmund Rolph will neglect any duty for the safekeeping of the Stuart!" He let her go then, so suddenly that she stumbled. His manner changed to that of bullying authority. "You will stay here and be civil to me, but don't imagine that I will let you go down into Newport again, promising to deliver letters to please some fancy lover!"

He had evidently no suspicion that the man whom she strove to please was in the castle. Without a backward glance Mary sped across the courtyard. Her cheeks burned, her limbs were shaking and there were tears of fury in her eyes. Behind the wellhouse she ran blindly into Firebrace, coming from the keep. He steadied her gently. "Thank Heaven that drunken fool did not draw suspicion upon you!" he whispered.

"I felt sure I should be sent away!" she cried, momentarily clinging to him.

"We could not have spared you," he told her, disengaging himself because there were several people about and their encounter must not seem anything more than an accidental contact.

"We!" echoed Mary, glaring at him through her tears.

"With our plans for his Majesty's escape so nearly completed," he explained guardedly.

"His Majesty! Oh yes, always his Majesty!" she flung back at him hysterically, feeling she hated the King they were pledged to help.

Firebrace turned in genuine concern. "Why, Mary my sweet, what is it?" He would have gone after her, but she was already half-way towards the household entrance, her tawny head held high and her back like a ramrod. Puzzled, Firebrace went on his way to his master. Something must have upset her, he supposed. Women had odd moods. But Mary was usually so sweet-tempered...

Up in her aunt's deserted room, Mary flung herself on the bed. "Couldn't he have been glad for us?" she sobbed, torn by a surfeit of recent and varied emotions. "Even that brute Rolph wanted to keep me here for *himself*!"

# CHAPTER FOURTEEN

———◦◦◦◦———

W E CALCULATED WELL. IT is the darkest night imagin-
able," reported Mary, peering out from the window of
the housekeeper's room.

"*And* a Monday, when the Governor should sleep soundly after
all those tedious hours in the Court Room," said Mistress Wheeler.

"If only the Rolph beast sleeps soundly too!"

"Come into bed, child. I can almost hear your teeth chattering,"
urged her aunt.

It was already March, and Mary's shivering was caused more
by nervous tension than by cold. Obediently, she climbed into
the high bed beside her aunt. Because they had not dared to light
a candle neither of them was fully undressed, and they made no
pretence of settling down. Mistress Wheeler lay propped high
against her pillows, while Mary sat with her knees drawn up under
the bedclothes and her hands clasped tightly round them. Both
of them were listening for sounds from the room below. Some
evenings they were able to hear the murmur of voices, although
never the actual words spoken. But now all was quiet. Harry
Firebrace must have finished undressing his master, Herbert and
Mildmay been dismissed, and his Majesty gone early to bed.

"To think that the night we have planned for all these weeks
has come at last, and that by to-morrow morning the King will be
gone!" said Mary, trying to keep a shaky, high-pitched tremor out
of her voice.

"It is to-morrow morning I dare not think about," confessed the housekeeper of Carisbrooke, shuddering momentarily as if someone had walked over her grave. "The state the Governor will be in, and what will happen to us all!"

"But the men will all be back in their beds by then, or preparing to go on duty. Brett will not be able to get in to make up the fire, and Captain Titus will pretend to be amazed and give the alarm. Harry Firebrace and Master Dowcett and Richard Osborne have covered every eventuality so exactly that the Governor won't be able to prove a thing against them," declared Mary.

"Four drunken guards with a flagon of strong wine apiece will take some covering. Especially if Captain Rolph goes his morning rounds early!" pointed out Mistress Wheeler, who never had liked that part of the scheme because she was afraid it might involve her brother.

"Heaven send he does not force them into telling who gave it to them," agreed Mary, thinking of Rolph's bullying ways and of Harry Firebrace's danger.

They said no more until the chapel clock struck ten. "Midnight is the time fixed," Mary whispered then, wishing that her voice would sound more ordinary.

"Try to go to sleep," advised her aunt. "There is nothing we can do."

"That is the worst of it." Mary remembered how even when she had had to slip a letter into the King's clothes chest with the Governor standing in the room she had not felt so strung up as now.

By mutual consent she and her aunt had left both window and bed-curtains undrawn; but the night was so dark that they might have been lying in a tomb. "If only I could see the smallest star!" thought Mary, feeling that its calm light might cheer and steady her. Anything, anything might happen on a night like this; and she would see nothing, be able to do nothing.

The long minutes dragged by. After a while deeper breathing beside her told her that her aunt was asleep. Soon it would be midnight. Mary's thoughts turned to Firebrace. Perhaps even now he might have taken up his appointed place down in the courtyard. What must *his* feelings be, who was responsible for the whole dangerous enterprise? Did he realize that she was awake and not far from him, wrapping him about with her tender concern? But probably he had no time to think either of her or of his own danger, but only of the King's. She had seen that look of devotion on his face and knew that in this matter he was capable of complete selflessness. His enthusiasms were the most lovable part of him, and she blamed herself for ever having resented them. Soon—so very soon now—he would have got the King safely away from his enemies, and would have time to relax and to think of her, and of his own life. Mary closed her eyes and prayed soundlessly. "Lighten our darkness we beseech Thee, O Lord, and defend us from all perils and dangers of this night." Somehow the familiar words which she heard every Sunday evening seemed to have taken on a very real and desperate meaning.

Immediately below her the man she specially prayed for had taken up his stance beneath the King's window. Dressed in a borrowed suit of black and pressed against the wall, he would have been completely invisible even had the Governor thought it necessary to set guards in the courtyard. The darkness was like a cloak, the silence of the night almost tangible. Where, even in the most rural parts of the mainland, he wondered, could one experience such a weight of silence? When had he ever known the blood to beat so loudly in his veins? He had embarked upon this scheme with the light-heartedness of any adventurous young man, and during most of the time realization of its magnitude had been obscured by small day-by-day preparations. But suddenly, on the brink of achievement, the thought of its far-reaching results appalled him. To-morrow the whole castle would be in an uproar, then London. Then—fast as horses could gallop—the news would spread to Wales and Scotland. It was heartening to picture the joy of family reunion if the King reached France in safety; but depressingly easy, standing beneath his window at this crucial moment, to share Charles's misgivings as to whether any court in Europe would welcome the embarrassment of his arrival.

Firebrace wished that he had not taken up his stance so

early—that he had left himself less time to think. And then some trooper's horse neighed in the stables, and was answered by a faint whinny from outside the south wall, reminding him that Worsley and Osborne were waiting too. Instantly he became his own cool-headed self again, with all his wits about him. His concern was only for the immediate present. Methodically, his mind went over every point of his plan.

Before he had left the King for the night, Dowcett had come in with the rope beneath his cloak and hidden it under the valance of the bed. Titus was on duty at the main door ready to give warning in case of any unusual stir in the house. An hour ago Edward Worsley had flashed a lantern from Whitcombe hill to let them know he was on his way from Gatcombe with the horses. Legge and Ashburnham would be waiting with more horses on the mainland, to reach the ship for France. Several times during his Majesty's walks round the battlements, he and Titus had managed to point out the exact spot where the horses would be waiting. It had, of course, made things more difficult Mary no longer being able to visit the "Rose and Crown" regularly and leave messages for John Newland. Messages about times and tides and the chosen night. If there were any hitch about the boat they would indeed be undone. But Osborne had seen to it all in her stead. He had talked a lot about some cousins who were staying at the inn on their way from Guernsey, and then gone out quite openly to sup with them. And he had not returned. He was out there now on the other side of the moat with Edward Worsley—an efficient pair, with loaded pistols in their holsters for their sovereign's protection during their short but perilous journey to the north shore. Firebrace's thoughts followed the three riders almost visually to a deserted creek in the shadow of Quarr woods, where one of John Newland's boats would be waiting. With such a fine, loyal team what *could* go wrong?

To his horror, his sharp ears distinctly caught a snatch of maudlin song from the direction of the guardroom. God send those fellows were not so drunk as to arouse Rolph in his quarters across the courtyard! If only a breeze would get up with the tide, instead of this cursed stillness which betrayed every snapped twig or voice or footfall! Dealing with the guards had been the chanciest part—that and the bars. Funny how Mary, who knew every part of the castle like her own hand and who was so full of commonsense, had immediately picked upon the difficulty of the bars!

Firebrace stepped out away from the wall and, turning, looked up towards the King's window. Not that he could see anything; but he had studied it and measured it so often that memory served as well as sight. Five tall arched casements, the stone mullions of each now divided by a central iron bar. Only a small man could possibly squeeze himself through. Firebrace had wanted to send to London for one of those new-fangled files so that he could cut away some of the iron frame of the middle casement, but the King had, quite reasonably, been afraid that his tampering would be noticed and their whole plan aborted. "I have tried it," he had said each time the subject was broached, "and where my head will pass my body must pass also." And one could not argue with a king, or override that immovable obstinacy so often to be found in a gentle person like Charles Stuart.

The chapel clock struck twelve. All was quiet again in the guardroom. Firebrace went swiftly across the courtyard and up the ramp to the battlements, looking along them in either direction to make sure that no one was about. The darkness beyond the walls was impenetrable. He groped along the ground for a pebble or two and slipped them into his pocket. And as he went softly back towards the Governor's house the thought came to him, "Next time I walk here—in a matter of minutes now—it will be done. The King will have escaped."

Carefully judging his distance he tossed up a pebble, which was the agreed signal to let the King know the coast was clear. In his tensed state he thought the faint tinkle it made against the glass sounded loud as the crack of doom. He wondered if Mary had heard it from the room above, and whether she was thinking of him. And presently came the creak of one of the King's casements being pushed cautiously open. Something struck with a soft flop against the stone wall a foot or two above his head. He reached up a hand and found it to be the knotted end of a rope. Once more he took a swift look round. There was no sign of light or stir anywhere about the castle. So far all was going well. He had only to wait until the King climbed out. He waited for what seemed a long time. He remembered that Charles was unaccustomed to doing manual tasks for himself. In the darkness it might take him some time to make sure the other end of the rope was securely fastened to a bedpost. But surely not so long as all this. He should be out of the window by now. Firebrace jerked gently at the rope to assure him that he was there, waiting to guide him to the ground. But there was no answering jerk and after what seemed an eternity he heard a groaning. The suppressed but continued groaning of a man in desperate pain or difficulty.

Sweat broke out upon Firebrace's forehead. "He is stuck fast!" he thought in panic. "I was right about the bars being too narrow, and now he can neither come out nor pull himself back again."

His first instinct was to get back into the house and tell Dowcett or Titus so that they might go to the King's aid. But of what use, since the State Room door was locked from the inside? He dared not call up and question the King himself. There was nothing he could do to help. He could only stand still, listening to that laboured groaning until it suddenly ceased and all was silence. Desperate with anxiety, he decided to climb up from the outside and see what was wrong, though his weight on the rope might make matters worse. He reached up for the end of it, but even as he did so it was jerked from his grasp. So at least the King must be sufficiently recovered to see the necessity of hauling it in and hiding it. Relief and dismay strove almost ludicrously in Firebrace. Conscious only that he had grown very cold waiting in the night without any kind of cloak, he stood there not knowing what to do.

Presently a light glowed above him as a candle was lighted and set in the wide window. By the light of it he could see that each of the casements was now fast closed, and knew it to be a sign to him that all further attempt at escape was impossible. He stared upwards, still hoping against hope; and when after a few minutes the light was put out, it was as if all his high hopes were put out with it. He guessed that his master had undressed and gone to bed.

Involuntarily, Harry Firebrace's mind skimmed over all the hastily exchanged scraps of information, the difficulties overcome, the excitement and the comradeship of the past three months; and suddenly he felt very tired.

His thoughts went to Osborne and Worsley, sound Royalists who would be as disappointed as himself. Slowly, without any excitement at all, he retraced his steps to the south battlements. Helplessly he stood at the appointed place. The cord by which he had hoped to lower the King was wound about his waist, but without some trusty friend to hold it he could not lower himself down sheer wall and escarpment. Although Osborne and Worsley would be on the alert for the slightest sound, he dared not call to them. He stood there, hands in pockets, shoulders hunched against the midnight cold. And as his mind groped for some means of communicating with them his right hand encountered the remaining pebbles in his pocket. How often as a boy had he not skimmed stones across some lake? Using his thumb as a cata-pult he skimmed one now, through the air across the moat. And then another and another. And at last to his relief an answering stone struck the masonry of the gun embrasure behind him. He hooted softly, mournfully, in what he hoped was a fair imitation of an owl. And presently the long, whirring call of a nightjar answered from the direction of the trees. Three times in succes-sion the reassuring realistic call came until he was certain that its originator must be Edward Worsley, who was familiar with the call of every bird on the island.

Soon he heard the chink of a bridle farther away towards the road to Gatcombe. They had understood. They were moving off. There was nothing more to stay for. Harry Firebrace let himself into the house by the window which Mary had left unlatched for him. He tiptoed upstairs and threw himself fully dressed across his bed.

"So it is all to do again!" he yawned, being young and optimistic.

# CHAPTER FIFTEEN

W ELL, AT LEAST WE were none of us caught. Friend Rolph is as accommodating as ever, and not a breath of suspicion anywhere," summed up Osborne, when they were all gathered together in the housekeeper's room on the following Monday.

"Though how you managed to get back and appear on duty as usual I cannot imagine," smiled Mistress Wheeler, who had taken a reluctant liking to the deceptively indolent-looking young man.

"It was thanks to your brother, Sergeant Floyd. He sent the sentry off on some errand and let me in at the north postern. Remembering what you said, I would not have asked him—"

"Then how did he guess?"

"It seems he found the guardroom looking like a disreputable fairground, and Wenshall and Featherstone solemnly cavorting round their stacked pikes under the impression that they were dancing round a maypole. After pouring the vials of his wrath and a bucket of water over them he had the presence of mind to change the guard ten minutes before Rolph went his morning rounds."

"Then it was Floyd who really saved the situation?" said Titus, appreciably.

"And got reprimanded for turning out his men ten minutes too soon."

"Captain Rolph always has his knife into my father," said Mary.

"I would not willingly have brought him into it," apologised Osborne a second time. "But it is clear where his heart lies."

"Is the King himself very much disappointed about last Monday's failure?" asked Mistress Wheeler.

"He seems more depressed about not having news from the Duke of York," Firebrace told her. "On the whole he keeps up his spirits wonderfully. He is now agreeable for me to send to London for some *aqua fortis*."

"What is that? " asked Mary.

"A kind of acid which will eat away the iron of the centre bar."

"A pity he did not listen to you before about the file!" she muttered.

Being a woman, her aunt agreed with her. But the men evidently regarded as disloyal a remark so full of outspoken common sense. "The *aqua fortis* should be here in a few days' time," Firebrace hastened to say, in order to cover her lapse. "So we can try again next time there is no moon."

"Things should go all the better for our last—rehearsal," prophesied Dowcett cheerfully.

"How *could* the King go calmly back to bed?" asked Mary unabashed. "I was so terrified when I heard him groaning—and then that awful silence! I shook my aunt awake and clung to her—"

"'Aunt Druscilla! Aunt Druscilla! Someone is murdering the King!'" mimicked Mistress Wheeler; and they all laughed, except Firebrace. "It is easy enough to laugh about it now," he said ruefully.

Osborne got up and strolled to the window. In passing he laid a sympathetic hand on his friend's shoulder. "It must have been a grim enough hour for you, Harry," he said. "But that hooting owl… really, you unobservant townsmen!"

"I thought it was rather good myself, Dick."

"So it may have been. But poor Worsley was nearly having a seizure. He says there are none of those *ti-whit ti-whoo* creatures on the island. Only shriek owls."

It was Firebrace's turn to provide the laughter. "Well, how was I to know?" he protested good-humouredly. "Did someone get that letter away to Ashburnham and Legge explaining why their horses on the mainland were not wanted?"

"Yes," Dowcett assured him.

"Where are the gentlemen now?" asked Mistress Wheeler.

"Still lying low at Netley, in Hampshire, where they can be extraordinarily useful," Osborne told her. "But Berkeley has managed to get away with messages to France."

Because they were all relieved at having avoided suspicion and because there was nothing more they could do for the moment, a sense of relaxation began to inform them. Their conversation turned to topics of more ordinarily personal interest. Dowcett had discovered by chance that some of Mistress Wheeler's relations by marriage were known to his wife in Windsor. Richard Osborne stood near them, alternately joining in their conversation about Court personages and encouraging Patters' exuberant family to climb up his long legs. Before long Titus excused himself because he was due for duty. Mary and Firebrace were left to themselves on the high-backed settle. Completely at ease, for once, they had an opportunity to talk about themselves.

"Are you indeed such a townsman as Master Osborne makes out?" asked Mary, set upon finding out more about her companion's life.

"I lived in Derby as a boy, and went to school at Repton. Yes, I suppose you would call me a townsman," agreed Firebrace, "for by the time I was thirteen my family moved to London. We lived in the parish of All Hallows, Barking. It is near the Tower, you know."

Mary ought by rights to have taken up some lace which she had offered to mend for Mistress Hammond in order to save the old lady's failing sight and out of gratitude for her kindness to Libby. But instead she sat with idle hands, regarding him with rapt attention. "And what did you do there, Harry?"

"My father apprenticed me to a legal scrivener."

"But you were so young!" she cried, picturing a bright-haired boy trying to tame his eagerness to the drudgery of a desk in some dreary city office.

"It was the best my father could do for me. I had five older brothers. I was supposed to be studying for the law."

"That too!" murmured Mary, thinking of the summer evenings when he should have been out at play as she had always been. Yet in a way she was glad because his comparative lack of wealth seemed to bring their backgrounds a little nearer. Judging by his gay clothes and manners, she had always supposed his youth to have been so privileged as Osborne's.

"I, too, have always had to work," she said gently.

Appreciating her unfailing kindness, he touched her hand with one of his light, charming gestures. "Oh, but I have been extraordinarily fortunate," he told her cheerfully. "Partly because I really *did* study, but largely through the good offices of my sister."

"I did not even know you had one."

"We have had so little time to talk."

Mary was immensely interested, feeling that one day she and the Firebrace girl would surely meet.

"She was in the household of the Countess of Denbigh and together they persuaded the Earl to take me as his secretary. When the war came he was on the Parliamentary side, but a finer man never lived. But that is enough about me. Let us talk about you, Mary."

"But my life has been so ordinary. Dull, I suppose you would call it."

"I do not find your island at all dull."

"No," agreed Mary, with a little spurt of laughter. "But then you and dullness never come within hailing distance! You are like a gunner's match!"

"A gunner's match?"

"You set light to the rest of us—who are only the priming—and then everything goes up in light and flame and—excitement."

"As long as it does not just go up in smoke!" laughed Firebrace.

"But seriously, I have enjoyed my life here," went on Mary, her eyes alight with a repletion of happiness. "I love my island friends, of course. And the little bays, the valleys and the hills. I love them as I shall never love any other place on earth. When Frances and my other friends talked of their longing to go to the mainland, they used to laugh at me because I always said I could not live anywhere but here."

"And now?" asked Firebrace, thinking he had never seen her look so lovely.

"Now—"

The question of the future was left hanging in the air. Whatever she had been going to say was interrupted by Dowcett. "I am carrying Mistress Wheeler off to see my painting of my wife. There is just time before supper," announced the excitable little Frenchman. "Do you wish to come, Mary?"

It was one of the endearing things about him that he was always telling them how beautiful his wife was. At any other time Mary would have been most interested to see her portrait, particularly as she also had forwarded royal letters from her home in Windsor. But the present moment was too precious to be lost. "Some other time, if I may, dear Master Dowcett," she replied absently.

The Frenchman looked disappointed, and Osborne, hearing her decline the invitation, put down the clamouring spaniels. He stood for a hesitant moment or two regarding the couple on the settle with a queer, twisted smile. Their happy absorption in each other was patent. "My servant's spavined mare needs some attention," he remarked rather inadequately; and Mary, looking up briefly, saw him follow the other two out of the room. But her mind did not recognize his dejected altruism nor consciously register the exact moment when she and Firebrace were left alone.

"Then you only joined the Parliamentarian forces because you happened to be in that kind of household?" she prompted, plunging back into their interrupted conversation.

"Partly," admitted Firebrace. "Though because of my legal training I saw—in fact, I still can see—how arbitrarily the King sometimes behaved."

"Then how did you come to be his page?"

"It is rather a long story." Firebrace settled himself more comfortably, stretching his legs to the blaze and his arm along the settle-back behind her. "When his Majesty set up his standard at Nottingham, Denbigh was appointed Commander-in-Chief of the Midland counties for Parliament and I went with him. A young man has to do *something* on one side or the other. I got my commission and after a battle or two I had the good fortune to be made secretary of his war councils. Our headquarters were at Coventry but I was always being sent from place to place. I got to know people."

"Important Roundheads, you mean? Like Cromwell and Monk and Fairfax?"

"Scarcely such *very* important people," said Firebrace, smiling at her flattering idea of his own status. "But quite useful men on both sides. You see, I had to do most of the writing for the negotiations at Oxford and Uxbridge; though unfortunately the two armies could come to no agreement. My earl was not one of these anti-Royalist fanatics. He believed that if he could only persuade his Majesty to make a few concessions he would be peaceably restored to the throne, and the whole country saved any more bloodshed. He hoped this so fervently that after the negotiations were officially closed I was sent back and forth with private messages between them. So you see, my sweet, that must have been when I acquired my deplorable penchant for intriguing with secret letters!"

"And when you fell a victim of the Stuart charm!" teased Mary.

"It was difficult not to. King Charles was always so courteous and so thoughtful for people who did him even the smallest service. But I have always wanted to explain to you about men like Titus and myself, who must seem to you to be turncoats. It is not so much that we have changed our convictions as that we have found many of the men from whom we imbibed them now want to go to far more brutal lengths than we could ever have accepted."

"Even here, some of them seem almost crazed with spite. Specially those who find all the curses but no love in the Scriptures. Were you in great danger carrying those secret messages?"

"Milord Denbigh seemed to think so. He used it as an argument when trying to get months of back pay which in the end was never refunded to me. But it was interesting work. When the war was nearly over, as you know, the King gave himself up to the Scots. I happened to be at Newcastle at the time; and after they had sold him back to the English, the Earl of Denbigh used his influence to get me a place in the royal household there, in the hope that I might still persuade his Majesty to make some of those concessions."

"Anyone can see that the King likes you."

His devoted Groom of the Bedchamber modestly shrugged the

valued compliment aside. "Thank God, he *trusts* me," he said. "But I have long ago come to realize that the Queen herself could not persuade his Majesty to make any concession which went against his conscience."

Mary gave the matter her grave but immature consideration. "Does not that sometimes make things very difficult for other people?" she ventured to suggest.

But the bell clanged for supper and Firebrace did not answer. For the moment he seemed to have forgotten all about his master. He rose reluctantly, pulling her up with him. "I shall always remember this firelit room," he said.

"So shall I," said Mary softly. "You mean when it is really all over and the King has gone?"

"Yes. When I leave here."

"Leave here?" she repeated, with a small catch in her voice. She had so much hoped that now, on this peaceful evening, he would have talked about the future as well as the past. "Where will you go?"

Firebrace bent down to throw another log on Mistress Wheeler's fire before they left it. "Back to my wife, I suppose," he said, without any particular enthusiasm. "Had we not better be going down now?"

There was no answer, no movement. And when he looked up he saw Mary's face drained of colour, her eyes staring at him, dark and blind with pain. Her outspread hands were pressed to her breast. It occurred to him that had he driven his dagger into her heart beneath them she could not have looked more dead.

"Mary! " he cried, catching her by the shoulders lest she should fall.

But it was the familiar room, her world, the whole of her life that was falling. Her lips parted but no words came. As Richard Osborne had said, she was so young, so inexperienced. She knew no comparison by which to lessen the sudden blow, nor any subterfuge with which to mask the shame of her total, unasked-for love.

Harry Firebrace's face whitened too. "God forgive me for a brutal fool, I did not know!" he cried. He pulled her to his breast and held her close, so that he could not see those desperate eyes. His mouth, which had so carelessly dealt the blow, was pressed in loving contrition upon her hair.

A door slammed, voices suggested some laughing encounter, hurrying footsteps died away upon the stairs. Down in the hall people would be cheerfully eating supper. Somewhere at the back of his shocked mind Firebrace realized with relief that for an hour at least the firelit room would be theirs, undisturbed. He drew Mary down on to the settle, still holding her so that she did not have to look at him and trying to still her violent trembling. "The tragedy—the absurdity—of it is," he muttered into the gathering dusk above her head, "that I could have loved you. *How* I could have loved you! I must have been blind—blind. Why, all along, from the day I first knocked into you with that absurd ink-pot, and we looked into each other's eyes and laughed, I have never been so happy with anyone!"

His flexible young voice had begun to take on the exultation of a glad discovery so that her shame was eased. She raised her head a little and sat staring unseeingly into the fire. "Why did you never speak of—her?" she asked tonelessly at last.

"If I did not, I swear it was not of intent."

"Did you never think of her—long for her—as Abraham Dowcett does for his wife?"

"I thought of her sometimes," admitted Firebrace soberly. "But—she is an invalid."

Mary's head came up a little higher. "You mean—an incurable invalid?"

"The doctors do not know. Only time will tell."

"So she cannot—you do not—live as man and wife?"

"She lives with a kind old body at Knightsbridge."

"Where is that?"

"It is a village just outside London," Firebrace told her wearily. He passed a hand over the springing strength of her curls, and got up quickly as though stung by some comparison which he could not bear.

"What is your—what is her name?"

"Elizabeth," he said, leaning an arm against the spandrel of the fireplace. "She is insane."

The words dropped hopelessly into the silence of the room. They, and the pity they evoked, brought life back to Mary as nothing else could have done. She leaned forward and took his list-lessly hanging hand into her cold one and pulled him back beside her. "The years must have been hard for you," she said, the words at once a forgiveness and a comforting.

He sat forward on the settle, hands locked between his knees. "There was a man who used to visit her," he began incoherently. "Before I even knew her he wanted to marry her. It seems such irony—now. He even bought her clothes and things when I was away at the war."

"And you were not jealous?"

"I was glad for her sake."

"Then you could not have loved her."

"I did once. But it has gone on so long—her sickness and my being away. And, God forgive me, life has been so full of more exciting things... Lately I have even hoped that she—that they... But my wife is a good woman. I do not believe that she was ever actually unfaithful."

Mary got up and walked about, as though she must have the physical relief of movement. But she walked without lightness, like an old woman. "Richard Osborne knew you were married?" she asked, arms tight across her breasts as if to keep out the cold.

"Yes. Why?"

"He once tried to warn me. He said 'what did I know of you?'"

"Yet he did not tell you?"

A new understanding of Osborne's dilemma came to her. "No. I suppose it would have been what you men call disloyal. He only hoped—"

"Yes?"

"That I would not get hurt."

Mary laughed with a bitterness so alien to her that it seemed to wipe out all her childish innocence, and Firebrace's arms were suddenly round her. Too late, they were the arms of a lover.

Neither gentle, nor compassionate, but demanding. "Let us forget that you know," he urged. "A while ago we were so happy. Let us go on from there. My sweet, my very dear accomplice, we have this hour…Afterwards, if you like, I will take you away with me to the mainland. Anything you wish. We were made for each other, Mary, and I cannot bear to see you hurt."

With closing eyes, she almost let herself be swept into the rising tide of his passion. There would be ecstasy, and forgetting. Everything that her body had been awakening for. But the moment had come too late. Her senses had been bludgeoned with the blow to her heart, so that her mind and all her careful training gradually took charge. Involuntarily she thought of Libby, remembering that for herself there could not be even a belated marriage. "It seems I must get hurt either way," she said faintly between his kisses.

"All these weeks how could I not have seen—"

"Perhaps because you are not very conceited. You must not blame yourself. It has been something which—just happened." Pride came to her rescue, and she withdrew herself resolutely from his embrace. "Go now, and leave me alone," she entreated. She knew that she must begin to learn to find her way about a new empty kind of world in which no older relatives could advise or help her to bear her burdens any more, and when Harry Firebrace would have taken her into his arms again her small, strong hands held him off. "No, no. I love you too well to have resolution for us both," she reproached. She leant back against the table, the firelight warm on her hair, candour in her eyes and pride in the lift of her chin. There was a new dignity about her. She looked somehow taller, a grown woman, done with girlhood's illusions. There was raillery in her voice, but it was kinder, less bitter, with half the mockery for herself. "Better go now," she advised, "and take with you your charm and your enthusiasms and your laughter— everything that has been my foolish heart's undoing—and spend them in the service of the King."

# CHAPTER SIXTEEN

———∞∞∞———

THE MAKING OF THE bowling green was a blessing to most of the inhabitants of the castle. It gave them something fresh to think about and broke the grim routine of winter. Soldiers from the over-crowded barracks were able to spread themselves in the pleasant acres of the place-of-arms within the outer walls.

It was Mistress Hammond who first put the idea into her son's mind. The King loved to talk to her because she was part of his old life and had known his children when they were small, and to her in some relaxed moment he had confided laughingly that without his usual hunting he feared he would grow fat, and how much he would give for a game of bowls.

"He must miss so many other things which he never does complain about," she had sighed, repeating a part of the conversation to Hammond. "I know you cannot let him ride abroad but there is room and to spare for a green on the place-of-arms, Robert, and if you can see your way to give his Majesty that much pleasure it would please your father to hear of it."

There were few ways in which Robert Hammond could please a revered father, since their political persuasions lay so far apart. And here was something he could do for Charles which in no way clashed with his duty to Parliament. So after supper that night he cheered his royal guest by telling him of his intentions; and soon the inner ward was humming with activity.

Sergeant Floyd spent willing hours measuring and levelling. Pikemen gladly dug instead of being drilled. The island men among them, accustomed to scythe and sickle, cut the sweet grass short. Those who were townsmen from the mainland rolled it again and again with a heavy iron cylinder loaded with stones. Cooks and scullions took time off from the hot kitchen to fashion short flights of steps in the banked-up sides. Discipline was temporarily relaxed, and out beyond the postern gate which separated the two wards friendly shouts gave an illusion of freedom and eased tension. Everyone, whenever possible, went out to watch. "It will be better than the bowling alley at Whitehall!" prophesied Thomas Rudy, forgetting his republican prejudices as he marked out the rinks under the King's personal direction. And, warmed by a sense of his own magnanimity and the King's obvious gratitude, Hammond, in a final burst of generosity, instructed the carpenters to build a little pavilion at the southern end where players could rest or shelter from a sudden shower.

"Our Governor is too much the fine courtier," sneered Rolph, raging because his men were weeding grass for aristocrats when they might have been trying out the new brass cannon sent from Southampton or practising signalling with the horse-guards who now patrolled the hills. But only the sourest of his men really grudged their prisoner a chance to forget his troubles in the game he loved.

The weather was dry and when it was found that play could begin almost at once Herbert and Mildmay and the rest of the King's attendants were glad for their own sakes as well as for their master's; and the small coterie of people planning for his second attempt at escape were only too thankful that so many fresh activities diverted attention from their own.

April on the island was an enchantment. The kind gaiety of nature pushed through the ugly cruelty of party strife. The maidservants went out and gathered kingcups in the mill-pond meadows. Birds singing in the hedges of Castle Lane made a mock of roaring gun practices and did their best to drown the sharp sound of military commands.

But for Mary sunshine and bird-song made a mockery. She was

enduring her first taste of grief. The future which had beckoned so enticingly had suddenly become an unthinkable blank, the present a penance to be lived through. From task to task, from hour to hour, was the longest measure of existence which her mind could contemplate. With pathetic young dignity she tried to draw the cloak of everyday cheerfulness about her, hoping to hide her unhappiness from an uncaring world.

From her father she could not hide it. Too deep a bond of sympathy ran between them. And after a day or so, because he had not probed the raw wound with questions, she found that she could tell him spontaneously about the misfortune of her love.

Being a man of fundamental strength and simplicity, Silas Floyd offered her no easy platitudes. He recognized the irreplaceable quality of first love. He did not say "You are so young, you will get over it," or "My dear, there will be others." He knew that however many men there might be, or however deep their love, no one of them could ever be the same. He knew that for his tender-hearted maid something tremulously beautiful had been broken—that the first brittle, shining wonder of it could never come again. There might be better things in her life—he prayed there would be—but never, he knew instinctively, would there be anything so innocently close to heaven.

So he spent all the time he could with her, walking with her in the sunshine when he was dog-tired and sitting with an arm about her of an evening so that she should feel assured of his love.

And old Brett, who could be as deaf as an adder when it suited him, was not deceived. He remembered the lilt in her voice and the lightness of her step whenever she and that pleasant Master Firebrace had used his wellhouse as a nice quiet spot in which to exchange their secret notes and their hastily whispered bits of news, and he noticed her lagging footsteps now. She came as often and cared for the donkeys as assiduously, but when the last bucketful of water had been raised and Jonah called out from the wheel, the old man watched her with troubled eyes. When she stayed so still in the shadows with her cheek against the little beast's rough, grey neck he guessed that she was crying.

For a week Mary had avoided Firebrace and felt miserably sure that he was avoiding her; and when another Monday evening came round she excused herself from the usual meeting in her aunt's room to which she had always looked forward so eagerly. She was very tired, she said. But Mistress Wheeler remembered how tirelessly her niece had worked since the King's arrival, and how healthy she was, and looked up at her with shrewdly anxious eyes. "Go gather me some primroses, and get some colour back into your cheeks!" she bade her, with brisk kindliness.

So Mary gathered up Pride of the Litter and wandered out through the postern gate to a small wild piece of land beyond the new bowling green. Obediently she gathered a few primroses, then sat listlessly upon a log with wild violets and anemones starring a fragile pattern about her feet and the small dog dozing on her lap. During that hour before the household supper, when King and courtiers were at table, people strolled in twos and threes about the grassy inner ward. In her loneliness Mary had a sudden longing for Frances and for Mistress Trattle's comfortable kindness. She had not seen them for so long and saw no hope of doing so without giving in to the Captain of the Guard's importunities. But she was not left long alone. A shadow fell across the grass and Richard Osborne joined her. Startled, she wondered if Harry had told him what had happened between them after he had left them together a week ago. But his manner was as nonchalant as usual. He merely admired the bunch of flowers lying on the log and, seating himself beside her, began to talk casually of this and that as anyone might do upon so sweet an evening. He told her how his servant's lame horse was doing, then spoke of his growing understanding of the Wight and of his liking for Edward Worsley, asking her if she knew him.

"To say good-morning or curtsy to, as we all do," she told him. "I meet him out riding on the downs sometimes. I think he must love them as I do. And sometimes in the previous Governor's time he used to come up here to dinner. He is considered one of the handsomest young men on the island."

"By you?" he teased.

"Certainly by my friend Frances Trattle. Did you see her when you went to the 'Rose and Crown,' Master Osborne?"

"I did. And a ravishing sight it was."

"Was she wearing her tabbed crimson gown?"

"And a lace cavalier collar that became her."

"It seems true what they say about your having an eye for pretty women. You know that she is to marry Master Newland?"

Osborne stretched his long legs and looked down upon her disapproval with amusement. "So she informed me when I would have kissed her."

"And so you deserved!"

"But she had the good sense not to tell me until it was too late."

Mary had to laugh, picturing the engaging scene. It sounded so like Frances. "If you should see her again I pray you have the kindness to explain why I have not been to see her, and tell her how much I miss her."

"I will make it my business to see her," he promised.

"In order to kiss her again?" asked Mary, with an unaccountable prick of jealousy.

"No. To give her your message." Having brought back the adorable dimple to her cheek and banished the desperate unhappiness from her eyes, he judged it time to say what he had followed her out there to say. "You do not need to sit here all alone, my poor gallant child. There is no rogues' meeting being held this evening in your hospitable room."

So he had guessed about her and Harry. She looked up in surprise and asked him why there would be no meeting.

"The Governor has had a letter from Derby House. One of those letters which put him into what your islanders call 'a fair firk.' The Major of the new foot company brought it. You must have seen them come marching in this afternoon."

"Why, yes. But I was thinking—of something else—" Seeing the unusual gravity of her companion's face, Mary jerked her mind back from personal grief to practical issues. "Does he suspect about—that Monday night?" she asked with uncanny intuition.

"Only a general suspicion, I think. After all, there is nothing he can pin on any of us. But we thought it wisest not to meet."

"Of course." Mary sat pondering for a moment or two, then

tumbled the spaniel almost roughly off her lap. "Is it anyone in particular this time?" she asked, remembering how Napier and the little tailor had been sent away.

"Captain Titus, I fancy. And Harry." Hearing the sharp little gasp that escaped her lips, he picked up the bunch of primroses and buried his nose in their sweetness in order to give her time. "They were both sent for and questioned an hour or so ago. Oh, they gave nothing away, I assure you. But those of us who are in this thing must be careful not to be seen too much together."

"My father?" she asked quickly. "Did anyone see him let you in?"

"No. Definitely no, Mary. I am more grateful than I can say for that."

She called to Pride of the Litter who was attracting attention to them by yelping excitedly down a rabbit hole, and Osborne, slipping her posy with masculine carelessness into his pocket, got up in his leisurely way to pull him out for her.

"How could news about anything we do here come in a letter from London?" she asked, absently watching his efforts.

"I do not know. But Cromwell's espionage system is most efficient." Heedless of the earth on his expensively tailored coat, he tucked the disobedient little creature firmly under his arm. "Harry asked me to explain that if he keeps away it is so that he may not draw suspicion upon you. Upon you particularly, who have been suspected before."

Even that small message was of comfort to her. She began to walk back towards the Governor's house and Osborne fell into step beside her. But as they were about to pass through the postern gate she paused uncertainly. "Thank you for coming to tell me about—everything. But would it not be wiser for you to wait a few minutes so as not to be seen with me?" she suggested, thinking for the first time of *his* safety.

But Osborne only laughed. "You do not have to add me to the list of your tender concerns, my sweet. Do you not realize that I am hand in glove with the Captain of the Guard, who is so much in favour at Westminster that he has this very day been recommended for his majority?"

"Oh, no!"

"And that I shall make it my business to be on good terms with this new Major who has arrived to-day—whose name happens to be Cromwell?"

"Cromwell!" At sound of the all-powerful name Mary stopped short in her tracks.

"Oliver's nephew. And therefore vaguely related by marriage to our conscientious Governor."

"Is that why he has been sent here?" asked Mary, in her innocence.

Osborne shrugged, and in full view of Rolph and a grinning guard handed over the subdued spaniel. "Scarcely, I should imagine. More likely as a goad—or a watchdog."

And Colonel Hammond, standing gloomily before his window in the officers' quarters, had come to much the same conclusion. Those bureaucrats at Derby House might have spared him this, he thought. True, he was glad enough of the extra company of well-trained men but he had no need of a ranting Puritan always at his elbow. Did Parliament consider him disloyal or inefficient because he tried to preserve courtesy towards his prisoner? And now they wanted him to obtain and to send them secretly a copy of the terms offered to the King by the Scottish Commissioners. And no doubt had sent this self-righteous young sprig of the Cromwells to make sure that he did so.

Robert Hammond took an angry turn or two about the room. To *obtain*. Why did they not say outright to *steal*? Charles must have those terms in writing somewhere, but he would certainly keep them under lock and key. Did the coarse-grained hypocrites expect him to pick the lock of his Majesty's writing desk like a common thief? And rifle through his private papers? If so they had better relieve him of his command and give it to some low fellow like Rolph. And allow him, Robert Hammond, the son of the learned divine, to retire to some quiet place where he could at least live with some remnants of his self-respect.

That they were beginning to consider him inefficient Hammond could not doubt. Back by the window, he paused in his angry striding to draw a much-folded letter from his pocket and to read it through for the third time. Once again the busybodies at Derby House were presuming to know more about what went on in his household than he did. They were urging him to have a very careful eye kept in those about the King, lest some of them should help him to escape one of these dark nights. As though he himself had not taken every precaution. A conservator approved by Parliament at each of the King's bedroom doors, bars fixed at his window and guards set all round the battlements. In this last letter they had even gone so far as to hint at the untrustworthiness of Captain Titus, with his fine republican war record, and at Firebrace, one of the most capable and popular officials in the whole castle. Two men who never made trouble with either party. He had felt obliged to question them, and a rare fool he had looked. Was he in any way dissatisfied with the way in which they performed their duties, they had asked; and there had been absolutely nothing he could find fault with.

Hammond crumpled the letter impatiently. Why, as soon suspect that young *flaneur* down there bowing like a lord to the Sergeant's daughter. Or the girl herself, with her useful domestic ways and her honest eyes. Though to be sure, her name *had* been mentioned in connection with the Bosvile affair. But there could have been nothing in that because even now, since she had been forbidden to take in the linen and Bosvile was gone, the Derby House people seemed so certain that letters were still getting through. Well, decided Hammond, thrusting the irritating letter back into his pocket, he must watch them all. But what a way to live, mistrusting everybody about one…Sometimes he began to wonder if that clod Rolph were the only one he could really be sure of.

The man and the girl down in the courtyard went their separate ways, and it was not until her aunt asked for the primroses that Mary realized that she had not brought any. "I must have left them on the log where I was sitting," she confessed.

"Mooning, you mean!" snapped her exasperated aunt. "What is the matter with you these days?"

Mary could not tell her; nor could she know that the poor flowers were still crushed in Richard Osborne's pocket. Or that when he found them later he smoothed out their crumpled petals with strong, pitiful fingers. "They are like Mary herself," he thought. "Fresh and sweet and humble—and so easily crushed beneath the first heedless heel."

Most of the women he had known had been of a much gaudier type.

# CHAPTER SEVENTEEN

———∞∞∞———

MARY, COMING FROM THE laundry, waited until the King and all his gentlemen had trooped out to the bowling green before taking the freshly-ironed shirt up to his Majesty's room. She had hoped to see the Governor go with them, but he was usually too busy these days. He must be dealing with his correspondence, she supposed, or gone into Newport.

At the bottom of the backstairs she met Brett, coming down with his bucket of ashes. He always took the opportunity of giving the great hearths what he called "a fair rake" at this hour of the morning when Presence Chamber and bedchamber were sure to be deserted. "So as not to make a terbul smother for the gentry," he said.

"Have you seen Captain Rolph or the new Major anywhere about?" she enquired cautiously, before going up.

Brett shook his greying head. "Everything be prid near quiet an' peaceful as the weather," he grinned. "Though even that do be but a breeder, I reckon. They gurt black clouds pilin' up Yarmouth way'll bring a storm avore long."

Mary went upstairs congratulating herself that she had plucked up courage to deliver the letter this morning. With her free hand she felt in her pocket to make sure it was there, folded small just as Harry had shown her so that it would fit into the crevice of the State Room wall.

She was almost happy because she was doing something to help him again. The letter was important and had come two days ago,

Aunt Druscilla had told her; and Harry himself was being so closely watched that he could find no opportunity to deliver it himself. Mary would know what to do, he had said.

She had put on her softest shoes and went silently as a shadow along the passage. To her surprise she saw light coming from the King's door, showing that it was partly open. Brett, cumbered with his load, had probably failed to shut it properly. As Titus was not on guard at the end of the passage no doubt he had gone to see to it. Certainly a man was standing just inside the doorway but he was broader than Titus and wore Cromwellian armour. His back was turned and he had not heard her. And between the buff cloth of his sleeve and the jamb of the door Mary could see into the room. She stopped dead and gasped.

She could see the brightly burning fire and the wide-mullioned window. And full in the light of both, the Governor of the Wight rifling through the contents of the King's desk. That beautifully carved escritoire brought from Hampton, with an instrument of some kind still dangling from the picked lock. She could see the pulled-out drawers, the papers scattered round them, the little piles of letters still neatly tied with ribbon and the open letter in his hand.

Instinctively she drew back before the man in the doorway had time to turn. He was a stranger and from his broad regimental sash she guessed him to be young Major Cromwell. His shock at seeing her was obvious. He stepped out hurriedly into the passage, closing the door behind him almost furtively as though anxious not to disturb the Colonel so busily employed inside. "And what may you be doing here?" he asked. His expression was more surprised than angry, and Mary felt certain that he did not know what she had seen.

"There was one of his Majesty's shirts forgotten," she said, with all the stolidity she could muster. "I am supposed to leave all linen with the conservator on duty."

He had none of Rolph's roughness, nor any of his leering way with wenches. "Captain Titus has gone on an errand for the Governor and for the moment I am relieving him," he said. "Better leave it on his table."

He was new to the ways of the castle and evidently had no idea who she was. Feigning nervousness before his authority, Mary let the shirt slip from her hands and then wasted time carefully refolding it. Never taking her eyes off his back as he strolled impatiently along the passage waiting for her to be gone, she managed to push the much-folded letter into the chink in the wall where it would lie hidden from anyone inside by the arras until evening, when the King himself would look for it. Meekly she turned to go. But suddenly there came the sound of raised voices from within. Major Cromwell swung round in alarm, brushed her aside and reopened the service door.

The main door facing it had been opened too, and just inside it stood Thomas Herbert, rain dripping from his hat and indignation on his pointed, scholarly face. Robert Hammond still stood by the desk, letter in hand, fairly caught. "Because of the storm I ran ahead to fetch his Majesty's cloak," Herbert was saying—almost shouting. "And I find you—"

But the words were taken from his mouth because the King, wet and breathless, had already hurried past him into the room. The fury on his face was something which it would take a brave man to face. "Is this your hospitality? The 'fulfilling to your utmost of my just desires' that you p-promised?" he cried, going straight up to Hammond.

His face was white, his eyes blazed. It had never occurred to him that in a gentleman's house such an indignity could be offered to him. He seized the half-read letter from his gaoler's hand. "So you would even read a letter from my wife?" he said, his voice like ice. "Violating a decent privacy which even the meanest of my subjects enjoys!"

Hammond's face was red with shame. That a merciful God should have allowed such ill fortune! That he, an upright man, should be found at the one detested, despicable moment of his life! "The most of it is in cypher, and the only part that concerns me is about a ship to get you away," he said, with a kind of dogged courage.

"I know of no ship!" blustered the King, knowing full well that the coded letter was full of it.

Anger flared in Hammond, ousting all feeling of respect. "Yet I find all these letters—recently dated—secretly received…You do not suppose that I am interested in the harmlessly personal parts of your correspondence, do you? Or that I have read them?"

"Because our sudden coming prevented you."

The Governor tried to get a grip on himself. "It was not your Majesty's private letters, however hard some of your correspondents strive to make my duty here, that I came to seek," he repeated. "But by the order of Parliament—" His fine swordsman's hand stretched out suddenly to grasp a sheaf of thicker, more important-looking documents. But Charles was too quick for him. He grabbed them first. He glared defiance at his aggressor, so much taller than himself. For a moment it looked as if Hammond would wrest them from him by force. "If they are the terms of the Scottish treaty—" he began.

Herbert sprang forward towards his master, and from outside the room Mary watched aghast.

But Charles ducked beneath the Governor's outstretched arm and dodged behind him. As he did so his slight lameness betrayed him so that he stumbled, bumping his forehead sharply on the carved corner of the desk. But he succeeded in throwing the papers into the blazing heart of the fire so lately replenished by old Brett. Hammond reached for the shovel, hoping to rescue them; but the Stuart stood in his way, like a dog on guard, and he dared not lay a finger on him. Because of what had happened there could never be anything but antagonism between them. Because Hammond's soul abhorred what he had been seen doing, his sense of having been misjudged would always make him speak with bitter sarcasm. And even though he offended his masters by his humanity, the King would never again trust him.

There was blood now upon Charles's bruised brow and the beginnings of a small, cool smile on his lips beneath their smooth brown moustaches. The papers, whatever they were, flared up and then died down into a mass of quivering, charred flakes behind him. That round had certainly gone to the King.

Herbert's sigh of relief was audible. Cromwell's nephew, who had been absorbed in watching the sudden drama, came to his everyday senses and slammed the service door; and Mary saw no more.

But up in the room above she described it all to her aunt, and before long rumours of it had spread all over the castle. And because no one had had the story at first hand the rumours were wild and varied.

"You should have seen the Governor's face when he came down!" said the sentry at the main door of the house. "And heard that finicking pendant Herbert berating me for not preventing him from going up in the King's absence—as if the likes o' me could stick my pike in a Colonel's belly!"

"I could see the bump on the King's forehead, big as an egg, when I took in the roast," reported a servant returning to the kitchen. "I reckon the Guv'nor hit him."

"And how the alleged brutality will be seized upon by the Royalists as a tid-bit for the London news sheets!" prophesied Rudy, discussing the news after lights out in barracks.

"Whatever he does he's bound to be wrong with one party. Governor or no Governor, I do not envy him," ruminated Sergeant Floyd, leaning over the battlements beside the master-gunner.

All the King himself said when Herbert was bathing his forehead was: "What a mercy we were able to send those terms of the treaty to Ashburnham for safe keeping a fortnight ago! But it would have been worse had I not managed to burn his map and plans for getting me to the Essex Coast."

For the handful of people who were plotting the King's escape the painful encounter was more than a matter for gossip. It affected them too closely. "Finding so many letters which must have been received since his Majesty came here, the Colonel will be bound to suspect someone," said Mistress Wheeler.

"The King should have destroyed them," muttered Mary fiercely, noting the worry on her friends' faces.

"He did burn most of them," said Dowcett. "But a man's letters from his wife—they are all we have when we are parted—" With quick sympathy he patted the pocket bulged by his own letters.

The six of them waited fearfully for what would come. And

they did not have long to wait, nor did Hammond have long to wonder. Yet another letter came from Derby House telling him more or less what had happened on that dark night of the attempted escape. A very considerable personage had had word of it, they said. One of their own conservators, Captain Titus, was thought to have helped and a young man called Firebrace had waited beneath the King's window to lead him to safety. How, they did not appear to know.

Somehow Anthony Mildmay had learned what was in the letter, and showed his goodwill by warning them. For a stolen moment or two Firebrace, Osborne, Titus, Dowcett, Mistress Wheeler, and Mary managed to meet in the housekeeper's room. The six of them looked into each other's faces, and knew as surely as they knew their own souls, that not one of them would have betrayed the rest. Of those outside, Worsley, who had come into the project voluntarily, was above suspicion, and Newland, already in trouble with Mayor Moses because he had been absent from so many evening Council meetings, had too much to risk. Sergeant Floyd and Brett, who must have had some inkling, were both honest men.

"His Majesty must have been in correspondence again with the Queen's crony, Lady Carlisle. That treacherous bitch is altogether too friendly with the Scots," growled Titus, seeing himself back again at Bushey trying to explain his dismissal to a stern Puritan father.

"Mildmay says Cromwell's spies got hold of that last letter his Majesty wrote to the Duke of York," Firebrace told them. "It sounded like any ordinary family letter, and he swore it was; but they demanded the code."

"Lord Wharton tells me these Parliamentary foxes have an amazing mathematician who can break down almost any cypher," put in Osborne.

"For as long as he dared young James kept it from them," went on Firebrace. "But when they threatened to put him in the Tower the poor faint-heart handed it over."

"He is not yet sixteen, is he?" murmured Mary, imagining the lad's lonely struggle against such hard persuasion.

"And there is something about the Tower that makes human blood run cold. Maybe most of us would have done the same," suggested Osborne tolerantly.

Firebrace looked up at the tall, almost foppishly elegant figure with a sudden warmth of affection. "I can see *you* doing it!" he jeered laughingly, sore at the thought of having to leave him.

"Well, however the story leaked out, it is done now," sighed Mistress Wheeler, steering the conversation back to practical essentials. "And this morning the Governor gave orders that the King is to be moved into more secure apartments. So all the domestic turmoil is to do again. You and I will have to bestir ourselves, Mary."

Everyone was taken aback.

"Did he tell you *which* apartments?" asked Firebrace, quick as a gun shot.

"In the old part along the north wall, using the upper hall of the officers' quarters as a Presence Chamber. He and Colonel Hammond will simply change over, I imagine."

"Hammond should have been made a general for his strategy!" remarked Titus, speaking as if, for him at least, the whole matter was over. But Firebrace's energy, in spite of his dismissal, appeared to be unabated. "When is his Majesty to make the change?" he asked.

"It will take some time. The walls of those old rooms are in a bad state of repair, and there is all that fine arras from Hampton to be rehung."

For the first time Mary and Firebrace allowed themselves to exchanges glances. "What sort of windows are there?" he wanted to know.

"I am not sure," said Mistress Wheeler. "But in any case they are barred."

"There are two smaller windows on the stairs and one in a kind of lobby," volunteered Mary, who had often followed her father around in all manner of unexpected places.

"I must find some excuse to go there and reconnoitre. Hammond is allowing me to stay on for a few days. But for your sakes I dare not be seen with you now." Lest he should not see her again to say good-bye, Firebrace kissed Mistress Wheeler's hand, whispered something to Mary, and was gone.

"Why did the Governor allow him to stay?" asked Dowcett.

Titus shrugged. "Because he likes him personally, and the fellow has a persuasive way with him, perhaps. Or, more likely, because Hammond hoped that, given rope, he will inadvertently betray the rest of you."

"I doubt if it is such sound strategy after all, if only because it *does* give Harry more time," said Osborne.

"You mean he will plan the whole thing all over again from these new rooms before he goes?" asked Mary, torn between fear and pride.

"And leave us the joy of carrying it out, my pretty gosling!" laughed Osborne, rising and lazily stretching his long limbs.

They all wrung Titus's hand in silence. "To think I once doubted him!" sighed Mary, watching him walk dejectedly away, and considering how few of them would be left.

"You doubted me, too, I think?" said Osborne softly, as Mistress Wheeler and Dowcett followed him to the door. When Mary did not answer, he stood grinning down at her confusion; then, suddenly grown serious, held out his hand. "In spite of all my grievous shortcomings, I hope you trust me better now?"

Mary put her hand into his. "You know I do," she said, feeling that without him she could not face the lonely blank ahead.

But for the moment nothing mattered besides the fact that Harry Firebrace had whispered in passing, "I will see you again *somehow* before I go."

# CHAPTER EIGHTEEN

⸺⧉⸺

**M**ARY SLID CAUTIOUSLY DOWN the side of the vast bed and drew her cloak over her night shift. She paused to listen again to her aunt's deep even breathing; then crossed the room and silently drew the bolt. Barefoot, she felt her way along stairs and passages and once past a dozing sentry. Her heart thumped in her body when she reached Harry Firebrace's room; but it was the only way to see him alone.

To-morrow he would be gone. His shrug and lift of the brows at supper time, so eloquent of frustration, had told her that he was being too closely watched to manoeuvre a meeting. The King would be moving into his new apartments in a day or so, and Dowcett was desperate because he could find no opportunity for a final word with Firebrace about the new escape plans. And even Aunt Druscilla, who would have struck her senseless sooner than let her go traipsing like a trollop to a man's room at midnight, must realize how necessary it was for *someone* to have word with him.

A light showed beneath the door and Mary overrode every tenet of her up-bringing and pushed it open. If Harry would not endanger her by being seen in her company, she must go to him—whether as lover or confederate she was not sure. But she was honest enough to know that her heart drove her harder than her reason.

She found him standing by his bed in shirt and breeches, putting the finishing touches to the packing which his servant must have begun earlier in the day. He himself had been so busy about the King's affairs, she supposed, that he had not until now found a moment for his own. He looked up sharply and the smile she loved suddenly lighted his tired face.

"Mary!" he exclaimed, with a delight which she could not doubt. He dropped the holster he was holding and came to meet her, taking both her hands. "I did not dare to hope—that you would come *here*."

"I am not the prude men like Rolph think me." Freeing herself, she walked to the garment bestrewn bed, instinctively hiding her embarrassment in the performance of some practical task. "Not riding boots on top of your cravats!" she chided. "And cannot your man pack a coat better than this? It is your best blue velvet and will crumple so that it is not fit to be seen. Let me fold it properly for you." As methodically as if she were his wife she began putting order into the chaos he had created and packing his possessions into a leather saddlebag. Because she would never have the right to pack his things it gave her peculiar joy to do so, and the very domesticity of their occupation eased the memory of the last moments they had spent alone.

The softness of candlelight was on her face and Firebrace stood watching her, thinking how sweet such wifely administrations could be and how, during most of his married life, he had had to be dexterous for two. "You are so clever with your hands," he said, unaware that he was echoing a dictum of her aunt's which she still hated because at one time it had been used disparagingly.

Mary lingered over the last shirt and smiled tenderly at the gaudiness of a handkerchief. "But not so clever with my head as you. That is why one of us had to see you. The others, being more important, are being watched like felons until you go. But not even Captain Rolph would think of my coming to you in the middle of the night!"

Hearing the gallant laughter in her voice, Firebrace was filled with admiring gratitude. "Mary!" he exclaimed again, and could find no more to say—he who was so seldom tongue-tied!

With his arms about her she scorned to excuse her motives. "I had to come," she repeated with softer emphasis. Because no previous giving had drained the sweet, strong current of her desire,

the response of her senses made her defenceless against his close-
ness. Her hands reached up to caress his disordered hair; her eyes
and lips invited him. But that way, he knew, lay irrevocable regret.
Because he had inadvertently cheated her heart, all that was decent
in him resisted the temptation to enjoy and then discard her body.
How could any man so requite her loyal help? Remembering that
she was only seventeen and recognizing her innocence, he kissed
her with leashed passion and let her go.

With unsteady hands he began fastening the straps and buckles
of the saddlebag. With an effort he concentrated upon the more
practical reason for her nocturnal visit. "Will the King's new apartments be ready by to-morrow?" he asked, picking upon a question
almost at random.

"To-morrow or the next day, Aunt Druscilla says," Mary
answered automatically, her whole being concerned only with her
frustration. Without full understanding of what she had desired,
she knew that he would never take her now. She knew that this
was the real moment of their parting. Although they might go
on exchanging words for a while longer—might even catch sight
of each other the following day—they would never again come
into that close sharing of ecstasy. By her own quickened pulses she
gauged the cost of his abstinence; and, young as she was, appreciated vaguely that the incompleteness of their union would preserve
its quality of radiance.

"There is so much we must talk of," he was saying, with unnat-
ural briskness. He made her sit in his only chair before the hearth,
and knelt to coax a flame from the dying fire. Because the early
hours of the morning were cold he spread his travelling cloak about
her. "The file has come at last," he said, drawing a small piece of
metal from his pocket and throwing it lightly into her lap. "You or
Dowcett will have to find means to give it to his Majesty."

"I thought you intended to use acid."

"Mistress Whorwood sent it but it never arrived. Probably
Parliament got to know about that too."

"Who is this Mistress Whorwood I have been hearing about
lately?"

There was a flatness in their voices and the spirit seemed to have gone out of their enterprise. Firebrace was leaning against the narrow window of his room, too far away to touch her; and Mary had the feeling that they were both talking for safety's sake. Safety from their own passions, not the safety of Charles Stuart.

"Jane Whorwood used to be about the Court and is devoted to the King," he told her. "She got the stuff through a celebrated astrologer called Lilly. I should not care to have dealings with such men myself. But she is one of those people who is never daunted, and has written to his Majesty promising to send us some more by a different messenger. You are to look out for a lean peddler, bringing Woodstock gloves to the castle."

"I promised Master Dowcett I would find out somehow what you and the King have decided about the window."

"It will have to be the one in the bedchamber. There are too many people up and down the stairs. After all," mused Firebrace, remembering his nerve-racking hour in the courtyard, "it is all to the good that the windows on that side are on the outer wall. Once his Majesty has let himself down by a rope he will have only the moat to negotiate and the horses will be under the beech trees in the lane."

Firebrace was becoming absorbed in his project again and it was easier to seem to share some of the excitement. "The only buttress on that side is close beside his window," said Mary.

"And should provide a certain amount of cover. Don't forget to tell Osborne that we think it will be best for his Majesty to make his way close under the wall to the bowling green and get down to the outer escarpment from there."

"There is a kind of gully which should serve him."

"You know every blade of grass, don't you?"

"It is my home." There was a proud defiance in Mary's voice, daring anyone to imagine that she had ever dreamed of any other.

Either Firebrace did not notice it or knew of no comforting answer. "And there Osborne and Worsley will be waiting as before. But this time it will be under the north wall—instead of the south," he said, on that note of contentment with which any craftsman, having done his best, may lay down his tools. Hearing the chapel clock strike, he roused himself and took his cloak from Mary. His hands were steady and he no longer took such care to avoid touching her. "For initiative and resolution this Mistress Jane Whorwood is really worth all of us put together," he said, as Mary stood up. "If she should write you or even come here, trust her in everything, Mary. Dowcett knows her. He will tell you the same."

Mary had no present interest in Mistress Jane Whorwood. "Will you go straight to the mainland?" she asked.

He walked with her to the door, his manner resolutely unemotional. "I shall try to stay a few days in Newport. I should like to see the end of this."

"Take care of that fiend Moses," she warned. "Perhaps Master Trattle will take you in."

"I will go there."

"And then you will be going back to—her?"

Firebrace was careful to answer her question only in its literal sense. "Not while I can be of any use here on the Hampshire coast. Next Sunday is the night his Majesty has decided upon."

"Not a Monday this time?" A presentiment of calamity lent fear to the words.

"It is a matter of moon and tides. I have consulted Newland."

"I hope you will be—somewhere close."

Seeing her shiver he turned at the door and laid a comforting arm about her shoulders. "Do not be frightened, sweetheart. Osborne and Dowcett will make all the arrangements. There will be nothing for you to do on the night of the escape unless it be to leave some door unlocked, as you did for me."

"Who will deal with the sentries?"

"Leave everything to Osborne. And never be deceived by his pretensions to indolent lunacy. He is far cooler headed than I in an emergency."

"And the Captain of the Guard?" thought Mary. Once again Rolph was the incalculable factor. In his zeal he had taken to going round the battlements several times a night, her father said. But she would not add to Firebrace's anxiety by telling him so. "I must go back now in case my aunt should wake," she said instead.

He wanted to accompany her, but both of them knew that it would be madness.

"You think you will remember? Next Sunday, the bedroom window, the peddler, the gulley by the bowling green?" he recapitulated quickly.

"Yes, I shall remember—everything," said Mary, trying to learn his smile so that she could keep it for ever in her heart.

"You have been wonderful. God bless you always." The door was open, and the cold dark passage yawned before her. "I shall see you again," he whispered. "Somehow I shall come back."

They did not meet again before he left the castle. The workmen from Newport had finished preparing the old rooms in the north wing for the King's use, and Mary was up early seeing that the maids swept and polished every corner before the furniture was brought in. Then there was the arranging of it, under her aunt's supervision, while Charles himself was out on the bowling green. At the Governor's orders an extra bar had been fitted in the window and a shelf built for the King's books. Master Herbert himself brought in the precious volumes and arranged them while men with ladders rehung the arras and the bed tester, and soon the maids were scurrying back and forth with ewers and basins and bedclothes. If Mary's face was pale and her eyes smudged with sleeplessness, no one had time to notice it.

"The Governor does not seem to mind our being in the room by ourselves any more," she said, when the others had gone and she was helping her aunt to make the royal bed.

"I imagine he has more disturbing things to think about," said Mistress Wheeler. "And then there were all those letters you say he found in the King's desk. He must have realized they went on being delivered after you were forbidden to bring the linen into the room."

Mary looked across the room at the arras now covering the solid thickness of mediaeval stone and thought sadly that there would no longer be any way of slipping them through the wall. A casement stood open and as she stood with raised head she could hear the clip-clop of horses. The sheet she was unfolding slipped to the floor. Had it been the Canopy of State she would have let it fall. She ran to the window and was just in time to see Harry Firebrace and his servant trotting down the lane. She could see their heads bobbing up and down behind the greening beech trees on the other side of the moat.

"The King's lace-edged sheet on the floor!" scolded Mistress Wheeler. "Whatever are you staring at, child?"

"At Harry Firebrace going away." The trees and the sharp descent of the lane stole him from Mary's sight. She drew in her own head and went back listlessly to the bedside.

"Pass me the other pillowcase. I do not know what we shall do without him," said Druscilla Wheeler.

"No," agreed Mary, plumping up the King's pillow.

After her aunt had gone she stayed to straighten the body linen in the chest at the bottom of the bed because it had been shifted about in the moving; and presently Brett came in with a taper to light the fire. Again she thought she heard hoof beats and half rose from the floor where she was kneeling. But this time it was only someone hammering. It went on for some time accompanied by the sound of men's voices. She had not slept all night and her nerves were taut as fiddle-strings. She had never felt like this before. "What is that hammering?" she cried in exasperation.

"Hammerin'?" repeated Brett, at his deafest.

"Surely you can hear it? All that noise underneath the King's window!" She got up from her knees, went to the window again and leaned out. Two soldiers were digging holes in the sharp slope of the grassy escarpment, while two more drove in stakes. Downer, the head carpenter, was measuring a pile of planks while his mate sawed them into equal lengths. "Come and look, Brett. Whatever can they be doing on so steep a bit of ground?"

But old Brett, who had spoken to the men when he fetched the donkeys in from grazing, came reluctantly; and before he joined her Mary saw that Captain Rolph was down there directing operations. He was leaning against the bastion looking remarkably pleased with himself, and when he heard her voice he looked up and grinned and pulled off his steel helmet in ironical imitation of the way Osborne had swept off his plumed hat to her in the courtyard. Mary drew in her head quickly, pushed Brett impatiently out of the way, slammed down the lid of the great carved chest, and went up to the housekeeper's room in the other wing.

There, as she had hoped, she found her father. He had been present at the friendly send-off given to the popular young Groom of the Bedchamber, and had hurried to be with her as soon as he was off duty. He had expected to find her tearful, but not so tempestuous. "What are Downer and the rest of them doing on the escarpment immediately outside the King's bedroom window?" she asked brusquely.

Floyd was slow in answering. He was watching her stricken face. "They are building a platform," he said.

His sister swung round from the inventory of royal chattels she was checking. "A platform?" On that slope? What in the world for?"

"To mount a guard on."

"You mean—all day?"

"And all night. Three sentries, I heard one of those cocksure lieutenants say."

Aunt and niece exchanged glances and the older woman sank down on the edge of a chair. For once she was shaken out of her habitual composure. "Oh, Hammond is clever! How clever the man is! " she wailed, her deep voice husky with tiredness.

"Unless that fox Rolph suggested it," said her brother.

"Then everything that Harry worked for—" began Mary, forgetting that she must protect her father from participating in their plans. She stopped short, met his understanding smile, and ran sobbing into his arms.

# CHAPTER NINETEEN

ⷦⷦⷦ

ALTHOUGH IT WAS A May evening the King was arranging his personal possessions in his new quarters instead of taking the air. The weather had turned cloudy and there were few people on the bowling green. Osborne and Dowcett, hoping for an opportunity to be alone, were engaged in a desultory game of singles; while on the next rink Anthony Mildmay, finding himself odd man out, was fulfilling a friendly promise to teach Mary to play.

"How is she doing?" called Dowcett, as they passed each other halfway down the green.

"She has a marvellously straight eye," encouraged Mildmay, who had always been particularly kind to her.

"My father taught me to shoot when I was twelve," laughed Mary, "but a pistol is not weighed more on one side than the other!" She was evidently finding it difficult to control the bias, but Osborne was glad to hear her laugh again. She had often watched her father and his friends playing nine-pins and could not fail to feel flattered that a middle-aged friend of the King's should spare time to teach her a game traditionally reserved for the gentry. But then Mildmay always called her Mistress Mary, meticulously remembering that although she was a sergeant's daughter she was niece by marriage of the late Sir William Wheeler.

As the sun moved westward beyond the gatehouse tower a chilly wind blew up, and people who had been strolling about or watching the play drifted back to the castle. Soon Mildmay himself had to go in to wash and change before carving the King's meat at supper. Mary would have put away the woods and followed him, but the two men on the next rink stopped playing as soon as they were alone and Dowcett called to her to stay. "It becomes still more impossible to talk indoors now that this Cromwell watchdog has been appointed Groom of the Bedchamber in Harry Firebrace's place," he complained.

"One cannot help admiring Hammond's cleverness there," remarked Osborne, stooping to pick up the jack.

"Yet even that fresh difficulty is not insurmountable. After all, the man must eat and sleep *sometimes*. But there is nothing we can do about this accursed platform."

"Except wine or bribe the sentries," said Osborne.

Mary looked at him in surprise, a bowl poised on either palm. Like Dowcett, she had supposed that the guarded platform finished all chance of carrying on with Firebrace's plan. "You mean that in spite of all these new precautions you would risk another attempt?"

"Only because I have recently learned of an even graver risk." A few drops of rain were beginning to fall and Osborne, who usually seemed to regard himself as immune from suspicion, drew them both into the privacy of the little pavilion. He relieved Mary of her two woods, then loped swiftly back across the green to gather up the rest so that if they were interrupted they might appear to be wiping them and putting them back on their racks. "The boredom of my hours with Rolph has at last borne fruit," he told them. "Believe me, it's hard work trying to drag information from a Puritan who gives nothing away in his cups. But since Harry was sent away Rolph has taken me closer into his confidence. With genuine intent to console me, no doubt, as well as to gain his own ends. The man has his points, oddly enough, in spite of his murderous mind."

"Murderous?" echoed Mary.

Osborne stood there carelessly throwing up the jack and catching it, but there was a grim set to his jaw. "He has invited me to join him in a pleasant little plot to kill the King."

"*Nom d'un chien!*" Dowcett stayed poised, horrified, in the act of swinging his short Parisian cape about his shoulders; and Mary felt befouled because she had more than once been held in the would-be murderer's arms. "But surely the Governor—"

"The Governor is not to know," explained Osborne. "Rolph excuses his villainy by telling me that some of the more rabid elements in the army have already offered Hammond a bribe if he will put the King out of their way by having his food poisoned. And that Hammond has not even deigned to answer."

"The only way to treat such an insult!" declared Dowcett, particularly appalled because catering for the royal table was his responsibility.

"But you cannot expect a man of Rolph's mentality to appreciate that. He thinks Hammond ignored them because he is afraid of losing a well-paid appointment which he himself covets."

"And you think the story of the bribe is true?"

"Probably, because Rolph seems confident that the army will make him a colonel at least if he outwits Hammond and does the gruesome deed for them. So he has asked me to try to persuade the King to escape. Imagine being asked to do that by our precious Captain of the Guard and having to keep a straight face!"

In spite of their repugnance the other two had to smile.

"How easy it could be with his connivance!" sighed Dowcett.

"He will connive at nothing until he is sure. In fact, he will watch more closely than ever because he is afraid his Majesty might get away before he can arrange it. His idea is to lure him into some hiding place under pretext of taking him to a ship for France, and then—as he so self-righteously expresses it—to 'root the evil man out of the land of the living'."

"But surely, however much you may have hoodwinked him, he does not seriously think that *you* would do *that*?" exclaimed Mary, horrified by such wickedness.

"It is scarcely flattering, I admit," grinned Osborne. "But it seems he has already found someone who will. He has not yet trusted me with our fellow-conspirator's name; but there are to be three of us, I understand."

"Heaven defend us, have we another murderer in our midst?" said Dowcett.

"I wonder if it could be Thomas Rudy, whom he brought over with him and who so cheerfully runs all his errands?" speculated Mary. "My father says that although the man is popular he stirs up more trouble than anyone else in the barracks and is never short of money—though the plausible wretch seldom gives a groat to his wife!"

"If so, you should be in fine company, Osborne!" Dowcett went to the door of the pavilion to make sure that no one was about. "What did you tell Rolph?"

"That I would do my utmost to encourage his Majesty's escape and that he would hear more about it later. He wanted me to take an oath on it."

"And did you?" asked Mary; and for a moment had a glimpse of his contemptuous anger.

"I told him that for centuries his betters had accepted the bare word of an Osborne. Whereat he became disgustingly servile. Ah well," he went on, recapturing his usual debonair manner, "Titus will be ready at any time with horses on the other side, and Harry knows of our new dilemma and will be working from London, so we ought to bring off an escape, and Rolph will certainly hear of it—although too late for him to interfere, please God!"

They could see Major Cromwell's square-shouldered figure descending the long flight of steps from the keep, and dared stay no longer. With Gallic politeness Dowcett transferred his cloak to Mary's shoulders and they went out into the rain. "We should like you to tell Mistress Wheeler of this," he said, as they walked back towards the castle. "And I am sure she will be relieved to know that the ship Mistress Whorwood has chartered lies ready in the Medway. Explain to her that since the Prince of Wales left Jersey for France in accordance with the King's wishes, the hospitality of my country is more strained; and it is thought best to convey his Majesty to his eldest daughter's court in Holland."

"What is this energetic Mistress Whorwood like?" asked Mary, finding herself more able to take an interest in the lady than she had been when Harry Firebrace first mentioned her.

"A tall, forthright, dependable sort of woman. Everything, in fact, that the treacherous Lady Carlisle is not. In riding breeches, Jane Whorwood might well pass for a man. Not unhandsome either, though unfortunately her face is covered with—how do you say them?—*taches de rousseur*."

"Freckles." Osborne supplied the word absently, his mind evidently on his plans; and before reaching the postern gate they parted company and went their separate ways.

Several days passed before Mary saw either of them to speak to again, and still fresh difficulties presented themselves. The darkest night and the most likely guard never seemed to synchronize. Jane Whorwood had been obliged to change the berth of the ship when suspicion fell on her skipper because of the length of time he had spent unloading; but Firebrace sent word that he would meet the King's party at a certain point on the road and direct them to the new and more secluded mooring. Trattle had managed to convey the reassuring message to the housekeeper along with his account for yeast delivered to the castle bakery.

News of Firebrace's doings, however impersonal, was precious to Mary. News that he was working in conjunction with Jane Whorwood meant that he had not yet returned to his wife—and that, to her shame, she found doubly precious. When all the bustle of the King's moving was over, she was able to return to her normal occupations with a better heart. Seeing the Reverend Troughton in earnest theological discussion with the King reminded her that it was days since she had cleaned the altar plate, a duty of which she had lately relieved her aunt. And because she had a longing to be alone she gathered up some soft linen rags and went across the courtyard to the old chapel of St. Nicholas.

But it seemed she was not to be alone. As her eyes accustomed themselves to dim light after sunshine she became aware of a man kneeling in the quiet shadow of a pillar, and glancing a second time at the tall figure with the reverently bent brown head she saw to her surprise that it was Richard Osborne. It seemed difficult to connect his usual careless pose with devoutness; but she supposed that he might be asking a blessing on their coming enterprise.

Not wishing to disturb him she picked up the ewer from the font and withdrew to a narrow bench in the porch. She could feel the warmth of the sun and hear the birds singing as she worked, and before long Osborne joined her there.

"So my being here has driven you outside?" he said, as taken aback as she.

"No, no. It was just that—I was surprised to see you."

"To see me praying?"

I suppose so."

"Though who should need more desperately than I to seek a better way of life?" he said. So perhaps it had not been the King's escape that he had been praying about after all. He stood bare-headed, watching her with that quizzical lift of an eyebrow. "I suppose people have warned you that my reputation is dangerous?"

Mary breathed upon the ewer and gave its fat sides a final rub. Though other women might fear for their virtue in his company, she herself had always felt remarkably safe. "Perhaps it is mostly their invention," she suggested.

"They do not underestimate my vices, of course."

"Neither do you encourage the world to do so."

"Touché," he admitted with a smile, and sat down beside her. "For their sins my forebears have always held important positions at Court, and like most young men in that sort of family I was sent far too young on a tour of Europe with a tutor who had little control over me. And then—like most younger sons—I was placed in a nobleman's household with a view to a position at Court. My father persuaded that fabulously rich old libertine, Lord Wharton, to take me. It was considered a very good move socially, but my mother begged almost with her dying breath that I should not be sent there." He stopped short, as though aghast at his own garrulity. "I assure you I have never before tried to excuse myself to anyone—"

Mary sat with bent head, compassion and understanding in her heart. Compassion had always flourished there, but a measure of understanding had seeded itself from her own new suffering. Even if God had denied her the lover of her choice, she thought, He had been generous in allowing her to inspire liking in a variety of people. "Did you adore her?" she asked, not knowing what else to say.

"My mother?"

"Yes."

"She was the only woman who has ever really meant anything to me. She had a tender-hearted goodness which I have been seeking ever since—until now." He added the last two words so softly that Mary was not quite sure whether she had heard aright. For the first time she wondered half incredulously whether he had sought her out of late for his own sake and not, as she had supposed, because he was sorry for her for vicariously accepting a situation which was in some sort his friend's responsibility. Osborne sat silent a while and then, as if to contradict the serious mood which lingered with him from his prayers, he challenged her flippantly. "Surprised as you may have been to find me in church on a Monday morning, you cannot accuse me of being altogether godless. Consider how patiently I sat last Sunday through one of those denunciatory sermons Rolph delights in, and how edified they all were when I commended the preacher afterwards! His text, if I remember rightly, was 'Vengeance is mine, I will repay, saith the Lord.' If God is really as vindictive as they make out there can be little chance for sinners like me!"

"Are you so great a sinner?" smiled Mary, comparing him with her hateful recollections of Rolph. "Surely kindness and tolerance count for something? Frances and I were once reprimanded by the vicar of Newport for dancing in the Square, and she was brave enough to remind him that Miriam danced before the Lord. I thought it clever of her, but he only told her not to be pert. These Puritans are so certain they are right!"

"But so, for that matter, is the King," pointed out Osborne. "There might have been no civil war had he not tried to force the Church of England Prayer Book on the Presbyterian Scots."

Mary had heard the same opinion expressed far more crudely in courtyard and kitchen of late, but she was surprised and not a little shocked to hear it from the lips of a Royal cavalier. Her aunt and the Trattles never had criticized the King, nor would they ever say a good word for the Parliamentarians, and until recently she had accepted their opinions unquestioningly. Before the King came the whole rebellion had seemed so remote—just something that was happening over on the mainland. But now, having seen the extremes of hatred and fervour and danger to which men were driven by the strength of opposing convictions, she felt that it was something which a grown woman should understand. She had heard people discussing the Long Parliament and the Rump Parliament, and the removal of the Court to Oxford, and the battles at Marston Moor and Nazeby, of course; but even her father, who admired certain aspects of Cromwell's discipline, had not really been able to explain to her the rights of it all. Whenever she had ventured to discuss the King with Harry that dedicated look had come into his face. For him the King could do no wrong; or if he could, it was one's duty to defend it. But here beside her was Richard Osborne, a man who must have heard other people's views in London and in foreign countries and who always spoke with cool detachment. Perhaps he could explain what had always puzzled her—how one side or the other could be completely wrong when each felt so passionately. If only he did not laugh at her, and had the patience to put things simply…

"Of course I know about the war, but how did it all *begin*!" she asked, laying down the ewer. "I am not clever like Frances, and can only read the simplest things. We scarcely ever see the London news-sheets here, and when we do they are so violently for one side or the other that I can make little sense of them."

"Oh, my precious Mary, which of us can? I suspect that if some of us pretend to understand all the forces which have brought England to this bitter pass it is only because we lack your refreshing honesty."

He was not laughing at her at all. There was no jibling on that wide, reckless mouth of his and she had noticed, when she first met him, the kindness of his eyes. Womanlike, she was more interested in the protagonists than in the facts. "It seems so strange that a king who beheaded his wives should have been allowed to go on reigning, and yet all this cruelty should have been shown to a good man like King Charles."

"A good man does not always make the best kind of king. For instance, the late King Jamie's ways may have been coarse, but he was a realist. He knew just how far he could push his subjects, both here and in Scotland. Whereas King Charles has always been so hedged about by ideals and dignity that he does not understand when he is pushing them too far. It is only fair, of course, to remember that he was not trained for kingship."

"You mean until his elder brother died?"

"Yes. I have heard my father say that before then Charles was left up in Scotland with his tutor. He stammered and his leg always dragged a bit. But when he became Prince of Wales and came down to London he made valiant efforts to conquer both disabilities. By sheer determination he made himself the best horseman in the two kingdoms, so that seeing him mounted one forgets that he is a little lame or small. That is the kind of courage he has. The kind that draws out the devotion of men in personal touch with him like Harry. And yet his Majesty can be so painfully irresolute over some things."

This was the sort of thing Mary wanted to hear—the personal aspect of the struggle rather than the political. "He has never loved any woman but the Queen, they say. Is she so very beautiful?"

"Not beautiful. But charming and vivacious and—a little too capable."

"Then why do people hate her so?"

"Because she is French and a Catholic—both obviously unfair reasons. But also because she was always meddling and trying to get the best appointments for her friends. Parliamentarians like Hampden who really had the good of the country at heart deplored her influence at Court."

"Then was it she who caused most of the trouble?"

"I would say that money and religion were the two main causes. I am sure no sovereign ever wanted more earnestly to rule well than King Charles, but he believed so firmly in his divine right that everything had to be cut to his pattern and kept under his personal authority. So he tried to rule without Parliament, with the result that he was never voted adequate money to carry through his reforms, and the still more dangerous result that he began levying taxes in all manner of arbitrary and unpopular ways. There was all that trouble, for instance, about Ship Money being levied on inland towns."

"I remember the outcry about Tonnage and Poundage. The Customs men were always talking about it."

"Yes. But the bitterest quarrels always seem to grow out of differences in religion. He and Archbishop Laud tried to force everyone—in Scotland, Ireland, and Wales as well—to worship according to the rubric of the Church of England. They wanted the churches to have dignity and beauty—candles and vestments and the altar in the sanctuary instead of the Communion being taken from a table in the middle of the church as many people wanted it. The Puritans accused his Majesty—quite unjustly—of favouring Rome because he was civil to his wife's Catholic friends. And so God-fearing families, sooner than attend the Established Church, began holding prayer meetings of their own. Laud interfered and the bitterness grew."

"We heard about the Presbyterian women up in Scotland throwing the kirk stools at the Anglican preacher's head."

"Of course there were many more issues after that. And then we had all those years of civil war."

"With so many young men killed! And even now—"

"Now, as we all know, the whole thing has rolled beyond the control of those who began it, and the power is often in the hands of men who either want it only for revenge or at best are not sufficiently accustomed to it to use it without cruelty."

Mary sat thinking over what he had said while outside the sound of marching feet from barracks to guardroom seemed to emphasize the King of England's sorry plight. She got up from the bench with a sigh, remembering that she had still the altar plate to clean. From where she stood she could see inside the little chapel which had remained so peacefully outside the worst of such stormy arguments, and thinking of the kind of sermon that Osborne had had to listen to she was thankful that here, at least outwardly, things had been left unchanged. Things which the King stood for and which the Governor, whatever his personal preferences, had not suffered his chaplain to alter very much. Then her gaze came back speculatively to her companion. "You do not regard the King with the same devotion as Harry does," she said.

Since they were alone, he answered without caution. "Not with the kind of devotion which blinds me."

"Yet you risk so much for him."

"For the monarchy—the Stuart cause—for the civilized order of existence to which my kind is accustomed. You must remember that I was never a Parliamentarian like Harry. They say that converts to any cause outrun the rest." Osborne stopped being serious and went on speaking with a kind of exasperated amusement. "I could wish sometimes that his Majesty did not complicate our efforts by writing so many letters and instructions—or that he had the common touch as well as the Stuart charm. Like the younger Charles—"

Like any other girl, Mary was full of curiosity about the young Prince of Wales whose adolescence and young manhood had been so full of unfortunate adventures. "Did you know him?" she asked.

"I fought with him when he was a lanky lad of sixteen—before he was sent to Jersey. He was dragged from battlefield to battlefield, but he never lost his cheerful sense of the ridiculous."

There was a warmth in Osborne's voice which made her look up quickly. His smile showed reminiscent affection for a fellow human being rather than any blind devotion. "And now as an exile I suppose he will be dragged from country to country," he said regretfully. "It will probably mar him much as I was marred."

# CHAPTER TWENTY

ON THE LAST SUNDAY in May Osborne left the castle early. He was supping with the Leighs at Thorley Manor, so he had told all and sundry, and he had leave to spend the night. And before going he made as much commotion as possible. Just as he reached the gatehouse he remembered that he had a long ride before him and sent his servant back for his thickest riding cloak. Captain Rolph sauntered over from his quarters to twit him about forsaking gay colours for an elegant new suit tailored in black like his royal master's, and the two of them stood talking and laughing familiarly. Islanders on guard pricked up their ears hopefully when they overheard Osborne remind their Captain facetiously that he ought to allow them an extra pint of liquor next day because it would be the Prince of Wales' birthday, and some of the Model Army men looked sourly disapproving when he went on to describe the luscious charms of Barnabas Leigh's young sister. Before the cloak could be found the new horse Osborne had bought was plunging and rearing impatiently. So after all he rode off by himself, calling to the guard that he would not need the cloak and that his man could have the evening off.

Once at the bottom of the lane and on the road to Thorley, he branched off left in the direction of Gatcombe and rode leisurely to sup with Edward Worsley. And as he went his expression sobered and he looked to his brace of pistols.

He hated having to leave the two women and Dowcett to see through the first part of the scheme, but there were only the four of them left now. "Keep about as late as possible in case there should be anything you can do to hearten Dowcett," he had advised Mistress Wheeler and her niece. And already he regretted having said that because if any heartening were needed it should have been for them. He had almost quarrelled with Harry once because of the risks he had allowed Mary to run. But she was so quick and calm and sensible, whereas Dowcett, for all his zeal and courage, was excitable and highly strung.

Well, there was nothing she would be likely to be called upon to do during this momentous night, he supposed; nor anything more he himself could do for that matter, until he and Worsley should find themselves actually helping the King up the far side of the escarpment into freedom. Apart from the fact that the escape would be carried out from the north wall instead of the south, and that there would be no courtyard to cross, everything was to be carried out so much in accordance with Harry Firebrace's original plans that playing one's individual part in it had become almost routine. Walking his horse along a narrow woodland path which Worsley had shown him, he went over the stages of the plan much as Harry must have done. John Newland down at the creek with a boat. Titus on the Hampshire coast with horses. A safe night's lodging arranged for him and the King at Arundel. Harry waiting on the road somewhere in Kent, and Jane Whorwood's ship all set for Holland. And this time the bar of the window had been successfully loosened, so that the King would only need to lift it. The only other difference was the matter of the sentries. He and Dowcett had decided that, since their co-operation was needed rather than their negligence, to fuddle them would be useless. Most reluctantly they had been obliged to take the three men into their confidence.

This time they had to use money instead of wine. A hundred pounds apiece, raised by Sir John Oglander, the Worsleys, and himself. Worsley had it in safe keeping at the manor. It would mean a fortune to such men—particularly to an islander. And two of the men whom they had persuaded to it were islanders—the same two pikemen, Wenshall and Featherstone, whom Harry had made so drunk before. They were Sergeant Floyd's men, of the original garrison, and had no liking for Puritan ways. If only he could have had Floyd himself for their third man! He liked him and the King had suggested him as being a man with initiative whom they could thoroughly trust; and now, having come so close to the climax of the adventure, Osborne felt that he should have insisted upon approaching him. But the man was Mary's father; and Mistress Wheeler, who had helped them so loyally, had stipulated that he should not be drawn into the affair. And so he had persuaded instead a recently recruited young Londoner whose father had been killed fighting on the Royalist side at Nazeby, and who was baited and wretched in the Cromwellian army. A thin, sandy-haired young man called Tilling, whose ambition was to buy a mercery business in Cheapside, and whose eyes had lighted up like pale agates at thought of the money.

Osborne found it was good to be in a private household again with the kindly family at Gatcombe Manor. But relaxation in that homely atmosphere was all too short. After supper the spare horse was saddled, and boots and a pistol brought for the King; and as soon as it was dusk Worsley led him through his own woods and by various sequestered field paths back to Carisbrooke, where they took up their appointed place beside the lane.

"It is not nearly so dark as we had hoped," whispered Worsley, looking up in the direction of the King's unlighted window. "I could almost see anyone climbing out."

"We decided not to use the rope after all. It is only a ten-foot drop and his Majesty can easily let himself down on to one of the sentries' shoulders."

"Hammond will not expect any activity to-night since he has heard so much about your courting Barnabas's sister at Thorley!"

"Everything should work out well this time," whispered back Osborne cheerfully.

But in spite of an eventuality important enough to change history, the ordinary events of everyday life went on.

In the early hours of that Sunday morning, Libby's baby had been born, and Rudy had been allowed to go down to the village to see her. The child was lusty and a boy. So in his parental pride Tom Rudy had called in at the "Castle Inn" and brought back enough wine for his comrades on night-watch to celebrate the event The barracks had become even noisier than they usually were on a Sunday night, when disputes over the day's sermons invariably ended in a brawl; and although Wenshall, Featherstone, and Tilling saw no particular cause for rejoicing over the reproduction of a Rudy, they were only too glad to avail themselves of his generosity. All three drank deeply in order to keep up their spirits for a night's adventure which each of them secretly feared. Meanwhile Rudy, more full of himself than of wine, mounted a table in order to harangue his fellows. He excelled himself in exposing all the shortcomings, real and imaginary, of the King, and kept the barrack-room in an uproar with all manner of amusing anecdotes which had been going the rounds of London taverns about the defeated cavaliers. It was the personal kind of propaganda which men who would not listen to the preachers' violent sermons lapped up with a drink and an easy laugh. "What does any man, just because he happens to be borne a Stuart, need with a Gentleman Carver, a Gentleman Usher, and a Groom of the Bedchamber to draw on his breeches for him? And why should all these royal minions bring servants of their own, when we who are trained soldiers have to clean out the stables?" demanded the glib orator. "Look at that idle, feather-brained fop, milord Rakehell Osborne! Allowed out any night he feels like wenching. Apes his master in a new black suit, and then sends his servant back for his best cloak to dazzle some innocent island girl he was boasting about seducing. And in the end is too impatient to get to his lechery to wait for the poor fellow!"

Because they were drinking his wine the three sentries due for platform duty had to listen. By sheer chance Rudy had picked upon the very man who had offered them their bribes. And had they not all heard tales of the Gentleman Usher's levity?

"You reckon this Osborne is to be depended on?" whispered

Wenshall behind his hand, huddling closer to his two comrades on a corner bench.

"Real gentleman, he be. Not the new, blusterin' sort. Didn't his uncle hold that gurt Guernsey fortress for the longest siege in the war?" Featherstone reassured him, with more certainty than he really felt.

"Don't seem right ter me, his goin' out wenchin' and leavin' us to do his dangerous work," grumbled Tilling.

"Anyways, he b'aint here to know whether we does it or not," muttered Wenshall.

Rudy, still astride the table, was well launched upon his usual tirade against the privileged classes whose lives were all pleasure and no work because they had the money, and for a time the three men in the corner exchanged congratulatory winks, for would not they soon find themselves in that felicitous company? They would be able to buy themselves all the boats and cattle and wine and wenches they wanted. And a trip to London to see some of the fine sights Rudy was always bragging about, maybe, the two islanders thought. Featherstone's ideas of pleasure could go no further, but Wenshall's livelier imagination had begun to work in a more sombre and immediate direction. "Master Osborne did say as how they would bear us out if we was to swear we saw nothin'; but come to think on't, even a hundred pounds b'aint much good to a man once he be a noddy," he remarked, with the gloomy kind of prognostication which drink always engendered in him.

"Wot's a noddy?" asked the pale-faced Cockney.

"A dead 'un," said Featherstone.

Tilling took a deeper swig at his tankard, hoping to imbibe some much-needed courage. He was young and, unlike Featherstone, suffered from a surplus of imagination. Moreover, he stood in vast awe of the keen-eyed Captain of the Guard, who had frequently sharpened his wits on the subject of his inadequacy with a musket. He wanted that mercer's shop and a girl he knew in Barking. He wanted to see his mother again. And he definitely did not want to be a noddy. He passed his tankard to be refilled. Seen through a haze of Burgundy this Rudy fellow was a good sort and free with his money. He was also a fellow-Londoner and probably knew what he was talking about better than a lot of outlandish yokels whose speech he could scarcely understand. That fine big gentleman and his fellow sentries had talked as if letting your prisoner escape were an easy way to get all that money, but now he was not so sure. He would give anything not to go on duty to-night. Perhaps if he could go sick or have some sort of accident—something that would incapacitate him, but nothing serious, of course. Drawing his knife and screwing up his courage, he made a slash at his trigger finger, but his hands were unsteady and the knife slipped, cutting deeper than he had intended. The blood gushed out and someone guffawed at his clumsiness. And because he was not accustomed to the expensive kind of French wine which was smuggled into the Wight he was soon lying prone along the bench with red blood and red Burgundy dripping unheeded to the floor. His two mates were in no state to consider the consequences, and in any case were now too deeply engaged in some earnest half-whispered discussion to heed him.

He was still lying there when Sergeant Floyd came in to quell the noise. Mistress Hammond had complained of it and the Reverend Troughton had added his opinion that such an uproar was a disgrace to a Christian castle on the Sabbath. "That trouble-maker Rudy again!" thought Floyd, weary of this new, contentious world. But remembering that the girl Libby had given birth to a son he was as lenient as possible. He made sure that all of them would be sober enough to turn out for night duty—all except one young fool in the corner who was too far gone even to come to attention. "What's the matter with him?" he asked, seeing that pool of blood.

"He's cut hisself," volunteered the fool who had guffawed.

"Any road, Sergeant, he be too drunk to go on duty," said one of his own men more helpfully.

"An' what now if us gets a tale-bearing Roundhead posted along o' us this night?" thought Wenshall and Featherstone. And the hideous probability became a deciding factor in their whispered discussion.

"Put the fellow in the guardroom lock-up," ordered Sergeant Floyd.

Seeing the cut was more serious than he had thought, he followed them and bound it up himself, and before he had finished, the young man, still maudlin and weak from loss of blood, sat up and begged to be kept in the lock-up until morning. Floyd had no intention of doing anything else, but he brought his lantern and looked at him more closely. Tilling was not one of his men but his experience of all types told him that here was a weak but decent lad, with a spot of real trouble on his mind. He asked a leading question or two and because his manner was less bullying than the recently arrived sergeants' he soon had the whole amazing story. "You'd certainly be better selling silk than playing at soldiering!" he told Tilling brusquely, wondering whether Osborne had picked on him because of the account the lad had to square with Parliament for his loss at Nazeby or merely because he and Dowcett had been unable to find anyone else. He locked the door and walked up and down outside for a while digesting the information which had come to him so fortuitously.

So there was to be another bid for the King's escape to-night? He had always suspected that some of the royal household discussed their plans in his sister's room, but had half hoped that with Firebrace's dismissal their enthusiasm would have waned. His own private opinion, based upon his knowledge of the Captain of the Guard's efficiency, was that the time had passed when such an escape might have been safely effected. The Governor knew too much about their previous efforts. But since they meant to try again to-night his first thought was for Mary, and how far she might be involved. He guessed why Osborne had gone out, and hoped with all his heart that the King would get away this time. Going about his duties, Floyd had heard enough to know how bitterly some of the propaganda-ridden soldiery blamed King Charles for the state of the country and for their own long exile from home, and how willingly a small minority of them, inflamed by such leaders as Rolph and Rudy, would treat his Majesty with violence.

He wished that Firebrace and Osborne had taken him into their confidence in the first place and asked him to help. There were so many ways in which he could have done so. But he suspected with a glow of gratitude why they had not. And now, with a part of their scheme come by accident into his hands, it rested with him to decide for himself how much he would swerve from his immediate and apparent duty, how much he would risk.

If now at the last moment, and without time to sound him, any other man were to be sent as the third guard he would almost certainly give Wenshall and Featherstone away and jeopardize the King's last chance of escape. So instead of calling another muske- teer or pikeman Floyd decided to go himself. He wished he could have had a word with Dowcett about it first, but it was impossible. Floyd had once helped Charles Stuart to fire off the castle cannon, and he was prepared to help him in a much bigger adventure now. And if there should be nothing in particular which he could do, at least his presence on the platform should steady Wenshall and Featherstone more than that frightened Cockney lad's.

The guard was due to change in half an hour. His thoughts heavy within him, Floyd went back to the barracks to make sure that all was quiet and to get Tilling's musket. He had been round by the guardroom lock-up longer than he intended and had not seen Wenshall and Featherstone cross the courtyard and slink in at the back door of the Governor's house.

The long summer evening had faded into night at last. But for Floyd's sister and daughter there was no thought of going to bed. Mary could not stay still indoors and had gone to the wellhouse. Sitting on the coping of the well with the door ajar she could see whoever came and went dimly outlined against the lesser dark outside. Dowcett, she knew, had made some excuse to pass the sentry at the north postern so that he might take a final look round beneath the walls and make sure that Worsley and Osborne were in their appointed place on the other side of the escarpment. Waiting for his return, Mary allowed her thoughts to project themselves into the future. By this time to-morrow the King would have seen Harry, and she felt that their meeting would be some sort of link between Harry and herself. "The King will tell him how I managed to put that letter behind the arras almost under Major Cromwell's nose, and how happy it made him to hear of the young Duke of York's escape," she thought. "And he may tell him, too, how I went on helping as I promised." Sitting there in that quiet place which had so often been their happy rendezvous, she could almost see the way Harry's face would light up with approval.

She heard Dowcett's footsteps and softly called him inside. It was too dark in there to see his face, but she knew at once by his restless movements that he was worried. "I saw Rolph out there," he said. "Isn't it enough that he must needs sit at the foot of the King's stairway half the day, without poking round outside the walls at night? Do you suppose he suspects anything?"

"He is much more likely to be working out his own horrible scheme for getting the King away," she told him, with an optimism she was far from feeling.

"It is to be hoped so, but I do not like it. There seem to be more people than usual about to-night. Did you hear all that noise a while back from the barracks?"

"That at least had nothing to do with us," Mary was able to assure him. "Brett tells me Libby's baby was born early this morning. Rudy had been down to the village to see her and the men were probably celebrating. You remembered to remove the rope from the King's room?"

"I hid it in my own clothes press."

"Then everything is ready. The platform sentries will be changing over any minute now."

"If only we could be sure that that cursed Captain of the Guard had settled for the night! He has gone back to his quarters now, but who knows?"

"I suppose we had better go to ours, even though we cannot sleep," sighed Mary. "Of course Master Worsley and Richard Osborne have arrived?"

"I barked in fine imitation of your Patters and Worsley gave one of his famous bird calls."

Mary laughed. It gave her a sense of security to know that they were out there. She bade the worried Frenchman good-night and went up to her aunt's room, hoping to find her resting in her chair;

but Druscilla Wheeler was walking about looking distraught. "Your father has gone on guard instead of that young overner," she said the moment Mary came into the room.

Mary stopped short. "How do you know? You cannot see from here."

"I heard them marching out and went to that little staircase window on the north wall and looked down, just to make sure that Wenshall and Featherstone had not been put on to some other duty as they were last Sunday. And there was your father with them."

"Are you sure? In the dark?"

"I heard his voice."

"But what reason can there be for the change?" asked Mary, coming to the hearth and putting her firmly into a chair.

"I can think of nothing—unless the young man is sick. But even so, a sergeant does not usually—"

"Well, at least father will betray nothing. Imagine if it had been some Roundhead!"

"If Master Osborne asked your father to do it, after all I said—"

"He must have wanted to, but I am sure he did not." Seeing her aunt so upset, Mary fetched a skillet and went to the fire to warm some milk; and as she waited for it to heat she milled the matter over in her mind. She recalled that in her first shock at hearing about the platform she had let slip some words about its undoing all Harry's plans; but she felt sure that her father had had a pretty shrewd idea of their plans all along, and that he had wished them well and would have liked to join them. But why, to-night, had he taken Tilling's place? Had he done so purposely, knowing what was going to happen? If so, perhaps it was all for the best. Young Tilling might have bungled things. She gave her aunt the hot milk and blew out the candle, and they both sat by the hearth waiting. Dowcett, whose room was in the older part of the building, was going to try to give them a signal when the King was well away.

But Mistress Wheeler was still restless and anxious. Calm enough in facing dangers for herself, she could not face them for her beloved brother. She kept glancing at her precious clock, and when an hour had passed and it was nearly midnight she went to the window overlooking the courtyard and looked out. She had not been there many minutes before she turned and called Mary sharply to her side. "Look! A man has just come out from the officers' quarters. You can just see him standing there. Oh, please God it is not Rolph!"

It was difficult to discern anyone at all, save for a faint luminous glow from a steel breast-plate. Whoever it was stood still as if listening, and then turned back to close the door. And in that moment both women saw him clearly.

"It *is* Rolph!" said Mary, her heart seeming to turn over in her body.

From the open window they could hear his footsteps coming across the courtyard. "Going his rounds again!" wailed Mistress Wheeler.

"Only his ordinary rounds by the battlements, perhaps. If he turns off now toward the south ramp—" Mary leaned out as far as she dared, but her hope was short-lived. The footsteps came straight on. Then he stopped. She could see his face as a white blur in the darkness as he looked up at the windows, and realized that probably he could see her too. She felt that he was staring specially at their window and was glad that she had snuffed out the candle.

"If he goes on round by the wellhouse he can only be making for the northern postern," Whispered her aunt, moving away as if she could no longer bear the suspense.

"He *is*. He is going outside the walls again," gasped Mary. "And any moment now the King will be—"

Her aunt, who so seldom lost control, gripped her wrist in panic. "Merciful God, what can we do? How can we stop him?"

There was only one way that Mary knew of, and even that might not succeed. Edmund Rolph was such a strange mixture of devotion to duty and reluctant sensuality. But there was certainly nothing anyone else could do. Now, in the last stage of the game, it was left to her to make the final move. Only she could make this last bid for success. And it was not for her to count the cost. The Captain of the Guard had always desired her, and with each frustration that veiled hunger in his eyes had grown. "I will go to him," she said almost calmly, freeing her wrist.

Their minds were so closely fused in the tension of the moment, that Druscilla Wheeler could not mistake the full significance of that ordinary phrase. For a moment or two one fear seemed to oust another. "Mary, you cannot—you must not—" This tune she gripped her niece firmly by the arms. "I will not let you go!"

Although Mary recognized it as a last chance to carry Harry Firebrace's cherished plan to success and to save the King, in that moment her only conscious motive was to defend her father. "If he is caught he will be shot," she said.

Druscilla Wheeler had always had her own strange foreboding. And were they not both pledged to this cause? She gave no spoken consent, but the strength went out of her restraining arms. Mary broke from them and sped down the stairs and out into the night.

She went straight to Rolph and was enraged because he did not even show surprise. He must have seen her at the window and supposed that her interest in his movements was purely feminine. "So you had to come sooner or later, now that you can no longer get to that fancy lover of yours in Newport?" he said. "I suppose a girl starves the same as we do."

She could have killed him. Instead she let him jerk her to him, cupping her chin in his hand. His greedy apprizing glance passed slowly from the white oval of her face to the darker outline of her body. "And what if I tell you I do not want you to-night, my pretty? What if I have more important things to do?"

She knew how he must have enjoyed saying it after all the times she had broken away from his desire. But she was beyond the lash of insolence. All she knew was that she must keep him away from the King's window—keep him somehow for the next half hour. She summoned to her aid all those wiles she had watched and wondered at in Libby—Libby, who had this very day given birth to a child. Putting that frightening thought from her, she lifted enticing arms and forced herself to touch the man. "Is there anything more important than ourselves this summer night?" she whispered invitingly.

# CHAPTER TWENTY-ONE

ARY CROUCHED TERROR-STRICKEN ON the bed. She stared numbly round the room—a man's room, bare and orderly, with an army cloak lying across a shabby chair and a pistol lying on the table. At Edmund Rolph standing beside the bed she dared not look. He had thrown off his tunic and she heard the impact of his swordbelt as he threw it across the foot of the coverlet.

No sense of triumph sustained her now. At the last minute she had found the sacrifice too great and would have cheated him if she could. Once in his room, she had tried to cajole him with promises, to flatter him into talking—of the way he had risen in the world, of his promised majority, his hatreds and ambitions, of anything. But as well try to stave off a rutting stag. Ambition and lust always strove in him for mastery, and by her own doing lust was in the ascendant. He had been too urgent to drape desire with the veneer of conversation. Desire had blotted out his ever-present bogy of hell-fire. With hot hands he had stripped the gown from her shoulders and pushed her to his bed.

Past events and the world outside had been driven from her mind by present horrors; her thoughts were only of her shame and how to meet the future. She thought of Libby who had that very morning paid the natural price of some such impassioned moment. But with Libby and her man the passion had been mutual, whereas she herself felt only repugnance. Her glance went wildly to the pistol. Its owner was the sort of man who would always keep it primed. It lay within her reach, but Rolph was nearer. Would God do nothing? But why should He, when she had brought this thing upon herself? She closed her eyes and heard, without believing, a knocking on the door.

Rolph, with a hand already on her naked shoulder, stood motionless between her and the candlelight. "Go to hell!" he bawled out savagely. But the knocking only became more peremptory and a man's voice, sharp with authority, called to him to unlock it.

"The Governor!" breathed Mary, drawing the worn coverlet about her in yet deeper shame. Yet gratitude and relief strong as joy warmed her cold body. That God should have sent him at such a moment! Until she learned the reason it seemed too fantastic to be true.

Rolph knew that voice as well as she. He came to the foot of the bed, and she saw him look from her to the door, wretchedly irresolute. One could not disobey the Governor. And only some crisis could have brought him to his officers' quarters in the middle of the night—he, who was accustomed to sending for people when he wanted them. Reluctantly, Rolph shrugged himself into his uniform again. With coat still unbuttoned he motioned to her to keep quiet, and pulled the worn, seldom-used curtains about his bed as silently as he could.

As he went to the door Mary's numbed mind began to work, too. She realized the circumstances which had driven her to such dangerous shame, and lay trembling behind the thin screen of worn tapestry. If Colonel Hammond found her there it was no immediate fault of Rolph's. He could say with truth that she had enticed him like a common harlot. But much bigger concerns than her morals must have brought him. The door closed and she knew that he was in the room. "Thank God you are not yet undressed!" she heard him say. "The King is attempting another escape to-night."

"To-night?" She knew that the dismay in Rolph's voice was not for the plan but because he had not been told of it. "How do you know, sir?"

"Two of the platform sentries came and told me."

Mary sat up in the bed, both hands on her racing heart.

"But they should be posted by now. I was just going out to make a surprise inspection. These fellows need watching." Rolph still sounded flurried.

"I suppose they lost their nerve. They came and made a clean breast of it at the last minute. They'd been bribed at a hundred pounds apiece to let the King come out of his window and get away."

The chair creaked. Evidently, the Governor had sat down. It was easy to differentiate between his crisp, cultured voice and Rolph's rougher speech with its ineradicable Cockney accent.

"Are you sure they haven't got it muddled, sir? That it isn't something planned for some other night?"

"Why should it be? They tell me the bar has been tampered with. Those indefeasible fools who help the King must have got a second bottle of acid through after we dealt with their first effort."

"Who bribed the sentries? That crafty Frenchman, probably. I met him prowling about out there earlier in the evening."

"He is probably in it. But they both say the man who persuaded them to it was Osborne."

"Osborne!" A foul oath ripped out of Rolph. "But he went out to supper—he was talking to me of some girl he was going to see. He—" The Captain still found it hard to believe that during all these weeks he had been fooled.

"He hoodwinked us all pretty thoroughly."

"May the Almighty let me lay hands on him!"

"He probably will if you carry out my orders with despatch. The time set for the royal departure is midnight and it is almost midnight now."

"Who were the men?"

"Wenshall and Featherstone."

"Islanders!" The word was so charged with contempt that it sounded as if the Captain spat. "No men of mine, God be praised!"

"I understand the third was a Londoner," said the Governor, drily.

"From the new company Major Cromwell brought, no doubt."

"I told the two who came to me to go on duty as though nothing had happened. To speak of it to no one—not even to their fellow-sentry. So if you watch what happens we ought to find out for certain who is involved in this and catch them red-handed. There must be someone *outside* the castle with a horse for the King."

"Osborne, I'll wager! A pox on his luscious wench and his supper party!"

"Send a dozen of your musketeers to set an ambush on the far side of the lane. Let them go out by the main gate and creep down through the copse from above."

"And I'll see to it that every man of them is a good shot!"

"Then go yourself immediately and hide in the angle of that bastion a few yards from the window. Take what men you need—men who will obey you implicitly."

"I shall not need many." The grimness of a threat was in Rolph's tone.

"Wenshall and Featherstone will not raise a finger. I have told them to maintain their guard but to take no part in the affair. So you will have only one sentry to deal with. Let the King get to the edge of the escarpment before you take him so that we see who comes to meet him and help him down. Give your men orders to fire on anyone who resists, but forbid them to show any violence to the King himself. Only make sure that he is taken."

Personal issues were momentarily forgotten. To both men it was merely an absorbing military manoeuvre. "And the third sentry?" enquired Rolph.

"Arrest him and bring him to me, unless he is seen actively helping the King. In that case shoot him at sight."

The shabby old chair creaked again as the Governor got up to go, so that neither of them heard Mary's smothered cry. "I will come with you, sir. I have only to collect my gear." Rolph seemed to have forgotten her. Whatever other opportunities the night might bring he was eager to get to them.

The clink of steel told her that he was buckling on his armour. His swordbelt was still lying across the end of the bed, and his pistol on the table. Leaning across the pillow she reached out a stealthy hand between the hangings and drew the heavy, lethal weapon into the half darkness of her hiding place. She thrust it under the bedclothes to deaden the sound of the catch, and emptied out the powder. As stealthily she reached out and put it back.

Almost immediately she saw Rolph's strong, hirsute hand appear and grope for his belt, then heard him stride to the table and pick up the pistol. "I should put on this dark cloak so that the King will not see you," advised Colonel Hammond. Then the door closed behind them and she was alone.

Instantly Mary slipped from the bed and ran to the door, tugging her torn dress about her as she went. Memories of fatherly loving kindness and small shared jokes impelled her. Rolph would have to collect his men, she calculated. "If I run now to the north postern one of our garrison may be on duty. I will beg him to let me pass. Those old men have never refused me anything, I will tell him my aunt has been taken ill and that I must see my father."

She might yet be able to warn him and he in turn could warn the King. She pulled at the door but could not open it. She pulled again with all her strength, and then began banging on it in a frenzy of frustration. But Edmund Rolph had locked it from the outside.

He had not been able to prevent her from overhearing the Governor's orders, but he was taking no chances about her giving warnings. She supposed that if his mind had sufficiently recovered from the shock of Osborne's duplicity, he must surely have realized by now that she, too, had been duping him. Had they opposed him openly in a matter of duty he would probably have borne no particular grudge. As Osborne had once said, the man had his points. But with understanding of her purpose the bubble of his masculine conceit would be pricked, and for that he would never forgive her. He would never lose an opportunity of paying off the score. And because he had basked in the belief that he was on intimate terms with a gentleman of the class which he envied, abhorred and hunted—because he had publicly boasted of it and must now look a fool—he would be Osborne's sworn enemy for life.

Mary ran to the window overlooking the courtyard, but it was small and barred. "Most certainly he will pick all his best marksmen for the ambush!" she moaned, sinking down on the low window seat. She remembered how often Richard Osborne had tried to comfort her, and for the first time, in the midst of her terror for her father, her thoughts reached out in a passion of protectiveness to that tall reckless figure, all unaware of Cromwell's musketeers closing in around him in the darkness of the copse.

What a puffed-up fool she must have been to suppose that she could interfere! And at what might have been such an irremediable price!

# CHAPTER TWENTY-TWO

$$\text{\textasciitilde}\!\!\text{\textasciitilde}\!\!\text{\textasciitilde}$$

T ANY MOMENT NOW the chapel clock might strike the hour. Alone in his room, Charles had made his final preparations. Earlier in the day he had complained of a chill and asked Brett to light a fire so that he might destroy such documents as he could not take in his pockets. He had burned his wife's letters. "Dear Heart," she had called him in every one, and it had felt like severing his last link with her. It was four years since he had last seen her, but by God's help he would see her again this very week and there would be no more need of all this difficultly contrived correspondence.

He took a last look round the room at his few possessions. When he had left his treasures in Whitehall he had felt beggared. Yet in a few minutes now he would be a fugitive possessed of nothing save what he stood up in. He passed his hands over his defenceless body, almost nervous of being out in the world again. Had he remembered everything Harry Firebrace had told him that first time? The black suit that would not show in the darkness, the dark grey stockings drawn up above the rosettes at his knees. How easy Harry's enthusiasm had made things seem! How cold these old rooms were without his smile! And that sweet-faced girl who helped with the letters—she must miss him too. "They have all served me so well," thought Charles. "If ever I come into my own again I will remember them."

Only at the last minute did he remember to take off his glittering George, so accustomed was he to wearing it as sole ornament and as a silent reminder to the traitors about him to keep their place. He slipped it into his pocket, took it out and laid it aside with nervous indecision, then put it back again. In Holland it would be safe to wear it, and he must remember that he was a poor man now. Or if anything should happen to him before he got there Ashburnham or someone would sell it for his younger children's needs—clever, delicate Bess and eager young Henry. If anything should happen to him…

Although it was almost June he suddenly felt chilled indeed and wished that he need not leave the comfort of Brett's fire. But it was time to go. His jewelled watch told him so. Time to leave this castle of his which he had once thought so pleasant and which had become a hated prison. He hoped he would never see it again. In order to steady his nerves he urged his thoughts out beyond its walls. To-morrow he would celebrate his eldest son's birthday by riding once more through the lovely shires of his kingdom. And afterwards—who could say? Protecting each flame with a fine, tapering hand, he blew out the candles.

He knelt for a moment or two in prayer before cautiously opening a casement of his window. The dividing bar was still hanging in position, but had been so cleverly treated with acid that with one smart tug it came away from the top as Dowcett had assured him it would. Charles laid it down, careful to make no noise, and leaned out. There was no wind and the sweet scent of May trees came up to him. It seemed to him that the whole summer night smelled of freedom.

Below him, close under the wall, he could see the figures of the three sentries, and beneath their feet the new wood of the platform glimmering whitely above the steeply sloping grass. Two of them stood motionless at the far end of it. It seemed they had not heard him. The other—the shorter man with the broader shoulders— looked up. He turned at once and came closer. He propped his musket carefully against the wall and took off his helmet lest its wide, upturned sides should get in the way, then stood expectantly holding up his arms. Charles, with eyes uninured to the darkness, could not be sure which soldier he was, but he was there and ready to help him down and that was all that mattered to a man tortured by a horror of heights.

He mounted a stool and thrust first one leg over the sill and then the other. The aperture was narrow but this time it would suffice. Sitting on the sill with the scented night air all about him, he leaned forward and reached down with his hands. The hands that grasped them were warm and strong, and the man's upturned, smiling face was so close that now he could discern the features. It was Sergeant Floyd's face, with the same steady eyes and crisply curling hair as that girl of his—and now the corners of the eyes crinkled into an encouraging smile. So Osborne had roped him in after all Charles was glad. It was like finding, as he set off alone on a strange journey, someone whom he had known since boyhood. The jump into the darkness was going to be nothing after all—no more unnerving than a joyous vaulting into the saddle with his own groom holding the stirrup. Instead of being a nightmare, this was the beginning of an adventure—a splendid adventure like firing off the castle cannon.

Charles' swinging feet felt for Sergeant Floyd's shoulders. His muscles, which he had kept supple with swift walking, tensed themselves to spring. And as his breast came forward a sharp crack sounded from a few yards away, followed by a smothered oath. It could have been the snapping of a dry branch suddenly trodden beneath a boot, or the release of a trigger—but if it were a trigger no fire came. Both of them turned their heads instantly and became aware of figures moving in the shadow of the bastion. Charles could have sworn they were not there before. They must have been watching and crept round from behind it. For a moment or two he and Floyd remained rigid, listening.

"At the ready! Present arms! " ordered Floyd. He was burdened, bareheaded and unarmed, his back offering a perfect target to an enemy, but Wenshall and Featherstone, at the other end of the platform, made only a poor show of fumbling with their matchlocks.

"Go back, sir!" warned Floyd, hoisting the King upwards with one hand while he reached for his own musket with the other. But before he could reach it someone fired from another angle, murderously close. There was no mistaking it for a snapped branch this time and the shot got him between the shoulder blades. Charles had already managed to pull himself back into his window. His own efforts excluded other sounds so that he did not hear the groan and thud, and was unaware that Sergeant Floyd had slumped down on to the platform and that Wenshall and Featherstone, quick enough to bend over him in shocked remorse, were hastily unbuckling his breastplate. The King closed his window and moved instinctively behind the shelter of a wall. But his reaction was incredulity rather than fear. That it should have come to this! That they should dare to fire at him! All his sense of kingly dignity was outraged. He stood there, with fast-beating heart, listening for what would come next. He could hear the other sentries talking down below. The shot seemed to have raised them from their incompetence. "Small wonder Cromwell's soldiers beat us if all my men were as slow as they!" he thought irrelevantly. And then a sharp volley of musket fire rattled through the copse across the lane, followed by another and yet another. Then single pistol shots barking in return.

"Osborne and Worsley!" he lamented bitterly, in the darkness. "How many more men must die for me!"

It seemed to his tried experience that no two men could live through such a murderous fire. But the firing was coming from farther away now, growing fainter and more spasmodic. "Edward Worsley is an islander. Perhaps, after all, they may get away," he thought on a faint uprising of hope.

Finding that his legs were trembling under him he sat down at his desk. With angry daring he lit a candle and sat by the uncurtained window. If any of his subjects wished to kill him let them do it while he sat, as became him, in his own room. Not while he was climbing like a thief from a window. Even if it should mean the end of freedom he would never attempt that means of exit again. Because it was so alien to him, he thought, it was doomed to failure. To-night had been but a repetition of that first night when young Firebrace had talked him into making the attempt from that other window. Only then there had been a much bigger drop and no steadying hands, and he had been secretly glad when the space had proved too narrow. In a rare moment of shamed retrospection Charles wondered whether that secret relief had had any connection with his reluctance to test the space first. But even so, when it came to the point, he had tried his utmost. Always, since his lonely boyhood in Scotland, he had fought that ridiculous horror of heights. Now he would fight again for his freedom. And for his rights. But by some method more suited to an intelligent mind. Some dastard might have shot him this night but God had miraculously stayed his hand. He was sure now that the first sharp sound he and Floyd had heard was a pistol which for some reason did not go off. He did not mean to die if he could help it. He would write again to Parliament suggesting that in the interests of the country he and they should try again to settle their differences. He would write now. He picked up his pen and pulled some paper towards him. While there is life there is hope. The words had been so often in his mind of late. *Dum spiro, spero* he wrote idly across a corner of the paper while he considered what proposals to make.

Everything was quiet now and to his amazement he heard a key turn in his lock. Was there then some master key? Failing to shoot him, had they come here to murder him? His mind went back to other kings, in eras which were supposed to be more savage, who had been foully put away in remote castles. He sprang to his feet, his gaze fixed in horror on the opening door.

But it was Colonel Hammond who stood on the threshold. Of course, this had been his room. He had probably retained a key. And one did not associate murder with Colonel Hammond. A deep breath of relief issued soundlessly from Charles's lips. He stood still, pen in hand, beside his desk, waiting for an explanation. It was only impertinence, not regicide, he had to face.

The Governor offered no explanation. He bowed formally and walked deliberately across the room to the window. He was standing close beside Charles and looked pointedly at the space where the bar should have been. Comment was unnecessary.

Being left to speak first put Charles at a disadvantage. "What have you come here for, Hammond? What is the matter?" he asked.

Hammond turned towards him politely but without any particular deference. "I am come to take my leave of your Majesty as I hear you are leaving us," he said, with the beginning of a smile curving his thin, clever lips.

The words were not unfriendly. Their eyes met and Charles laughed like a good loser. Hammond picked up the bar and examined it as he might have examined a good piece of gunsmithery. In that moment they came nearer to liking each other than at any other time. Fate had tipped the balance of power from guest to host, but each recognized in the other a reasonable, civilized person. For the first time Charles spared a thought for the difficulty of the man's position. He was even sorry that he had purposely quickened his pace one frosty morning and then laughed when the Governor, trying to keep up with him, had slipped painfully full length on his back. And Hammond, in spite of his irritation with the King's obstinacy and all these intrigues which made it impossible for him to alleviate captivity with any of the small privileges he would have preferred to grant, was human enough to appreciate the King's disappointment. "I had to make sure that your Majesty was safe," he said, almost apologetically, laying down the bar and preparing to depart.

"What was all that shooting?" asked Charles.

"I regret that it should have been necessary. But if it is of any comfort to you, your friends have got away—for the moment."

"What friends?" asked Charles, refusing to be drawn.

Hammond's smile was more grim. "Your Gentleman Usher and—I suspect—Master Edward Worsley from Gatcombe." It was royalist sympathy in the island that he feared.

Charles sat down and picked up his pen again, pretending to be occupied with his writing. He managed to preserve a non-committal silence until Hammond was almost at the door. But there was something which concerned him more closely still. Something which he had to know. "And that other musket shot—which I imagine was meant for me?" he asked, without raising his head.

"I assure you it was not. My orders were that no violence was to be shown you."

"But that first misfire—" began Charles, sure now that it had been from a pistol and remembering how urgently Sergeant Floyd had warned him, and how much more clearly he must have been able to see. But naturally the Governor would know nothing about it and at least he would not lie. "Then whom was the musket shot intended for?"

Because Hammond's heart was heavy within him for the loss of a good man he looked back at the King without any vestige of his momentary liking. "For a sentry who disobeyed orders," he answered curtly. "They are bringing in his body now."

# CHAPTER TWENTY-THREE

⟨⟨⟨⟩⟩⟩

MARY KNELT BY HER father's grave in the village churchyard, a slight desolate figure in black with summer
daisies mockingly starring the grass around her.
Although Sergeant Floyd had been shot for disobeying orders, the
newly-turned mound of earth was covered with flowers. There
were wreaths from his sister and from the Trattles, an unobtrusive bunch of roses which had come anonymously from Mistress
Hammond, children's wilting posies, and a profusion of simple
country blooms from cottage gardens. Some of his men had made
a rough cross on which the master-gunner had whittled the words
"Faithful unto Death," and after the officer in charge of the burial
party had gone the coffin bearers had hurriedly fixed it at the
head of the grave. It meant more to Mary than any stonemason's
impersonal slab which might come later; for these men had known
and understood her father and shared the memories from which
her grief had grown.

Mary herself had brought no flowers, only her passionately
unhappy heart.

When Rolph had released her because the Governor was
asking for her, she had found her aunt distracted with grief. Seeing
Mistress Hammond and the Chaplain with her, Mary had guessed
the news they had come to break. She had tried to comfort poor
Aunt Druscilla and then gone about her ordinary duties in silence.
Her father was dead, and she had been too stunned to listen to the

comfort people tried to give her. Obediently she had put on the black gown which the Governor's mother had had made for her in Newport, and had even stood at the window to watch her father's coffin being carried out towards the drawbridge. Aunt Druscilla, burdened with grief and sick with that past anxiety for her niece of which she could not speak, lay all that day on her bed behind drawn blinds, and it had not been thought seemly for either of them to attend the funeral.

But the following morning Mary had gone boldly to the Governor's room and asked leave to go down to the churchyard, "You may go there at any time. Why do you ask leave of me?" he had asked, trying not to meet her tragic eyes.

"Because Captain Rolph has given orders that without your written word the guard are not to let me out of the castle."

"You probably gave him good cause, trying to bring in letters."

"I am to be allowed out only if I go with him," she had added, thinking how strange it was that heart-break could so quickly eat up fear.

Hammond had looked up sharply, scrutinizing her white, set face before taking up his pen. "Here is your pass," he had said. She was not to know how often he wished that he had his mother's gift for conveying sympathy. "If there is anything more I can do for you, always come to me."

She was not to know either, that as soon as she had closed his door he had sent for Anthony Mildmay, choosing him as the kind of watchdog who would not intrude upon her. "She is taking it too quietly. Follow her at a distance—particularly should she go near the mill pond," he had ordered uneasily. "But see that no other man follows her."

She had walked out past the sentries and no one had stopped her. Rolph, parading his company in the courtyard, had called out to know where she was going and, armed with the Governor's chit, she had walked past him as though he had not spoken. She could still take pleasure in the men's covert grins at his discomforture, and she was not the type to seek oblivion in millponds. Unaware that Mildmay kept her within sight, she had gone down the lane beneath the dappled shadow of the beech trees, and by the stone clapper bridge over the brook. Because it was June, ladies' laces flung creamy bridal veils against green hedges along the village street, and the scent from an old lilac bush had drifted down to her as she pushed open the churchyard gate. And now, kneeling among the daisies beside that sad, unresponsive mound, she thought that nothing that happened in June could ever matter any more.

How could so much sorrow have come about, she wondered, staring at the wilting flowers and the little wooden cross? Surely it had all begun on that Sunday seven months ago? If the King had not come to the Wight they would all have gone on living their quiet uneventful lives. The happy lives which Frances had thought so dull. Her father would have been up at the castle now, drilling his men or seeing to the stores. There would have been none of that bustle and excitement, no introduction to a world of ceremony and fashion, no falling in love, no pain of parting, no useless attempt to barter her body, no final desolation. Why, why—out of all the castles in his kingdom—must King Charles have chosen to come here?

The soft, salt-laden breeze that stirred the grass seemed to carry a faint echo of the voice which her heart strained to hear. "What does it matter, my foolish one?" her father had been wont to say when her small world went wrong. "What does anything matter so long as we face it together?"

And now she was alone, with a world of fear and loneliness to face. During the last few days there had always been people with pitying faces, and her own aggressive pride, because everyone knew her father had been shot like any defaulting sentry. But here she could for the first time give way to her emotions. She was at an age for joy, but although the sun warmed her and the birds sung overhead, life loomed like a grey emptiness before her. She covered her face with both hands and sobbed.

When she was worn out by the wildness of her grief she felt herself being lifted from the grass by arms strong and gentle as her father's. Blinded by tears, she made no resistance. She allowed herself to be carried to a low wall screened by the dipping branches of an old willow tree, and found herself in Richard Osborne's arms. Too tired out by suffering to speak, she leaned her head against his breast and went on weeping silently.

He held her until her shaking body grew still, then set her down on the wall beside him; but he kept an arm about her so that she could rest against his shoulder. "That you should have been the one called upon to pay—and so bitterly!" he said, kissing her wet cheek as gently as he would have comforted a child.

"They shot him as though he were a t-traitor."

"It was the world that changed, my sweet, never his loyalty. It is the same with all of us who are on the King's side."

"How did you know about it?" she asked dully.

"The Gatcombe bailiff heard about the funeral when he came in to market. I knew you would be sure to come here so I came through the woods and waited in the priory ruins."

She roused herself and would have pushed him away, suddenly remembering his danger. "You know they have been searching for you for days. At any moment they may be out again." But he did not move, and looking up at him for the first time she saw the roughly bandaged wound high up on his cheek. "You got that when they ambushed you?" she asked, touching it with a pitiful, exploring finger.

"It is not deep," he assured her. "Although Worsley seems to think I shall always bear the mark of it. Mary, what happened that night? What went wrong?"

She explained it all to him as best she could, piecing her story together from what she had overheard from Rolph's bed and from what she had learned afterwards. "I was frantic with anxiety when I heard all that shooting. The firing party sent out were the best marksmen in the garrison. How did you get away?"

"By being a rather better marksman, I suppose. And Edward Worsley knows every bush and bypath. There is no need to worry about *us*. We have gone to earth in a snug lair in his father's woods and one of their servants brings us food. Mary, were you allowed to see your father before—the firing party—"

She shook her head sadly. "There was no firing party. The Governor's orders were to arrest the third sentry unless Rolph should see him actually helping the King, but in that case to shoot at sight."

"This must have been a terrible shock for Mistress Wheeler. How did she take it when she first heard?"

Mary looked down, picking at the wall with aimless fingers. "I was not with her."

"Not with her? That night?"

"Not until the morning." She hurried on without giving him time to question her further. "She took to her bed and will not speak to anyone. Not even to me. She still thinks that you persuaded my beloved father to go on guard, even when I tell her that Wenshall and Featherstone both say it was because of Tilling being drunk."

"So you have been defending me?" He sounded inordinately pleased, but at mention of her father Mary's tears had begun to flow afresh. "I have no one now," she murmured in her desolation.

"You have me."

"But when I go back you will not be there. And poor Abraham Dowcett is under close arrest. They found the rope in his room."

"If you can get a message to him through Brett or someone tell him that when I reach the mainland I will try to see his wife," promised Osborne.

"Will you have to go abroad?"

"I shall try to join the Prince in Holland."

"It really is not safe for you to stay here with me any longer," she reminded him anxiously.

"No, I suppose not," he agreed; but he spoke absently as though his mind were on something else. "How did you *know* what orders the Governor gave Rolph about your father?"

"I—overheard."

"Overheard? How could you, possibly? You say the sentries only went to Hammond at the last moment." He withdrew his arm and looked at her in perplexity. "Where *were* you that night?"

She realized that in her agitation she had betrayed herself, but could not bring herself to lie to him. She sat looking straight before her as she told him. "Dowcett was worried as you feared he might be. He had seen Captain Rolph prying round outside the walls. We all went to our rooms and, as you know, Dowcett's is at the other end of the castle. Just before midnight my aunt and I saw Rolph from our window. He was going out to inspect the platform guards again. We knew my father was there—and that any minute would be helping the King to get out of the window. Rolph would catch them in the act. Somehow we had to stop him. I had to do something—"

"Go on." Osborne got up as if the better to bear some blow.

"I went down to him."

"And he took you instead of the King? I know the bestial hypocrite!"

"No—I promise you! The Governor came to his quarters and by the mercy of God I was saved from that."

"But he meant to seduce you?"

"It is true that he has been pestering me for months, but this time the blame was not his. He said he had some important duty to attend to and I—I enticed him from it. I let him take me back to his room. You and Harry were not there and *someone* had to keep him away from the King's window. Oh, say you understand!"

Osborne understood only too well. "I will half kill him," he said.

"Oh no! For then you will never escape."

"Leave that between him and me." He stood staring out over the churchyard wall, his hands thrust deep into his pockets as though to keep them from violence.

"The Governor came for him and he hid me behind the bed-hangings. He could not prevent me from hearing all they said."

"So that was how you came to be so remarkably well informed—and why you were not with your aunt," said Osborne bitterly.

"Oh, Richard, what else could I have done?"

Her voice and eyes implored him. Without his friendship she would be utterly bereft. He turned at last, but not before he had fought down his fury and forced his features into some semblance of a smile. Instead of answering her question he asked another. "When I am no longer hunted like this, will you marry me?"

It was surely the most abrupt offer of marriage a girl ever had, but few suitors, she supposed, were so cruelly pressed for time. "Marry you?" she repeated, almost as surprised as if the Governor himself had asked her.

"You have no man to care for you now."

Colour came into her cheeks and a tremulous smile to her lips. "I always said you were kind, Master Osborne."

"No, you disliked me at first. But I am not asking you out of kindness and my name is Richard," he answered gruffly. "It is true you are bereaved, but God knows I am in trouble too! I suppose no woman would choose to marry a man who is on the run, and who will almost certainly be exiled or imprisoned if he is caught? A man who is on the losing side anyway, and whose life has been anything but blameless." He came and looked down into her grief-marred face and took her hands in his. "I am not good enough to touch you, sweet, let alone marry you," he went on, with rare tenderness. "But now it seems that we two can give each other all that we most need."

She looked up into those kind brown eyes of his, and saw that his mouth looked neither reckless nor cynical. "But I do not love you."

"Not as you loved Harry, perhaps."

"You knew—about that?"

"I cared so much that I could not help knowing. But it need not make marriage impossible. I would try to be patient."

"I do not think you are a very patient kind of person," she told him, managing a small smile.

"But then I have never been in love before," he said, smiling back at her. "And you on your side would have plenty to forgive."

Mary slid slowly down from the wall. "It is a wonderful thing to know, in my grief, that any man can care for me like this—"

He took her in his arms and for a brief and blessed moment the rest of the world seemed to be blotted out. "Isn't it time that someone cared for you—you who are always making crazy sacrifices for other people?" he said, tenderly smoothing back her disordered curls. "And, besides, I am not any man. One day I hope to be your husband." He kissed her again as if indeed he were. "When I am able to come back for you—"

"Oh, but you must not take the risk!"

"I shall manage it somehow—even if life drives us apart again for a time. I should know then that at least I left you with some money and the protection of my name."

"And you would have nothing."

"This very day I shall have something sweet and lovely to live for if you will promise to wait for me."

The comforting thought of his protection tempted her, and she was too tired to resist. She knew that all her life long unbidden thoughts of a slender, auburn-haired young man, of the shining warmth of his enthusiasms, or the sound of his sudden laughter, would catch her unawares, quickening memories which would make all other men look slow and drab. But one had to live. If one was young one's senses must be taught to forget. One's heart could not go on aching all the time, until one came to die.

"I cannot promise what is already spent—" she began, with reluctant honesty.

"I am not asking you for that. Perhaps I am not good enough to want the kind of love you gave Harry. But if you will give yourself to me, my little love, I shall know how to make you happy."

In the end it was she who clung to him when he would have let her go. "How shall I hear from you if you go abroad?"

"I have changed my mind. I shall not go now. I shall stay and try to justify myself and your father and all of you, and bring that lecherous murderer to book."

They could both hear a company of horsemen approaching from the direction of the castle, and Osborne picked up the battered steeple hat he was wearing and pulled it down over his bandaged forehead. At the last minute Mary caught at his sleeve. "Richard."

"My love?"

"When I was behind that man's bed curtains—"

He put a hand over her mouth. "I forbid you to speak or think of it."

"Only this once. Because there is something you should know—something which might strengthen your case. While the

Governor and Rolph were talking I emptied the powder from his pistol. It did nothing to save my father, but could it have—made any difference?"

Though the sound of horsemen was coming closer he stood looking down at her with admiration and surprised attention. "It could have saved the King's life," he said, remembering Rolph's intentions. But he dared no longer. He vaulted over the wall and strode swiftly towards the cover of the forest. Mary walked slowly back to her father's grave. She remembered how he had once said that he liked Osborne, and now, at the far end of the dark tunnel of her loneliness, a light glimmered steadily.

As she left the churchyard and crossed the village street the search-party, headed by Rolph, trotted briskly past in the direction of Ashey Down, and Anthony Mildmay was coming casually out of the smithy. With his usual courtesy he fell into step beside her and accompanied her up the lane to the castle gates. He had carried out the Governor's orders, and if in the execution of them he had happened to see Richard Osborne he deemed it no part of his duty to report the fact.

# CHAPTER TWENTY-FOUR

AVE FOR THE CHANGING of the guard and the sharp sound
of routine orders a new quietness seemed to have settled
on the castle. Men of the original garrison were shocked by
their Sergeant's death. The excitement and tense expectancy of
the last few weeks had given place to gloom and boredom. There
seemed to be no further likelihood of the King trying to escape,
and everyone felt certain that Osborne and Worsley had got away
to the mainland. The daily manhunts had been given up and discipline was partially relaxed because Rolph lay sick in his quarters.
No one quite knew what had happened to him. One evening when
his zeal had driven him to follow some trail ahead of his men he
had been picked up bruised and semi-conscious in the Gatcombe
woods. Some said that a wild animal had attacked him, others that
he had slipped and cut himself on the stones of a disused quarry.
Only Mary guessed that the man whom he stalked had lain in wait
and half-killed him. Rolph himself would say nothing, feigning not
to remember. He bore his painful bruises stoically and although
Doctor Bagnell from Newport was attending Mistress Wheeler he
refused to see him. Only Rudy was allowed in his room, and even
he reported that the Captain's temper was unbearable.

There had been yet more dismissals and the King's apartments
seemed almost deserted. Since the exposure and failure of his plans
only two or three of his gentlemen were allowed to remain with
him. He and the Governor avoided each other, and because of the

awkwardness between them Charles no longer passed a part of his time in theological argument with the castle chaplain. Dowcett was still under arrest, and Major Cromwell had been recalled to attend some military conference. Mistress Wheeler kept to her bed and her niece never seemed to come into the State Room when his Majesty was there. Libby had been allowed to come back because of her husband's appeal to Captain Rolph, so Brett told him, and it was she who for the last few days had brought his clean linen. Indeed on wet days it was only through the bent old servant that the King received any news at all; and it was Brett, with tears in his eyes, who told him that Sergeant Floyd had been shot—a piece of sad information which his Majesty's gentlemen had been carefully keeping from him.

Since the disappointment of that Sunday night Charles would stand silently looking out of the Presence Chamber window. From his former apartments he had been accustomed to see all that was going on in the courtyard, and who came in and out through the gates, so that here he felt still more caged. Yet the old rooms that faced northwards had a far more beautiful view. Nostalgically beautiful to him because he could see across open country to the Solent, and beyond that the mainland of his kingdom. On a clear day he could pick out the hills and houses on the Hampshire coast, and even the ships, like tiny black dots upon the blue, passing in and out of Southampton water.

He would stand there for half an hour or more at a time unheeding the presence of his attendants, and they, guessing at what his thought must be, did not like to interrupt him. With the long eye of memory he looked much farther than the Hampshire coast, imagining what a crowd of republican vandals might have done to his carefully collected art treasures, or trying to get the feel of the grassy rides of Windsor. How long would it be, he wondered, before he rode there again? Or enjoyed the company of his wife, whom he liked to remember as gay and vivacious, not ill and worn as he had last seen her. How long before he would see his children? In spite of so much loyal help, was he destined never to get free?

At least Osborne and Worsley had got safely away in spite of that murderous fusillade. And Hammond seemed to have turned a blind-eye towards the merchant Newland, against whom nothing could actually be proved and without whom the castle would get no sea coal. Charles roused himself from the melancholia which had begun to enwrap him since he moved into these duller rooms. He reminded himself that no monarch ever had been more blessed in his personal servants. He turned and smiled at Herbert who was looking up some passage for him in a book. "How one misses Harry Firebrace and his irrepressible cheerfulness!" he said.

Mary, who was bringing the warming-pan into his bedroom, looked up at mention of that name and saw him through the open door. She thought how much his Majesty had aged. Woman-like, she noticed that his clothes were not quite so immaculate as when he first came, and that his rich brown hair was greying, and his little pointed beard unkempt. It seemed to her both pitiful and foolish that since his own two barbers had been sent away he should have refused the services of any other. Probably it irritated the Governor too, because he had sent his Majesty an expensive set of razors which were still there on a shelf unused. In a man as fastidious as Charles, such slovenliness looked like a deliberate gesture designed to underline his wrongs.

Moving the warming-pan up and down between the sheets, Mary put the hard thought from her. It might well be that sheer weariness of spirit made the poor King negligent, and he too was missing Harry—and his family, of course, and all his interests and pleasures. "His Majesty seems very low-spirited to-night," she remarked to Mildmay, who in the absence of a Groom of the Bedchamber was laying out the royal nightshirt.

"I have been trying to persuade him to let me ask the Governor once more if he can have a morning's hunting. Though I am afraid it will be useless," Mildmay told her. "His Majesty does so miss his dogs and horses."

An idea came to Mary—one of those impulsive ideas which endeared her to so many different kinds of people. For the first time, moved by compassion, she wanted to do something for the royal prisoner for his own sake. "Master Mildmay—" she ventured, a little breathless at her own presumption.

"What, Mistress Mary?"

"Do you suppose the King would like to have one of my father's—of my—young spaniels? They have no pedigree, of course, but the mother came from the Oglander kennels." She remembered how often she had held Pride of the Litter's warm body close during the misery of the past few days. "It would be company—" she urged.

"I think it is an excellent idea," said Mildmay, wondering why none of them had thought to get the King a dog before.

Mary withdrew the warming-pan from the bed, emptied the cooling coals on the fire, and prepared to go. "Then if I bring one of them will you give it to his Majesty?"

Like most courtiers, Anthony Mildmay seldom missed an opportunity of presenting personally anything likely to please his master. But there was something about this girl which brought out his better nature. He had often thought how pleasant it would be to have such a daughter. "Bring the dog and give it to his Majesty yourself. Bring it one rainy day when he cannot get out to play bowls," he said.

So the next afternoon Mary stood hesitantly just inside the door of the Presence Chamber. The weather had broken completely and the day had turned so chilly that a small fire had been kindled, and the King was sitting by the hearth reading. Master Mildmay, who was in attendance, had—rather meanly, she thought—gone out of the room as soon as he had admitted her.

Her courage nearly failed her, but in her nervousness she unwittingly clutched the little dog so tightly that he yelped. The King looked up and saw her standing there in her sad black gown and having now learned the cause for it, he rose and went to her as if she had been a queen, and led her to the fire. "They have just told me about your father," he said. "He was a friend of mine and now I shall always be his debtor—and yours. God grant I may be worthy of such sacrifice!"

Because of the real kindness in his voice her eyes suffused with tears. She could think of no adequate words and as soon as he had seated himself again she held out Pride of the Litter. However much she hated to part with him, being Mary, she had brought the best. "I thought perhaps your Majesty might deign to accept him," she said. "Your Majesty must often be lonely too."

"Very often, Mary."

He snapped his fingers invitingly and without the smallest respect for royalty Pride of the Litter leapt onto his knee, licking his hands and sweeping aside his bookmarker with one eager wag of a freshly brushed tail. "Little rogue!" laughed the King, as Mary retrieved it from beneath the bookrest.

"He is not very obedient yet, sir," she apologised. "But he is so affectionate that he can be a great comfort."

"Do you not need the comfort yourself?"

"There are three others in the litter."

"Then he shall be called Rogue and come for walks with me," said Charles.

"And if it should please your Majesty I will come and fetch him for his exercise when it is wet."

Mary would have curtsied herself out, but he motioned to her to stay and enquired after her aunt. "And I have to thank you for the letter you managed to convey to me after Harry Firebrace left. It contained news of the Duke of York's escape from St. James's Palace to Holland, which was of great comfort to me. Firebrace has spoken very highly of you, and I have no doubt you too miss that volatile young man."

"I do indeed, sir," admitted Mary. "But I interrupt your Majesty's reading."

Charles smiled at her and for a brief span she, like Harry, was to come beneath the spell of his charm. "I have a great deal of time in which to read, but few fresh people to talk to. And as you stand there you remind me that I have a daughter not much younger than yourself, whom I love very dearly."

"The Princess Elizabeth?"

"The Queen thinks she is cleverer than any of our children. Like me, she loves books and pictures; whereas her elder brothers and sister are more practical outdoor sort of people. Although she is only fourteen, it has made a bond between us."

Evidently he liked to talk about her and while he sat there caressing Rogue, Mary knelt on the hearth before him. "I am here by the Presence Chamber fire talking with the King of England!" she thought incredulously, and wished that her father could see her. But having always been interested in the younger princess, she was soon completely absorbed in what he was saying.

"When my little Bess was quite a child she slipped and hurt her leg while running across the floor at play, and although Sir Thomas Meyherne, the celebrated physician, has done all he can, she has never been over strong. She has not always been able to play with the others and it has made her more serious. Little Temperance, her big brother Charles calls her. Like yourself she is always caring for other people."

"Perhaps because she has known suffering and loneliness herself," suggested Mary.

"Her elder sister Mary, who is now Princess of Orange, tells a story of how, when Bess was quite small and fidgeting in church, they gave her a prayer book with pictures to keep her quiet. But soon everyone in the royal pew was distracted from their devotions by the sound of heart-rending sobs, and there was my little lass passionately kissing a picture of the crucified Christ and crying over and over again 'Oh, the poor man! Oh, the poor man!'"

"I wish I could see her!" said Mary.

"Perhaps you may some day. Who knows? Perhaps you may even come to London."

"It is scarcely likely, sir. And still less likely that her Highness would ever come here."

"God forbid!" Charles sighed and began stroking the sleeping spaniel's silky ears. "Ever since the rebellion began, have not she and young Henry been moved about from place to place by Cromwell's orders? I could pursue my plans to escape from this country with a more easy mind were I sure that someone was with her who would be kind."

Mary did not like to ask him where he might be going, and as he seemed to have fallen into a reverie and Rogue was asleep she quietly took herself off.

But there were many other afternoons when she came to fetch Rogue. Rain fell day after day, blotting out the landscape. It was the worst summer the Wight had known for years. The hours dragged and sometimes, beguiled by her fresh youthfulness, the King would talk to her. She had the still quality of a good listener and sometimes she thought he almost imagined himself to be talking to his beloved Bess, while at others he seemed to be merely speaking his thoughts aloud. Anthony Mildmay had gone to the mainland on business and she suspected that Master Herbert and Master Harrington, the two over-worked gentlemen left, were only too glad to retire to the ante-room and doze while she knelt before the fire listening to the King.

He told her about the wonderful masques his family had produced at Whitehall, the splendid paintings a Dutch artist called Van Dyck had made of his family and of the stolid conscientiousness of James and the drollery of Charles. To an only child it was like looking in upon the tantalizing warmth of home life. Because his own mind so often dwelt there he described his palaces and the fine buildings of London so that Mary was enthralled. But the conversation that was to stay most vividly in her memory was when he told her something of his youth in Scotland before ever he had expected to become a king.

Rain lashed the casements at Carisbrooke, the wind rose with the tide and whistled down the old chimney, every now and then blowing gusts of smoke out into the room. Instead of playing, Rogue whined dismally and crept with his tail between his legs beneath the table. The King had been telling her how he had had to overcome his fear of horses.

"You—who are the best horseman in the land!" she had exclaimed involuntarily.

"I suspect that most people have fears to overcome. Foolish, personal fears to which they are subject all their lives, and to which they would be ashamed to confess." And then, as the storm raged outside, he told her of an absurd nightmare he had had as a child. Instinctively she knew that this was the first time he had ever spoken of it. Perhaps when one has a strong, brilliant elder brother one would never talk about such a thing—except, perhaps, on the spur of the moment to some sympathetic, unimportant stranger. "If it had been but once," he was saying almost to himself. "But it was so many times. I would wake up t-terrified, but too proud to cry out for my nurse. I was always going out through some window—and the drop outside was deep and d-dark—"

"Then how your Majesty must have hated the manner of both those attempts at escape which Harry planned!"

"He was not to know. Another man would have thought nothing of it; whereas I, who am accustomed to hard hunting and have so frequently been on battlefields, had to nerve myself to climb out of an ordinary window!"

"And that is one fear which your Majesty never has overcome?"

"Oh, but I shall—just as I learned to master horses," said Charles confidently. "When I was so close to the adventure last time and your father grasped my hands the absurd fear left me. That second time I came almost within sight of conquering the horror of my old nightmare."

"Perhaps the third time—" said Mary without considering the unlikelihood.

The King laughed. "It seems absurd to suppose that I shall ever have to go out of a window like that again. But I have a feeling that if I do I shall go out without any fear at all, and find that there is nothing on the other side except an adventure which finally kills all fear.

# CHAPTER TWENTY-FIVE

W ITH LIBBY BACK AT work and Aunt Druscilla recovered
from her illness, Mary had more leisure. Taking advantage of a fine afternoon during that wet midsummer,
she sat on a stool near the laundry door with Libby's baby on her
lap. He had his mother's bright, dark eyes and was amusing to
play with, but now, bored with a surfeit of attention, he had fallen
sound asleep. So soundly that he did not stir when Wenshall came
clanking round from the well-house with the water pails.

Mary had never brought herself to speak to either him or
Featherstone since their betrayal of the King; and she knew that
several of their old comrades, sore from the resultant loss of their
Sergeant, avoided them. But only these two men who had been on
the platform that night could possibly answer the question that so
often tormented her. Acting on impulse, she called to him.

"Who actually shot my father, Wenshall?" she asked abruptly,
as he pulled up short with his slopping pails.

Taken aback, he was slow at answering. "'Twas Captain
Rolph—" he began.

"But he could not possibly have fired the shot," said Mary out
of the certainty of her secret knowledge.

"'Twas he as gave the order, an'—sorry as we might all be,
Mistress Mary—you know none of 'em durst disobey."

She knew, too, that the order, as the Governor had given it, was
right and just. A soldier had been caught in defection from duty.

But that the execution of it had been carried out with anything but zeal, she doubted. "Surely you or Featherstone must have *seen* who fired. You were so close," she urged.

"'Twas midnight," Wenshall reminded her. "When the King was half out o' window us *heard* a trigger click, one that didn't go off like. Someone cursed the plaguey thing—maybe Capt'n himself. Then he give the order, an' next us knew was the King had nipped back quick, there was a crack from one o' they new muskets and Sergeant was lyin' there groanin'. But if you was to ask me—"

But Mary was no longer asking him anything. She could not bear to hear about that groaning. And she had seen his troubled glance rest on the babe in her lap and knew, without his saying so, that it had been Rudy who had fired. She waved the old soldier away and he trudged on, shame-faced yet relieved, through the kitchen door.

Carefully, but without tenderness, Mary put Rudy's small son back in his basket, and sat there in the fitful sunshine, thinking. Surely public opinion would not condemn her father, or Osborne, or Dowcett or any of them if only they knew that this time they had been trying to save the King's life? Not even honest Republicans, like General Fairfax and the late John Hampden, could blame them if they knew of Rolph's dastardly plot.

And this public recognition of the King's danger was what Richard Osborne was working for. Though she knew, better than anyone, how much revenge and self-justification entered into his purpose.

Immediately upon his arrival on the mainland he had written to Lord Wharton, in whose household he had been, asking him to lay the matter before Parliament; but the cautious, pleasure-loving old man had merely put the letter in his pocket. Through Trattle, Osborne had managed to let her know of this and of his disappointment. And then, determined not to be thwarted, it seemed he had boldly sent the same written statement to Parliament. The Commons, not being wholly ignorant perhaps of the Army's violent plot, would have ignored the matter, but the Lords had insisted that any possibility of danger to the King's person must be looked into. And so Osborne had been promised a hearing and offered safe conduct to London.

This was common knowledge on the Wight because in consequence Rolph had been summoned to answer the charge. Although he was better and about his duties again, he was still a sick man and had tried to excuse himself on the grounds that he was not yet fit to travel. But Parliament had insisted.

The next excitement had been when Dowcett was fetched, also under safe conduct. Osborne had asked that he and Worsley might appear as witnesses. Worsley had gone into hiding and could not be found, and his friends thought that he had probably doubled back on to the island and did not want to bring trouble on his family for harbouring him. But Dowcett, having a beloved wife on the mainland, went willingly enough. Before leaving he had been allowed to bid good-bye to Mistress Wheeler and Mary who had been preparing his clothes for the journey, and he had left with them a rough copy of the statement he had prepared as evidence for the Committee of the House of Lords.

"I am ready to take oath," he had written, "that Mr. Richard Osborne told me the King's person was in great danger, which information was the cause of my engagement in this business." He had described Rolph's plan to lure the King away and kill him and had added, "I am ready likewise to depose that the said Rolph came to me when I was a prisoner in the castle, and in a jeering manner asked me 'why the King came not down according to his appointment?' and then with great indignation and fury said that he had waited under the new platform with a good pistol to receive him if he had come."

And now the trial was going on in Winchester. Everyone was talking about it—people on the mainland because it threw light on what had been happening to the royal prisoner on the island, and people on the Wight because they knew the protagonists. And public favour was swinging towards Osborne, as it always must towards a man who goes out openly to claim justice rather than to a man who makes excuses when asked to come forward.

The court, rumour said, would be packed with Rolph's supporters, and even now the verdict might be going against her friends. Dowcett's poor wife must be frantic with anxiety and Mary found herself caring for Richard Osborne's safety more than she would ever have thought possible. He had asked her to marry him when she herself was unhappy, and now concern for his danger so occupied her thoughts as to turn them even from the all-absorbing emotions of first love and first irrevocable loss.

Although both King and Governor were personally interested in the trial, neither of them had received any reliable information for some days. Dispatches took so long to reach the island. Mary had never realized the frustration of it until now, when she had close friends on the other side. Her thoughts were so much with them that she scarcely noticed the arrival of Trattle's cart or the stir caused by the weekly supply of liquor being unloaded until one of his men, bringing a few sacks of bran to the laundry, dropped one almost on her feet. Because the strain of the last month or two had told upon her, she jumped nervously and gave vent to an exclamation of annoyance. But instead of receiving an apology she heard a pleasant voice enquiring whether by any chance she were Mistress Mary Floyd.

She looked up into a likeable, fresh-complexioned face which showed more refinement than she would have expected in a dray-man's mate, and was filled with compunction because the fellow seemed to be sweating unduly from his labour; and suddenly it occurred to her that the sack might have been dropped purposely. She got up eagerly, hope flaring in her. "Have you a message for me from Master Trattle?" she asked eagerly.

"Not *from* him, although it is by his connivance that I am able to bring my news. It will take a long time to tell, and this is scarcely the place."

The coolly amused voice was no labourer's, and for the first time Mary noticed the freckles. She looked more attentively at the well-built figure clad in fustian with a floury sack flung across the shoulders, and recalled what Dowcett had said about an intrepid woman who, in coat and breeches, would easily pass for a man. "You are Mistress Jane Whorwood!" she stammered in surprise.

"And Trattle's drayman has instructions to lay a life-size dummy of sacks at the bottom of his cart and drive off without me."

Jane Whorwood's buoyant manner would have cheered anyone. Mary carried Libby's baby into the laundry where his mother was working and hurried her unexpected visitor up to the housekeeper's room. She was amused to see how readily her aunt made friendly contact with a woman as decided and practical as herself. They had worked in the same cause for so long that it seemed like finding a missing piece of the game, Druscilla said.

"If this escape business had been left to us women in the first place, the King would have been free months ago!" laughed Jane Whorwood in her forthright way. "And now I will strike a bargain with you both. I will give you first-hand news of all our mutual friends if you will help me to see the King." But before coming to the purpose of her visit she expressed her sympathy for their bereavement with the sincerity which endeared her to so many people.

"Master Dowcett told us that you have known his Majesty for years," said her hostess.

"My father was Surveyor of the Stables to the late King James, and my step-father was a Groom of the Bedchamber, so I was often at Court. And that is where I met your Governor's mother. I came up here with Mistress Hopkins, the Newport schoolmaster's wife, yesterday, to pay our respects to Mistress Hammond, but although the old lady spoke for us to her son, he would not allow us to see the King."

"He knows too much about your activities with the ship," said Mistress Wheeler.

"My good friend Harry Firebrace warned me of that."

Mary looked up apprizingly. Although this woman of whom all men spoke so highly was comely enough, she must be nearly forty. And past love affairs—or so it seemed to a girl not yet eighteen. And any friend of Harry's must be served. "I could take his Majesty a message or a letter," she offered.

"Thank you, but I must see him. William Hopkins tells me that his Majesty has been asking for me continually. They all want me to impress upon him the wide rift there now is between Parliament and Army, and that it is from the Army that he stands in most danger. Besides, I know what Charles *is* once a correspondence about some plan is started. He never *could* make up his mind."

"Then you have yet another plan for his escape?" asked Mary, impressed by her familiar reference to the King.

"Master Hopkins and I have. And we want it all settled *now*. The Hopkinses and those two useful Newport men, Newland and Trattle, whom I met in their house, are convinced that there is strong Royalist sympathy here, and we mean to rouse the whole island and hold the Governor captive while we get the King away."

Neither of her listeners made any comment. They had heard so many plans discussed and knew the difficulties better than she did. And Mary was impatient to hear news of Osborne.

"And now is the moment to do it," went on Jane Whorwood unperturbed. "With that brute Rolph away and a wave of sympathy stirred up all over the country by Osborne's bold revelation. We must be ready to act *now*, the moment he is vindicated."

Mary turned to her, caring little for the plan but radiant with excitement. "Then the trial is over? And he has been successful?"

"As successful as a loyal subject is ever allowed to be in courts set up by those sanctimonious Roundheads! The fact that no action is being taken against him proves that they are powerless to disprove his accusations. Because of the strong feeling in his favour neither Parliament nor the Army dare molest him openly. They dismissed the case, but he asked me to tell you that he will have to lie low for a while."

Mary picked up her skirts and executed a triumphant little *pas seul*, and her aunt, who was in her confidence and full of a new gratitude to Osborne, sat down with a sigh of relief. "When they appointed Sergeant Wild as judge we scarcely supposed he had a hope," she said. "He was that inhuman wretch who condemned poor Captain Burley to death."

"This trial was just as much of a farce. I went to the Assizes myself. The judge harangued the jury in Rolph's defence and read out a laudatory letter about him, written by Colonel Hammond. And even though no one could disprove the truth of Osborne's statement or of Dowcett's corroborating evidence, the Commons proposed that Rolph should be paid compensation. But the Lords vetoed that."

"Anything you and the Hopkinses plan to do should be done before Major Rolph returns," warned Mistress Wheeler. "For he will certainly come back more full of venom and self-confidence than ever."

"So he is a Major now? Oddfish, how the man steps up!" Standing tall and crop-headed before the window, the indomitable Whorwood woman appeared to enjoy her brief excursion into masculine freedom.

"He will not be satisfied until he is Governor of this castle," prophesied Druscilla Wheeler. And when the other two looked at her in startled protest, she merely added "Mark my words!" and went on to ask about her favourite, Dowcett.

"Firebrace tells me they took him back to the prison where he was lodged pending the trial. But his wife is allowed to visit him and he is hoping for an early release."

Mary bent down to adjust a loose buckle on her shoe. "And Harry himself?" she asked, as casually as she could.

"I left him in London with Titus. They are prepared to come back here and help if we can find enough supporters to take the castle." Aware now of a lack of warmth for her fantastic scheme, Jane Whorwood added with truth, "It will be a manner of escape much more suitable and attractive to Charles than disguises and climbing out of windows."

"And cause the death of many more men," Mary remarked with bitterness.

"Poor Burley thought he could take the castle," sighed her aunt.

"But that absurd rising was not properly organized. Why should it be impossible?"

"We had a garrison of twenty then, and half our guns were obsolete. Whereas now we have over two hundred of Cromwell's picked troops," said Mary.

"And more than two thousand secret Royalists living round about. And, between ourselves, Mistress Hammond told me that her son does not sleep too well at night for thinking of them! You have a very fine militia, I am told—trained by loyal local gentry like the Oglanders and the Worsleys and the Leighs. And I tell you that now is the Heaven-sent moment because several ships of Cromwell's Navy have gone over to Prince Charles in Holland."

Jane Whorwood had the same infectious kind of enthusiasm as Harry Firebrace, so that somehow her scheme did not sound so hare-brained now.

"We had not heard that. How wonderful it would be if the Prince were to come sailing across the North Sea and rescue his father!" exclaimed Mary. "I will try to get you into the King's room to-night."

"In those clothes!" objected the royal laundress.

"It could only be *done* in those clothes," decided Mary. "That is what gave me the thought. You remember, Aunt Druscilla, the Governor gave orders for that piece of the old wall to be patched up. The piece where the plaster fell when the new bookshelf was fitted. And the plasterer is coming out from Newport to do it while his Majesty is at supper."

"Well?"

"Mistress Whorwood can *be* the plasterer. I will take her in and hide her in the garde-robe. I am afraid, Mistress Whorwood, you will have to wait there while the real plasterer does his work."

It seemed that nothing ever deterred Jane Whorwood from her objectives. "What a surprise it will be for Charles!" she exclaimed delightedly. "He was furious because Hammond would not let me in yesterday. But how shall I get out?"

"I will wait for you at the foot of the stairs. Major Rolph usually sits there in the doorway of his room, but now he is away the guards are getting lax."

It was always with difficulty that she could bring herself to mention the man's name.

After the King had supped and locked himself into his bedroom as usual, Mary waited a long time. Much longer even than it should take for so concise a woman as Jane Whorwood to convince the King of his danger and to give him a clear idea of the proposed plot. So long that the shortening summer evening had grown dark and Mary was beginning to worry lest the friendly sentries at the gatehouse would be changed before she came. But at last there were cautious footsteps on the stairs and the King's visitor joined her with just that nice margin of safety which suggested that the whole business would indeed have been better left in her hands, She had the air of one whose visit has been successful, and seemed as humorous and unruffled as before. "They will think you are letting out a lover!" she said, with her deep gurgling laugh as Mary flung a cloak about her. "Do you not mind?"

"I have been called upon to do so many unlikely things since the King came here that I think I have come past minding," said Mary, half-rueful and half-laughing too.

Before leaving the shadow of the building Jane bent and kissed her. "You are very sweet, as Richard Osborne and Harry both said you were," she whispered. "Sweet enough for all the happiness which I am sure is coming to you."

Mary drew back abashed. "Oh, so they have been talking about me!"

"People do tell me things, you know. Besides, I was to give you this."

Mary felt a small packet pushed into her hands. "From Harry?" she asked involuntarily.

"No, from Richard. All Harry asked me to tell you was that his wife is almost cured of her distressing malady. It may well have been out of generosity to his friend that he sent you the message."

"Do you suppose that he will go back to her?"

"Being Harry, he will probably do what is right. But at the moment he is concerned only with the King's cause."

As they crossed the starlit courtyard Jane thanked Mary cordially for helping her to spend those hours with the King, but before they reached the gatehouse she added with a gentleness which sat oddly on her capable buoyancy, "Life must have grown very complex for you, you poor child. But there are two things you will do well to consider. That when a man who has acquired some reputation for philandering does not so much as look at any other woman for weeks, beckon she never so sweetly, he is probably very deeply in love. And that even though it may not bring the same ecstasy, it is always less painful to be deeply loved than to be extravagantly loving."

Mary was still remembering the words next morning, rather resentfully. What right had an exuberant, middle-aged woman who went to such lengths to spend three hours in a married man's bedroom to offer her good advice?

"Aunt Druscilla," she said, as they were making the King's bed.

"Yes, child?"

"Do you suppose that the King and Jane Whorwood—"

"No, I do not," answered her aunt crisply. "Not on her side, anyway. Though I admit that many people might, seeing all she has done for him."

"She must feel very flattered that his Majesty is so anxious for her company."

"Probably he is starved for the society of women from his own world. He may even, in his loneliness, have conceived a romantic attachment for her. She is a very attractive woman." Mistress Wheeler jerked the bed-hangings to just the right daytime position, which she considered that neither her niece nor that scatter-brained Libby ever achieved. "Besides, I understand she has a lover in Oxford."

All of which left Mary feeling that life was more complex than ever. Her hand went to her throat to finger the locket which Richard Osborne had sent her. The feel of it, warm against her flesh, was strangely comforting. It was solid gold and heart-shaped and plainly uncomplicated as to its meaning.

# CHAPTER TWENTY-SIX

———

A<small>S</small> M<small>ISTRESS</small> W<small>HEELER</small> <small>HAD</small> said at the time, it was difficult for an overner to know the precise difficulties or to
assess the chances of a scheme prepared for the island.
But although nothing came of Jane Whorwood's bold plan for
attacking the castle, conditions within it seemed to improve from
the time of her visit.

Druscilla herself began to think of something besides her
bereavement. Missing Agnes Trattle as she sometimes did, she
had found comfort in talking to another congenial woman, and
hearing news of mutual friends had revived her interest in people
and places she had known on the mainland. "If the Governor
can spare me, I might accept Mistress Whorwood's invitation to
stay awhile in Oxfordshire," she remarked one day. And Mary,
thinking how good it would be for her, had promised to do her best
to perform her aunt's duties during the time she would be away.
Not for worlds would she herself have risked leaving the Wight lest
Richard Osborne might not know where to find her.

Jane's unexpected visit had done wonders for the King too.
Apart from the pleasure he took in seeing her and talking over
old times, she had left him with fresh hopes and interests. He
began one of his lengthy correspondences with the Master of the
Grammar School about the details for his escape; but the clear
picture of the mounting differences between Parliament and Army
which Jane had drawn for him had started in his mind the idea

of playing one off against the other to his own advantage. This had been his policy before when Scots and English had fallen out among themselves, but it had ended disastrously. The Scots had handed him over to the English and so, by way of Holtham House and Hampton Court, he had come to this captivity in Carisbrooke.

Now, learning that the Parliamentarians were finding it difficult to hold their own against the dictates of an all-powerful Army, he wrote to Westminster, suggesting the possibility of further negotiations for agreement with himself. With Hammond's willing concurrence he sent the letter openly, and felt that once again he had something to hope for. September had brought a belated summer and in the golden weather he went out daily to play bowls. He resumed his walks round the battlements with Rogue at his heels, and quoted still more frequently those Latin words *Dum spiro, spero* which had puzzled Mary until Master Herbert told her they meant "While there is life there is hope."

Then came the glad day when three Commissioners arrived to discuss plans for drawing up a treaty. It was a glad day for all men of moderate thought because it brought the first gleam of hope that Charles might be allowed a controlled monarchy and that internal peace might be restored to their long-tortured country.

"And who do you suppose has come with them?" cried Mary, rushing into her aunt's room. "Master Titus! And they have allowed him to bring Babington, the King's barber. They say they will come up here to see us as soon as they can find a free half-hour."

"It will be good to talk to someone from the outside world again," declared Mistress Wheeler. "Never did I think I should be penned up in a country castle for the best part of a year!"

"Titus says that if a reasonable basis for a Treaty can be arranged it will take place over here. There will be a kind of armistice and all the King's friends will come flocking back. Even Harry Firebrace, perhaps, and Richard Osborne."

"Firebrace, very likely; but surely not Osborne, child. Not now with that fiend Rolph back here and having more say in things than ever!"

It was a happy if brief reunion with Titus. Babington was

allowed to stay and—most important of all—the preliminary talks went well. Charles Stuart began to look a different man. With hair and beard neatly trimmed, and his old lightness of step, he set about his preparations. Now that new clothes were being made for him Mistress Wheeler was officially reinstated as Laundress and Mistress of his wardrobe, and one of the first things he did was to ask her to have a new pair of boots made for him because he might soon be riding again. It had been definitely decided that the Treaty would be made in Newport and the Mayor and Corporation were putting their Town Hall at the disposal of both parties, which meant that Charles would be free to leave the castle and stay in the town. William Hopkins immediately offered him the use of the school house, an arrangement which his Majesty accepted with alacrity. Although it would be very small to accommodate him and his immediate suite, the King found interesting employment in discussing the necessary alterations.

After ten months of captivity these brighter prospects seemed to him like an answer to his constant prayers. He would soon be free to ride or walk about the island—free as he had been at Hampton Court—save that now he must give his parole not to try to escape. "This time next week, by the Grace of God, you will no longer be my gaoler," he told Hammond, unaware perhaps of how fully the sorely tried Governor's relief matched his own.

Being by nature no idler, Charles was glad to be busy again. Apart from his devotions and his exercises, much of each day was now taken up in preparing speeches which he would make during the Treaty discussions, and much in quiet thought. Instead of dwelling upon plans for escape his mind was determining just how far he would allow his enemies to push him, and what terms he could bring himself to accept. But the pleasantest task of all was making a list of the people who had served him so well in the past and who were to be allowed, during the negotiations, to serve him again. Colonel Legge and Dowcett were still under restraint, and with Major Rolph now in charge of all troops stationed on the Wight it would be madness to include Osborne's name. But although his Majesty was under the galling necessity of submitting his list for the approval of Parliament, he forgot no one. Among the first names which he wrote were those of his old friend Ashburnham, of Firebrace and Cresset, of Titus and Murray—and, of course, of Mistress Wheeler "with whatever maids she chooses to bring."

The extra work of packing up the King's clothes and their own was a blessing to both Druscilla and Mary as it took their minds off the loneliness of those off-duty hours which Silas Floyd used to spend with them. At the Governor's request they went on ahead into Newport to arrange the King's possessions; regretting only that by so doing they missed the moving moment when the best horse in the stables was brought round and his Majesty rode out from the castle again for the first time since his visit to Sir John Oglander.

The excitement in Newport and the coming and going between there and Cowes was reminiscent of those November days when he had first arrived, but this time all was on a far larger scale. Every day shiploads of friends and officials came over until it seemed that half the population of London must be crowded on to an island only twenty-four miles long. Titled families, accustomed to living in large mansions, hired ordinary small houses in Newport streets. Solemn-looking, soberly-garbed Commissioners booked all the bedrooms at the "Bull." Cavaliers in their worn finery made the "George," opposite the Town Hall, their headquarters. Trattle at the "Rose and Crown" could have let even his attics twice over, while a whole army of clerks and servants found themselves lodgings wherever they could. Shopkeepers and householders made more money in a week than they usually saw in a year, the grammar-school boys enjoyed an enforced holiday, and market days were like Bedlam let loose with Puritans in steeple hats, fine ladies in ruffs, soldiers, drovers, and beasts all blocking the narrow streets. The great farm manors in outlying villages sent in cartloads of produce to feed them all, the small river harbour was packed with barges, and even merchants like Newland and brewers like Trattle found their resources so strained that they had to be augmented from the mainland.

The Earl and Countess of Southampton, who had given sanctuary to the King on his flight from Hampton Court, hired a house in Lugley Street, hard by the school, and Mistress Whorwood joined them there, so that the King was able to enjoy their company. And because Master Hopkins's house was so over-crowded they offered to take in the King's Laundress and her assistant, an offer which pleased and flattered Mistress Wheeler immensely.

Once the Treaty negotiations had begun, the King would saunter forth each morning along St. James's Street, turning left past church and Square along the High Street to the Town Hall, and the loyal visitors at the "George" opposite would wave their hats and handkerchiefs and break into rousing cheers. He looked just as dignified and immaculate as they remembered him, though a little aged perhaps. He looked, in fact, just as everybody expected their King to look. But to Mary, who had knelt listening to him by the fire during some of his darkest hours, the transformation seemed little short of miraculous. Even with awed recollections of his first coming, it was difficult to believe that this composed figure, dressed with such quiet distinction and followed respectfully by a posse of courtiers could be the same unkempt and ageing man whom she had tried to comfort. All who had been in close attendance upon him must have felt the same, she supposed.

"That the likes o' I should 'a had the uppishness to yoppul away to a real King like 'ee!" exclaimed old Brett, finding himself standing beside her in the street as the impressive little procession went by.

"I am glad it was given to both of us to help him a little," said Mary, with tears suddenly stinging her eyes. "His Majesty is gone out of our reach in a manner of speaking, but please God he may stay that way! May he never be so cast down again!"

During those dreary days when he had been in and out carrying fuel Brett had come to know his sovereign better than many in more exalted stations. "Zo a wull if Treaty be proper trigged up. But that calls for givin' ground on both zides, I reckon. An' that be a game King b'aint more'n middlin' at," he muttered wisely.

King and courtiers and waiting Commissioners passed into a Town Hall which looked far too small to hold them all. And, as the watching crowds dispersed and the daily business of the place went on again, Mary shivered. It might have been because a cloud had passed across the October sun, or because a humble old servant's remarks had reminded her of words she had recently overheard on the lips of more important people in the King's over-crowded ante-room, where privacy was at a premium. "Being sick of this state of affairs and secretly afraid of the Army, members are in the mood to meet his Majesty *now*. But more concessions will have to be made by both parties," Titus had said anxiously.

"His Majesty will never make concessions where his religious principles are involved," the Earl of Southampton had answered.

Apart from the grander manner of the phrasing the words had meant much what Brett was meaning now, but although they had filled her with a sense of foreboding she had not stopped to listen to any more at the time because she had heard Harry Firebrace's voice, crisp and cheerful, on the stairs. Filled with sudden panic, she had caught up her cloak and run out with the others who were going to watch the daily spectacle.

But what wisdom decreed, her heart denied, and it was impossible to avoid meeting him for long. He was the born aide-de-camp, and had been one of the first people the King had sent for. And next day they came upon each other without warning in one of Mistress Hopkins's rooms.

His delight at seeing her again was boundless, sincere, and unembarrassed. He would always like being with her, and yet she felt sure his heart had not been rent as hers had been. Otherwise how could he have come straight to her and taken her hands as though she were the most precious being on earth—and then so rightly let them go? "He never loved me as I loved him," she thought. "He only found that he *could* have loved me had he been free. There will always be a small scar on his heart, perhaps, made by the pity of it. When he is alone sometimes of a summer's evening he will know the sadness of regretting. But his is the spontaneous kind of nature which can love and give happiness to so many."

He spoke of Richard Osborne's courage in pressing his case, of Dowcett's joy at reunion with his wife, of the anxious time he and Titus had had while waiting on the mainland for the King, of everything but their last meeting when she had unwittingly revealed her love. And all the time he kept thinking, "Dear God, how sweet she is, and how desirable! If I took her to live with me in sin I could make her wildly happy for a week and then—who knows?"

But even in the first half-hour of their reunion he was still caught up in pressing duties for his royal master. And in spite of everything he could still set her laughing about it with something of the old, crazy gaiety.

"What in Heaven's name, Harry, are you doing with that business-like account book and that basket of tired-looking mushrooms?" she asked, noticing for the first time that he had been carrying them.

"His Majesty has asked me to take over Dowcett's work as Clerk of the Kitchen."

"As well as being Groom of the Bedchamber?"

"Only until Sir William Boreham arrives, who understands the ordering of food for the King's table."

"Which obviously you do not!" laughed Mary.

"I told his Majesty so and begged to be excused. I even found a man who had just arrived here who had been Comptroller in one of the palaces, and who was yearning for the appointment. Not knowing one end of a sheep's carcass from the other myself, I tried to push him forward, but the King would not hear of it."

"Yet why? For seriously, Harry, it must be most difficult for you. From hearing my aunt ordering for the Governor's table, and from being with my father when he was in charge of the garrison stores, I know how much experience it needs. One has to know, for instance, how long fruit and vegetables will keep and what is in season—"

"And not order asparagus in October, as I have just startled one of your Newport tradesmen by doing!" Suddenly Firebrace's light-hearted gaiety deserted him, and he glanced over his shoulder to make sure that no one was listening. "The King, as you know, is an abstemious eater, and it has occurred to me that at the moment he may care less about my incompetence than the fact that he can trust me. Osborne and Dowcett both told me that they believe Rolph would have shot him; and I have wondered, Mary, whether his Majesty may be afraid that such enemies might now resort to poison."

Wild as the suggestion was, Mary did not find it difficult to believe any evil of Edmund Rolph. "In that case, if only to set the King's mind at rest, you will certainly have to do your best until this Sir William Boreham arrives," she said. "And with what slight knowledge I have gleaned I will help you. Let us give those mushrooms decent burial and go down and see what is already in the store room."

So once again she found herself working with Firebrace, and during the next few days they were thrown together far too much for her peace of mind. Too much for his, as well, she found.

She had tried to plan a series of appetising meals without being aware that he was looking closely over her shoulder, and had fought down the almost maternal tenderness that rose in her at sight of him striving to look coolly knowledgeable while ordering the necessary delicacies from the trades people or giving orders to the cook. But inevitably the day came when, at the end of a busy morning, the clamour of their senses destroyed all domestic pretence. He stood aside to let her pass through the still-room door. The room was small, the doorway narrow and both of them were young. She had to brush against him in passing, and he had only to stretch out his arms. "Let us get away from all this and ride up on to your beloved Downs this afternoon," he begged impetuously.

He had taken up much of her time and what more natural than that he should offer her some small excursion? But he had his Elizabeth, and Osborne's golden locket lay warm against her throat. "I am sorry," she murmured with averted eyes. "This afternoon I am going to see my friends the Trattles."

Recognizing it for the unpremeditated excuse it was, he had the sense not to offer to accompany her; and so that her purpose should not weaken, Mary went straightway to her aunt. "After dinner I am going to the 'Rose and Crown,'" she said.

"It is high time one of us went," agreed Mistress Wheeler. "Now that everyone knows we are free to come and go they might be offended if we do not."

"You will not come with me?"

"No. This afternoon Jane Whorwood is going to present me to the Countess of Southampton. But give them my love and tell Agnes I will come later. There is so much to do."

"You can manage without me until supper time?"

"Why not? We are all tumbling over each other in these cramped houses as it is, and in any case when I want you, you are always down in the kitchens or somewhere with that ubiquitous young man Firebrace."

Although Mistress Wheeler spoke with asperity, Mary was well aware that her aunt was so much taken up with her new friends that she was only too glad for her to go in her stead. Crossing the Square after dinner, she slipped for a few minutes into the church. "To be loved is always less painful than to love extravagantly," that woman of the world, Jane Whorwood, had said. But to accept love without honouring it was base. One must transmute it into a kind of spiritual armour; and for this one needed grace and strength.

Almost next door to the quiet empty church the "Rose and Crown" was full and noisy, but pushing open the door was like a homecoming. The public rooms were packed with strangers, all arguing loudly about the morning's proceedings. Peeping into the homely, familiar parlour, Mary perceived that it had been let to some wealthy family. She finally found Mistress Trattle, knight's daughter though she was, basting a fowl for some latecomers in the kitchen. Her quilted silk skirt was bundled up above her petticoat, she had a long iron spoon in one hand and a smudge of flour on her hot cheek, but she held out her arms and gave the orphaned Mary a daughter's welcome. "My dear—my poor dear—you have come at last!"

It was not until that moment that Mary realized how often of late she had longed to come. "Aunt Agnes! Oh, Aunt Agnes!" she cried brokenly, burying her face against that comfortable bosom.

The chicken was left to the hustling and harassed maids, and Mary was taken up to the Trattle's bedroom because there was nowhere else to go. Trattle was summoned from his serving and Frances came running from her improvised attic.

"Oh, Mary, it is wonderful to see you again! We thought that horrid Governor would never let you come," she cried, hugging her excitedly. "And you have come in time for my wedding. I always vowed I could not be married without you as my chief bridesmaid."

"Perhaps Mary scarcely feels like weddings," suggested Edward Trattle, drawing his late friend's daughter against his side. "You look different somehow, child—"

"I am several months older," laughed Mary.

"But I do not think it is only that." He looked at her searchingly, thinking of all the events which must have changed her from a carefree child to a woman. "You have done some fine work for the King, Mary. Major Bosvile told us about the letters. And he was more concerned for you than for himself when that wretched ostler of mine turned up drunk. Your father would have been very proud of you."

"Offering the King a damask rose was nothing!" declared Frances generously, kissing her again.

Mary would have liked to tell them about emptying Major Rolph's pistol, but shame prevented her. Perhaps one day when things were in less of a turmoil she would tell Mistress Trattle everything—and it would be as if she were talking to the mother she had never known. For the present it was balm to be welcomed, loved, and petted.

"Bosvile is staying here," Trattle told her. "He has brought official despatches from the Prince in Holland. He says it feels as dull as flat ale to be delivering letters *openly*."

"And the kind man has brought me a roll of French silk for my wedding-gown. I must show it to you, Mary."

"Perhaps I can come in my free time and help with the making," offered Mary, thinking that it would keep her from the dangerous joy of spending idle hours with Harry. "When is the wedding to be, Frances?"

"It was to have been on Lammas Day but now it cannot be fixed at all."

"John Newland has been under suspicion, as you know, and the Mayor has been making things as difficult for him as he could," explained Trattle. "And now with the town full like this—"

"But as soon as the Treaty is signed and his Majesty safely back in London, perhaps we poor islanders will have time and space to consider our own affairs," said Agnes.

"At least you can come and see the silk, Mary," invited Frances, drawing her away for a bedroom gossip as of old. "I thought we should have been hearing of *your* wedding, my dear, with all those handsome gallants about the castle! Did you know," she asked, as soon as they were alone in her attic, "that that tall exciting Master Osborne came here?"

"On his way to the mainland? He risked his life by taking his case to court," remarked Mary noncommittally.

"He came here twice. And believe it or not," confided Frances, raising her rosy face from the clothes chest she was opening, "he kissed me. Not at all as John does. I am sure you cannot imagine how different it was."

"Perhaps he has had more experience," suggested Mary, with a delicious smile twitching the corners of her mouth.

"Of course, I reminded him I was betrothed."

"Of course," agreed Mary solemnly, remembering Osborne's jocund description of the event. And remembering, too, rather to her surprise, how very exciting his kisses could be.

"And what happened about that nice auburn-headed young man—Firebrace or some such name—whom you brought here last Christmas? I thought you were having an affair with him?" persisted Frances.

"He is already married," Mary heard herself saying quite steadily.

"Well, with *all* those good-looking young men about the castle, I must say you seem rather to have wasted your time!" laughed Frances. "But then you never were much interested in love affairs, were you?" The bride-to-be lifted the shimmering silk from the chest and laid it reverently across her bed. "There, isn't it lovely?" she breathed ecstatically. "Like a real Court lady's, Mistress Bess Oglander says. And it will be all the lovelier when your clever fingers have worked on it, my pet. Oh, how I ache to wear it!" The Trattles' pretty daughter went pouting to her mirror. "Imagine having to wait all this time for one's wedding, just because the King came to Carisbrooke!"

Mary picked up a fold of the lovely stuff with envious fingers. "So many things have happened—because the King came," she said.

# CHAPTER TWENTY-SEVEN

———⌾———

I N SPITE OF ALL the overcrowding and inconvenience, high
hopes of a national settlement and a better way of life insured
cheerfulness and good nature in Newport. During the first week
or so people of violently opposing persuasions went out of their
way to be polite to each other. But as the forty days allowed for
negotiations dragged by and every clause was bickered over and no
settlement reached, anxiety on both sides mounted and tempers
became more strained. There were arguments at street corners and
free fights in the taverns, and the soldiers frequently had to be
called upon to restore order.

The terms offered to the King were bitter as gall. They
included the maintenance of Presbyterianism for three years and
Parliamentary control of the Militia for twenty years, which would
have reduced his status to that of a puppet. Charles opposed each
clause with practised logic, and all present marvelled that there was
no stammering hesitation in his voice. But gradually he was forced
to make concession after concession, until it came to the matter
of his Church where he finally stood firm. By the end of October,
when he was very weary and the allotted time was running out,
he even agreed to the abolishment of bishops, a concession so
unpopular with some of his supporters that soldiers had to be sent
to quell their demonstrations at the "George"—demonstrations
which Charles himself deplored. He confessed to his friends in
private that he had made the concession solely in the hope of

delaying matters. He knew that the Commons were determined to reject his own proposals on religious matters and that the success of the Treaty was already doomed. And that therefore his only hope lay in effecting an escape during the few days left to him before he should be taken back to Carisbrooke.

Each day when he returned to William Hopkins's house the serene front which he had put up before the world gave place to preoccupied silence. This time escape was so desperately necessary that, once free of the strain of discussion, he could think of nothing else. To his vast relief Parliament decided that the negotiations might go on for another fortnight, and he was still allowed to walk about the countryside, although always within sight of his guards.

"Even if his Majesty can find the opportunity he will be too proud to break his parole," declared Mistress Wheeler. But Jane Whorwood explained that the King no longer considered his promise valid because he was not being allowed the same freedom from surveillance which he had enjoyed at Hampton Court. He had openly said as much to the Governor.

Whatever his inward feelings, Charles's outward fortitude remained unchanged. He spent hours at his desk as a man will who must clear up his affairs. He was there one evening early in November when Mary, hearing Rogue barking resentfully at the sentries and fearing the noise might be disturbing his Majesty, carried the little dog into the Presence Chamber. She set him down before the hearth and was going out again as quietly as possible when the King called her back. "Do you know where Richard Osborne is?" he asked.

"No, sir," she answered, hoping with all her heart that he would be able to tell her.

"Unfortunately, neither do any of us. But Master Mildmay suggested that you might know."

Mary stood there wondering why Master Mildmay should suppose any such thing, and saw that the King was pointing with his pen to a particular sentence in the letter he had just signed.

"I shall be glad if you or Mistress Wheeler can find means to send this to the Prince of Wales in Holland," he said. "But before I seal it, there is a passage here which I should like you to read, Mary. Should you ever meet Osborne again I should like him to know what I have written. It may prove useful to him."

His manner was gracious although not at all intimate as it had been when he had talked to her before the fire up at the castle. Mary knew that, considerate as he was, he did not usually speak intimately with any but his friends. She came to his side, still mystified as to why he connected her with Osborne and not a little confused lest she should be unable to decipher the passage. But it was very brief and his writing exceptionally clear. Looking over his shoulder, she read his request to his son. "If Osborne (who has been in trouble for me about one Major Rolph's business) comes to you, use him well for my sake."

Relief and gratitude welled up in her. "Somehow I will get it away," she promised, with shining eyes.

He sealed the letter and handed it to her with a smile. "Osborne may be a very reckless young man, but I should never hesitate to trust him," he said, in so calm a voice that she was not sure whether he was merely making a statement or giving her advice.

Seeing little hope for himself, it seemed that his Majesty was thinking a great deal just then about those who had risked their lives for him in the past. When the Army, growing impatient with Parliamentary discussions, sent their own ultimatum, the King refused it unconditionally because it contained a clause calling for the death penalty for some of his most loyal friends. Major Rolph, knowing well that he had the backing of the generals on the mainland, took more and more upon himself and, although the King complained of his offensive surveillance, Colonel Hammond dared not interfere with measures for watching his Majesty's movements, because he knew that both Rolph and he were dealing with a desperate man.

When Jane Whorwood, determined to find out what the generals were planning and the exact extent of the King's danger, set out for the mainland, Hammond made no objection. Foreseeing trouble on the island, he even asked her to take his mother with her so that the old lady might return home.

Jane found that the King's danger was great indeed. A Remonstrance had been drawn up by General Ireton and others, with the all powerful Cromwell's agreement, demanding that his Majesty be brought to justice for the bloodshed and mischief he had caused and that his two elder sons should surrender themselves for trial.

She hurried back to warn him, and somehow managed to cajole the officials at Portsmouth into providing her with a pass. Since the King had now defied the final demands of both parties, she begged Hopkins to help him to immediate escape. "Though let it be by some door and not from the top of the house or by means of ladders," she counselled, being more in his confidence than most.

But already the net was closing and it was too late for Hopkins or anyone else to act. Still more troops had been sent over to prevent any possible rising of the island Royalists, and General Ireton was trying to persuade Hammond to put the King back into captivity in the castle.

On the last Saturday in November when the sittings in the Town Hall terminated, the violent arguing of the inhabitants of Newport gave place to a feeling of helplessness as dreary as the weather. "My Lords," said Charles, in bidding farewell to the Commissioners, "you cannot but know that in my fall and ruin, you may see your own. I am fully informed of the plot against me and mine; and nothing so much affects me as the suffering of my subjects and the miseries that hang over my three Kingdoms, drawn upon them by those who, under pretence of good, violently pursue their own interests and ends."

He walked quietly back to the grammar school and everyone wondered what would happen next.

As a servant of Parliament, Hammond refused to change the King's lodgings without their orders, and General Fairfax was persuaded by fellow officers less moderate than himself to summon the Governor of the Wight to Army Headquarters at Windsor to discuss the matter. As a soldier, Hammond dared not disobey, but he immediately sent young Major Cromwell to Westminster with the General's letter, and with much misgiving left Rolph as his

Deputy, and Captain Boreman, who commanded the local militia, in charge of the castle and of the King's safety. He knew only too well that while Parliament was still debating the question of the King's future residence, the Army intended to seize the moment to strike and that all they wanted was to get him out of the way.

"So unpredictably turns the wheel of life," he said to Mildmay, in a moment of rare expansion, "that only my presence, which his Majesty has so often resented, now stands between him and his bitterest enemies."

All the members of the King's household who had spent the past year in the castle regarded Robert Hammond's departure with dismay. "It seems strange to think how my dear brother and all of us hated the appointment of a Parliamentarian Governor," said Druscilla Wheeler.

"And how we tried to hoodwink him," grinned Firebrace.

"He is very young for a governorship anyhow, and I do not think any man could have loathed his unexpected responsibility in this matter more," mused Anthony Mildmay, who had come nearer to being Hammond's friend than most.

"And if he does not come back we shall all be at the beck and call of Major Rolph!" said Mary, shivering at the thought.

The weather alone was enough to make anyone shiver. The elderly Earl of Southampton had begged leave to be excused duty in the school house and had taken to his bed next door with a chill, and the Solent was a fury of white-capped waves. Yet in spite of a tearing gale two senior army officers managed to get across soon after the Governor's departure. Although they landed as secretly as possible, they were met by Rolph, who conducted them straight to the castle. Everyone was agog to know what was going on up there and rumours soon spread that the few selected men they had brought were a force of thousands. Towards evening one of the officers, Colonel Cobbett, rode down into Newport and was closeted with Rolph, whose own company were now all billeted in Newport. The town seemed to be full of soldiers, and householders barred their windows uneasily and kept their wives and daughters indoors.

That evening the Earl of Southampton was taken worse and the women of the household were up late doing what they could for him. By nightfall his temperature had risen and his wife was seriously alarmed. "I will send one of the servants for Doctor Bagnell," offered Mistress Wheeler, knowing that both the Countess and Jane were strangers to the town. And when Mary went down to the door to direct one of the Earl's men how to find the doctor's house she was surprised to see Lugley Street and St. James's Street full of soldiers. The grammar school at the corner was surrounded. Although the rain fell in torrents they stood in groups about the doors and windows with the water pattering on their helmets and streaming from their cloaks, and when she looked out at the back she saw that there were more of them waiting silently in Master Hopkins's little garden. One of them pounced on the amazed servant and asked him for a password. Mary stood in the shelter of the doorway, filled with alarm. She saw the man point upwards to the lighted window where his sick master lay, and a corporal came and questioned him before they were satisfied as to his business and let him go. Bolting the door, she ran upstairs to tell the others.

"What are they all doing out there?" she asked Doctor Bagnell when he came. "What does it mean?"

"According to the Sergeant in charge it merely means that Major Rolph has doubled the guard because we are cursed with so many troops that there is nowhere left to sleep them," said the doctor, with a sceptical laugh. "But I never heard of troops yet who couldn't sleep soundly enough in a barn."

"Then it has come," muttered Jane Whorwood, losing all interest in the patient and pacing ceaselessly up and down her room. When the Earl had been given a sleeping draught and the house was quiet again, Druscilla and Mary, although wildly anxious, went to take what rest they could. But it seemed to Mary that she had only just drifted into an uneasy sleep when she was being jerked back into frightened consciousness by someone holding a guttering candle before her heavy eyes and shaking her by the shoulder. "Get up, child!" her aunt was saying between chattering teeth. "They have come for the King. And I am to go along to see to his clothes. You had better come with me."

Mary sat up, staring dazedly at her half-dressed relative. "You mean we are to go back to Carisbrooke? Now, in the middle of the night?" she asked, groping blindly for her clothes.

"No, God help us! It is almost dawn and the messenger from next door said they are taking him to Hurst."

"Hurst Castle!" exclaimed Mary, jolted wide awake by horror.

"Where is Hurst?" asked Jane Whorwood, coming in at that moment with another candle. She set it down on a tallboy and Mary noticed how her strong, capable hand was shaking.

"It is that grim-looking castle you can see sticking out into the Solent on a long spit of sand from the Hampshire coast. Opposite Sconce Fort, just past Yarmouth haven."

"Do you know anything about it?"

"No, except that the Captain of the castle is a black-bearded bully of a man called Ayers, and I have heard my father say that the place is in a shocking state of disrepair."

"Rolph's orders are that we are to be ready in a quarter of an hour," warned her aunt, gathering up what possessions she could. "The dear Lord knows what will happen to all our things up at Carisbrooke with all those plundering Ironsides!"

She and Mary made themselves as ready as they could for the journey, too much agitated to know what to wear or take. And all the time Jane Whorwood stood there trying to give them a picture of the night's doings and to marshall plans for their future meeting.

"I managed to see Harry Firebrace for a moment by the garden gate. They were as alarmed as we were at seeing the soldiers last night. The King sent a friendly Roundhead officer up to the castle for Captain Boreman, but he found him and his men practically prisoners. So the men next door were sure Rolph meant to make a *coup* of some kind. The Roundhead officer, may Heaven bless him, offered to get the King out under an army cloak as his servant, and Harry Firebrace was prepared to take his Majesty through the streets and knock up John Newland for a boat."

"Heavens, what a risk!" cried Mary, fumbling at the buckles of her shoes.

"No worse than being murdered like rats in a trap, as they half expected. But it wasn't as bad as that, God be praised! It seems a crowd of Rolph's men broke into the house—even into the King's bedroom—and told him to get up and dress and come with them. Before anyone was about, of course. He must be almost ready by now."

"Listen! There is a coach and some other vehicle being brought along," said Mary, leaning out of the window. The rain had ceased but dawn had not fully come, and only by the rumbling and creaking and the movement of feet as the troops made way could they be sure.

"They will not let either Harry or me go with him. They are afraid we should somehow get his Majesty out of their clutches," said Jane, helping Druscilla make up a parcel of her possessions. "So as soon as the Earl is fit to be moved we are going over with them to Titchfield. Try to get in touch with us there, Druscilla."

There was an impatient knocking on the door and Mary and her aunt had to pick up their bundles and go. Both of them stopped to embrace Jane who leant against the open doorway, all her brave hopes and splendid self-confidence broken at last. Her face looked aged and ravaged in the grey dawn light, and the extent of her caring was plain for all to see. "What will they do to him?" she moaned. "I implore you send me word how they treat him!"

Regardless of her grief, or of their reluctance to leave her, a couple of troopers hustled them down into the street. A coach stood before Master Hopkins's door surrounded by fully armed soldiers. More soldiers kept back a muttering crowd. Early as it was, the Royalists at the "George" must have heard the arrival of the coach and hastily dressed townspeople had run out from their houses, some of the women barefooted and with cloaks thrown over their nightshifts. And as they stood shuffling and craning to see what was going to happen to their King, a continuous muttering arose from their throats, rising to a frightening, dangerous growl every time a soldier pushed them back with musket butt or pike.

Mary, told to wait by the baggage wagon with her aunt, could see Rolph giving directions and Rudy, already mounted, holding his horse. Presently he disappeared with an air of importance into the school house, and Firebrace came out carrying his master's bible and a jewel case, which he placed carefully inside the coach. As he stepped back he turned his head as if looking for someone. Seeing Mary, he went to her, taking her hand in hurried, wordless farewell. His young face was white and drawn as she had never seen it. "His Majesty has had no breakfast," he said. "I had it prepared for him but the swine would not let him stop to eat it. He is coming now."

Both of them were quivering with nervous tension. Although they had no idea when they might meet again, their thoughts were not fully upon each other, and the gaze of each of them was on the open, closely guarded door.

After a moment or two Rolph reappeared in buff coat and crimson sash, with a fine plumed hat instead of a helmet on his closely cropped head. He was now Deputy Governor of the Wight, and wished all to know it, and seemed to consider it reason enough for swaggering out with his head covered before the King.

The crowd fell silent as Charles himself appeared, pale and proud, drawing his cloak about him against a sudden gust of wind. Though the guard hustled him he made them wait while Harry Firebrace knelt on the pavement to kiss his hand, then climbed without ceremony into the coach, leaning forward for a last sad look at his host and the little company of bare-headed gentlemen in the doorway, then with a gracious gesture invited Herbert, Harrington and Mildmay to join him. But Rogue, following closely at his heels, was scared by the concourse of people and the vehicles. He streaked between the wheels and ran to Mary. She picked him up and ran forward. They were all in the coach now and Rolph was already approaching as if to order the driver to move forward. The King would need all the comfort he could get at Hurst. Careless of all the eyes upon her, she outdistanced the Major to the coach and lifted up the little dog. Master Mildmay, sitting with his back to the horses, saw her coming and reached down and took Rogue from her. And at that moment she felt herself pushed roughly aside.

To her amazement the new Deputy Governor, with his hat still on his head, was about to swing himself up into the coach. Mary saw his well-polished boot on the iron step, his strong body braced to spring upwards—and apparently the King of England saw it, too. Just as Rolph was about to enter he shot out his own lightly shod foot and neatly dislodged him and, leaning across Herbert, slammed the door in the intruder's face. "It is not come to *that* yet, sirrah!" he said in that clear, far-reaching voice of his, "Get you out."

Rolph, taken by surprise, missed his footing and stumbled, his impudently retained headgear falling ludicrously over his eyes. And Mary, standing within arms length of him, almost hysterical with strain, suddenly laughed aloud with delight. Too late, with Rolph's dark eyes blazing at her, she clapped a hand over her mouth. The rapidly augmented crowd of Newport citizens, though the tears still stood in their eyes, took up her laughter. The delectable little incident would be told over and over again about the hated upstart.

The coach started with a lurch, and before jumping on to his waiting horse the man who had barely failed to seduce her caught Mary's arm in a cruel, twisting grip which made her cry out. "I shall be back, and I will have you yet, you haunting daughter of Jezebel," he swore, his working face too close to hers for any but Rudy to hear. "And if that play-actor Osborne dares to show his face on this insubordinate island again I will let the castle hounds loose on him!"

# CHAPTER TWENTY-EIGHT

———∞∞∞———

MARY WOULD ALWAYS REMEMBER that strange journey, taken with furtive haste in the chill half-light of early morning. She and her aunt were put into a covered waggon with the baggage and a hastily packed chest of the King's clothes. With soldiers riding before and behind it, they lumbered and jolted over rough country roads. They knew that they were making for the wilder, less inhabited western part of the island, instead of for Cowes. Every now and then, when the canvas flapped back in the wind, Mary caught glimpses of familiar country—the lovely village of Calbourne, snug under its hills, the thatched inn at Wellow famous for its smuggled wine, and Thorley Manor to which she had once ridden with her father with a message for the Leighs. But Rolph had more sense than to push on over the drawbridge into Yarmouth. Popular Captain Burley, in his heyday, had held Yarmouth Castle for the King, and most of the inhabitants were King's men still. There might be sympathy, opposition—all the things which Major Rolph and the officers from the mainland were trying to avoid. Already, now it was light, farm-hands were stopping work in the fields to stare. So after a hurried consultation Rolph sent a sergeant into the town to charter a ship, while coach and waggon and the handful of horsemen turned southwards along a narrow lane, crossed the river Yar by the causeway which alone connected the western peninsula of Freshwater Isle with the rest of the Wight, and then hurried back again along the far side of the river to Sconce Point. And there, stretching out before them from the mainland, less than two miles away, lay Hurst Castle, grey and formidable on its spit of sand.

The King rested in his coach until a little brig was seen tacking out from Yarmouth haven, and then made his way with the rest of them down the narrow, rough chine to the deserted beach where, a little farther westward, a copse of stunted, windswept oaks grew down to the edge of the low cliffs. And while he was standing there a man came out from the shelter of the trees to kiss his hand. "God go with your Majesty!" he said simply, bowing his young, bared head.

"Why, look, it is Master Edward Worsley—in one of the Gatcombe groom's clothes," Mary whispered to her aunt, as they waited by the baggage. "Surely Major Rolph will arrest him!"

But Rolph was giving last-minute instructions to his men, and either did not notice or did not care; for what could one more misguided island Royalist matter when the King would soon be securely in his hands on the other side of the Solent?

"It may well be that Rolph has never seen him and does not even know it is one of the men he was trying all those weeks to catch," whispered back Druscilla.

"And even then his mind was set only on catching Richard Osborne," agreed Mary, realizing with relief that only they two were likely to recognize Worsley.

They saw the King speak to him and give him something which he held reverently in his hand. Then Rolph came striding towards the King, Worsley disappeared, and all eyes were on the small boat which had put off from the brig to fetch them aboard. Already eager hands were hauling her bows on to the beach. The King's embarkation was secret and hurried, and this time he had to put up with Rolph's company. His Majesty's gentlemen climbed in after him, and Mary noticed that he never once looked back. "There cannot be very much that he wants to remember," she thought, regretfully jealous for her beloved island.

She and her aunt sat apart upon some baggage. Badly jolted by such sudden uprooting, Druscilla's methodical mind was on all the things left undone or left behind. Mary thought of the sad grave in Carisbrooke churchyard and remembered that Richard Osborne was somewhere on the mainland. She wondered if she would ever get to London and see all those wonderful places which of late she had heard so much about. It seemed strange to think that it was exactly a year ago since old Captain Burley had taken her to Brighstone Down and she had amazed Frances by saying that she did not want to visit the mainland. Now, with her father no longer here and so many people she knew on the other side, Mary began to think that it might be exciting after all. But what a strange, sad way to go there!

Chin in palm, she huddled herself against the wind, gazing across the water at the inhospitable walls and towers of Hurst. Presumably, the poor King must be as hungry as she was. Would they give him a meal directly he got there? Would they have enough food in that isolated place? Her domestic speculations were interrupted by someone calling her impatiently. The boat had returned for them and Rudy had been sent back. "The King is asking for that white dog he sets such store by," he was shouting through cupped hands. "They seem to think the little beast may have run back to the coach. Major Rolph says it will come to you if you call."

Mary had supposed that Rogue had gone with the King, and blamed herself for mooning there looking out to Hurst instead of making sure. While Rudy helped her aunt into the boat she ran back up the chine, whistling and calling. Breathlessly she made enquiries of the soldiers who had been left up there with the vehicles, but they were just on the point of leaving and had seen no sign of any dog. Probably he had chased off among the trees after a rabbit. She pictured the foul temper Rolph would be in if kept waiting at such a time, but she must call to Rudy to wait while she searched the little copse.

But when she emerged from the narrow chine onto the beach again the little boat had pushed off and was already halfway to the ship. Urged by a hail from her deck, the two boatmen were rowing hard and the tide was with them. Mary could see her aunt waving frantically and being held in her place lest in her agitation she should upset the boat. And then she saw Rudy standing in the stern looking back at her plight. Across the dividing water she heard him laugh suddenly and loudly as she herself had laughed in Newport at the Major's discomfiture. And seeing him wave derisively she knew that she had been tricked.

To have told Frances that she did not want to leave the Wight was one thing, but to be left behind without home or relatives or money in a place where Edmund Rolph would soon be back as Deputy Governor was altogether another. There was not another boat on that deserted strip of beach, or in panic she would have rowed after them. As it was she stood forlornly watching the distance widen until all the rest of the party were aboard and the Yarmouth brig setting sail for the mainland.

Footsteps crunched across the shingle and she turned to find Edward Worsley beside her. "That was a scurvy trick," he said. "Why did that Roundhead bastard do it?"

"Major Rolph's orders," she told him bitterly. "I laughed at him when he tried to get into the King's coach, and he swore he would get me. He wants to make sure I shall still be here, I suppose."

"Then you are Mary Floyd? Whom Osborne half-killed him for."

Mary nodded assent.

"And that lady in the boat would be Mistress Wheeler?"

"She will be cruelly upset."

"All of it is cruel," he said, glancing down at the treasured object in his hand as though he still could not believe it was his. "Imagine, even faced with the horrors of Hurst and—and the unknown—he gave me his watch. For what little I had done, so very unsuccess-fully. Would you like to see it?"

Mary smiled, glancing down at the familiar timepiece. "I have seen it so often," she reminded him. "It was always on the table beside his bed."

"Why, of course. It must be worth a great deal, but for me and my family its value will always lie in more than workmanship and gems." He put the beautiful thing carefully in his pocket and, in spite of his unashamed emotion on the King's behalf, courteously turned his attention to her problems. "I could perhaps persuade John Newland to have one of his men row you across."

"And be jeered at and refused permission? Or—worse still—admitted unprotected by men like the Captain of Hurst and Major Rolph?"

"No, I see that would not do."

"And Colonel Hammond has gone and the castle, where I live, is full of Cromwell's soldiers."

"Have you no friends you could go to?"

"There are the Trattles at the 'Rose and Crown'."

"You must go there, Mary. They are good people. If you will ride before me on my horse I can take you part of the way. Although being but a fugitive on my own land it can only be through the backways, as far as Gatcombe."

"Oh, Master Worsley, would you be so kind? But why should you bother at all?"

"Richard Osborne is a friend of mine. Had he been here just now and seen how they treated you there would have been murder."

He led her to the tree where he had hitched his horse, and they were soon riding quietly inland. "I heard about your father. All my family were grieved. It was a great loss to the island." Although gentle and cultured his voice had something of the broad native lilt. Mary and her friends had always been accustomed to think of him as one of the gentry to whom one merely curtsied, but now she felt completely at ease with him. "How did you know so much about me?" she asked, as they re-crossed the river causeway.

"Osborne once described you to me."

"What did he say of me?"

"He said you had a gallant bearing, golden-brown curls and the kindest mouth in Christendom. It must have been one of those nights when we were hiding in the woods and there was a romantic moon!" Dodging an overhanging bough he looked down to see if the description tallied and was evidently satisfied. "He said, too, that you had the look of a stained-glass saint waiting to be wakened."

Mary gave a little burst of laughter. "I—a saint? And wakened to what?"

"Now that I have seen you I know what he meant."

They rode on until the great Manor of Gatcombe was in sight. "*He* ought to have had the watch. He took far more risks than I," said Worsley, suddenly grave.

"The King has already remembered him," said Mary, and told him about the letter.

"He will be glad of it. If I know him he will want to go and fight for young Charles again."

A tremor of fear went through Mary. "Where is he now?" she asked.

"In London, as far as I know."

"Do you think he will come back?"

"Yes, I feel sure he will," said Worsley, who knew what it was to be in love. For was he not creeping about in borrowed clothes like this because he hoped, when the present trouble had blown over, to marry an island girl and settle down on the Wight.

His words made Mary feel more reconciled to having been left behind. She thanked him with her most charming smile and he set her down at the edge of his father's land, a mile or so from Carisbrooke, and she walked on towards Newport. She had had little sleep and no food, and as she went wearily past Trattle's Butt, where the townsmen had always practised their archery, she was thankful to see Trattle himself coming out of the gate.

"Why, Mary, what are you doing here?" he exclaimed in surprise. "We heard you and Mistress Wheeler had gone with the King."

"Aunt Druscilla went."

"Is it true that they have taken him to Hurst?"

"Quite true. I saw them set sail."

"And he is to be imprisoned in that hole?"

"I suppose so. Father told me the windows are so small that the candles have to be lit at noon. But I could not bear to tell Mistress Whorwood that."

She told him all that had happened and he was furious. "That jumped-up bootmaker thinks he is God Almighty! Is there no redress?" he cried, banging a mighty fist on the top bar of his gate.

"I had no definite permission," admitted Mary. "We only took it for granted that if Aunt Druscilla was ordered to go I should be allowed to accompany her." As full realization of her situation flooded over her she caught at his arm. "Oh, Master Trattle, do you think I could come back with you? I would work—I would help Aunt Agnes. You see, I dare not go back to the castle now. And I—I am so *hungry*..."

He did not wait to hear more. He took her by the arm and hurried her towards the Square. "Who wants you to work?" he said brusquely. "As long as I own a house with a roof to it, it is your home."

# CHAPTER TWENTY-NINE

———⊗⊗⊗———

MARY SAT SEWING IN the parlour of the "Rose and Crown," using the last of the January afternoon sunlight. The inn was her home now. The only home she had. And now that Frances was married, Agnes Trattle was doubly glad of her company and help. "More help than that dear, undomesticated daughter of mine ever gave me," she would say, laughingly. "And with all the fine folk from London gone, I might as well go out junketing or sit with folded hands as I used to do in my father's manor."

Mary was happy enough with such kind friends, and the cheerful coming and going of an inn kept her from brooding over her recent bereavement; but she missed the new friends she had made and all the exciting conspiracy that had gone on up at the castle, so that the past two months in Newport seemed like some strange backwater of existence which did not belong to her former life.

She seldom went out except to the shops or to visit Frances in her fine new home in Harbour Street. Major Rolph was back and she did her utmost to avoid him. At first she had worried very much about her aunt's welfare and natural anxiety on her behalf, but Jane Whorwood had been able to set their minds at rest. Soon after the King's arrival at Hurst Druscilla Wheeler had been allowed to visit Titchfield, taking letters from his Majesty in which he had written to his friends there that he was civilly used, and Jane had been able to tell her that Mary was with the

Trattles. The first arrival at Hurst had been horrifying, Druscilla had said. Lieutenant Colonel Ayres was as brutish as her brother had described him; and the roughness of his manners might have been abetted by Rolph, but Colonel Cobbett, who had been sent by Cromwell, had insisted upon reasonable respect and comfort for the King. His Majesty had been allowed to take his daily exercise along the two miles of sandy causeway to the mainland—which information had, of course, immediately fired Jane's and Harry's fertile minds with thoughts of rescue.

But whatever hopes they had entertained must be damped down by now, for three weeks later Charles had been taken to Windsor. How glad he must have been to get there, thought Mary, embroidering a crown-encircled rose on one of the inn's best table-cloths. But what a lonely homecoming, unless they had allowed his two younger children to be with him for Christmas. She had liked to picture him walking on the lovely terrace he had once described to her. But before long they had taken him from Windsor to closer captivity at St. James's Palace in London.

"What made them move the King like that just when he must have felt a little happier?" she asked of Mistress Trattle, who had come into the room followed by her husband bearing two lighted candles. Whatever their ordinary occupations those days, the minds of all of them were upon the momentous events going on from day to day on the mainland, from whence reliable news came so exasperatingly slowly. And whenever they met again after a short separation they would go on discussing them.

"I do not think it was done out of spite, but rather as a necessary safeguard for their own ends," said Trattle, answering for his wife. "Parliament had protested that the abduction of the King from here to Hurst was against their orders, and some firebrand named Colonel Pride led a troop of soldiers to Westminster and forcibly prevented any Members from entering who were likely to vote for the rescue of the King from military custody. 'Pride's Purge,' the Londoners called it. William Hopkins calls it a trick for bringing the King illegally to trial."

"Then was there not some trouble about some letters from

the Queen?" asked Agnes Trattle, seating herself near Mary and picking up her own needlework.

"William Hopkins says that she persuaded the French Ambassador to deliver a letter to General Fairfax imploring him to let her come and see her husband before the trial."

"And the inhuman wretch would not? I used to think he was the kindest of the generals."

"He might have done, had she not secretly sent a second letter to the King full of last-minute suggestions for his escape. The prying bloodhounds found it in his Majesty's State Room, it seems, and that was the final argument for his being brought to London. They did not mean to lose their quarry just before their hard-fought-for trial began."

"And now it is going on," sighed Mary, letting her work fall upon her lap. "What *can* they bring against him?"

"Every wickedness that is mentioned in the Old Testament, if I know anything about them," said Trattle, getting up restlessly and going to the window. "It began last Saturday, so we should be hearing the result any day now."

"Never have I minded so much living on an island!" lamented Agnes.

"'Hearing the result'," echoed Mary. "Just as one hears the result of a bowling competition or a wrestling match! How can a pack of subjects find their King guilty? And if they should—what will the result be?"

Both the Trattles looked at her in silence. Whatever they feared, they could not put it into words. Least of all to Mary, who had seen the King every day for a year, who had laundered and mended his linen and given him her dog—who knew him as a vulnerable human being who had likes and moods and habits as other men. "We shall know soon," muttered Edward Trattle. "Sooner than we thought," he added, suddenly alert as he caught sight of a familiar figure turning into the Square. "For here comes our new son-in-law, hurrying as if a bull was after him!"

A minute later John Newland burst into the room. He was not much younger than his father-in-law and more heavily built, and had been hurrying hatless all the way from the river. He sat down on the nearest chair and buried his greying brown head in his hands.

"They are going to behead him," he said.

The terrible words came out between his laboured panting, and were spasmodically expelled as though he had scarcely managed to hold them in so long. And no one needed to ask of whom he spoke.

Presently he lifted his head. "The court adjudged that the said Charles Stuart, as a tyrant, traitor, murderer and public enemy, should be put to death by the severing of his head from his body," he quoted, staring before him as though the words were written visibly on the parlour wall.

The two women sat motionless, speechless. Trattle went to him and shook him by the shoulder. "How do you know?" he asked, almost angrily.

"One of my skippers. Just come up on the tide with a Gravesend barge. London is shocked silent as if they had the plague, he says." Newland mopped his sweating forehead and Trattle automatically poured some wine into a glass and pushed it into his hand. "The travesty of a trial was all over by Friday," Newland told them, gradually recovering his breath. "His Majesty had no chance from the first. They would not let him speak."

"How has he taken it?"

"I know no details. Only what my man told me."

Agnes, white-faced as the sheet she had been hemming, tried to put into words the question in the minds of all. "And when—when will they—"

"To-morrow. The last day of January." Newland passed a hand through his hair and set down his empty glass. "They have taken him back to St. James's. Only Master Herbert and the Bishop of London are allowed to be with him now."

"There could be a reprieve. If the Londoners are so shocked they could *do* something! It is their turn. They could rise up and kill those cruel murderers—" It was tender-hearted Mary who was speaking, half-hysterically, with the fine linen napery screwed up like a dishclout in her shaking hands.

"Unfortunately the murderers are armed. The best-armed force we have had within living memory," Newland reminded her bitterly. He got wearily to his feet, looking round for the hat which he must have left somewhere down at the harbour. "I must be going home to tell my poor, pretty Frances—"

"Who gave him the rose," added Agnes, and burst into tears.

The terrible news was soon confirmed officially by the Mayor, and unofficially by every ship putting in from the mainland. It was known up at the castle, and Rolph posted small detachments of soldiers in market squares and at cross roads to prevent demonstra-tions. No one talked of anything else. Or thought of anything else. Even the Puritans who had shouted loudest for Parliament during the Newport Treaty were awed and shocked. Many of them, however firmly assured of the righteousness of their convic-tions, would not have shouted at all had they known it would end like this. On the day which was fixed for the King's execution men went about their business as heavily as though a plague had struck the Wight, women whispered fearfully in little groups, and families who were known to be strong supporters of Mayor Moses and the rabid preachers now had sufficient sense—or shame—to stay indoors.

Mary went about as though stunned, her thoughts far away across the Solent. What must Harry and Jane and the rest of them be feeling, who had done everything humanly possible to save their master from such a tragic fate? And men like Thomas Herbert and Anthony Mildmay, who had always loved him in spite of their unswerving loyalty to Parliament? By now, she supposed, the poor Queen might know in France. And his Majesty's daughter and exiled sons in Holland. And what of those two lonely children left in England? Because the King himself had talked to her about his beloved Bess, and because she herself knew so well how it felt to lose a father by violent death, Mary found herself thinking frequently of the young Princess Elizabeth.

"If only we knew whether it has really happened! Whether someone tried to avert it, and whether his children were allowed to see him," she said over and over again to Agnes Trattle.

"We are bound to hear in time," Agnes comforted her, "because some of those Royalists who were with you in the castle must be in London."

"Do you suppose Aunt Druscilla is with them?"

"If she is she will be able to tell us everything."

But it was not Aunt Druscilla who brought them the news they were so anxiously waiting for.

A few evenings later, after the inn doors were closed for the night, the three of them with John Newland and Frances were sitting round the parlour fire. William Hopkins and his wife were with them, having come over to know if Trattle had picked up any news from his customers. They had not lit the candles and were, as usual, speculating about what must be going on in London. "Will Cromwell let them bury him in Westminster Abbey like a king?" asked Frances.

"And will they—Uncle Trattle, when someone who has been executed is buried—is the head—" Mary's voice trailed off into silence. She closed her eyes against the rising tears, caught by the memory of Charles's comely head above the wide, lace-edged collars which she used to launder so carefully, and shrinking from the thought of how it must look now—severed, separate and bloody.

And at that moment, before anyone could answer, there came the knocking on the wooden window shutter. Everyone started, and then sat rigidly silent. Trattle pulled himself together and went out to unbar the street door, and they heard his voice warm and hearty with surprised welcome. And the next moment a small white dog streaked across the floor and sprang into Mary's lap.

"It is Rogue!" she exclaimed incredulously, gathering him into her arms and kissing his silky head. And when she looked up there was Richard Osborne standing in the doorway watching her delight. "Spare some of the welcome for me!" he called to her laughingly.

"Oh, Richard!" she cried, too much surprised to hide her feelings.

The others were crowding about him, pressing him for news—asking him if he had been in London and why he had come so quickly.

"I came to bring that foolish little dog back to Mary," he said lightly, and came and sat down beside her and—to Frances's surprise and envy—calmly removed one of her fondling hands from Rogue and held it in his own.

"Were you—there—on Tuesday, sir?" asked Trattle.

"No. I was pursuing his Majesty's spaniel through the packed streets of London." Osborne's voice lost its habitual note of levity. "But I was able to see Thomas Herbert afterwards."

"Could you please tell us?" asked Frances, from the settle where she sat within the shelter of her husband's arm.

Their unexpected guest went to the hearth to warm his hands, and she would have risen to light the candles, but her mother stayed her with a gesture, sensing that they might hear things which it would be easier to bear by firelight. Osborne stood absently fingering an hour-glass which stood upon a little ledge above the chimney-piece. By the look of his mud-splashed boots he must have been riding hard. It seemed as if, in the expectant silence, he was turning his mind back to those harrowing scenes at Westminster, and trying to condense into a few ordinary sentences a drama which must have moved him to the soul—sentences with which he could make these loyal people gathered in a faraway inn parlour see them too.

During the expectant silence Mary found time to recover from the joyful surprise of seeing him and from her happy embarrassment at the way in which he had made no secret of his interest in her. She was able to forget her own affairs in the vast importance of his news. "It was unbearably sad seeing his Majesty taken away to Hurst Castle," she said.

"It was at Hurst that he seemed to realize it was the end and to compose his mind, Herbert said. At Windsor, it was more like a homecoming. The King had his own rooms. But the army got the upper hand after Pride's purge. You will have heard of that even over here?"

Most of those present made a sound of assent and Osborne swung round, with his face in shadow and the firelight outlining his tall, loose-limbed body. "So they took him to St. James's Palace that he might be at hand for that travesty of a trial," he said, absently turning the hour-glass up and down between his hands. "I have little time to tell you of it now. Bradshaw, a Lancashire man, was President, and most of the judges were new. In any case, I saw only a part of it."

"I was told that they would not let the King speak in his own defence," said Newland.

"I think it was more that his Majesty refused to recognize their authority to try him and—at the beginning at any rate—refused to plead. By refusing to defend himself before an illegal court he was upholding the rights of his people, he said."

"Did no one protest at the obvious illegality?" asked William Hopkins, the thoughtful-looking schoolmaster.

"No one who was likely to protest was allowed in! The doors and streets were thick with Ironsides. Cromwell had seen to it that his most fanatic regiment was in London. But when they were calling the roll and came to the name of Thomas Fairfax a woman's voice called down from some gallery, 'He has more wit than to be here!' It was the General's wife, but the soldiers hustled her out."

There was not a sound while Osborne described the scene.

"The last day was sheer drama. Cromwell sat there square-jawed, forcing himself to what he calls the grim necessity. Everyone knew by then that it would be the death sentence. I wish I could show you the solemn beauty of Westminster Hall. The King stood there, in black, with only his glittering George and that silver-headed cane he always carries. On the steps where the second Richard, who restored that lovely place, was brought to bay two and a half centuries ago. The same kind of curs yelped now for Charles's blood. A shaft of sunlight from one of the windows was upon him and he looked more kingly than I have ever seen him. It may have been his proud quietness and the splendid setting, or merely my imagination, but the divine right in which he believes so strongly seemed to ring him about with light—to set him apart. Even the soldiers gazing at him from the back of the hall seemed bemused and had to be struck before they remembered to obey orders and yell for his destruction.

"Not until he was faced with death did the King ask for a hearing, and then it was too late and he was denied. Bradshaw solemnly reiterated the list of his crimes in the name of the people. 'It is a lie—not half or a quarter of them!' interrupted that courageous woman's voice again, and was roughly silenced."

"Could no *man* do anything?" demanded Agnes.

"Very little. When the King asked to be allowed to address the Lords and Commons in the Painted Chamber, a man called John Downes tried to delay the sentence by moving an adjournment—"

"May his name be remembered down the ages," murmured the schoolmaster's wife.

Osborne shrugged despondently and turned to set the hourglass back upon its shelf. "The end came quickly," he said, as if reluctant to speak much of it. "All the bloodshed of the war was laid upon him. It is almost ludicrous to think that he, the King, was sentenced to death as a traitor!"

"How did his Majesty take it?" asked Hopkins, who had been his friend and host.

"Without flinching. But he found that he would not be permitted to speak after the sentence, as he had hoped, and he lost that marvellous self-control for a while. For the first time he stammered and beseeched. But there was no pity. 'Guard, withdraw your prisoner,' ordered the President.

"'If I am not suffered to speak,' said his Majesty, all dignity again, 'expect what judgment others will have!'

"He turned and walked out, and when the sedan chair bearers came bare-headed as usual to carry him to the rooms prepared for him in Whitehall, they were jeered at and told to put their hats on their heads again because Charles Stuart was now just a man like themselves." Osborne turned from his audience and, without noticing what he was doing, put the old-fashioned hourglass back. "It was like the scene outside Pilate's Praetorium," he said a little incoherently. "One of Cromwell's soldiers spat in his face."

There was silence in the firelit room, broken only by Mistress Hopkins's smothered sobs.

"Were the children—Princess Elizabeth and little Prince Henry—allowed to say good-bye to their father?" asked Mary, after a while.

Osborne came and leant over the back of her chair as if this part of his narrative were specially for her. Like most big men he was gentle-hearted towards children, and it had been some childlike quality about Mary herself which had first attracted him. "Yes, my sweet, they were brought to St. James's," he assured her. "Bishop Juxon said it was heart-rending. The boy is scarcely old enough to comprehend, but for the little Princess it must have been a cruel ordeal. And after they had gone the King was so affected that they had to get him to bed. That old weakness which makes him limp sometimes came back so badly that he could scarcely stand."

Mary's tears dropped quietly on to the little dog curled in her lap. "The Princess herself is not strong," she recalled.

"Judith Briot told me that she had almost to carry her to the coach."

"Who is Judith Briot?"

"Her gentlewoman."

"Oh, I hope she is kind!"

Osborne shrugged, and Mary had the impression that in any other circumstances he might have found her question amusing. "She would not be willingly unkind," he said, after a moment's hesitation. "Herbert had complained about the troops being posted even in the King's bedroom," he went on, as if to change the conversation. "And Cromwell had the common decency to have his Majesty moved away from the hammering. That is how he came to be back at St. James's."

"What hammering?" asked Frances, in an enthralled whisper.

"For the scaffold," her husband explained shortly.

"Where did they erect it—to do this terrible thing?" asked Agnes, who knew London and could picture it all.

"At Whitehall. They built a platform outside one of the windows of the banqueting room, and the block was put on that." Osborne saw Mary's whole body stiffen, but had no clue to the cause. "It was built so high above the ground and so railed round that although the crowd stretched away up to Charing Cross and down to Westminster, they could not really see. The trouble was to find an executioner. The official headsman refused. London is full of rumours as to who it was who did it, all muffled up in mask and wig.

"As I told you, I was not actually there. Herbert told me afterwards that the King had made his peace with God and striven to forgive his enemies. The sun came out from behind the clouds and his Majesty stepped out through the window onto the platform as though he saw no fear. 'Death is not terrible to me,' he had told Bishop Juxon."

To everyone's surprise Mary sprang up, tumbling Rogue to the floor. "Then it really came true!" she cried; and Osborne saw that although her cheeks were wet with tears like the two elder women's, her eyes were shining.

"What has come true?" they all asked.

"What the King said—about going out through the windows." But of course they would not know…She turned eagerly to Osborne. "You remember how each time you and Harry planned an escape it was by way of a window. Well, after you left the castle, when his Majesty was so hopeless and alone, he used to talk to me sometimes. He told me about a nightmare he had as a child, and how he had no head for heights and how he really dreaded climbing out like that. We did not know, of course. And that last time when my father reached up to help him escape, his Majesty began to feel as though he were going out to some splendid adventure. If he should ever have to do it again, he said, he was sure he would find there was nothing there to fear after all."

"Perhaps there really is not—for all of us," suggested the Newport schoolmaster. And each of them fell silent, coming to more kindly terms with death.

A more practical aspect was troubling Trattle. "Working here unobtrusively for the King's cause, and finding so many of my customers in his favour, it amazes me that as a nation we have let this thing happen," he said thoughtfully. "Between the passing of sentence and the execution, did no man raise a hand to stop it?"

Osborne, who realized just how much he had done so unob-trusively, laid a hand upon his shoulder. "Yes, one man. His eldest son. Without counting the cost he signed a blank sheet of paper, offering those traitors any terms they liked if they would spare his father's life."

"The Prince of Wales did that?"

"Whatever their faults, Trattle, the Stuarts are loyal to each other."

"Perhaps it did not arrive in time?"

"Oh yes, it did. Cromwell looked at it and passed it on to the others. But the hunt was on, the taste of blood almost upon their lips. They shook their heads. Efficient as he is, Cromwell blundered badly there. They might have gotten all they wanted without labelling themselves murderers and creating a martyr. The last word the King said on the scaffold was 'Remember.' And no command of his will more inevitably be obeyed. And now I suppose the blank sheet of paper is filed away among the rest of their dusty records—that warm, spontaneous offer of a young man's personal hopes and heritage!"

# CHAPTER THIRTY

---

HE SCHOOLMASTER AND HIS wife rose to go, refusing the meal which Mistress Trattle had ordered. They had heard all Osborne could tell them about the tragedy of their recent royal guest and, being people of sensitivity, they felt that there might be more personal things which he had come to talk about.

"I am ravenous," he had confessed smilingly to Agnes. "But you must forgive me if I eat and leave you. I had hoped to go on to Gatcombe to see Worsley, but someone recognized me on my way here and, having urgent business in hand, I must get back to the mainland before your Jealous Deputy Governor lets his blood-hounds loose on me."

"I will go and see about a boat," offered Newland, recognizing the danger in which he stood. Trattle and Osborne went to see the three of them off and in the stir of departures, while they were all talking together by the inn door, Frances seized the opportunity to speak to her friend alone. She could scarcely contain her curiosity about Osborne and, kneeling beside Mary, almost shook her in her impatience to know. "You called him Richard, and he brought your dog back, and while he was standing there behind your chair his hand was on your hair," she said in an urgent whisper. "Are you going to marry him?"

There was little of romantic interest which escaped Frances. Mary laughed and blushed. "I really do not know. He once asked me, but it was all mixed up with so much unhappiness and danger."

"Imagine hesitating about becoming Mistress Richard Osborne! Why, Mary, you would be one of the rich gentry!" Frances clapped her hands, then pouted a little, uncomfortably conscious of having been a shade patronizing when showing her friend the solid comforts of a well-to-do merchant's house.

"Oh, no," denied Mary. "Richard made it quite clear that he will be poor now, even though he won his case. You must remember he was in the pay of Parliament when he was caught helping the King to escape, so now, with Cromwell in complete power, he runs the risk of a heavy fine—or worse—"

"Then you may go abroad with him?"

"Truly, dear Frances, I do not know."

"And to think you never talked it over with me! I used to think it was that charming red-headed young man."

"I used to think so myself."

"Until you found he was married? Oh, my poor darling!"

Mary bent down and kissed her. "We were all so busy before your wedding. I did tell your mother about—a number of things. And I promise I will tell you more about Richard. But not now. They are coming back."

Frances stood up hastily to rearrange her skirts. "You must have had a wonderful time up at the castle!" Remembering that Silas Floyd had been shot up there, she added hurriedly, "But it was Edward Worsley I always wanted. And even with him you seem to have been riding round the country! You, who always pretended you were not interested in men!"

"Not quite riding round the country!" laughed Mary. "But I assure you he was very kind."

A hasty meal was brought into the privacy of the parlour and over it Osborne was able to give them news of Druscilla. "She is staying at the Whorwood's town house in Channel Row. It is only a stone's throw from Whitehall, and two days before the King was executed he asked Herbert to go there to fetch that locked box which Jane had had in keeping for him. It contained his Majesty's private jewels, and they are for his two younger children. Jane, it seems, was out; but Herbert saw your Aunt, Mary, and in spite of her grief she was well. And quite happy about you, since you are here with such good friends."

"Jane must have been sorry to miss seeing Master Herbert!"

"The King sent her that emerald ring he always wore."

"Oh, I am so glad! She served him better than any of us," said Mary, remembering the kind sincerity of the advice Jane had given her.

Osborne told them of other precious last-moment legacies. Of the silver bedside clock given to Herbert, the familiar tasselled cane left to Bishop Juxon and how—at the last moment of all—the King had taken off his George and handed it to Juxon for his eldest son. And in return Mary was able to tell him how Edward Worsley had risked arrest to say "good-bye" and been given the King's watch. "He said it should have been for you," she told him.

"He gave a keepsake to Harry, too," said Osborne, without envy. "A ring set with a miniature painting of his Majesty."

"How sad your friend must be after all he did to save the King!" said Agnes.

"But, being Harry, he said he would have done the same again ten thousand times over, only done it better!"

They laughed, and Mary asked him how he had come to be searching for the dog.

"I was waiting in St. James's Park—much as Edward Worsley waited to say good-bye, I imagine. Though in my case the crowds were so dense that there was little danger of being recognized. It was a bitterly cold morning. Herbert told me afterwards that the King had asked for an extra shirt lest he should shiver and the people think he was afraid."

"He, afraid!" scoffed Trattle, setting down the carving fork.

"I saw him coming across the park in a little procession of people, though he would not let it look sad or funereal. He was walking briskly as he always did, and somehow Rogue must have got out and followed him as usual. Except for the soldiers and the crowds he might have been taking one of his usual walks with a few friends, with the little spaniel at his heels. But some low, vindictive fellow kept walking backwards before him, jeering at him and staring in his face. This was clearly bothering his Majesty, whose thoughts must have been on far higher things. I saw Herbert speak to one of the officers, and the man was driven off. But just as I was going to step forward and kiss his Majesty's hand, I saw the mean wretch pick Rogue up and dive off with him into the crowd. Everyone was too busy staring at the condemned King. Rogue was struggling frantically and I knew how much you loved the little brute, Mary, and so—"

"And so you missed making your farewell to the King." Mary touched his hand as it lay beside his plate. Sorry as she was, it was sweet to know that she came first.

"I shouldered my way through after the man, but people were jostling each other so that I soon lost sight of him. Afterwards in a tavern I heard some men talking about the money some opportunist was making with a little booth down the river. Westminster was full of people from all parts that day and he was charging them a penny a time to see the King's pet dog—and a handkerchief dipped in the King's blood which he had sopped up from the scaffold."

"How horrible!" shuddered Agnes.

"What did you do?" asked Trattle.

"Threw the man into the river and took the dog."

No one wanted to eat any more. Mary turned from the table and gratefully hugged Rogue to her. And when Trattle went outside to see if John Newland was ready with the boat, Agnes drew Frances from the room under pretext of putting away the dishes because the servants were all in bed.

Left alone with Osborne, Mary found her heart racing absurdly. "How can I thank you, Richard, for coming a hundred miles or more to bring back my dog?" she began, to cover her embarrassment.

"Dog be damned!" laughed Osborne. "Will you not understand that I came a hundred miles just to kiss you?" And kissing her hair and mouth and throat, he made sure that he had good value for every mile he had ridden.

"We are not even betrothed," she admonished him breathlessly, when at last she was released.

He stood grinning down at her unabashed. "I will write to your aunt if you wish, but I have had little opportunity for formal courtship."

The two distracting dimples so seldom seen of late dented her cheeks again. "You seem to have done remarkably well in the time!" she admitted.

"I flatter myself I have, for you are beginning to lose that remote look of a stained-glass saint!"

But she was still struggling against her awakening. "It was good of you to bring us all the news, too," she went on more sedately. "You cannot imagine how hard it was not knowing what was happening to people whom we knew so well. And how sad it is to feel we cannot help the King any more!"

"But we can still—indirectly. By helping those whom he loved."

"Is that what you are going to do?"

"Even to those faithful friends I could not speak of that. But to you, who God grant may one day be my other self, I can say this much—that I have orders from Holland to search out what chances of support there would be in Scotland and certain east-coast ports when the King is ready to land."

"The King?" Mary drew back, momentarily startled.

With an arm still about her, Osborne lifted his half-emptied glass from the littered table. "The King across the water," he said, tossing back the remaining wine in a hurried toast. "Dear foolish one, you surely did not suppose that we lack one? Or that he will not fight to get back his own?"

Mary looked up into his confident young face and a new, warm hope of happier days began to stir in her. "King Charles the Second," she said softly, testing the sound of the new, unfamiliar title.

"I am to go to Holland with whatever information I have gleaned."

"And you should have a very good reception, for his late Majesty wrote commending you to his son because you had been in trouble for his sake. He showed me that part of his letter, and bade me tell you if I should ever see you again."

"That was better than any keepsake," said Osborne, well pleased. "But everything here must be done with so much secrecy that it may be weeks or months before I am ready to sail. And until

young Charles gets back his crown mine will be a poor, hazardous
life. With little money and much fighting, I imagine. I have no
right to ask any girl to marry me."

"But I seem to remember you already have."

"And you said no. You did not love me."

"There were other things then—"

"I know."

"Now you have made it more difficult to refuse—"

"A man fights for what he wants."

"I am not afraid of being poor and have grown used to hazards.
And I think I could no longer say with truth 'I do *not* love you',"
she said softly, consideringly.

He kissed her again with triumphant passion, then forced
himself to patience. "It is utterly unlike me, I know; but I care for
you so much, Mary, that I want you to take time and think—to
be sure. If it is humanly possible I will come back to the island for
your answer."

"Before you go to Holland?"

"At least I shall write to you."

He held her tenderly, his cheek pressed down upon her curling
hair. Remembering his reputation, she wondered how many other
women he had held like that. "Richard, what did you mean about
that Briot woman?" she asked suddenly, fidgeting with a button of
his coat.

"Merely that if you were picturing someone motherly in attendance on the King's daughter you were mistaken. She is fond of
the Princess, as who would not be? Judith is too frivolous to be
ill-natured. But being an artist's daughter, she is more conscious of
her beauty than of her duties. Her father is that clever designer of our
coins, and she told me that is how she came by the appointment."

"You seem to know her well."

"Quite well. Most men do who have been about the Court.
She has lovely breasts and hair like a red-gold sunset fresh from
her father's palette."

"And a mind like a conceited pea-hen's?"

He swung Mary round so that he caught the feline glint in her eyes, and laughed delightedly. "Now, you could not possibly be jealous?" he enquired.

"I was concerned only for the Princess," she lied with dignified aplomb.

And then the boat was ready and it was time to part.

The weeks passed and the island settled back into its quiet ways. News came of the private funeral at Windsor, with snow making a white pall for the King's coffin. "White for innocence," the people said, when out of hearing of their new rulers. Herbert and Mildmay had been two of the bearers and Harry Firebrace one of the twelve gentlemen allowed to follow. Young Elizabeth had nearly died of grief, the Trattles heard; but Cromwell, who had always liked the Princess for her piety, had shown pity. He had arranged for the two fatherless children to be put in the care of Lady Sydney at Penshurst, where it was hoped that the country air and the gentle atmosphere of that cultured home would restore her.

England was now a Commonwealth.

Frances Newland grumbled because country fairs and May-day revels were forbidden, and her prettiest dresses frowned upon as being devices of the devil. The severe deep linen collars and quiet colours which a Puritan world deemed suitable did not suit her.

To Mary, living quietly at the inn, these things scarcely mattered. For a whole year her youth had been robbed of normal gaiety by the violent dissensions of her elders, but she had had her fill of excitement. Now for the first time she had peace in which to sort out her own affairs. To school herself to accept the frustration of her first love and to attune her future to the proposals in Osborne's promised letter. As the months slipped by and spring spilled beauty over bays and meadows, the sight of lovers walking in the sweet glow of evening when fishing and farm work were done gave her, for the first time, a sense of sadness. Visits to Frances, blooming radiantly and reluctantly into motherhood, reminded her of her own physical loneliness.

By early summer a purple blue sea lapped lazily at golden sands, hedgerows were bridal white with ladies' laces again, and a whole year had passed since her father's tragic death.

Druscilla Wheeler had written from Oxford, where she appeared to derive vast satisfaction from being a guest of Sir Brome and Lady Whorwood. She had evidently settled back into the more sophisticated life of the mainland. There had even been mention of an admirer, a hint that she might marry again. Although there was no suggestion of her returning to the Wight, she invited her niece to join her. But that Mary could not do even if she had wished, for she had no means of letting Richard Osborne know, and might miss him if he came.

At last, on a hot midsummer evening, another letter came for her which she felt sure must concern him. Hearing a clattering in the Square below her dormer window she looked out to see two soldiers before the door, and one of them dismounting with a letter in his hand. She heard Agnes calling up the attic stairs to her, and for the moment felt faint with fear. "It is something official. They must have arrested him. Do I care as much as this?" she asked herself, finding herself trembling as she ran swiftly down to the parlour.

The letter was for her, but neither from Richard Osborne nor about him. The Cromwellian corporal who handed it to her made a stiff little bow as though she were a person of some importance and then withdrew.

Having called both men into the taproom for a drink, Edward Trattle came quickly to join his wife while Mary read her letter. They all sensed that it must be something of moment. "It is from Master Mildmay. He wants me to go back to the castle—as housekeeper in Aunt Druscilla's place," she told them, flattered and incredulous. "He has orders to bring Princess Elizabeth and her brother to Carisbrooke."

"Oh, no, even the Army Council could not be so cruel!" cried Agnes, aghast. "Imagine what that poor girl's feelings will be!"

"They are coming almost immediately."

"But why take them from the care of good Lady Sydney?"

"It is probably because of that rising in Scotland," said Trattle. "Young Charles is clear-headed and vigorous and since his father was murdered more and more Royalists have sneaked out of the country to join him, so that ever since the Scots proclaimed him King of Scotland, Cromwell and his crew must have been in a dither lest he should land. The presence of those two poor fatherless children is bound to create a lot of Stuart sympathy. They want them out of the way, I'll be bound."

"I think you should go," said Agnes, turning anxiously to Mary. "After all Major Rolph is away on the mainland and likely to stay there for a while."

"But I am so young."

"You always said that Master Mildmay was kind, and he says specially that for the Princess's sake there should be some sympathetic woman in charge of the domestic arrangements," pointed out Agnes, to whom Mary had handed the letter.

"Only a very simple establishment...The Prince's tutor, a gentlewoman for the Princess and an equerry'," quoted Mary, reading it through again over her shoulder. "'Henry of Gloucester to have the same bedroom as his late father first had, and the lady Elizabeth that ante-room leading off the original Presence Chamber, which was once my own room,' he says. I'm thinking that all the rooms will need a world of scouring after being occupied by half Cromwell's army!"

"He says you can have whatever help you like."

"But you might need me."

"Not nearly so much as that poor child Elizabeth will need you."

"No," agreed Mary, thinking of frivolous Judith Briot and of what Osborne had said about helping those whom the late King had loved; and of the word-picture the late King himself had made, sitting unshaven by the fire, of his beloved, misfortunate Bess.

# CHAPTER THIRTY-ONE

———∞∞∞———

MARY STOOD AT THE door of the Governor's house ready to welcome the travellers from Kent. Her Puritan grey gown had a wide linen collar and she had hidden her curls beneath a severe white cap. She was trying to look older than eighteen and to conceal her nervousness.

Brett, overjoyed at having her back, grinned proudly at the pleasing sight of her as he crossed the courtyard on some last-minute errand. Libby, whose husband had not taken her with him to London, remarked that "those Stuart children" might not arrive for hours, and brought Mary a stool to sit on.

It had been a busy week getting the rooms back to the point of cleanliness which Mistress Wheeler would have exacted, and clearing out as far as possible all trace of military occupation. But to Mary's relief nothing in the housekeeper's room had been tampered with.

"Directly you left I locked it and lost the key," Libby had told her with a grin, producing it from her pocket.

"Anyways, they gurt overnors was prid near scared to pass the door once I'd told 'un our last housekeeper had died o' the plague!" old Brett had chuckled.

It was such old familiar loyalties that made Mary glad to be back. Although there were new faces among the garrison, the place was home. It was full of heartache at times, but she had wanted to see it once more as it used to be, with the courtyard sleepy in the

sun and long silences broken only by island voices, before having
to leave it perhaps for ever.

Waiting in the doorway, she thought how tired the travellers would
be, and wondered anxiously if there were anything else she could have
prepared for their comfort. She thought too how pleasant it would be
to see Master Mildmay again, and how proud her father would have
been that her services had been chosen to ease the Princess's stay.

At the sound of approaching wheels she stood up and tucked
back the last recalcitrant curl, and Libby, hovering in the back-
ground to get a glimpse of the proceedings, hastily took away the
stool. A couple of guards stood to attention under the gateway arch,
but there was to be no military or ceremonial pother. Parliament
had sent strict instructions that the royal visitors were to be called
plain Elizabeth and Henry.

Anthony Mildmay rode first into the courtyard, middle-aged,
comely, and quietly assured. Then came the coach, rumbling and
swaying over the flagstones. Apart from a small escort sent from
Cowes, it was accompanied only by a well-mounted young man
who must by the equerry, and a small sickly-looking person on
a spiritless horse who might be the Duke's valet. The equerry
dismounted and opened the coach door with a flourish and a
lively boy of nine or so scrambled out, full of interest in his new
surroundings. Castles and guns, thought Mary, were probably more
to his mind than quiet country houses. He was followed by Lovall,
a youngish-looking tutor in holy orders, and then—like a flash
of colour among the old grey walls—out stepped a young woman
who could be no one but Judith Briot. She sprang down lightly
with a laugh, landing almost in the handsome equerry's waiting
arms. Then both of them, with the tutor, turned solicitously to
help someone still inside. Obviously, they expected to have to
lift the Princess out, but a small hand waved them aside and a
frail, black-clad little figure stepped down with shaky dignity. The
vigorous health of her companions and their lack of all signs of
travel strain emphasized her sickly pallor, but she took Anthony
Mildmay's proffered arm and followed her young brother into
the Governor's house. Mary curtsied as she passed and Mildmay

presented her. The Princess managed a small, gracious smile, but her dark eyes looked blind with weariness or weeping. Only when she came to the high-backed chair by the empty hearth did she pause as though her attention were really caught by something. "Is this the chair my father used?" she asked. And when she was told it was she sank down in it, leaned her fair head against the worn red velvet and closed her eyes. Her ringless hands, flaccid and outstretched, came to rest caressingly on the arms of it.

The effort of the journey had been too great for her to take any part in the polite exchanges of arrival.

"Your Highness must be hungry with so much sea air," said Judith, forgetting her instructions to omit a title. "I am ravenous. Are you not, Master Lovall?"

"I am," declared Henry Stuart. "I climbed part way up the rigging to get a better view of all those big ships in the Solent."

But whether his tutor was hungry or not, his shrewd, kind eyes rested as anxiously as Mary's on Elizabeth's exhausted face. And when at last her blue eyes opened it was to look fastidiously at her travel-soiled hands. "I should like to wash first," she said.

"I have had hot water sent to your Highness's room," said Mary, repeating Judith's absent-minded error, unrebuked by Mildmay. With an impulsive gesture of compassion Judith threw an arm about the girl, and Mary showed them the way to the Princess's bedroom. But after a quick glance round to make sure the servants had brought in the clothes chest she departed. Her thoughts were already on the first meal she had had prepared for them on her own responsibility, and her anxious mind outran her footsteps to the kitchen. But she need not have worried. The party from Penshurst ate together informally in the Presence Chamber, with Mildmay at one end of the table and the young Duke of Gloucester at the other and they seemed pleasantly surprised to find such good fare at Carisbrooke, and all but the Princess did full justice to it. But afterwards when Mildmay, who had not been without some anxious qualms himself, came in his kindly way to congratulate her, Mary, although flushed and triumphant, remembered Elizabeth's almost untouched plate. "She should have been put straight to bed," she could not forbear from saying.

"Her gentlewoman should know," he excused himself. "Perhaps a good night's sleep will make all the difference."

But what with her exhaustion and the strange room and her horror of the place, the Princess scarcely slept at all. Next morning found her hot and listless, and she had a hacking little cough. For all her determination of the day before she did not attempt to get up, nor could she touch the peaches and milk which Mary brought for her breakfast.

"Do you not think we should call in the doctor from Newport?" suggested Mary, following Judith Briot from Elizabeth's room to her own. "He is very kind and quite clever."

But the Princess's gentlewoman did not seem to think it necessary. "She is just tired out from the journey, poor sweet," she said negligently, intent upon polishing her finger nails with a wad of rose petals. "And she has not really recovered from the shock yet. Of the execution, I mean."

"But she looks so peaked and ill."

"She often looks like that. She is delicate, of course. But she changes so. She is absurdly sensitive and for some reason or other dreaded coming here, though I personally find it quite amusing." Judith went to her mirror and tried the effect of a rose tucked into the comb that held up her luxuriant ringlets. "In a day or two Bess will be quite different. You will see."

"I will try to make something tempting for her dinner and try to coax her to eat then."

"That will be very kind. I am afraid I am not very good at sick nursing. Are you the housekeeper?"

"I am only taking the place of my aunt, Mistress Wheeler, who is away on the mainland."

"You are very young."

"I suppose Master Mildmay chose me because I have always lived here and was assistant laundress to the late King."

"Oh, then you must be one of those people who helped with smuggling in letters and all those amazing attempts at escape?" For the first time Judith looked at her with personal interest.

"I must be going. I have so much to do. I hope you did not mind my following you in here," Mary tried to excuse herself. But Judith was suddenly disposed to gossip. She threw down the rose and sat down on the bed. "Are you married?" she asked.

"No."

"You surprise me, living in a castle full of men. It must be most entertaining. And during the late King's captivity there must have been quite a number of personable young gentlemen here. Did you have a lover?"

"I had very little time for love affairs," said Mary crisply.

"But you could have," persisted Judith. "You are quite pretty and some of those young gallants are so persistent." She laughed reminiscently and wandered over to the window, so that Mary thought how blind those pleasure-hating Puritans must have been who had put her in charge of a strictly brought up Protestant princess. Casually, with her back to Mary, she asked, "Richard Osborne was here, wasn't he, mixed up with all that escape business?"

Mary stared at the beautifully gowned figure with high, rounded breasts and hair like a flaming sunset. "Yes," she said, envying and hating her.

"Probably you would not have seen much of him," decided Judith. "But he is very attractive." She turned from the window with an amorous sigh and her gown went swishing deliciously across the floor. "I have often wished—but, there, we were both of us too inconstant. A gallant young sea captain came along—"

Mary went out and closed the door upon any further confidences. The mug of untasted milk she was still carrying shook in her hand. If she were to be fool enough to marry Osborne would bits of his past always be being brought up before her like this? Would she often have to look at the bodies of women he had held? "But at least he never denied it," she told herself savagely.

"How beautiful and exciting she is!" exclaimed Libby, meeting her at the top of the backstairs.

"Who?" asked Mary, still wondering if Osborne's complete candour would make it any easier.

"Mistress Judith. That handsome equerry, Master Barmiston, cannot take his eyes off her."

Naturally, she would be just the kind of woman whom Libby would admire and emulate; and she would probably prove an easy-going, generous mistress to anyone who adored her. Libby would, soon be decked with discarded ribbons and trinkets, no doubt, which would make up for all her husband did not give her. "I should like you to look after Mistress Briot and take charge of her room entirely," she said, in a voice that sounded remarkably like her Aunt Druscilla's. "It will give me more time to do things for the ailing Princess."

Responding to Mary's care, Elizabeth seemed better next morning. "Will you not get up, Bess. It is far too lovely a day to stay indoors," urged Judith, looking out of the window while Mary shook up the pillows.

"There is no need for *you* to," said Elizabeth, with the gentle consideration she always seemed to show.

Judith turned and swooped down to embrace her with one of her ebullient gestures. "I was only thinking of you, Bess."

"All the same, it would be pleasant to explore the island with a willing escort. Is John Barmiston out there?" said the invalid with a smile.

"As it is our first day here Master Lovall has given Henry a holiday from his lessons. And they are all three going for a ride."

"Then you should go with them."

"I could not think of leaving you," protested Judith.

"I have my books."

"And I will look in from time to time to see if her Highness needs anything," volunteered Mary.

From behind the shadow of the half-drawn bedcurtains the young princess smiled at her gratefully, and, still protesting, Judith went to change into a becoming riding habit.

During the morning Mary made time to slip in several times between her duties. Once she brought a bowl of Aunt Druscilla's roses, and the second time she had the happy thought to bring Rogue. "He belonged to the King your father," she said.

"Oh, give him to me—here on the bed, please!" cried Elizabeth, feeling far less alone.

"While you eat this chicken jelly I will tell you all about him and how he went to London and came back," offered Mary, pulling forward a stool and carefully expunging all tragic details from the story. After she had finished with Rogue she made for Elizabeth word pictures of her father sitting comfortably by the fire discussing theology with Troughton or books with Herbert, or walking briskly round the battlements or playing bowls. And, listening intently, Elizabeth slowly spooned up the delicacies she had been brought while a faint pink came back into her cheeks.

"You have made it feel less of a prison and more of a home," she said, laying down her spoon. "Why are you so kind to me?"

Mary rose and took away the tray. "My father was killed—too."

"So that is why you seem to understand. Was it at Nazeby?"

"No. Although he was a soldier he was not killed in battle. It happened only a year ago." Mary came and stood beside the bed with folded hands. "He was shot for a traitor while trying to help his late Majesty to escape."

"Oh, Mary!" The Princess's thin arms were outstretched, the tears were in her eyes and the next moment they were clinging to each other with all thought of strangeness and rank forgotten. "Can you bear to tell me about it?" Elizabeth asked presently. "For a whole year I have been imagining, but never knowing, what happened here."

Then and at other times when she found the Princess alone Mary told her about the group of castle Royalists and of all their planning for her father's escape, even showing her, when she was up and about, the chink in the wall through which her own letters had been passed, until gradually the girl's nervous apprehensions about the castle gave rise to intense interest. "You cannot imagine how terrible it was never knowing what was happening to the different members of my family!" she said. "Even when those last battles were being fought I could get no news, or only news cruelly distorted by our enemies. For a short while after they took my brother James prisoner he was with Henry and me. He was able to tell me what had been going on and it was wonderful having an elder brother to talk to. But it seems that when the King kept trying to escape Cromwell intended to put an end to it by holding James as hostage, and our father sent urgent word from here that he must try to get out of the country."

"You must have missed him sadly, but it cheered the King so much to hear that he had got safely to your sister in Holland."

"How glad I am that I was able to help in that!"

"How did you manage it?" asked Mary.

"It was quite simple really. We were at St. James's Palace at the time, which is old and rambling. After supper one evening I suggested that we should play 'hide and seek,' pretending it was to amuse Henry. I had laid out some clothes of mine and when it was James's turn to hide I kept watch in the corridor outside my room and called to Henry to search in the opposite direction, James dressed up in my clothes and slipped down the backstairs and out into the garden. Someone had given him the key of a small gate into the street, and a Colonel Bamfield was waiting there with a couple of horses. My poor brother had to ride side-saddle all the way to the coast, but he made quite a creditable girl, Mary. His hair is fair like mine. A good thing it wasn't Charles, who is six-foot two and swarthy as a Spaniard!"

"Why, Bess, how lovely to hear you laughing again!" exclaimed Judith, coming in from a stolen hour with John Barmiston and relieved to find her charge looking so much better. "This evening you must play us those new dance tunes Lady Sydney taught you. It will do you good. You see how right I was, Mary."

It was true enough. And Elizabeth had not been in Carisbrooke a week before she was teaching Rogue tricks and playing the little organ in the Presence Chamber. "After all, someone who has been with her for months must know more about her health than I do," thought Mary. And that evening Judith even persuaded her charge to put on a pretty dove-grey, tabbed gown and had dressed her chestnut hair in becoming ringlets. After supper they must all dance, she said, so Mary told the servants to light all the candles they could find sconces for and produced an old leather-trunk full of clothes which some past Governor and his lady had left behind. Henry plunged into it with delight and insisted upon everyone dressing up. Even Anthony Mildmay and Lovall joined in to please him, and the equerry, who had a fine voice, sang some love songs and soon the old hall was a riot of noise and colour and kindliness.

"The room looks as it used to at Christmas and Twelfth Night in Lady Portland's time when I was a child," said Mary happily, feeling that Judith's high spirits and the children's laughter would somehow help to dispel the unhappy thoughts that must hang there.

It was the first time she had seen Elizabeth Stuart in anything but mourning, and as the girl sat at the organ with the candlelight on her hair, Mary wondered how she could ever have thought her plain.

"Bess must dance too. Master Lovall, you must play for us," ordered Judith, sparkling and generous as she always was when all men's eyes were upon her. And Lovall, more accustomed as he was to anthems and canticles, goodnaturedly allowed them to laugh at the jerky sounds he produced in his efforts at a coranto. Elizabeth danced as lightly as any of them, and laughed as gaily. "Dear Judith, how dull life would be without you!" she cried, as her gentlewoman set young Henry and the doting equerry capering in a country dance which Mary was showing them. But before long the young Princess's laughter turned to coughing, and she was lying back pale and exhausted in her father's chair.

"Should we not stop and have Mistress Briot take you to your room?" suggested Mildmay anxiously.

But Elizabeth would not hear of it. "No, no, they all look so happy," she insisted. "It was often like this at home. My brothers would dance with me for a short while and then I would have to sit down and watch. But I did not mind very much. They were all so amusing, were they not, Henry? 'I must dance with Little Temperance first,' Charles would say to my lovely elder sister Mary, 'because she will not last out as long as you.'" Elizabeth sighed and turned her cheek to the red velvet where her father's greying head had so often rested. "Oh, dear God, these last years have been so lonely! Let me last out until I see them all again!" Mary heard her murmur.

# CHAPTER THIRTY-TWO

TIRED AS SHE HAD been, Elizabeth was up betimes next morning, and when Mary and Libby passed through the Presence Chamber on their way to make her bed, she was writing diligently at her father's desk. It was a hot August day and Judith was trying to coax her to go out of doors. "I have something else to do," the Princess said with unusual sharpness.

"Surely, on a morning like this, you are not struggling with that Greek translation Master Lovall set you?" remonstrated Judith.

"No. I am writing in plain English. Something which I should have written down weeks ago. But there is no reason why *you* should not go out. Truth to tell, I would rather be alone."

Judith shrugged and left her.

To Mary it seemed miraculous that a girl four years younger than herself should be able to read and write in several languages. That she should be bilingual, having a French mother, was only natural; but she was frequently to be heard helping her young brother with his Latin or with a translation of some portion of the Scriptures. Perhaps now she preferred to be alone because she was making some entry in her Commonplace Book which she did not want anyone to see. But when Mary passed quietly through the room again she noticed, although Elizabeth was careful to turn her head away, that the page before her was smudged with tears.

An hour or two later Elizabeth called for wax and sealed two packets, one of which she handed to Mildmay, requesting him with quiet dignity to have it despatched to General Cromwell. The other she had locked away in her desk, and, after dinner, seeming much relieved at having finished her long tasks, she suggested a game of bowls.

"Master Mildmay is taking your brother to visit a Sir John Oglander, or some such name," said Judith. "And John Barmiston is to accompany them. So there will only be Guy Lovall and our two selves."

"I can play if you want a fourth," offered Mary diffidently. "I am not at all good, but Master Mildmay was kind enough to teach me when he was here before."

So together the four of them went out to the green. It was a sultry afternoon and they wore their coolest clothes, but Mary noticed the small clouds piling up over the mainland. "It looks like rain," she said, recognizing the climatic portents of what old Brett always referred to as a 'breeder.' "Shall I run back and bring her Highness's cloak?"

"What, on a lovely day like this!" scoffed Judith, who was in none too sweet a temper because Barmiston had been snatched away from her to accompany the Duke.

Elizabeth enjoyed her game and, partnering Lovall, won easily. "I was always practising in the hope that one day I should be good enough to play with my father," she said, when they congratulated her upon her skill.

"But you must not get too hot," warned Judith. "Let us rest a while in that little pavilion."

"Colonel Hammond had it built specially for the late King," Mary told them, as they seated themselves gratefully upon a bench.

"Then he was not quite the ogre the royalist pamphlets always made out?" said Lovall.

"We plagued him and outwitted him whenever we could," smiled Mary. "But looking back, now that we have Major Rolph as Deputy Governor, he seems to have been a very angel of upright-ness. Harry Firebrace told me that the Army had to get him out of the island before they could abduct the King. I hope that he and his kind mother did not suffer for it."

"I am sure you need have no anxiety on their behalf," the tutor said. "Colonel Hammond is known to be a fine soldier and will undoubtedly be given some good military appointment, particularly as he is related to Oliver Cromwell, who rules the whole country."

"This morning I took your advice, dear Master Lovall, and wrote him yet again entreating him to let Henry and me go to our sister in Holland," Elizabeth told him.

"I think you were very wise. Now that public sympathy has been aroused by your father's martyrdom they may listen."

"Was that what you were spending such pains over?" asked Judith.

"Not wholly. There was something much more difficult and now that we are away from—all that," Elizabeth waved a hand towards the massive pile of the castle rising from within the inner wall, "I would like to ask advice of you, my friends. As you know, before my father died Henry and I were allowed to say good-bye to him." She stood up as if the more easily to speak of that painful scene and her small face, which had been flushed a moment or two ago, was now alarmingly pale. "He gave me some messages for my mother and for the rest of our family. I was only fourteen, but there was no one else—of his own. 'Sweetheart, you are so young, you will forget,' he said."

Lovall laid a hand on her arm. "Do not distress yourself by trying to tell us—now that it is all over," he urged gently.

"But I *must* tell you. It is important. More important than anything my father ever asked me to do. You see, these were his last words to those whom he loved. And I promised. I said I would write down all that he said and let them know. But at Penshurst I was too ill. You remember, do you not, Judith, that at first I could not even hold a pen? And afterwards as time went on I could not bring myself to it—it felt like living that terrible hour all over again. The way he took Henry on his knee, and tried to speak cheerfully for our sakes, the way his hands could not part with us and then how he came back to embrace us again because, in my desolation, I could not stop crying." Elizabeth squared her thin shoulders and made an effort to speak less emotionally. "This morning I made myself write it all down as well as I could remember. But how am

I to send it? That is what I want your advice about. I am not even allowed to write to my mother in Paris."

"Bishop Juxon, perhaps," suggested Judith.

"But how can I be certain that he would be allowed to send it out of the country?" She turned to Mary and caught at her hand. "I thought perhaps Mary, who sent all those letters for my father, might know of someone—of some way."

"There is Mistress Jane Whorwood," suggested Mary, after a moment's thought. "She would have done anything for his Majesty, and it was she to whom he entrusted those jewels he left you. I have her address because my aunt is staying with her in Oxfordshire."

"But, my dear child, the world has come to a pretty pass if such sacred messages must be sent clandestinely," the tutor reminded Elizabeth. "They were not in any way political, I take it?"

"Oh no, Master Lovall. They were just the personal messages which any man condemned to death might send to his wife and children."

"Then why not give your record of them to Master Mildmay as you gave that other packet—openly, officially?"

"He is very kind," added Mary. "Although he never entered into our plans against Parliament he has more than once warned us of danger, and whatever he may have seen he never gave away."

"I do not doubt him. It is those fiends who employ him," Elizabeth sighed, consideringly. "But I will do as you think best, Master Lovall."

They got up to play again, but the sky had darkened while they had been discussing the Princess's problem. There was a rumble of thunder and she was at the far end of the green when the storm broke suddenly in heavy drops, which soon became a downpour. Lovall took off his doublet and put it about her shoulders, but the storm increased so that they were obliged to run the last part of the way across a soaked courtyard. By the time they reached the Governor's house, laughing and panting, the girls' frocks were all bedraggled and the tutor, in his shirt sleeves, was soaked to the skin. Elizabeth's wet hair clung to her cheeks and the water squelched in her thin shoes.

"Oh, my poor new flowered gown!" lamented Judith, who had recently had it as a present from her father.

"Go and change it and Libby will iron it out for you," called Mary. "I will see to the Princess."

Wet as she was, she stopped to change every garment Elizabeth had on and sent for a basin of hot water to bathe her feet. She herself took no harm, but at supper Elizabeth ate nothing. She sat shivering, and went to bed early with two bright feverish spots on her cheeks.

"Her Highness got very hot playing, and then the rain came and she must have caught a chill," Lovall explained to Mildmay, when he and the Duke returned from Nunwell.

"She was upset talking about her father's farewell," added Judith, who knew how strongly the Princess's emotions could affect her.

All next day Mary cosseted her and put hot bricks to her feet, but as the feverishness did not abate Mildmay sent for Doctor Bagnell. His care and kindness were of great comfort, but her condition did not improve. Every day her brother would come in and talk to her as soon as his lessons were done, and although his high spirits and drollery delighted her, she tired far too soon. She had been at Carisbrooke less than a month when Mildmay, now thoroughly alarmed, sent an urgent message to London asking the Stuarts' family physician to come. The celebrated Doctor Mayerne was an old man and could not face the journey, but sent a younger man who had treated her before. He would be arriving immediately, the messenger said.

"Though what this Doctor Treherne can do for her that our beloved Doctor Bagnell has not already done, I do not know," sighed Mary.

It would be better not to leave her Highness alone, Bagnell had said, so they took turns at sitting with her. And one evening when Judith was at supper and Mary went into the sick room she found the Princess propped up against her pillows and looking a little stronger. "Oh, Mary, I have been waiting for you," she said. "It is about my letter—with those messages—"

"You must not worry about that. Master Mildmay sent it to Parliament days ago," said Mary, smoothing the sheets.

"Oh, I know you all think they will forward it," said Elizabeth, with the querulousness of sickness. "But how can you expect me to trust the men who murdered my father? Perhaps they will just destroy it as they ignored my brother Charles's offer of terms?"

"I know how you feel. It is hard that you should have been the only one to whom those messages were given."

Elizabeth put out a hot, imploring hand. Her eyes burned in her small face. "Mary, in case my letter should never reach them I should like you to know what was in it."

"Why not tell Judith or Master Lovall?"

"He does not know what it is to lose a father, and she might forget."

"But how could anyone as unimportant as I—"

"I have so much time in which to think, lying here. And I remembered last night that you once said you might one day go to Holland."

Mary could not deny the possibility. "Richard Osborne asked me to marry him, and he hopes to join your brother, the new King."

"You mean the man who helped in both my father's attempts at escape? And whose uncle was our loyal Governor of Guernsey?"

"Yes."

"Oh, Mary, I am so glad for you! Only sad for all the trouble and danger we Stuarts have caused him."

"Without it Richard and I could never have met." Although she smiled and spoke lightly, Mary began to pace back and forth between bed and window. "Our walks in life were so different. It is true that now he will be poor—and probably soldiering. Oh, Elizabeth, should I do right to marry him, do you suppose? Though my aunt was married to a knight, I am only a sergeant's daughter, with so little experience of life. You are younger than I, I know, but you must know more about such things."

"But what do I know of love?" For the first time Mary heard bitterness in Elizabeth's sweet voice, and realized more fully all she had lost. "Had life gone on happily as it used, I suppose I should

have been betrothed to some important European prince by now."
A smile passed over the patient's pale face, to be followed by a
fleeting sigh. "But I am sure my brother Charles would say that any
man would be more than lucky to have you. Your tender heart,
your good looks and—ah, how I envy you!—your good health."

"For all his wild reputation, I think it is Richard who has the
tender heart," boasted Mary, with a happy smile. "But I must not
weary you with my own affairs. Tell me about his late Majesty's
messages, and you will feel easier."

"In case I should not—as Charles used to say—'last out'? Henry,
I am sure, will always remember what our father said to him. Never
to let them crown him while his two elder brothers were alive.
Young as he is, Henry swore so valiantly that he would not.

"For the rest, listen carefully. My father said I was not to
grieve too much because it was a glorious death he would die for
the laws and religion of our land. He had forgiven all his enemies,
he said, and exhorted all of us his children to do the same. I have
tried and tried, but, oh, it is so difficult, Mary! He said he felt sure
God would restore the throne to Charles; and then we, and this
poor torn country, would all be happy again."

The steady, childlike voice was growing weaker. "He blessed
me," she went on as softly as if she were at her prayers, "and sent
his blessing to all his family and friends. And above all he bade me
tell my mother that his thoughts had never strayed from her and
that his love for her would be the same to the last. Somehow I feel
that it is that, most specially, which I must make sure is sent for her
comfort and never forgotten."

"I will never forget. And I promise you—if I ever get to
Holland—" It was Mary's voice which failed now.

"Specially, I think I want James to know that our father sent
him his love and blessing. Poor James! He was so shamed when he
first joined me in London because he had given away some code.
He is not the sort of person to do that. I shall always think they
threatened to torture him. We young Stuarts have had much to put
up with. But like St. Peter's denial, his youthful lapse and remorse
may strengthen his extraordinary loyalty to Charles." Elizabeth

gazed across the small quiet room out to the blue sky above the gatehouse as though she were looking into the future. But presently her head turned on the pillows and she closed her eyes. "I cannot talk any more now—"

"Sleep if you can," said Mary gently.

"Take Rogue now, and give me my Bible," murmured Elizabeth. "My father gave it to me and—before I fall asleep—I must try to forgive those enemies as he did."

The next day was Sunday and Judith, who had been sleeping on a truckle bed in the Princess's room, donned her freshly ironed flowered silk and went to chapel.

"How the green of it suits you, madame!" said Libby, hovering to hand her her book of devotions.

"Except that I am too pale from being kept so much indoors." And, glad to be released for a little while, Judith called back over her shoulder to Mary. "Doctor Treherne is coming to morning service, too, so you will not forget to give Elizabeth her medicine?"

"No," said Mary, standing at the door with Libby to watch the lovely creature cross the courtyard escorted by the doctor from London and John Barmiston, both of whom appeared to share Libby's admiration.

As the Princess was unable to attend chapel she had been reading from her Bible in bed, but when Mary returned with the medicine she appeared to have fallen asleep. "That, surely, is the best medicine of all," thought Mary; and being tired from all her extra duties, she sat quietly by the open window and let the peace of the summer Sabbath morning flow over her. From where she sat she could see the gatehouse and the white doves fluttering from their cote to settle on the chapel roof. Every now and then the sound of singing drifted up to her, interspersed by the murmuring of prayers, and finally followed by a distant drone of someone, preaching. For the first time for days she had time and solitude in which to wonder where Richard Osborne was and to wish that she might hear from him.

She must have been thinking about him for longer than she should. A shuffling of feet and the scraping back of stools roused her to realization that the long sermon must be over. "I must wake Elizabeth now, or Doctor Treherne will be angry," she thought reluctantly, reaching out for the little glass phial he had left and crossing to the bed.

All the peace in the world seemed to be gathered in the Princess's room. The curtains moved lazily in a faint breeze, casting a dancing pattern of sunlight and shadow on the wall, and a bee had buzzed in from the herb garden. Elizabeth's slight form scarcely moulded the coverlet and her pillowed head lay in the shadow of the half-drawn hangings.

"How tired she must have been to sleep so long!" thought Mary tenderly, standing phial in hand beside the bed.

"Bess, dear, your medicine," she said softly.

Her patient did not stir. "How frail she looks, and yet so peaceful. It seems cruel to waken her," thought Mary, pulling back the hangings so that the morning light fell across the pillow. Elizabeth was lying on her side with her chestnut-brown hair straying in tendrils across the open pages of her Bible, which must have fallen from her hand. Mary leaned across to see what she had been reading. "Come unto Me all ye that travail and are heavy laden and I will refresh you," she read. Refreshed indeed, thought Mary, as the compassionate Christ had promised. Although all the natural joy of her youth had been crushed by men's hatreds, and she had been so weary that she scarcely seemed to breathe. And now, in the revealing light, looked so alabaster pale!

A sudden terror gripped Mary. She put out a hand, fearfully, and touched the white hand on the coverlet and found it cold as death. "Bess! Bess, *dear!*" she cried, her voice rising in panic. And in that moment knew that Elizabeth had gone to join her father.

Breaking the stillness of the morning almost simultaneously with her cry came the swell of organ music through the opened chapel door and the voices of the congregation streaming back to their duties across the courtyard below. Mary blessed that human contact.

She ran to the door and caught sight of Brett going about

some household chore. "Fetch Master Mildmay and the doctor. Quickly, Brett! Doctor Treherne is coming from chapel now but Master Mildmay may be with those messengers from the mainland. Only hurry!"

For once Brett's old bones moved quickly, and soon the Stuart's attendants were all gathering in that modest little room. The doctor leaning over the bed, Lovall and Barmiston standing bareheaded at the foot of it, and Judith, down on her knees and all forgetful of her flowered gown, sobbing in abandonment. Somewhere in the doorway Libby and some of the other frightened servants gathered. In their consternation they had momentarily forgotten young Henry of Gloucester. He pushed past them all and flung his arms about the gentle sister who, burdened beyond her years, had for so long tried to mother him. It was his first sight of death. "Bess! Bess! Why will you not speak to me?" he cried, unable to believe that she had gone beyond his loving importunities.

His tutor tried to calm him as Anthony Mildmay came hurrying into the room. He had an opened letter with a heavy seal dangling in his hand, and stood there stricken.

"She has been dead an hour or more," the doctor told him.

"And I was on my way to show her this. I thought it would cheer her," said Mildmay, holding out the official-looking letter. "It is from Parliament granting leave at last for Bess and Henry Stuart to go to their sister, Princess Mary of Orange, in Holland."

"And after all this time it has come too late!" sobbed Judith Briot.

# CHAPTER THIRTY-THREE

PRINCESS ELIZABETH'S FUNERAL WAS over, with its sad little cortege wending its way down from the castle to St. Thomas's Church in Newport Square. Mildmay had had the Princess's slight body embalmed, and it had been carried in the same coach which had borne her father on that cold winter's morning to Hurst. People had gathered from all over the island, local women had stood weeping at their doors and even the Mayor, rabid recusant as he was, had ridden out to meet the King's daughter whose gentle soul had been incapable of harming anyone. Followed by the small company of those who served her, her frail body had been laid to rest before the altar.

A ship bound for Holland had put in at Cowes and Mary was packing the bereft young Duke's belongings ready for the long-hoped-for journey of which so much of the joy was marred. Henry's tutor had asked for her help because the boy's valet had been taken ill. "Though I strongly suspect that his sickness has suddenly become worse because he does not want to go to Holland," said Lovall, dragging forward a clothes chest in an effort to help.

"Are *you* glad to be going?" asked Mary, making a neat pile of Henry Stuart's hose.

"I suppose it is the goal of most of us younger Royalists now. What else is there for us here? And God knows a high-spirited youth will need spiritual guidance in a foreign land!"

"I believe you saw Harry Firebrace before you left London," said Mary, bending over the half-filled chest. "Does he, too, want to go abroad?"

"I would say that his devotion was more personally directed towards the late King than to the Stuart cause, for he is back serving the Earl of Denbigh again. There is some talk of his going to manage the Earl's large estates in Warwickshire, and his wife, who is wonderfully recovered, will join him there. Honest Denbigh never lost his hope of bringing King and Parliament to terms, and if you ask me he worked Firebrace into the royal household with that end in view. But, as you know, Firebrace came completely under the King's spell and when danger threatened, served him with undivided devotion. A most engaging fellow, I thought. Did you not find him so?"

"Yes," said Mary, sure that the tearing pain she used to experience in speaking of him had grown fainter. She cared little for the worthy Earl's intentions and had learned all she wanted to know. She went on with her task feeling in an odd, detached sort of way that she was folding away more precious and intangible things than a boy's hard-worn garments.

Lovall strolled to the hearth and stood looking round the room where Charles had first come as an honoured guest. "I wonder what they will do with all this handsome furniture which you say came from Hampton?" he speculated idly.

Mary straightened up from her packing and looked about her at the familiar pieces. "I suppose really Henry should inherit it," she said, considering the matter for the first time.

"But I make no doubt they will sell the stuff! Anthony Mildmay was saying only the other night at supper that if they should come under the hammer before he leaves he means to bid for those red and blue tapestries by the door."

"Oh, I am so glad!" exclaimed Mary, marvelling, not for the first time, at how much Mildmay must have known of that year's activities.

"Why? What is special about them?" asked Lovall.

But Mary did not answer. She was standing stock still in the middle of the room listening to another man's voice, and there was an expression of horror on her face. "Do you not hear him?" she said.

"I can hear a great deal of commotion, and some blustering fellow making himself felt."

"It is Major Rolph. He has come back."

Not understanding her consternation, Lovall went to the door and looked out into the Presence Chamber from which the sounds were coming.

But Mary clung to his arm. "Please—please, Master Lovall, do not leave the door open. Or let him come in here."

"Why, Mary, what is he to you?" asked the young tutor, looking down amazed into her whitened face. "You are trembling. I will stay with you if you like."

"No. no. It is not only for myself. But his coming here now could endanger someone—for whom I care. If you would slip out quietly and find out what he has come for—and how long he is going to stay—"

"It is natural enough that he should have been sent to see to the Duke's departure. After all, Lord Sydenham, your newly appointed Governor, is not in residence. But I will find out."

Knowing how little time there was before the ship sailed Mary tried, as soon as he was gone, to concentrate on finishing his pupil's packing. But her thoughts flew wildly from one possible danger to another. What if Richard Osborne should return? Even with Mildmay's protection, was she herself safe from Rolph's vengeful lust? Automatically she filled and closed the chest ready for the servants to put upon the baggage cart.

"What have you found out? Have you the key to lock this?" she asked in agitation, when Lovall returned.

He crossed the room heavily and slumped down upon the chest. "We shall not need the key," he said.

"Not need it? Going all the way to Holland?"

"We are not going there after all. Nor anywhere else. That son of Belial, Rolph, must have put his spoke in somewhere. I do not know the reason *why* it is we are to stay, He has been arguing with Mildmay for an hour or more, and when I reminded Mildmay that the horses would be round immediately after supper he told me curtly that the Duke would have to wait a while."

"Then the Army must be trying to override Parliament's decision. Is Major Rolph staying here?"

"Yes, and he was furious to find that Henry has his room."

"*His* room?" Mary looked round the pleasant State Room which had housed a king and various lordly governors before him, involuntarily comparing it with that bare and shabby room where Rolph had slept when Captain of the Guard, every detail of which would always remain crudely clear in her memory.

"He was most offensive, talking about 'that Stuart brat' in the Deputy Governor's bed. But Mildmay stood firm on *that* score. I would he had stood his ground as firmly on the question of departure! We could have been away to-night."

"The delay may be only for a few weeks. They cannot go back on their word," consoled Mary, wrenching her thoughts from her own predicament.

"Well, I shall have to go and break the bad news to Henry," said Lovall, getting to his feet. "If they do not let him go soon I shall ride to London myself and plead his cause. Or get him to write and badger them as his sister did." Lovall got up, zealous for his beloved pupil. "Has not the boy been deprived of enough already? Do they want to kill the whole family, one by one?"

Being island bred, Mary looked instinctively towards the chapel weather vane. Both wind and tide would serve. "The chance of a ship bound for The Hague may not come again for months," she said. "Could you not leave all this baggage and slip away now and board her?"

But Lovall, though shrewd and conscientious, was no Osborne or Firebrace. He had served the Stuart cause as priest and scholar, not by amateur soldiering.

"Rolph has brought a detachment of his own men with him and must have been in an uncommon hurry to see that Henry—or somebody—does not get off the island. Their poor mounts are wet with sweat. And now he is bawling for his supper. The audacity of that man! As though the castle belongs to him. Mildmay had to remind him that his own appointment from Parliament still holds and that he is in charge so long as either of the late King's children remains there." Striving to subdue his personal loathing to a charity more befitting to his priesthood, Lovall remembered the other part of his errand. "Master Mildmay wants you to go and see him. About the arrangements of the rooms, I imagine."

"To go to the officers' quarters?"

Lovall was man of the world enough to guess at the cause of her reluctance. "I heard Rolph shouting for hot water so probably he is at his ablutions," he said, and without being asked walked along with her before going to find his pupil who had just come in with Barmiston from Nunwell, whither he had gone to bid good-bye to the Oglanders.

In the room that had been Colonel Hammond's, Mary found Anthony Mildmay writing a letter at his desk, with his personal servant waiting for him to seal it.

"The Deputy Governor has arrived," he said, glancing up briefly at Mary. "I would like you to have the late Princess's room made ready for him."

"Yes, sir," said Mary, hoping that Elizabeth's gentle ghost would haunt a man whose ferocious activities had helped to hound her to her lonely end.

"And there is no need to go on packing the Duke's possessions. He will not be leaving us just yet." He handed the letter to his man with directions to have it despatched immediately to Westminster. Although his manner was calm, Mary could see that he was still white from recent anger. And as soon as the door had closed behind the man he got up and walked over to the window.

"But the young Duke *will* be allowed to go?" she ventured.

"Eventually, I make no doubt of it," he said, with his back to her.

She stood there, uncertain whether she should go. And he, it seemed, had been making up his mind whether to speak or not. "I heard yesterday that Richard Osborne is on the island," he said at last.

He must have heard Mary's quick movement behind him. "Where?" she asked, in a small strained voice.

"At Gatcombe. He intended coming here after dark to-night. To ask leave to accompany the Duke to Holland, I suspect." Mildmay turned and smiled at her. "And to see you, perhaps. Now, with the Deputy Governor arrived, it would of course be disastrous."

"You could not possibly—warn him?"

"I have already done so. I sent word to say that if he has any sense he will get aboard that ship *somehow* before she sails. And that I would tell you. He is probably on his way to Cowes by now."

There was silence in the room while the full implications of his news sank into Mary's startled mind. "How did you know—about us?" she asked, in a low voice.

"Hammond asked me to follow you that day you went down to the village to visit your father's grave."

"And you saw us together? And never spoke of it?"

"Only to the King."

"Even though Major Rolph was searching for him for days?"

Anthony Mildmay shrugged her gratitude aside. "It would be difficult to give away so likeable a man as Osborne. And I gathered that Hammond thought Rolph was the type that might follow you that day." Mildmay came back to his desk. "Are you still afraid of him, Mary?"

"Richard half-killed him—"

"So that was the cause of his mysterious sickness?"

"And I laughed, you remember, when the King pushed him out of the coach. And to keep him away from the platform the night the King was trying to escape—I went to his room. I emptied the powder out of his pistol. I tricked him, letting him think I desired him as he desired me. He would never forgive that. He did not have me—but he has sworn that he will—"

It was much as Mildmay had surmised and his face was stern. After a moment or two he jerked open a drawer and drew out a little leather bag of money. "I had meant to give you this to-morrow, thinking my duty here would be finished and I should be leaving. It is what Parliament owes you for satisfactory service." His businesslike manner changed, and he looked away as a man will when embarrassed by his own goodness of heart. "The ship

leaves at midnight, and in half an hour we shall all be at supper."
Because he knew how much he would miss the sweet candour of
her smile he found the words surprisingly hard to say.

Mary stood with the little bag cupped between her hands. It did
not represent merely money to her. It was as if her father's protective kindness were reaching out to her through another. "Why are
you so good to me?" she asked.

"Because it is time you found carefree happiness. Listen, Mary.
We none of us wanted to come here. Least of all, the King. For most
of us it meant exile from our homes and families. And during that
year when his late Majesty was here you always seemed a part of
Carisbrooke Castle, and for most of us you made it a happier place."

The smile he would miss spread over Mary's face. "What a
beautiful thing to say!" she said and because she, too, recognized
the moment as a parting, she reached up impulsively and kissed
him, and knew that he was inordinately pleased.

Meeting Libby on her way back to the housekeeper's room
she told her to take one of the other maids and prepare the late
Princess's room for the Deputy Governor. Then she sent for Brett.
"The others are all busy over the Major's arrival. Will you saddle
my horse for me?" she asked.

"Happen it be zum extra viands from village you be needing', I
could go get 'un," he offered.

"Not this time, Brett," she said gently, and hurrying on to her
room she put a few things into a basket, threw her cloak about
her shoulders and tucked Rogue under her arm. The courtyard was
quiet and all the household at supper when she stepped on to the
mounting block before the door. "There is something you can do
for me to-morrow," she told the faithful, bent old man. "Try to
find means to go down into Newport and see Mistress Trattle at
the 'Rose and Crown,' and give her a message from me. Give her
my love, Brett. Give them all my dear love. And tell her that the
Duke of Gloucester will not be going to Holland after all, and so
this evening I am going for a sail with the friend I was expecting
from the mainland."

"Goin' for a zail, Mistress Mary? Zo late in the day?"

"Yes. I think she will understand. And Brett—" Her hand rested lingeringly on his shoulder as he held out a toil-hardened palm to mount her. "You must always be proud that even a King found comfort in your humble company."

She was aware that the old islander who had done her small kindnesses ever since she was born was looking after her in a puzzled sort of way.

And so she rode out under the castle gateway for the last time, the muted thud of her horse's hooves on the wooden drawbridge seeming to echo all the happy hours and recent griefs of her past. And the laughter of a young man whom she had loved. So great was the wrench that once outside she dared not look back, but cantered briskly towards Cowes.

They would all be at supper now, she thought, as she looked steadfastly at the road ahead through a blur of tears. And Judith, who was leaving for London in the morning, would be making eyes at Edmund Rolph. Judith, whose lovely body had been held in the arms of Richard Osborne…the man to whom she was going—alone, unwed, with little money and no shame.

Swiftly changing events had left her no time in which to think. For better or for worse, she had had to lay hold of destiny. She had chosen instinctively. Putting behind her all her known way of life, all assured comfort and security, for a man whose kindness had never failed her. She remembered that her father had liked him. And clearly from the past came the comfort of the late King's words, "Richard Osborne may be a reckless young man, but I should never hesitate to trust him."

In the wide mouth of the Medina river the little merchantman lay at her moorings, her sails already being unfurled. Mary left her horse at the little "Sloop Inn" where the late King had slept when he first landed on the island. The proprietor was related to Edward Trattle, and when she did not return he would see that the animal was sent back to him. She went down to the shore, but there was no sign of Osborne. At least she could get away from Edmund Rolph. And she must find the new King Charles and give him the messages which Elizabeth had entrusted to her.

But what should she do—she who had never so much as been to the mainland of England—alone in a foreign land where people spoke some incomprehensible language? If Osborne had failed her, she would have landed herself into a yet more difficult life. But nothing would matter so much as the disillusionment of finding that he *had* failed her.

Resolutely she stepped into a boat which was just being pushed off with some other passengers, slipping a piece of silver into the longshoreman's ready hand. The stretch of calm water between boat and island widened. Already the "Sloop," with the lamps in its friendly windows, looked a long way off. A moment of panic seized her. She half-rose from the thwart on which she was sitting and would have given anything to be able to swim ashore again. Then there came a shout from somewhere high above her, a rope was thrown and caught, around her people began to stand up. The little boat swayed precariously, and she felt strong hands guiding her toward a rope ladder. There was nothing to do but climb up the tall, tarry side of the ship. One arm was encumbered by the struggling spaniel. The basket with her last remaining possessions slipped from her grasp into the sea and floated away. At the top of the ladder she stumbled and a tall sailor in a red woollen cap with a freshly healed scar on his cheek caught her and lifted her on board. "Well done, my brave lass!" his deep voice said encouragingly and to her glad surprise, she found herself in Richard Osborne's arms.

All anxiety ended then. "Did you think that I should fail you?" he chided tenderly, finding a sheltered place for her upon a locker on the fo'c'sle. "Sit here until we are under way, and I can come to you. Since Parliament countermanded the passages of the Duke of Gloucester's party my only means was to bribe the Captain to take me on as one of the crew."

"What will they do if they find me?" she asked anxiously.

"I bargained for a passage for my wife," grinned Osborne.

One of the ship's officers was shouting for him and he had to hurry away. Through all the bustle of weighing anchor and setting sail Mary was thankful to obey him and sit quietly by the fo'c'sle rail. She was well placed, out of the way of passengers and crew alike. Once, looking up, she was horrified to see Osborne, barefoot, aloft in the swaying rigging; but remembered that, like young Charles Stuart, he had learned his seamanship as a lad in the Channel Islands. She was not sorry to be alone to take her last sight of the Wight. Already the friendly "Sloop" down on the waterfront was receding. In the gathering dusk the lighted windows of Cowes began to look like a necklace of jewels thrown carelessly down the steep cliff side. And gradually even the beacon lamps of the two castles, one on either side of the river mouth, began to fade, until finally the familiar outline of the Wight was only an irregular hump against the darkening sky. As night drew on activities on board ceased, passengers sought their rest and Rogue curled his small body comfortably on a coil of rope. The ship sped forward on a calm sea under gently bellying canvas, with the swish of water along her bows and the rhythmic creaking of her timbers only adding to the peacefulness of the night. The stars came out and Mary felt a man's arms, warm from exertion, fold about her as she leant against the rail. "So you love me enough to leave that enchanted island," he exalted softly. "It will be my main aim in life to see that you never regret it, sweet."

"It is only through Anthony Mildmay's goodness that I am here."

"He warned me, too."

"I know." Mary leaned back against her lover's shoulder. "He saw us that day when you were so kind to me in Carisbrooke churchyard."

"And never told!"

"When I heard Rolph shouting around the castle this afternoon and knew that you would be on this ship I came away just as I was, without anything but my dog."

Osborne turned her about and kissed her with all the gratitude that was in him. "And even he is not yours," he teased, laughingly to hide his deep emotion. "Did you not know that the late King left all his favourite animals to the Queen? But do not worry, my little love, for you may be sure that when her Majesty hears all that you have done she will let you keep him."

But a more strictly feminine concern had recurred to Mary's mind. "Even the few clothes I brought fell into the sea," she told him.

"We will buy some new ones in The Hague."

"Is the new King there?"

"No. In Breda. Come to think of it, I shall need some new clothes myself," added Osborne, glancing down ruefully at his own strange attire. "But I have something more important to do first."

"For the King, I suppose?"

He turned her face up so that she must look at him, and kissed the pout from her lips. "No. For Richard Osborne, this time. I must find a parson to marry us."

His quick ears caught her involuntary sigh of relief, and he shook her gently. "I suppose that Briot girl was at the castle and had to tell you about her conquests?" he demanded.

"One gathered things," Mary admitted, wondering out of her present happiness how she could ever have minded so much.

"Well, do not gather them any more. From anyone. That part of my life is finished and my lonely heart has come into port. From to-night you and I begin a new life together."

She reached up her arms and kissed him passionately of her own accord and their long embrace was a mutual dedication.

"Had I come to the castle I had intended to ask Guy Lovall to marry us," he said.

"But I came to you shamelessly unwed."

"I shall always be proud of the way you trusted me."

"And now," laughed Mary softly, "we shall not understand a word of our wedding ceremony in Dutch."

"We shall understand it in our hearts, beloved."

When she looked up again the island that held all her memories of the past was lost to sight. But, pressing closer into her lover's arms, she saw the future in the ardour of his eyes.

# CHAPTER THIRTY-FOUR

⟪ASTER AND MISTRESS RICHARD Osborne," announced the exiled King's servant; and the words were as music in Mary's ears.

He was showing them into a house in Breda where Charles Stuart and his small travesty of a Court had lodgings. It was an ordinary, unimportant-looking house and they had had some difficulty in finding it; but, like all Dutch buildings, it was kept scrupulously clean. Mary had not wanted to leave The Hague, where she had spent three rapturous days alone with her new husband, but she realized that he must make his report to the exiled King, and she herself had promised to deliver those messages entrusted to her by the Princess Elizabeth.

Both of them were shocked to find how poorly their fellow Royalists lived. "Are his Majesty's resources so low?" Osborne was asking with concern of an elderly courtier who came forward to receive them.

The man's scholarly face was as contented as his coat was shabby. "So low that sometimes we are forced to eat once a day like dogs," he chuckled. "But his Majesty is of such a cheerful disposition that I would sooner live with him on a couple of guelder a week than anywhere in the world without him! Your coming will make up to him in some measure for his disappointment about his young brother, Master Osborne, so I will tell him straightaway that you and your lady are here."

He passed through a door into a room where people were laughing and talking, and while it was open Mary caught sight of a middle-aged, apple-cheeked man sitting rather pompously at a table with some papers before him, and heard another man with a particularly pleasant voice arguing with affectionate exasperation. "Oddfish, Ned, why must you be so mulish? If Cromwell does not let young Henry come—" And then the door was closed behind the old courtier who, however hungry, seemed to find life tolerable with a penniless master.

Too agitated to sit still, Mary went to the window.

"I love these Dutch houses, with their little courtyards and tiled floors and their gables squared-up like steps," she said. "Do you know, Richard, they wash them outside as well as in!"

"You *would* notice that, my love!" he laughed, having eyes for little but the new radiance which happiness had brought her. As she leaned down to look into the street he followed her and kissed the nape of her neck where it showed beneath her curls. "Surely, not *here!*" she whispered in confusion, pushing him away and straightening his cravat with wifely concern. "I wonder you are not too nervous to be thinking of such things!"

"Why should I be?"

"At meeting the King."

"But I have met him several times before—when he was a lanky lad far too young to be on a battlefield."

"I remember how my knees shook under me when King Charles the First came to Carisbrooke and I had to go into his room to make his bed."

"You will find King Charles the Second very different."

"How is he different?" she asked, smoothing the lovely rose-pink gown which Osborne had bought for her wedding, and dreading having to make an entrance into that room full of exiled gentlemen.

But she need not have worried because, before Osborne could answer, the door opened and a tall young man of nineteen or so came in. He came in so unobtrusively and his black suit was so worn that until her husband went down on one knee and kissed

324 Margaret Campbell Barnes

his hand, she had no idea he was the King. And certainly no son could have looked less like his father.

"Why, Richard Osborne, it is good to see you again!" he was saying—and it was the same pleasant voice which she had heard through the open door. "My father wrote me of your good services and I knew you were the very man to sound the prospects of a good landing for us. I trust you bring good news?"

"Reasonably good, sir. I have much to tell you."

"Then we will talk of it after supper with milord Clarendon and those others who have thrown in their lot with me so loyally."

"Besides good news I have brought my wife," said Osborne, and Mary, having had plenty of practice, achieved a far more graceful curtsy than she had managed on being presented to his father.

"Fortunate man!" smiled Charles, assessing her as favourably as Elizabeth had said he would. "I did not know you were married."

"Only three days ago, in The Hague."

"Then nothing shall hold me from my happy privilege of kissing the bride," vowed Charles, striding across the room to do so with considerable enjoyment. "I would I could offer you better entertainment, Mistress Osborne."

"It is enough to see your Majesty," said Mary, finding her tongue as he bent down to fondle Rogue.

"Carisbrooke Castle is Mary's home," Osborne told him. "Her father was shot for trying to help the King your father to escape, and she herself, being the royal Laundress's niece, was instrumental in getting many of your letters in and out of his Majesty's room."

Charles looked at her with deep gratitude, and she observed that although there was frequent laughter on his full young lips, his dark eyes held the melancholy of a much older man—a man who has already known danger and suffering. "God send you be as happy with this good comrade of mine as you deserve!" he said gravely, and with his own capable hands set a chair for her.

He himself sat down with his back to the window and instantly the little spaniel, who was normally nervous of strangers, ran to him and sprang up on to his knees. "It seems as if he must know," exclaimed Mary, losing the last of her own shyness. "Rogue was the late King's pet during those last months at Carisbrooke."

"We have a whole history of that dog to tell you, sir," said Osborne.

"And the true details of all those attempts at escape, I hope, and all that happened to my father. No one has been able to give me personal inside information since Titus came—but I will not steal a march on him and the others. We must share your news. Though there is some which concerns me closely and which I cannot wait for." With the spaniel lying beneath his caressing hand, he turned to Mary. "Were you still in the castle when those callous murderers sent my sister there?"

"All the time, sir. And I had the great good fortune to be able to look after her—and nurse her."

"She was never strong, our little Temperance. It was cruel to send her there!"

"But your Majesty must not think of her as being ailing and unhappy all the time. We played bowls sometimes. And she had a gentlewoman, Judith Briot, who was beautiful and gay. She encouraged her Highness to dance and make music." Mary had spoken spontaneously, forgetting that she had ever held rancour against the woman and only grateful for the fleeting kind of joy she brought; and, looking up, saw her husband's eyes fixed adoringly upon her. She rose from the chair the King had set for her and knelt beside him, conscious only of her desire to comfort him. While well aware that no one would take a liberty with this shabby young man and go unscathed, she felt in him that intense humanity which had drawn her husband to his service. A humanity born of ordinary experiences and contrivances which do not normally fall to the lot of kings, and which would for ever make him more approachable. In that room in a foreign city with her mind back in the familiar rooms of Carisbrooke, she told him of small, everyday happenings which would be of interest only to himself and to members of his family. She told him of his father in captivity and of his young sister's last days and of her love and longing for him; and in a low, awed voice she gave him those last messages from his father which Elizabeth had not lived to bring him.

"To forgive our enemies," he repeated, his long fingers shielding the emotion on his face. "When I come into my own again please God I shall be merciful to men of other persuasions than my own. But to forgive his murderers—"

He sat for a while in silence trying to assimilate the magnitude of such a thought, then shrugged as though the matter were as yet beyond him. "No doubt these same enemies will see fit to send me dear Bess's written record of these heart-breaking messages in their own good time, but this has been the kindest way to hear them," he said, his hand dropping gratefully from his forehead to Mary's shoulder. "And in the meantime we must prepare to welcome young Henry and help him to forget such sad beginnings to his life." He stood up, strong and clear-thinking and unbeaten. "Well, I am still King of Scotland, and we must plan a landing there. Osborne."

"My sword and I are at your service."

The words sounded like a dedication, and as Mary looked from one to the other of them a shiver ran through her at the thought of what lay before them. They were of the same height and build, and the same deceptive air of indolence hid the purposeful courage of both of them.

As if sensing her fear, Charles turned and pulled her gently to her feet. "But you two are newly wed and it is like my clumsiness to talk of fighting," he apologised. "We have months of preparation to make yet and when the time comes, Osborne, I promise you that my sister, the Princess of Orange, who is the merriest soul alive, will take care of her charming namesake here. For dear Bess's sake and for all your Mary has done for my father, we must keep her in the family." The door opened and the same serving man appeared. "There is Toby come to tell us supper is served. Come and eat, man," invited Charles. "You must both be famished. Travelling and love-making are hungry work!"

"Oh, but sir—my husband and I could eat in the town. It is

wonderful what tavern wives will do for his smile and our few halting words of Dutch," faltered Mary, thinking how lean he looked.

"She is looking at the way my clothes hang on my long bones, and, womanlike, fearing I am half starved!" laughed Charles. But as long as I can come by a chicken and a loaf of bread I hope I may share it with my friends."

"And I hope my news may hearten them," said Osborne, with his arm about his wife.

"We shall get back to London, never fear," said Charles, as his man held wide the door. "You will find that fine-looking husband of yours peacocking it as royal Usher again. And as for you, my sweet Mary, I must appoint you royal Laundress at Whitehall."

"I shall hold you to that, sirs," laughed Osborne, as they followed him in to supper.

"With all my heart. But we Stuarts do not forget," said Charles, pausing in the doorway to take Mary's hand and lead her forward to meet his little group of friends, "Though God knows you may have to wait a long time for your appointment, Mary of Carisbrooke. For at the moment I have but one spare shirt, and that is borrowed!"

# BIBLIOGRAPHY

Allan Fea. *Memoirs of the Martyr King*. John Lane, The Bodley Head.

Burchell. *The Prisoner of Carisbrooke*. Macmillan.

Burton. *England's Eden*. Littlebury.

C. Aspinall-Oglander. *Nunwell Symphony*. Constable & Co. Ltd.

C. W. Firebrace. *Honest Harry*. John Murray.

Carola Oman. *Henrietta Maria*. Hodder & Stoughton.

Davenport Adams. *History and Antiquities of the Isle of Wight*. Nelson & Sons.

David Mathew. *The Age of Charles I*. Eyre & Spottiswoode.

Dorothy Hartley. *Food in England*. Macdonald.

Edward Hyde, Earl of Clarendon. *The History of the Rebellion and Civil Wars in England*. Oxford University Press.

Esme Wingfield Stratfield. *King Charles the Martyr*. Hollis & Carter.

Eva Scott. *The Travels of the King*. Constable.

G. W. Nichol. *Herbert's Memoirs*. W. Bulmer.

George Hillier. *Charles I in the Isle of Wight*. Richard Bentley.

George Macaulay Trevelyan. *England under the Stuarts*. Methuen.

Hugh Ross Williamson. *Charles and Cromwell*. Duckworth.

Jesse. *Memoirs of the Stuarts*. Nimmo.

*Letters of Dorothy Osborne*. Dent & Sons Ltd.

P. G. Stone, F.R.I.B.A. *Architectural Antiquities of the Isle of Wight*. The Author.

Philip Lindsay. *For King and Parliament*. Evans Bros.

Sir John Oglander. *A Royalist's Notebook*. Hogarth Press.

# ABOUT THE AUTHOR

MARGARET CAMPBELL BARNES LIVED from 1891 to 1962. She was the youngest of ten children born into a happy, loving family in Victorian England. She grew up in the Sussex countryside and was educated at small private schools in London and Paris.

Margaret was already a published writer when she married Peter, a furniture salesman, in 1917. Over the next twenty years, a steady stream of short stories and verse appeared under her name (and several noms de plume) in leading English periodicals of the time, including *Windsor*, *London*, *Quiver*, and others. Later, Margaret's agents, Curtis Brown Ltd., encouraged her to try her hand at historical novels. Between 1944 and 1962, Margaret wrote ten historical novels. Many of these were bestsellers, book club selections, and translated into foreign editions.

Between World Wars I and II, Margaret and Peter brought up two sons, Michael and John. In August 1944, Michael, a lieutenant in the Royal Armoured Corps, was killed in his tank in the Allied advance from Caen to Falaise in Normandy. Margaret and Peter grieved terribly the rest of their lives. Glimpses of Michael shine through in each of Margaret's later novels.

In 1945 Margaret bought a small thatched cottage on the Isle of Wight, off England's south coast. It had at one time been a smuggler's cottage, but to Margaret it was a special place in which to recover the spirit and carry on writing. And write she did. All together, over two million copies of Margaret Campbell Barnes's historical novels have been sold worldwide.

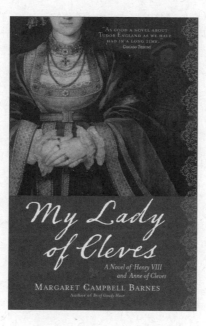

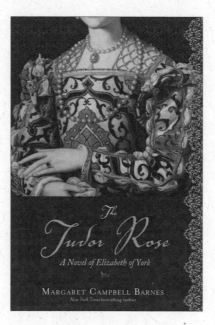

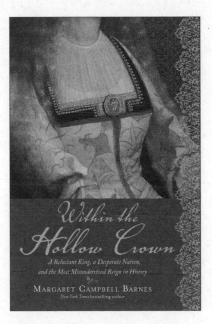